D0483021

the ISLANDERS

VOL. 3:

CLAIRE GETS CAUGHT *and* WHAT ZOEY SAW

KATHERINE APPLEGATE *and* MICHAEL GRANT

PREVIOUSLY PUBLISHED AS THE **MAKING OUT** SERIES

HARPER TEEN

An Imprint of HarperCollinsPublishers

HarperTeen is an imprint of HarperCollins Publishers.

Originally published by HarperPaperbacks as Boyfriends Girlfriends

ISBN 978-0-06-234080-1

Typography by Ellice M. Lee
❖
15 16 17 18 19   PC/RRDH   10 9 8 7 6 5 4 3 2 1
First Edition

CLAIRE GETS CAUGHT

PART ONE

"THIS IS IT," CLAIRE SAID. *"This has to be the end. It's either me or Wade. One of us had to lose and . . ."* She took a deep breath. *". . . He's already lost all he could."*

"Claire—"

"No, don't, all right?" she said harshly. *"This is hard enough. I really do care for you, and I know you care for me, so don't make me any sadder by saying it. There's just too much history between us. And to tell you the truth, I'm not a person who can go around for long feeling guilty. I'm sorry about what happened two years ago. I'm sorry you can't deal with this without trying to destroy yourself. But you can't. Which leaves only one solution."*

His arms tightened around her, holding her close. She pressed her cheek against his shoulder and blotted her tears on his shirt.

He took her face with his hand and forced her to look at him. He kissed her for a long, still moment.

Then she took another deep breath. She let the emotion run out of her, turning her thoughts away. She thought of her widow's walk. She thought of how much she liked to be up there, watching the lightning illuminate the darkness, watching snow drift down to settle on the little town below.

She had always been able to do what she had to. And now she pulled away, leaving the warmth of Jake's arms. She turned, and with dry eyes, walked away.

Claire left the dance, the sound of the music dying away behind her as she left the campus and headed down through the town, past the darkened storefronts and bright restaurants. It was a crisp, chilly evening and she walked briskly, her heels loud on the sidewalk.

It had gone pretty well, if she said so herself. Right now Jake was realizing what had happened: that she had given him up to avoid hurting him anymore. He was also realizing that he was all alone, staring at a room full of couples.

"I'm sorry you can't deal with this without trying to destroy yourself," she repeated under her breath. Perfect. Just the right touch of condescension.

Now to let him enjoy life without her for a while. See how much he liked it when he got what he *thought* he wanted. And then, she would simply wait until the right opportunity presented itself.

Claire smiled. It was unfair, it was dishonest, and it was certainly manipulative. But more important, with a little luck, it would probably work out just fine.

Zoey Passmore

I found the quiz in <u>Seventeen</u> or <u>Teen Vogue</u>, one of those, and tore it out. "How Well Do You Know Him?" with the word <u>Him</u> in bright pink letters. You're supposed to fill it out on your own first, guessing what your boyfriend's answer will be. Then later you ask your boyfriend, and if his answer is what you guessed it would be, great. If not, then you don't know him as well as you thought, right? Not that I take quizzes all that seriously. Still, I figured there had to be some validity to it or they wouldn't print it in a serious magazine like . . . like whichever one it was in.

Anyway. The first question was,

1. On the issue of sex, your boyfriend will say he is willing to: (A) Put it off until you are married; (B) Wait until you feel the time is right and not pressure you till then; (C) Pressure you to do it because once you try it you'll like it; (D) Leave you and go out with someone else if you keep saying no; (E) Not applicable, we're already having sex.

Well. Kind of cuts right to the heart of things, doesn't it? First of all, we can eliminate E right away. I am not sleeping with Lucas. I've never done it with anyone. Not that I haven't thought about it. A lot. Especially when he's kissing me and his hands are . . . See? I'm thinking about it right now.

But no. I don't know why, but that's like a step I'm not ready for yet. I think Lucas respects that. He doesn't respect it a lot; I mean, he's not thrilled by my saying no. Sometimes he's *very* not thrilled. But he wouldn't answer D. He also wouldn't answer A. I'm thinking he'll come down somewhere between a B and a C. Call it a C-plus. Although what he'll actually answer on the quiz is B, because he'll think that's the answer I want him to give.

Lucas Cabral

Forget E, unfortunately. If the answer were E, I wouldn't be taking really cold showers every night after I say good night to Zoey. If the answer were E, I wouldn't be bouncing off the walls and waking up remembering dreams that, believe me, you don't want to hear about. Nope. Not E.

Not A, either. D is a possibility; I mean, if this goes on forever. Seriously, say we're talking ten years, we're both in our late twenties? And I'm still not getting laid? I don't think so.

The true answer is C. Of course. But I have to answer B. I'm not an idiot.

Nina Geiger

Let's just set question one aside for a moment. Benjamin and I aren't even in the same room as that question. At least I'm not. I guess I don't know about him, given that we've only really had one date, which happened to be the first real date I ever had with anyone. I'm not exactly the source of true wisdom on this subject.

> 2. Your boyfriend's idea of a perfect date would be: (A) Going out for burgers and a movie; (B) Having a picnic on the beach and watching the sun go down; (C) Attending a rock concert; or (D) Hanging out with a big group of mutual friends.

Easy. He'd like the concert, of course, over a movie. Benjamin's blind and he's big on music. But the answer he'd give if you asked him is B. Get it? Blind guy watching the sun go down? That's Benjamin's idea of funny. Mine too, actually.

8

Benjamin Passmore

B.

Aisha Gray

Question one, C. Christopher isn't shy about asking. But then, I'm not shy about saying no. Question two, I'd guess B because B would give him the best chance of getting back to question one.

Ah, question three. How appropriate.

3. Will your boyfriend say that (A) You are both free to see other people; (B) He can see other girls but he expects you to be faithful; (C) He'll be faithful to you but he understands if you want to go out with other guys; (D) Let's just see how it all works out.

There it is, the question I never asked but should have. But would Christopher have given me an honest answer?

That's the problem with quizzes. They all depend on how honest he is, how honest you are, and how prepared you are to see the truth. I'm guessing he'll answer A. But I'm guessing what he really means is B.

9

Christopher Shupe

I've been living in Aisha's house while I recuperated from a very unfortunate run-in with some guys who didn't appreciate the color of my skin. I'm having meals cooked for me by Aisha's mother, and books brought to me by Aisha's father. Aisha's little brother comes around and plays video games with me. I would have to be a bigger toad than I am to answer A under these circumstances, knowing how Aisha feels. I guess if you really twisted my arm, I'd say my heartfelt answer would be B. But I don't know anymore. Aisha has stuck by me big time. That counts for a lot. I also happen to like her more than any girl I've ever met.

My answer is D. I guess. Ask me again later when I'm totally back on my feet.

ONE

THE WAVES WERE MORE GRAY than blue, and when Lucas stood up on his board, his longish blond hair was the only splash of color in a tableau of sea and sky that could almost have been a black-and-white photograph.

Zoey Passmore pulled the cowl neck of her sweater up over her chin and ears and slid her hands up inside the sleeves. The beach sand had lost all of the warmth from the sun that had shone so encouragingly earlier in the day, and she kept to the blanket. She'd collected driftwood from the beach and fallen limbs from the pine trees behind her and piled them with ex–Girl Scout expertise in a nice little pyramid. But she didn't want to light the fire until Lucas was with her for fear she'd burn up all her stash of fuel before he finally got tired of surfing.

Lucas fell from the board, diving into the water headfirst and surfacing moments later to shake the water from his hair like a dog. He grinned and held up a single finger, indicating one more wave.

She watched him reclaim his board and paddle back out, black rubber tight on his legs and butt, his feet bare and probably frozen by now. But she couldn't begrudge him the opportunity. There were rarely surfable waves on Chatham Island. This was a fluke, the result of a major storm far out over the Atlantic. It had brought them just the skirts of its clouds and enough of a surge to send Lucas scrambling to wax his old board and squeeze himself into a wet suit he'd clearly outgrown.

He caught a wave and had a good, long ride, bringing the board within a few feet of the narrow beach before he tumbled.

But he kept his word and emerged from the surf, lifting his board free of the foam that surged to within a couple of yards of Zoey's feet.

"Quick, light the fire!" he yelled. "I'm numb."

Zoey smiled. His hair was wet and tousled, his body outlined in perfect detail by the tight wet suit. She felt a definite twinge. He looked incredible. Too incredible for Zoey's own good. She fished in her bag for the matches, but without taking her eyes from him.

She tore her eyes away and found the matches. He planted his surfboard upright in the sand and flopped onto the blanket beside her, smelling of salt and laughing in sheer delight.

"Damn, I'd forgotten how much I loved that." He pulled the zipper halfway down his chest and inhaled deeply. "If only

I'd been able to breathe. I guess I'll have to break down and buy a new suit."

Zoey struck a match, but it was instantly blown out by the wind. *Don't say it,* she warned herself. *Don't say it.*

Then she said it anyway. "I think that suit looks pretty good on you." Her voice wobbled a little and she concentrated on lighting a second match, cupping it in her hands. She touched the flame to the dried grass kindling. It crackled loudly and caught fire.

Lucas rolled toward her and without warning stuck his hands under her sweater, pressing them to her bare stomach.

Zoey squealed and tried to push him away, but he held on. "Get those icicles off me!"

"I can't wait for the fire," he said. "I need warmth now. My hands are numb."

"I warned you it was freezing out there. You're the one who said 'Don't worry, I'll be plenty warm in my wet suit.'"

Lucas slid his hands around her back and drew her against him. Then he rolled onto his back, still holding her tight. "My lips are numb, too."

Zoey lowered her mouth to his and kissed his cold lips. She closed her eyes and kissed him again, more deeply, a vision of him rising from the surf still firmly fixed in her mind. Within seconds his lips were as warm as her own. She kissed his cheeks and pressed her hands to them. She kissed his eyelids and his neck.

"Now are you warm?" Zoey asked.

"Mmm. Now even other parts of me are warm," he said.

"Don't be crude."

"I meant my feet."

"Sure you did," Zoey said. She gave him a light peck on the lips and rolled off him. "Are you hungry?"

"That depends. Is there anything *else* on the menu? I mean besides food. You know, maybe something for some *other* form of hunger?"

"We have hot dogs and we have s'mores. That's what's on the menu."

Lucas sighed. "Okay, then I guess I'm hungry." There was no mistaking the pouting tone in his voice.

"Lucas, I thought we were going to give that topic a rest," Zoey said testily.

Lucas sat up and wrapped his arms around his knees. "I'm sorry. But you know, one thing kind of leads to another. We make out, we touch each other, first thing you know, I'm thinking about the next step. It's like . . . like saying hey, we'll get all dressed up, we'll drive to a fancy restaurant, we'll sit down and order this great meal, only, surprise, we're not going to eat anything."

Zoey was silent for a moment while the fire snapped and spread a glow around them. "You're using a food example. You must be hungry."

"I'm starving," he admitted ruefully.

"Look, Lucas, if every time we make out you're going to say I'm leading you toward sex, then what am I supposed to do?" She held up her hand quickly. "Scratch that question. My point is, I really, really like kissing you. Really, really. But I'm not going to be able to enjoy it if you keep saying step one has to lead to step two has to lead to step three when I'm not ready for step three. You know?"

Lucas shrugged and looked away. Then he looked back at her, dissatisfied but not angry. "So if I want one and two, I have to shut up about three."

Zoey sighed heavily. It wasn't like she never considered step three. They weren't all that different, not really, she and Lucas. Except that it was more complicated for her than for him. It must be nice to be a guy and have everything be so simple and straightforward—just be led around by your hormones and never have to think about consequences. "Lucas, don't you want this to be a choice I can make for myself, one way or the other, and that I can feel good about?"

He absorbed that for a moment and winced. "Yeah, yeah," he said, making no attempt at sincerity.

Zoey smiled and hugged him. "We can still do some more of steps one and two."

"Okay. But first, we eat."

Zoey said good-bye to Lucas as night fell over Chatham Island and the tiny village of North Harbor. He went off toward his home, tired from the surf and, Zoey was sure, still a bit disgruntled and unsatisfied. She herself was feeling edgy, as she often did after making out with Lucas. She'd intended to go straight home and finish the journalism class assignment that was hanging over her head, but she didn't feel like concentrating. She was full of pent-up energy. She waved her arms back and forth at her sides, realizing how strange it would look to anyone who might be out on the streets and saw her.

She decided to stop by Nina's house. Zoey hadn't talked to her since the night before at the homecoming dance. Normally Nina could be counted on to drop by on just about any day of the week, especially a weekend day. But so far the day had been Nina-less.

Zoey walked the length of Center Street, crossing to walk through the parklike center of the circle. An island car, muffler blasting, front bumper held on by string, came rattling by and Zoey waved. Mrs. Gray, Aisha's mother. There were few of the island's three hundred permanent residents Zoey didn't recognize.

She reached Lighthouse Road, the northern edge of the island where cobblestones, low picket fences, and neatly tended gardens ran into sharp-edged, slick-wet rocks and sudden explosions of ocean spray. She went in through the gate of the Geiger house and instinctively looked up at the widow's walk, a railed deck atop the third story of the old house. Sure enough, there was Claire Geiger, Nina's sister. She was wearing a bright yellow rain slicker. Her long, voluptuous black hair streamed out from under an incongruous yellow rain hat.

"Damn," Zoey said under her breath. She herself was still wearing just a sweater, no coat.

Claire peered down, leaning casually on the rickety-looking railing. "Hey, Zoey."

"Hi, Claire. It's going to rain, huh?" Zoey yelled up at her, craning her neck.

"Zoey, we are completely blanketed with nimbostratus."

"Uh-huh," Zoey said.

"Rain clouds. Nimbostratus. But forget these." She waved a hand dismissively. "This is nothing. What's great is that there's a monster Canadian cold front rolling down toward upstate New York and Vermont."

"Yeah, that's cool, all right," Zoey said dryly. If Claire hadn't had the good luck to be very beautiful and endowed with a natural elegance that emerged even from beneath a rain slicker, she would have spent her life as a nerd. Yet because she was the person she was, her fascination with weather, her natural solitude, her distant reserve all added to a sense that she was a unique individual, not to be judged by anyone's standards but her own. Whatever *those* might be.

"Snow," Claire said, her eyes glowing as if she were announcing the advent of universal world peace. "There's a serious possibility of major snow in Vermont. Say, around . . . Killington? And next weekend is a three-day weekend?"

Zoey clicked. "Ski trip? Are you thinking ski trip?"

Claire smiled her infrequent smile. "Very likely. I'll let you know."

"Excellent," Zoey said enthusiastically. She and Claire didn't share much (except for some ex-boyfriends), but they did both like to ski. And even though the school year was less than two months old, Zoey had been feeling hemmed in lately. A road trip would be just the thing.

She had no idea whether Lucas would like the idea. He'd never mentioned skiing. But snowboarding was very similar to surfing.

And yet, it brought up the question of spending a weekend

with Lucas away from family.

"Where would we stay?" Zoey yelled up.

"My dad knows a guy with a condo there. This early in the year he won't have rented it," Claire said. She smiled knowingly. "Don't worry, I'm sure there will be plenty of beds for whatever arrangement you want."

Zoey knocked at the front door and went on in. She followed the sound of the Strokes up the stairs to Nina's room. She banged on Nina's door.

"*Qué día tan hermoso!*"

She went inside and found Nina Geiger lying on her back on the bed, feet up on the wall, holding a Spanish textbook above her head. She was shouting phrases over the music, singsong Spanish intermingling with the cheerfully defiant obscenity coming from the stereo.

"*Cree usted que hara buen tiempo mañana?*"

"Nina!" Zoey yelled at the top of her lungs.

Nina looked alarmed, then smiled. "Zoey. *Chiquita. Como está?*"

Zoey sat on the bed and stretched to turn down the music. She and Nina did not share musical tastes. In fact, on a surface level they shared almost nothing. Nina was a year younger, louder, funnier, stranger, more vulnerable despite everything, and tended to dress like a refugee from Seattle by way of a rest stop in New York. The two of them had been best friends for years.

"I just stopped by to say hi," Zoey said. "You didn't come over today."

Nina shrugged and looked away evasively. "I am so behind on homework, Zoey. In history class I'm behind by an entire war. And in Modern Media I'm just media-ocre."

Zoey made a disgusted face at her pun. "Don't tell me you're hiding out because you have homework. Do I look dumb enough to believe that?"

"I thought it was worth a try."

"Come on, Nina. You didn't come over because you didn't want to run into Benjamin."

Nina rolled over and searched for her purse.

"That's not it," she said. "That would be silly and immature, and as we both know, I am the model of maturity."

"Things didn't go too well between you guys?" Zoey asked reluctantly. She had promised herself she would not, under any circumstances, get involved in the tentative relationship between her best friend and her brother. But this wasn't getting involved, exactly. She was just making conversation.

"Things went fine," Nina said. She continued to avoid Zoey's gaze, searching through her purse. She found a pack of

Lucky Strikes and stuck one in her mouth, as always leaving it unlit.

"Look, you can tell me. Nothing you say will embarrass me."

"Okay, Zoey, since you asked. After the dance Benjamin and I stripped naked and made love like animals in the mud in the middle of the football field."

For a split second, Zoey's heart stopped. Then she sighed. "Okay, there *are* some things you could say that might embarrass me," she admitted.

Nina looked pleased with herself, as she always did when she managed to get a reaction out of someone. "Actually, it was no big deal."

"It was your first date, Nina."

"Didn't Benjamin already tell you what happened?"

"I don't talk to my brother about his love life," Zoey said. "I talk to my best friend about my brother's love life. Now, I promise I will never get involved again, in any way, or even ask so much as a single question, but come on, Nina. I mean, this was a big thing for you."

After years of silence Nina had recently accused her uncle of molesting her as a child. One of Nina's deepest scars from that experience was a lingering fear of the opposite sex. Zoey knew that what would have been just a date for most girls was an act of courage for Nina.

"Well, we danced."

"I know. I saw that part," Zoey said patiently. "I was there."

"We held hands. It was sort of like you told me it would be. Only my hands kept getting sweaty, and I never knew when we were supposed to stop, or after we stopped when we should start again."

"That's good, though," Zoey said, feeling a wave of affection for her friend. "You got through it, right?"

Nina nodded. "Yeah. But it was close. I mean, when we kissed—"

"You what?"

"We went outside and, you know . . ."

"Is this another joke?"

"No. I kissed him, all right? Jeez. I guess I should have taken pictures."

"Where did you kiss him?"

"Outside?"

"You know what I mean," Zoey said.

"On the mouth. Actually, I missed on the first try and kissed his nose. But the second one was full lip contact. No tongue, though," she added helpfully.

This detail was just half a step too far for Zoey. "Okay, there is something sick about this. I mean, if it were any other guy, I'd be asking for all the gory details. But it's *Benjamin*."

"Yeah." Nina smiled wistfully. She nodded. "It was nice. I mean, a couple of times all the old stuff with my uncle started coming back, and I was getting panicky. A couple of times I was close to blowing punch and Doritos all over Benjamin."

"That would have been romantic," Zoey said, grinning at the image.

"But then I said, no, this is Benjamin, not someone else, and it's right now, not back then. And so then I was mostly liking it."

"Mostly?"

"Like papayas." Nina sucked thoughtfully on the cigarette.

"Papayas."

"You know, like it's unfamiliar, you haven't tasted it before, so you're cautious. It's not something you're sure of, like watermelon or apples. Then you start thinking, well, it's new and different, but it's not bad. I could see where over time I could develop a taste for this."

"That's good."

"Yeah." She looked up at the ceiling. "Yeah. Only . . . I don't know what Benjamin thought. I mean, he's tasted papayas before. He's tasted them with Claire, in fact. And she's a much more experienced papaya than I am."

"Oh, I get it. So you're worried about what Benjamin thought. Like did he enjoy it as much as you did."

"Or maybe it was just a pity date all along. And maybe he thought *no way*." She bit her lip.

"You shouldn't worry about him and Claire. I think that's over. It's Jake she's interested in now."

"Oh, *really*?" Nina said. "So how come she broke up with Jake at the dance?"

Zoey's mouth dropped open. "She dumped him? Poor Jake."

"Yeah, yeah, poor Jake. That's not what's important. Benjamin and Claire were a *thing* for a long time, as in years. Benjamin and I have been a *thing* for, let's see, almost twenty-four hours."

"I don't think Claire would go after your boyfriend, Nina," Zoey said, trying to sound convincing.

"Please. Claire would snatch a cookie out of the hand of a starving orphan. I'm not saying she would enjoy it, but if she felt she had to . . . I've tried to tell you," Nina went on, wagging her finger, "she worships Satan up there on that widow's walk. In fact, Claire gets Satan to do her homework for her. Last week he slept over and they made popcorn and stayed up all night watching reruns on Nick at Nite. Satan is especially fond of *Full House*, it turns out."

"Are you done?"

"Yeah, I think so."

"Look. If you're worried about how Benjamin feels, you

could just ask him," Zoey suggested.

Nina looked half-troubled and half-sly. "Or maybe someone else could find out for me." She batted her eyes.

"Oh no. I am not getting in the middle of you and Benjamin. No way."

Nina shrugged and fell serious. "I guess we'll work it out. I mean, Benjamin and I are good friends no matter what, right? One date, one kiss won't suddenly change everything. Will it?"

Probably, Zoey thought. "Everything will be fine," she said out loud.

TWO

CHRISTOPHER SHUPE WAS LIVING IN greater luxury than he had ever seen outside of a movie or *Cribs*. The bedroom was twice the size of any normal bedroom. It would have been possible to fit the entire two-bedroom project apartment where he'd grown up into this one room. The high, plush four-poster bed, as big as it was, with flowery draped fabric, voluminous matching down comforter, and some form of pillow covers that Aisha's mother insisted on calling shams, looked tiny in the overall space.

The floor was polished dark wood, partly covered with thick rugs. The walls were papered, trimmed in little flowery decals. The curtains were heavy and multilayered. He had a couch and a love seat and a coffee table. He had a tall oak dresser and a curved, oak-framed mirror.

And that was just the bedroom. He also got a separate dressing room, whatever that was about. And a monstrous closet that made his few articles of clothing look paltry.

But it was the bathroom that was truly amazing. There were

endless miles of tiled countertops and a stalled shower, but by far the coolest feature was the raised whirlpool bath. He could lie in the whirlpool up to his chest in hot, foaming currents, and look out the window, down over the lights of North Harbor.

At the moment he was doing just that, though his attention was drawn to the small TV showing a late-running football game. The remote control was on the tile beside him, alongside a cold soda.

It was a fine life, although very temporary. Too bad it had come as a consequence of getting beaten up. He still had to keep his bandaged arm and stitched face out of the water, but the heat felt wonderful on the bruises covering his legs and stomach and back.

Christopher heard a distant knock on the bedroom door and Aisha's voice.

"Come in!" he yelled.

The door opened. "Are you in the bathroom?"

"Yeah. But I'm jacuzzing. Don't worry. I won't show you anything you don't want to see."

Aisha Gray appeared, framed by the bathroom door, tall, thin, graceful, topped by a volcano of bouncy dark curls. "Stay in the water," she warned. "My mom wants to know if you think you can make it downstairs for dinner. If not, she'll bring you something up here."

"I can more or less walk up and down stairs," Christopher said. "But I don't know if your mom and dad and Kalif want to stare at my face through dinner." He indicated the stitches and the blood redness in one eye.

"You don't look so bad," Aisha said. Sweetly, it seemed to Christopher. She sat down at the far edge of the raised tile platform. "Besides, Kalif would love it. He thinks stitches are tough. He wants some of his own."

"Let's hope not, huh?" Christopher felt the cloud forming over him again. Suppressed rage and frustration that could only be kept under control by concentrating on the revenge he had promised himself. He forced a smile. "With all this luxury, you guys are going to have a hard time getting rid of me."

"I told my mom to put you in one of the cheap rooms," Aisha said. "But this room is her pride and joy. You know, in summer this rents out for five hundred and fifty dollars a day, not counting tax. Of course, a continental breakfast is included."

"Your mom is very cool," Christopher said with feeling. As soon as she'd learned of the beating Christopher had taken, Mrs. Gray had offered the facilities of the bed-and-breakfast as a place for him to recover. He had no family in the area, and no family capable of helping anywhere.

"She has that nurturing thing going big time," Aisha said

fondly. "But I told her not to be stuffing pastries down you, making you fat."

Christopher nodded. "How about you, Aisha? No nurturing instincts?"

"Why? You need additional nurturing?"

"I *need* you to come over here and kiss me."

Aisha gave him a dubious look. "You're taking a bath."

"So close your eyes."

Aisha slid closer but stayed just out of reach. "I don't know, Christopher. It's not like we've settled everything between us. We were broken up before this whole thing happened. And I seem to remember that it was your fault."

She wasn't exactly saying no. More like she was looking for some reassurance. "Aisha, do you really believe that I'm thinking about any girl but you right now?"

"Maybe not *right now*," Aisha said. "But five minutes from now?"

"Are you going to kiss me or not?"

Aisha looked him over thoughtfully. She had an uncanny way of slipping into an observational mode that reminded him of a scientist watching bacteria through a microscope. It was part of what made her so interesting—she was always precariously balanced between cool, skeptical reason and blind, impetuous romance.

Aisha bit her lip and shook her head ruefully, and Christopher knew that romance had gained the upper hand. For the moment, at least. She moved closer and put her hand to his bruised cheek. Her fingers were cool. She lowered her face toward his, closing her black eyes slowly. Her lips met his.

He returned the kiss, feeling it spread throughout his body like a painkiller. Her lips were so soft. Her touch so gentle. Her hair fell around his face, almost closing off the outside world.

Why couldn't he just tell her that he would be faithful? And mean it? She had been at his side the instant she knew he was hurt. She was at his side now. She was beautiful and passionate and he had never, with any other girl, felt the way he did at this moment with Aisha.

He opened his eyes and saw that hers were still closed. Through her curls he caught a glimpse of the TV, and of the St. Louis Rams cheerleaders.

Still, he reminded himself, there were so many girls in the world. Why should he accept limits? Even the delicious limits imposed by Aisha's full, soft lips?

Aisha pulled away, but only an inch. "I do love you," she whispered. "I wish I didn't, but I do."

What should he say? Did he love her back? Yes, he did love her. Yes, of that he was certain. It *was* love. But should he say it? Would she think it was some sort of vow?

The hesitation was fatal. She drew back, pushing her hair out of her face.

"Aisha . . ." he began.

She stood up, keeping her eyes averted. "Dinner is in about fifteen minutes," she said. "I'll have my mom bring it up to you."

Claire climbed down the ladder that led from the widow's walk back to her room, feeling wet and elated. The storm hadn't been much more than a lazy drizzle. A disappointment, as she'd been hoping for some good lightning. But Zoey had jumped at the idea of a road trip to Vermont. And Zoey would convince Nina to come along, and what Zoey and Nina did, Aisha could be convinced to go along with. That would mean all four girls, plus of course Lucas, who would certainly come with Zoey; Christopher, if he was well enough and getting along with Aisha by then; even Benjamin, if Nina hadn't found some way to alienate him on their one date. Benjamin and Nina. Claire shook her head. She might get used to that concept eventually, but it would take time.

Anyway, if the entire contingent of island kids went away for the weekend, wouldn't Jake want to go, too? Jake was the most fanatic skier of the group. Of course he'd go—as long as it looked like a nonromantic, noncouple, group sort of thing.

Claire shucked off her raincoat and hat and hung them on the closet hook. She spread a towel under them to soak up the dripping rainwater.

She would have to make clear to Jake that she considered it over between them. It wouldn't be about the two of them being together. It would just be about enjoying some early snow and being off the island. A group thing. And the trick would be getting someone else to invite him.

Then if, while they were off at some romantic mountain hideaway, things very innocently developed between Jake and Claire . . . Well, it would be Jake's own choice, wouldn't it?

Claire quickly changed her blouse and started downstairs toward the aroma of clam chowder and Janelle's homemade corn muffins.

She ran into Nina and Zoey on the second-floor landing.

"What are you grinning about?" Nina demanded, looking suspicious. "You look like you're up to something."

"Are you going to stay for dinner, Zoey?" Claire asked, ignoring her sister and wiping the telltale smile off her face.

"No, I'm heading home. But thanks."

The three of them descended the stairs. "Have you told Nina about the snow?" Claire asked.

"No. We were talking about . . . other stuff," Zoey said cryptically.

Benjamin, Claire realized with a surprising pang. *Stupid*, she told herself sternly. It was absurd to be planning to win back Jake while at the same time feeling a sense of loss every time Benjamin's name came up. Chatham Island was getting too small. Too many former boyfriends lying around.

"What about snow?" Nina asked.

"We're thinking road trip this weekend," Claire said. "There's supposed to be a snowstorm moving through Vermont, and with that, plus the man-made snow, Zoey and I were thinking maybe we'd head to Killington. Me, Zoey, and I assume, Lucas."

"Well, Nina, you'd come, too, wouldn't you?" Zoey said quickly.

Claire fought the urge to smile. The mental image of just the three of them—Zoey, Lucas, and Claire—hadn't set too well with Zoey. She wanted Nina along, too. But Nina was looking dubious. "Oh, Nina doesn't want to come," Claire said.

"You don't want me along, Claire? I'm hurt," Nina said.

They paused in the entryway. "It's not that I don't want you along, Nina—" Claire let the sentence hang. Of course she *did* want her sister along, if Nina could bring Benjamin and add to the sense it was just one big happy island family. But Nina would do the opposite of whatever Claire wanted.

"If you guys are going, *I'm* going," Nina announced.

"You don't even ski," Claire pointed out.

"Maybe I'll learn. I'm a work in progress, Claire. I intend to do lots of things in my life that I haven't done before. Be a roadie for Vampire Weekend. Get a tattoo on my left butt cheek. Shave all your hair off while you're asleep some night. It's a busy life, but I could probably find the time to learn to ski."

"You might even enjoy it," Zoey suggested helpfully.

"Don't push it, Zo," Nina said. "No offense, but only an idiot could enjoy hurtling uncontrollably down a slope while their ears freeze and break off."

"So, you're in," Claire said, trying to sound annoyed. Easy enough, really, since Nina had a natural talent for annoying her.

"Yeah."

Claire sighed and headed toward the dining room. Now, with her back turned, she could allow herself an impish smile. Easy. So easy.

"Well, then I guess one of you two should invite Benjamin," Claire called over her shoulder.

4. Which of the following ten descriptions would your boyfriend agree apply to you?

Claire Geiger

Well, what an interesting question. It would be even more interesting if I were sure who my boyfriend was. In my mind it's still Jake, though technically I broke up with him at the homecoming dance. But it isn't that simple. I mean, I broke it off because that's what he needed me to do. He couldn't reconcile being in love with me and blaming me for the death of his brother, Wade, two years ago. It was tearing him up, and me pressuring him to get over it wasn't helping.

So I told him it was over. I think the military phrase for it is <u>tactical retreat</u>.

Which of the following ten descriptions would my boyfriend agree apply to me? I'll give it a shot, though I'm not sure when or if I'll ever be able to get Jake's answers.

1. Manipulative. Yes, Jake would have to go along with that. And what can I do? Deny it? That would seem even more manipulative.

2. Vain. No.

3. Beautiful. Yes. And no, that does not prove I'm vain.

I know I'm attractive, but I honestly don't care that much.

Although it can be useful.

3. Giving. That might be stretching the facts a little.

4. Friendly. That would also be stretching the facts a little.

5. Romantic. More than people think, but I doubt Jake would answer yes to it. I genuinely am in love with Jake. Sure, I'm willing to be a little manipulative in pursuit of some happiness, but that doesn't make the emotion any less sincere. So, yes, I am a romantic.

Just not one who thinks romance is all about heavy sighs and soulful looks. Jake would answer no.

6. Intelligent. Yes. And Jake would say yes as well. In fact, I think he's a little intimidated.

7. Sensual. Less than most people think. I have the sense that people have an incorrect opinion of me here. Probably. I wouldn't really know because I don't spend a lot of time trying to guess what people are thinking about me. It would be interesting to see Jake's answer to this one, though. I imagine, like most guys, he would hope the answer is yes.

8. Funny. I don't know. I'm not Nina, obviously. And I don't remember Jake and me ever laughing much. We had a relationship that had about one good week before it entered this sort of continuing crisis. The Cold War, Part Two. Right now he'd answer no to this, just to annoy me.

9. Loyal. Another tough one. I don't think any of the guys I've gone out with would answer yes to this. Which I guess is too bad. I suppose the truth is that my main loyalty is to myself, and despite everything I've tried to do to show my loyalty to Jake, I doubt he would give me a point here. Someday, maybe. Not yet.

10. Good. Ah, there's a deceptively sneaky one from the old quizmaster. Am I a good person? Benjamin once told me that deep down inside I was fundamentally decent, and could be counted on to do the right thing. And Benjamin is a perceptive person. But he's also still in love with me, so perhaps his judgment is wrong. I don't think Jake thinks of me as a good person, though I know he's still in love with me as well. All I can say is that I always try to do what's right. As long as the right thing is also the thing that works.

THREE

"WHAT AM I SUPPOSED TO do? Do I sit with you? Do I sit with him? Do I say hi to him, then come sit with you? Do I ignore him unless he says hi to me, or unless he sits with me? I don't understand any of this. Isn't there a book somewhere that explains it all? *The Big Book o' Relationships?*"

Nina found the pack of Lucky Strikes in her purse and stuck one, unlit, in the corner of her mouth. The chill sea breeze fretted her dark hair, stinging her cheeks and eyes. She drew her jacket around her, comforted by the warmth and the satisfying groan of the leather. She glared across the deck of the ferry at Benjamin, who was listening to music through earphones and hiding his blank eyes behind black Ray-Bans.

"I am absolutely *not* going to get involved in your relationship with my brother," Zoey announced firmly. "I meant what I said yesterday. That was it. Never again." She was sitting beside Nina on the bench, shivering because, as usual, she had not dressed warmly enough. She'd spent nearly her entire life in

Maine but still clung to what Nina thought was an inappropriate optimism about the weather. Now Zoey was holding her wispy blond hair down with her hands, trying to keep her ears warm. "What you do with Benjamin is your problem, and his. I'm not advising, I'm not passing information back and forth, I'm not spying for either of you."

Nina gave her a dirty look. "Zoey, why do you have bare legs when it's this cold? You're a senior; figure it out. It's cold. And it's distracting, having to talk to someone who is turning blue and rattling. Especially someone who doesn't understand that girl-girl solidarity transcends mere sister-brother solidarity."

"*You* have bare legs," Zoey said. "I mean, those tights aren't exactly warm."

"Yes, but I have hot legs. I always have. My upper body gets cold, but my legs are unnaturally hot. At night sometimes I have to stick them out from under the blankets."

"I never knew that about you," Zoey said dryly.

"Oh, yeah. Hot-leg Nina—new from Mattel. I'll be Barbie's newest, coolest friend."

Zoey laughed. "See, this is why I can't give you advice. I have my own selfish interests. I mean, if you start sitting with Benjamin every day, who'll sit with me and keep me from doing my homework on the way in to school?"

"I notice Lucas doesn't always sit with us," Nina pointed out. "So I figured maybe there was some *thing* I didn't know about. Some secret agreement everyone but me knows about that says boyfriends and girlfriends don't sit together at certain times. A state law or something. Like at lunch it's always just you and me and Aisha. And Claire, whenever she feels like hanging with her inferiors."

Zoey shrugged. "These things just work out. I mean, I spend lots of time with Lucas. He's over every night. Wait, backspace—every *evening*. He's over every evening."

"Hey, Eesh," Nina said, reaching around Zoey's back to poke Aisha.

Aisha looked up from her notebook, where she'd been busily scribbling calculus problems. "What?"

"I just wanted to see if you were conscious," Nina said.

"I'm trying to get my calc done so I don't have to do it during lunch."

"Hmm," Nina said, nudging Zoey. "Aisha is behind on her homework. That's fact number one. And fact number two is that Christopher is now living with her. Do I sense a connection there somewhere?"

Aisha slapped her pen against her pad. "He is not living with me. I happen to live in a B&B. Strangers often stay there. It's the whole point of a B&B. Christopher is no more living with me than any of the old fart couples who come and spend a weekend."

"Touchy, isn't she?" Nina said gleefully.

"How is Christopher doing?" Zoey asked.

"He's recovering pretty well. Mostly he's living it up while my mom stuffs the latest recipe from *Bon Appétit* magazine down his throat."

"Do you think he'll want to go skiing?" Nina asked.

"Do I think he'll want to go skiing?" Aisha repeated. "Yes, Nina. That was the very first thing he asked for this morning when he woke up. He said, 'Hey, I'd like to go skiing.'"

"Ha," Nina pounced. "So you were there with him *when he woke up*."

"It was a figure of speech," Aisha closed her notebook with an air of resignation. "Christopher is unfortunately still a partial toad. He's an injured toad I am helping take care of out of the goodness of my heart, but he's still a toad."

"Huh. So, you guys don't want to go skiing?" Nina asked.

"What is this with skiing?" Aisha exploded.

"Claire says it's going to snow in Vermont," Zoey said.

Aisha threw up her hands. "It's like having a conversation with Tweedle Dee and Tweedle Dum. Would one of you explain to me what you are talking about?"

Nina raised her hand. "Can I be Tweedle Dee?"

"We're thinking about taking a road trip over to Vermont this weekend," Zoey explained. "It's supposed to snow, and Claire says she can get us all a condo at Killington. Claire and I both like to ski."

"It's an excellent way to make yourself into a paraplegic," Nina said.

Aisha shrugged. "I don't think Christopher would be up for skiing by then. Besides, I really doubt he skis."

"Lucas doesn't either, but I figured since he likes to surf, he'd probably get into snowboarding."

"I don't do either," Nina said. "I just drink hot chocolate and sing 'Walkin' in a Winter Wonderland' over and over until people threaten to kill me."

"Sounds like fun," Aisha said dubiously.

"First it has to snow," Zoey said. "Then we have to get all the parental units to go along."

"Are you asking Benjamin?" Aisha asked Nina.

"Sure," Nina said with more confidence than she felt. "I'll ask him later. Unless Zoey would just be a good friend and ask him for me."

"This looks like a boyfriend-girlfriend situation, *not* a brother-sister situation," Zoey said.

"Except for Claire, who is currently boyfriendless," Aisha noted.

Nina nodded thoughtfully. "Yeah. Unless for some reason Jake decides to come along." She glanced across the deck at Claire, who was sitting alone, reading a book. A shadow of suspicion crossed Nina's mind. This whole trip was Claire's idea.

But no, not even Claire was that subtle.

Benjamin ran his finger along the curved brass railing as he descended the stairs from the top deck to the bottom deck. One, two, three . . . fifteen stairs, counted off almost without thinking. He turned a sharp right, advanced to the next railing, and, so naturally that a casual observer would not have known he was blind, he trailed a finger along the painted brass to the gangway.

Once on the dock he needed a landmark to locate himself. The ferry landing was imprecise, and he needed precision. He unfolded his cane, swung it in a short arc and quickly found the bench he was seeking. Now, in a line with the bench, it would be fifty-two paces to the curb at the end of the dock.

He heard a person fall into step with him and guessed from a host of almost imperceptible clues that it was Nina.

"Hi, Nina," he said with a smile. "You can't fool me just because you change brands of soap."

"Damn," Nina said. "I went from Dove to Irish Spring. It's manly, yes, but I like it, too."

"Yeah, but you stayed with Lucky Strikes. The smell of tobacco but no smoke. Dead giveaway. Plus Doc Martens make a certain sound. So do tights when your legs rub together." He put on a cocky swagger. "Don't mess with me, Nina. I have powers far beyond anything you puny earthlings could comprehend."

"Oh yeah? What color underwear do I have on? And my legs do not rub together."

"White. All cotton."

There was a long silence. "Okay, I give up," Nina said.

Benjamin grinned. "Just a lucky guess."

"Okay. Try this. How many fingers am I holding up?"

"One. The middle one. That was too easy." He was rewarded by the sound of Nina's laughter, a sound that conveyed a sort of unforced, childlike delight. It was a sound that always touched a soft spot in Benjamin.

Laughs were telling, he had discovered. Claire's was rare and dryly appreciative. Bestowed like a pat on the back for a job well done. Zoey always sounded surprised, as if she hadn't been expecting to laugh but wow! now she was and she was glad about it. Aisha had two—a restrained, moderate one that was partly just politeness, and a wilder one that broke out like an escaped animal she couldn't quite get under control.

"So, look, Benjamin," Nina began in the awkward way she

had of shifting into a serious topic. "I was wondering. I mean, usually on Monday after school I come over and read to you."

"Yes."

"Well, do you want me to come over and read to you today as usual?"

"Sure. Why not?"

"No reason. I was just asking."

They reached the curb and Benjamin turned toward the crosswalk. In a corner of his mind the count went on, a subliminal reassurance that he knew where he was, could place himself in the invisible world. "I still want you to keep reading, unless you decide you don't want to."

"Do you *want* me to decide I don't want to?" Nina asked.

"No, I want you to decide that you *do* want to. Unless you really don't want to."

"I want to."

"Which? Keep reading? Or not?"

"Whichever you want," Nina said.

Benjamin groaned. "Nina, this isn't supposed to happen. Even though we went out together, we're supposed to go on being friends. Friends first. That was the deal."

"So . . . so you're saying the other thing, that was just the one time?"

"Is that what you want?" Benjamin asked.

"No fair. I asked you first. Come on, light's green."

They crossed the street. Benjamin could hear the idling car engines on his left and the electronic click as the light went to yellow. Some distance ahead he could hear Zoey's voice, raised in conversation with Lucas.

"I had a good time the other night," Benjamin said.

"Me too," Nina said guardedly. "The music was pretty bad, but it was fun anyway. I mean, dancing and all."

Was Nina trying to tell him something? Had she been turned off by the kiss they had shared? It was certainly possible. She was just starting to deal with the corrosive aftermath of the situation with her uncle. Maybe she hadn't felt good about kissing Benjamin. Maybe she wasn't ready to go that far.

Or maybe she just didn't like *him* in that way. Maybe it wasn't some general thing, maybe it was specific. She'd avoided coming over on Sunday. And just now, on the ferry, she hadn't even come over to say hello.

"Yeah, dancing," Benjamin said, distracted by his own thoughts.

A silence descended that lasted several minutes. "So. I'll come over this afternoon and read for a couple of hours," Nina said.

Was she sounding relieved? No, that wasn't quite it. But she sounded strange. "That would be great," Benjamin said.

FOUR

"THERE IS NO DOUBT THAT with the invention of the Internet there were changes in the craft of journalism," Mr. Schwarz said. "But the basics are still much the same. It is still a matter of conveying the facts, giving those facts context, and—"

The bell rang, ending first period. Instantly books were gathered up, feet shuffled, desks scraped on the floor.

"—I guess I'll leave you all in suspense until tomorrow," Mr. Schwarz said. "Zoey? Can you stay for a moment? The rest of you, take off. But don't forget I want your assignments on my desk by Thursday, no excuses."

Zoey hung back as the rest of the class rushed past. She picked up her books and papers and went up to the desk, wondering if she'd done something wrong or blown some test. But as she searched her memory, she couldn't imagine what it might be.

"What did you want, Mr. Schwarz?" He was, without a doubt, the best-looking teacher at Weymouth High: tall, fairly young for a teacher, with brown rock-star hair.

He wiggled his eyebrows suggestively. "I got a call from Lisa Soo at the *Weymouth Times*."

Lisa Soo was the assistant style editor at the city newspaper, which put her in charge of the twice-a-month youth section, written by students from all the high schools in the area. Zoey had done articles for her during her junior year.

"What did she do, find a misspelled word from one of my old stories?" Zoey asked, not wanting to seem too eager.

"No, she has an assignment for us, and I suggested you'd be the person for the job."

Zoey felt a thrill of anticipation. It was just the youth page, but it was for a real paper. Those kinds of clips, along with her contributions to the high school paper, would help get her on the student paper when she went to college. And that was an important step toward landing a serious reporting job when she graduated from college. Not the White House beat for the *Washington Post*, maybe, but a good starting job that might *lead* to the White House beat at the *Washington Post*. Followed by some time overseas covering wars and natural disasters. Then, after she'd proven herself as a serious journalist, a move to TV. Say, ABC bureau chief in Paris or Tokyo or Jerusalem. And during her spare time, she'd write steamy romance novels under a wittily chosen pen name. Only her closest friends would realize that the queen of romance and the serious, Pulitzer-prize-winning foreign correspondent were the same woman.

"Zoey?"

She snapped back to reality. "Sorry."

Mr. Schwarz smiled. "How far gone were you? *New York Times*?"

Zoey blushed. "I'd only reached the first Pulitzer prize."

"Uh-huh. Listen, this is a serious story, and she wants your best effort."

"What is it?"

"There are rumors of illegal drug use on our varsity football team. You go out with someone on the team, don't you?"

"I used to," Zoey said, feeling her heart trip.

"Are you still on speaking terms with this person?"

Zoey shrugged. "I think so. But I doubt if he'd know anything about it. Jake isn't into that at all." She hoped that was true. The night of the homecoming game Lucas had made some remark about Jake being high, but then, Lucas and Jake had never gotten along very well.

Mr. Schwarz nodded. "Still, it would give you a place to start."

"Yes, I guess it would."

"Give it your best shot. If you get a story, it could move right off the youth page onto the front page." He shook a warning finger at her. "But source everything. And triple check everything. No off-the-record quotes unless you talk to me first and clear it. This is serious stuff, and we don't want to make accusations unless we have it totally nailed down. This is not something I want you to hurry on. Take all the time you need. You understand?"

"Absolutely," Zoey said seriously. "All the time I need. Very careful." Her mind was already racing, trying to figure ways to get at the story. Ways that would bypass Jake, should it turn out that he was involved.

"Okay, take off. And don't let me down."

She turned and started off, deep in thought. Then she paused. "Mr. Schwarz?"

"Yes?"

"Thanks for giving this to me. I really appreciate it."

He winked. "Just tell me this—in the Pulitzer daydream, you're not some airhead anchorwoman, are you?"

"No way. Foreign correspondent. Trench coat and the whole thing."

She stepped out into the hallway and hurried toward her next class, practically buzzing with excitement. A real story. At least potentially a real story. Football and drugs. It would be hard to beat that combination for getting the reader's attention.

* * *

Jake McRoyan had set his alarm for four A.M. that morning. He had gotten up and pumped iron hard for forty-five minutes, working his muscles to the limit with the free weights. Then he had taken a six-mile run, circling the northern half of Chatham Island twice till his lungs were screaming and his heart was racing.

He had cooled down by viciously pummeling the heavy bag that hung on a swivel in the corner of his room. Afterward, sweating and flushed and so weary he thought he might not be able to stand, he'd showered and, in the full-length mirror, had checked his body, flexing the muscles, looking for signs of the weakness he knew must be there.

He had let the team down. He had let himself down. He had let the memory of his brother down. All because of Claire. All because, despite the lean, layered muscle in the mirror, he was weak. And no amount of pounding the punching bag would change that essential fact.

Even Claire had at last seen it. Why else had she dumped him at the dance?

That morning he had been alone on the ferry ride over to school. Alone on the walk up the hill from the dock to school. And for the first time in his life, he had entered the school feeling that he had to avoid the gaze of the people he met.

So many people would get pleasure out of ragging on him. So many people would enjoy pointing out the hypocrisy of straight-arrow Jake, suspended from the team for refusing to take a drug test.

He had waited for it to start in gym class, his second period.

And there *had* been some banter about the lost homecoming game, but no mention of the real reason—that the star running back had been hung over through the first half, and buzzed on coke through the last half.

No one had mentioned cocaine. No one had even hinted at his suspension. Were people feeling sorry for him? Was that it? Or had it reached the point where no one cared whether Jake McRoyan or anyone else used drugs? No. Weymouth, Maine, wasn't exactly Detroit or Chicago. Here, an accusation that a football player was using was still worth a pretty good scandal.

They ran a basketball drill in gym class, not Jake's best game, especially with sore, bunched muscles and a profound weariness from lost sleep. But although there had been one or two slams at his less-than-elegant hook shot, the dreaded word *drugs* had not been spoken.

Hell, if the situation had been reversed, *he* would have thought of plenty to say to an athlete who had blown an important game because of his own personal problems. Plenty. But there had been nothing. It was just strange.

He was leaving the locker room on his way to third period when BeeBee Hoyt fell in beside him. BeeBee was a sophomore who played tight end on the football team. Jake braced himself. Now it would start.

"Hey, Jakester. What's this I hear about you doing K-berger?"

Jake was utterly nonplussed. "What?"

"You and Louise Kronenberger, dude. After the game Friday. Is that why Claire Geiger split on you at the dance? Inquiring minds want to know."

Jake frowned. "I was at a party where she was." He concentrated. The party was a blur in his memory. It had come right after the game, right after he'd been suspended. He had drunk a great deal of beer, he remembered that. A great deal. Much later he'd managed to stagger to the water taxi and get back to the island. The next thing he'd known, he was waking up in Claire's guest room, sick and in pain.

"Tad Crowley's telling people you got faced and pranged the K-berger."

Jake hardened his expression. "Yeah, well, I guess it's open season on me now." Flashes of memory: sitting beside Louise on a couch. She had looked good. But that was all. Wasn't it?

"So, you're saying you didn't?" BeeBee pressed.

"What's it matter, BeeBee? Who the hell's going to believe

anything I have to say about *anything*?" Jake demanded bitterly.

BeeBee half-closed his eyes and affected a bored look. "I don't know what you're talking about, dude," he said carefully.

"Screw you, BeeBee. You know what I'm talking about."

"No. I don't. Coach says I don't, so I don't. I'm clueless. I wasn't even there. I was in some other state."

Jake stopped and gripped the smaller boy's arm. "What are you talking about?"

Now BeeBee looked a little scared. He tried to pull away. "Chill, big Jake. Coach said it stays in the team. No one says anything to anyone about him suspending you. Ever. He doesn't want a bunch of parents on his back, I guess."

"Are you telling me no one outside the team knows about this?" Jake tightened his grip urgently.

"Coach said he'd cut the balls off the first guy who said anything. Jeez, you're breaking my arm, man."

Jake released him. He drew what felt like his first real, deep, honest breath in days. Coach was keeping things covered up. He didn't want to hurt Jake's chances of getting into a college athletics program. Plus, like BeeBee said, he probably didn't want a lot of parents running around screaming about drugs.

The secret wouldn't hold forever, though. No matter what the coach said, some guys would tell their friends, others would tell their girlfriends. But this way it would come out slowly.

And dribbling out bit by bit like a piece of gossip, most people probably wouldn't believe it. After all, if anyone had a clean rep at Weymouth High, it was Jake.

"Sorry," Jake said, absently patting BeeBee's arm where he had squeezed it. "I'm a little tense, I guess." Then he shook his head in relief and amusement. "Forget that crap about me and K-berger. I'll admit I was drunk that night, but I'm not that stupid."

Jake felt a little flicker of life returning to him. A week from today he could take the drug test, pass it with flying colors, and be back on the team. He would stay sober. He would get himself back in shape. He would be up and ready for the game after next. All the crap of the last few weeks would be behind him.

FIVE

"THIS IS VERY CLOSE TO something that a human being could eat without having to run to the bathroom clutching her throat," Nina said, chewing a bite of the food from her tray. "Very close. I can't say it's good, but it doesn't make me gag."

Claire raised a skeptical eyebrow and looked across the round cafeteria table at her sister. "Are you just saying that, hoping I'll try some?" she asked.

Nina made a heart-crossing gesture. "It's honestly not awful."

Claire hesitated, waiting for either Zoey or Aisha to try a bite. Aisha obliged first.

"Huh," she said. She chewed slowly, with a thoughtful look in her eyes. "I wonder what it is?"

"It's tan, or you might prefer beige," Nina said, "with forest-green highlights that may be a type of vegetable material."

"It could be . . ." Zoey rolled her eyes to the ceiling. "I'm getting a sense of vegetables. Possibly spinach. Also, there's a hint of meat."

Claire tried it. It wasn't bad. It wasn't identifiable, but it wasn't bad. Very likely she didn't really want to know what it was. She shrugged and had a fleeting image of an entire school being hauled away in ambulances. "So. Chances of snow in the mountains have gotten better since yesterday," she said. She focused on Zoey. "Have you asked Lucas yet?"

Zoey looked uncomfortable and began playing with a tendril of hair. "Not yet. Actually, I was starting to have doubts about the whole thing. I mean, it's such a long drive and all."

"Long drive? It's like two hundred miles, even if we stick to the highway," Claire said. "We catch the seven-forty ferry on Saturday, we load up your folks' van, and we're making our first run by noon. Ski all afternoon. All the next day. Ski the morning after that, and we're back by dinnertime on Monday."

Zoey nodded agreement but still looked unconvinced. "Well, what's this condo like?"

"Why? You suddenly need five-star accommodations? It's a nice condo. Two or three bedrooms plus a living room, a fireplace, a Jacuzzi out on the deck."

Again Zoey nodded guardedly. "So, like how many beds are there?"

Claire smiled wryly. "Oh, so that's what you're worried about. Huge surprise. Look, there are enough beds and rooms and everything that I'm sure we can work out *whatever* arrangement you want."

"It would be easier with just two bedrooms," Aisha weighed in. "Then it would be guys in one, girls in the other. Three bedrooms brings up other possibilities."

Claire drummed her fingers impatiently. "Look, it's not like anyone is going to have much privacy. We're not talking No-tell Motel here. I mean, if everyone comes, it will be eight people in one condo." The second the word *eight* was out of her mouth she wished she could call it back. But no one had taken any notice.

"I guess you're right," Zoey said, "but what are the guys going to think? If I go to Lucas and say, Lucas, do you want to spend a weekend in the mountains with me? he's going to think . . . you know. And lately . . . well, anyway." She started eating again, keeping her eyes down.

Claire groaned inwardly. Good grief. So Lucas was getting a little frisky. Big deal. All Zoey had to do was say no. Or yes. Or whatever.

"I know what Christopher would think if I asked *him*," Aisha said. "I mean, he'd interpret it his own way, regardless of what I said. Besides, I'm not sure I really want to spend a weekend with Christopher."

"He's living right in your own house," Claire pointed out.

Why was everyone being so difficult? This should have been easy—a big group trip would make it seem only natural that Jake come along, too. After all, even though he wasn't with her anymore, he was still part of the group. And then, away from the island, with absolutely no pressure from her, the natural course of events would bring together the only two unattached people. Simple, really.

"I know he's living in my house," Aisha argued. "But so are my mother and father and my little brother. If we're all at some ski lodge, I have no one around but you guys. And anyway, that's not the only thing. I'm not even sure Christopher and I *are* Christopher and I. He has a whole different idea about how things are supposed to be than I do. At least I think he does."

"Maybe he'll come around more to your point of view," Claire said, trying to sound interested. The truth was, she didn't much care if Christopher and Aisha were together or not, except that the plan really only worked if it looked like the whole Chatham Island group was going, guys as well as girls. She certainly couldn't convince Jake to come if it was just the four girls and him. That would make it like a girl thing, not a *group* thing.

Aisha snorted derisively. "Christopher suffers from hound syndrome. I don't think there's a cure."

"So you guys are bailing? It's down to me and Nina?" Claire said distastefully.

"That's a horrible thought," Nina agreed. "It would end up like *The Shining*. I'd be going around saying *redrum* and she'd be chasing me through the snow with an ax."

"I could do that at home," Claire muttered. "What did Benjamin say?"

Now it was Nina's turn to look away. "I sort of forgot to mention it to him."

Claire threw up her hands. It was a clean sweep. Perfect. Now no one was going. Zoey didn't want to give Lucas the wrong impression. Aisha was trying to put distance between Christopher and her. And Nina? God knew what idea had gotten into Nina's head about Benjamin.

"Well, *I'm* still going," Claire said flatly. "By Saturday noon I will be there." *And so will the rest of you and your various boyfriends*, she vowed silently. And Jake, too.

Whether any of them liked it or not.

Jake's last period of the day was study hall, time he could use to go to the library, see his guidance counselor, or do homework. He had arranged his classes with a last-period study hall so he could work out in the gym and get ready for football practice. It wasn't technically an acceptable use of study hall, but no one had ever objected.

But this was to be a week without football. Which meant

that study hall was . . . whatever he wanted it to be. The study hall teacher barely knew Jake's name. He was free.

It was an unusual sensation. Football had been a big part of his life ever since Wade had made the team, back when Jake was still in eighth grade. After Wade's death, Jake had followed in his footsteps. It seemed utterly strange to think that all the guys would be out on the field this afternoon, running plays without him. His first instinct was to go out and at least watch the practice. But that would have just been pathetic. And he had been pathetic enough recently.

The depressing memories crowded in on him as he escaped from history class. Drunk before a vital practice, Claire sobering him up with coffee and a shower. Drunk after the game, waking up freezing on the North Harbor dock, surrounded by the faces of his friends—some worried and sympathetic, like Zoey, others, like Lucas, barely able to conceal their disgust.

He tried to shake off the memories and walked faster. He wanted to evade Zoey and Lucas and Benjamin, who were all in the same history class. Zoey had indicated that she wanted to talk to him after class, but he had very little to say to her. She was either going to say something sweet and encouraging about his breakup with Claire, or, despite the coach's warnings, some rumor about his suspension from the team had already leaked out. Either way, he didn't want to talk to her. He had loved

Zoey for a long time. Had imagined a future of them together. Her pity now, however well intentioned, would be impossible to bear.

He plowed smoothly into the anonymous hallway crowds of noisy underclassmen. A group of freshmen trying desperately to look tough were swaggering down the hall in front of him, but sensibly parted at his approach.

"Jake!"

A female voice. Jake decided to pretend he hadn't heard. It didn't sound like Zoey or Claire, but he couldn't be sure.

A soft hand touched his arm, and he had no choice but to turn and meet the person it belonged to. He fixed a scowl on his face.

"Well, you look fierce," Louise Kronenberger said, smirking at him.

Instantly he felt uneasy. BeeBee's insinuation was fresh in his mind. What were *not* fresh in his mind were the details of the party at Tad Crowley's apartment after the game. He half-tried to remember. He had a clear flash of sitting beside Louise on a couch and noticing that her skirt had ridden so far up that he could see her panties. But that was about it.

"Hi, Louise," he said, feeling something close to panic.

"Hi, Louise." She mimicked his nervous tone perfectly. "Don't want to be seen with me, huh?"

Louise glanced over her shoulder, took his hand, and drew him into a recessed doorway. She opened the door and peeked inside. Then she pulled Jake after her into the gloomy, vacant chemistry lab and closed the door behind them. To Jake's astonishment, she put her arms around his neck, raised herself on tiptoes, and kissed him on the mouth.

"What was that for?" he gasped. It had been a nice kiss, but it scared him. He was wobbling on the edge of a cliff, about to lose his balance.

"That was for Friday night," she said suggestively. "I didn't want to say anything to you at the dance, what with you being there with almighty Claire Geiger." She laughed her carefree, amused laugh, a sound that struck new chords of memory in Jake's brain. Why did that laugh sound so familiar?

"I guess we had a good time Friday night," he said guardedly.

Louise made a pouting face. "You *guess*? I know I enjoyed it," she said. "Except for the times when you'd blurt out Claire's name." She erupted in another round of amusement.

Jake felt the blood draining from his face. "Louise . . . Look, I was awfully drunk that night." Plus, coming down off two rounds of cocaine, a football game, emotional depression, a suspension from the team . . .

"We were both pretty well blitzed." She peered at him

closely, looking a little disappointed, as if he were a dunce stubbornly refusing to get a very funny joke. "You're not going to go into the whole regrets and second-thoughts thing, are you?"

Jake rubbed his hand over his face. It was hot and his hand was moist. "I don't know how to say this, but did something happen between us? I mean, something more than flirting on the couch?"

Louise stared at him, dumbstruck. Then a slow smile began to spread. "Are you b.s.'ing me? Are you telling me you don't remember?" The grin gave way to a delighted laugh. "Your first time and you don't even remember? It *was* your first time, wasn't it? You said it was, and guys don't usually lie about how *little* experience they have."

"Are you . . . Is this true? Because, you know, it would be a pretty sick joke to play on someone."

Louise made a wry smile. She began to pull down the neck of her sweater, revealing some of her left breast. A red, puckered mark lay against the white flesh. "Want to match the hickey to the mouth?" she asked. "I'll bet it's like snowflakes, or fingerprints—no two hickeys exactly alike."

Jake rocked back on his heels. Oh God, it was true. What BeeBee had told him. It was true. Fragments of disturbing—and explicit—memory were racing across his consciousness now.

"Don't heave a kidney, Jake," Louise said. "It's not that big a deal. I mean, it wasn't *my* first time. And it was my idea as much as it was yours."

"God, Louise . . . I . . . I was so drunk that night." His breath was coming short and fast. He gulped hard. What was he supposed to say? Thanks, I'm sure I had a good time? "I didn't mean to do it. Really. I mean, that's not me. I don't believe in . . . I don't know what to say."

Now Louise was looking annoyed. "Oh, grow up, Jake. I said you weren't my first. And, not that I want to break your heart or anything, but you won't be my last."

"Who have you told about this?" he demanded. Claire? Did Claire know?

She shrugged. "The people at the party had to know. Those who were sober enough to notice anything at all."

Jake shook his head despairingly. The day had begun with an unexpected reprieve, the news that Coach was covering up the drug suspension. Now it was ending with this.

What had he come to? It made him sick just to think of it. It was as if his life were spinning further and further out of control.

And worst of all was the fear that when Claire learned of this, any remote chance of their getting back together would be over.

5. Will your boyfriend say that he tells you the whole truth (A) All of the time, even if it reflects badly on him; (B) Most of the time, unless it reflects badly on you; (C) Only when it's something you need to know; (D) Only when it suits his purposes. (Try to get your boyfriend to answer at least this question honestly.)

Claire

Of all the guys I have ever known, Jake is the only one I think can honestly answer A. Possibly because he's never done anything he's ashamed of.

Benjamin will tell the truth and the whole truth . . . but only when he chooses. In other words, he's fundamentally honest, but he'll save up the truth for the time when it will do him the most good.

When I was going with Lucas, I don't know how much truth either of us ever told. He keeps his secrets. And so do I. Of course, that was two years ago. He may have changed. You'd have to ask Zoey that.

I have not changed. Jake has been through some bad times lately, but I don't think he's changed, either. I'm a D and he's an A. Probably that means we're not a very good match, but I don't live my life according to magazine quizzes.

Aisha

Too easy. The answer is D. If I could get Christopher up to a C, I think I could live with that. Anything more than that would involve transplanting a different brain into Christopher's body. Which might not be such a bad idea. I myself am a B. I'll tell anyone the truth as long as it isn't something that would really hurt their feelings. For example, I do tell Christopher he's immature. He is, he needs someone to tell him, and anyway he thinks it's just one of his cute character traits. I don't tell him his singing makes birds fall down dead out of the trees. That would hurt his feelings.

So I'm saving that for a time when I really need to unload on him.

Nina

I believe it was the immortal Curly who asked, "What is truth?" Or maybe it was "What is truth, nyuk, nyuk, nyuk?" Anyway, the definition of truth has haunted the great thinkers and philosophers down through the ages. Now it's my turn to deal with it, so we may start seeing some progress.

Does Benjamin tell me the truth, the whole truth, and

nothing but the truth? I certainly hope not. Like I want him saying, Gee, Nina, your breath smells of Velveeta and peanut butter, you sicken me? No. I think not. If he were an A, I don't think we'd last long as a couple. Not that we're likely to last long as a couple anyway, because I'm not sure we ever were a couple in the full sense of couplehood.

As usual with Benjamin, no single answer works. He's halfway between B and C. A C-plus, let's say. I hate to screw up his GPA like that, but maybe there will be a makeup test later.

Zoey

I think Lucas is very honest. At least about the things that involve us as a couple. He's certainly up front about where he wants the relationship to go, and how soon he'd like it to go there. And I'm equally honest about telling him that I have a slightly different vision of the direction and speed.

Yes, I trust him to be honest. That's not the problem. The problem is when he's honest, and I'm honest, and there doesn't seem to be any way for us to agree. Then what? Either someone gives in, or both people go separate ways, or you end up like some old couple who hate each other but are staying together for the sake of the kids.

SIX

CLAIRE WAITED UNTIL WEDNESDAY AFTERNOON to act. She had been waiting for two things. First, the weather. There was no point in going ahead with what she was privately calling *The Plan* until it was certain that the weather would cooperate.

And beginning at two a.m. on Wednesday, a Canadian cold front dumped an early blanket of snow from southern Quebec to western Massachusetts. At the lower elevations it melted away, but above a thousand feet it lay across mountain slopes like a big goose-down comforter. Between this natural snowfall and the man-made snow, Killington was in business.

Second, she had waited for some evidence that Zoey and Lucas, Aisha and Christopher, and Nina and Benjamin had come back around to the idea of the road trip.

The evidence was not good. On Tuesday morning Aisha complained that now that she was spending more time under the same roof with Christopher, she was beginning to think he wasn't as good-looking as she had once thought. On Tuesday evening Benjamin had called the house wanting to speak to Nina, and Nina, who had once quivered every time Benjamin entered a room, told Claire to tell him she was out. Then, just this morning, Zoey had shown all the signs of pouting after some sort of fight with Lucas, who was showing all the signs of pouting right back.

At lunch Claire had learned that Zoey, Aisha, and Nina were going to the mall after school. They had asked her along, but she had declined.

Instead, she rode the ferry home with Lucas, Benjamin, and Jake—all three of them former boyfriends, though she hoped Jake was less *former* than the other two.

She sat down beside Benjamin. He stiffened as he recognized her and pulled the earphones off his head with a deep sigh.

"What are you listening to?" she asked.

He made a self-deprecating gesture. "Opera, believe it or not. It's the only area of music I haven't gotten into before. I'm getting so I like it. It's so extreme."

"Opera," Claire repeated. "I don't think you want to go around spreading the word that you listen to opera."

"Oh, I don't know. Maybe I'll set a new trend. A year from today, MTV might be doing blocks of opera. Pavarotti could have a whole new career as a VJ."

"Uh-huh. Have you tried any of it out on Nina?"

Benjamin smiled impishly. "You know, that was really quite subtle. I like the way you were able to work with whatever conversation was available, even opera. A very smooth segue from what you are pretending to talk about into the actual reason you came over here to sit by me."

Claire gritted her teeth. She was beginning to remember one of the reasons she'd broken up with Benjamin. "You're getting to be a suspicious person, Benjamin."

"I know. It's a serious character flaw. I'll try to do better in the future. So, what about Nina?"

"Well, I know my credentials as a big sister may be a little in doubt—"

Benjamin laughed in overly quick agreement. "—but I am still the little psycho's only sibling. And I was just wondering what you had decided about the ski trip."

A blank look. "What ski trip?"

"She didn't even tell you?" Claire tried to sound shocked. "We're all going this weekend over to Vermont. Me. Zoey and Lucas. Aisha and Christopher. And supposedly you and Nina."

Benjamin looked thoughtful. He hunched forward and began pressing his fingertips together. "Okay, I give up."

"What?"

He sat up straight. "I give up. I can't figure out what you're up to."

Claire forced an innocent laugh. Benjamin was pound-for-pound the biggest pain in the butt around sometimes. He should think about a career with the CIA. "I'm just the one who has to make the arrangements for the condo. I want to know how many people are coming. Also, if there's some problem between you and Nina, well, she's totally inexperienced, you know, and I thought maybe I could help."

Benjamin did a double take. "You know, for a minute there I thought I heard you say you wanted to help."

Claire sighed. "Listen, Benjamin, you can think what you want about me, but I *do* care about Nina. I don't make a big thing of it, but I do care. She comes straight off the showdown with our uncle and plunges into her first big dating experience with a guy she's had a crush on for years but who, until recently, didn't even really know she was alive and treated her like his little buddy."

She was pleased to see Benjamin wince. *Take that, smart guy. I can play the guilt card as well as anyone.*

Now Benjamin looked genuinely uncomfortable. "Okay, not that I'm buying you as a concerned big sister, but the truth is I don't know what's going on with Nina and me. I thought everything was great at the dance. Then she blows me off all day Sunday. I see her on Monday and it's like she's sending signals that it was a onetime thing. She comes over and reads to me that day, but it's very stiff. And yesterday I call your house and . . . well, you were there, obviously . . . she claims she's out. You tell *me* what's going on," he ended in outright frustration.

Claire absorbed this information, none of it really surprising. "I think she's just new to all this boyfriend-girlfriend stuff," Claire said soothingly. "She doesn't know what is supposed to happen after a first date. But come on, Benjamin, she's been mooning over you for a long time."

"Maybe the reality didn't live up to the expectation," Benjamin said glumly.

"I'll feel her out. Find out what she's thinking. It's probably just nervousness and inexperience. If that's the case, do you want to go skiing with all of us?"

"Claire, just how in hell could I go skiing?" He grinned. "I'll admit it would be funny watching me try. Even better would be coming back to school afterward, telling people I'd spent the weekend skiing, and see who had the nerve to ask for an explanation."

"It's going to be a big group thing, Benjamin. You know, island kids only. It wouldn't be the group without you."

He nodded. "I'll come along for the ride. I can read and

73

listen to music and go out with you guys at night. But I still don't get it. Eventually I will figure out what you're up to, but I have to admit, I don't see it yet."

Claire suppressed the desire to laugh in triumph. It was such a rare pleasure, manipulating Benjamin. After him, the rest would be easy. "It is remotely possible that I just like going skiing, isn't it? And that at the same time I want to see my little sister happy?"

"Yeah, right."

Claire leaned over and gave him a kiss on the cheek. "You need to lighten up, Benjamin."

The smile dropped instantly from his face as she kissed him. And, to her surprise, his reaction was not unlike her own.

Yes, there was still something there between them. But it would fade, she assured herself. It would fade.

SEVEN

LUCAS GOT OFF THE FERRY and headed through the town toward his house, the image of Claire kissing Benjamin fresh in his mind. It hadn't looked like much of a kiss, more like a Hollywood *hello* kiss; still, it was the kind of thing Zoey would want him to tell her.

It was extremely annoying, the habit people seemed to have of revealing their secrets to him. Louise Kronenberger had told him at the dance about sleeping with Jake. Lucas didn't *need* to know that, didn't *want* to know that, and didn't want Zoey finding out that he knew that and somehow twisting it around to look like he was keeping things from her.

Zoey had already reamed him out over the time when he had known Christopher was getting different girls' phone numbers. Like it was Lucas's job to tell Zoey, so that Zoey could warn Aisha. Like it was Lucas's fault that Aisha had walked in on Christopher and some girl practically in the act.

And lately the secrets kept piling up and growing in

importance. The worst was that he knew the idiot skinheads who had beaten up Christopher. But if he dropped a dime on the guys involved, Lucas feared they might get back at him by hurting Zoey. So he'd kept his mouth shut. Not an easy decision, or one that gave him any satisfaction. Few things would have given him as much pleasure as seeing Snake put back behind bars.

Then Christopher had asked Lucas to obtain a gun. As if Lucas knew where guns could just be picked up. As if he were crazy enough to get one for Christopher so Christopher could try to hunt down the guys who beat him up. The very guys whom Lucas was shielding so they wouldn't hurt Zoey who, if she learned any of this, would lay on a guilt trip of such epic proportions that Lucas would be left feeling like untreated sewage and no longer be allowed to kiss Zoey's foot, let alone anything else.

Yes, it would be nice to get through the rest of the year without learning any more secrets. The responsibility was too much.

He reached his house but hesitated about going inside. Yesterday his mother had told him that Christopher had called while he was out. It wasn't hard to imagine why Christopher had called. Christopher would probably keep calling. Unless he could change Christopher's mind.

With a sigh, Lucas started up the winding road that led up along the crest of the hill. It was a steep ten-minute walk to the big bed-and-breakfast. Aisha made the walk every day. The girl must have steel knees.

Kalif, Aisha's little brother, opened the door and let him in, pointing the way upstairs to Christopher's room. Lucas knocked on the door.

"Come in," Christopher said.

Lucas opened the door and his jaw dropped. Christopher was sitting on the high bed like some ancient Persian prince, propped against a mountain of brightly covered pillows, a TV remote in one hand with the other resting near an artistically arranged fruit-and-cheese platter.

"Jeez, Christopher. Do I have to bow when I come into the room?"

Christopher grinned. "You peasants are so easily impressed. Would you care for a small wedge of Brie? Perhaps a fresh strawberry?"

Lucas walked around the room and peeked into the bathroom. "Oh, man. This makes me sick. My whole room could fit in your shower."

"How is everything going down in the village?" Christopher asked. "I so enjoy hearing of the comic antics of the simple folk."

Lucas pointed to an antique-looking chair. "Can I sit in that?"

Christopher waved a magisterial hand. "Yes, I'll just have the servants clean it afterward."

Lucas sat down and looked Christopher over closely. "You seem like you're doing better."

"I am. A little stiff here and there, but I managed to do some sit-ups and push-ups this morning." He smiled at the memory. "It gave me a good excuse to lie in the Jacuzzi for an hour afterward. Actually, I'm probably eighty percent back. I'd be doing my paper route again, only I'm letting Kalif take it for a week and keep the money."

"How about your seventy other jobs?" Christopher had graduated from high school in Baltimore, moved away from his ravaged family, and set about earning enough money to go to college. He delivered papers, cooked for Zoey's father at Passmores' Restaurant, was the equipment manager for the school's athletics department, and did fix-up work everywhere around the island.

"Everyone's being very cool about it. I figure after this coming weekend, I'll be back at it. Sort of a forced vacation, here."

Lucas looked down at his hands. "Any word from the cops on the guys who jumped you?" he asked casually. If the damned cops would just catch the creeps, then Lucas's worry and guilt would be over.

Christopher's smile disappeared. His eyes, normally quick and inquisitive, went dull as steel. "No. I didn't really think there would be. Zoey wasn't able to make an identification. And I never really saw them. But I *will* see them. Sooner or later I'll find out who it was and take care of them. That's why I called your house yesterday. I still need what we talked about that night at the hospital."

Lucas shook his head. "Christopher, I don't think that's the way to go."

"Yeah? Why is that?" Christopher asked belligerently.

"Look, I spent two years in YA, and probably half the guys in there are there because they got into some revenge or payback situation. Either their parents did something they didn't like, or else their girlfriend cheated on them, or some guy didn't give them respect. I mean, payback keeps jails and prisons in business."

"So I'm just supposed to shrug it off?" Christopher bristled angrily. "Some skinhead Nazi sons of bitches try and kick my teeth in and I just go, well, too bad, let's get on with life like nothing happened? I don't think so, man. Nobody does that to me and just walks away laughing."

"Okay, fine. I can't argue with that. They ought to pay. But first, you don't even know who these guys are, and second, they didn't *kill* you, right? Justice does not say they should die for what they did."

"So I'll just injure them," Christopher sneered. "Would that be more just? I'll put them in a hospital. They can have my old room."

"With a gun? Guns are for killing. You don't *injure* someone with a nine millimeter. And what about the other thing? You don't know who these guys are. Are you just going to shoot people without even being sure they're the ones who popped you?"

"Maybe," Christopher snapped.

"Christopher, look, you and I haven't known each other all that long, but I don't see you as being a guy who goes around just shooting people. And I'm real sure I'm not the kind of person who is going to help you get a gun."

"I can get one without you," Christopher said. "I'm over eighteen. It's legal."

"Yeah. But it would be stupid. I mean, you're supposed to go to college next year, right? You want to make it prison instead?"

"I have no choice," Christopher said in a more subdued voice. He met Lucas's eyes. "What would you do if it was you who'd been stomped in some alley?"

Lucas had expected the question, but he didn't have an easy answer. "I don't know. I guess if I knew who the guys were and for some reason the cops couldn't deal with them, I might do just what you're thinking about doing. Only you don't know who the guys are. You don't know who to go after."

Lucas could see Christopher's angry resolve beginning to disintegrate. He swallowed and looked away, and when he spoke again, Lucas was shocked and embarrassed to hear a rough trembling in his voice. "I just keep thinking if I could have got up off the ground . . ."

"Zoey said they caught you on the back of the head first. You were stunned. You were outnumbered." Lucas shrugged. "No one wins every fight. Sometimes all you can do is take your beating and try to survive."

Christopher looked like he was fighting back tears. He bit his lip and with sudden savagery said, "Easy for you, Lucas. What beating have you ever had to just take?"

Lucas smiled a twisted, sad smile. "The one my old man gave me with his fists about twice a week until I went off to the YA." He tried to stave off the wave of anger and bitterness that rose like a volcano inside him whenever he remembered those days. "Like I said. Sometimes you just take your beating and survive."

Lucas left Christopher behind in his regal convalescence and started down the hill. It had grown dark out, and through breaks in the trees Lucas could see the brightly lit ferry gliding across unusually smooth water on its way back from Weymouth. The six thirty. It would be at the dock in another fifteen minutes, give or take. If Zoey was on it, she'd be back at her house shortly after that.

Lucas decided to wait for her there. He felt sick at heart and desperately needed some time with Zoey. She would make him forget the memory of Christopher, trying so hard to sound tough, trying to cover a fresh pain that hadn't yet begun to heal.

Watching Christopher deal with that had just brought back all the similar feelings Lucas had so often experienced. He wondered if he was doing the right thing, not turning the two skinheads over to the cops. He hoped he'd at least convinced Christopher not to go the way of a gun. But sometimes life seemed to go off into a sort of hopeless area where there were never any good answers. Just a lot of choices between bad and worse.

He paced the gravel in front of Zoey's house, growing more morose by the minute and more anxious for Zoey to come and dispel his bad mood.

"Hey, Lucas. Want to come inside and wait?"

Lucas turned and saw Benjamin, appearing to look out of his open ground-floor window. Maybe his gaze was off a point or two, but it was close. And he had *known* it was Lucas. "You're not really blind, are you, Benjamin? This is all some elaborate practical joke you've been playing."

Benjamin got the self-mocking cocky look he put on when he knew he had impressed someone. "It had to be you, Lucas. Who else would be lurking in our front yard, muttering under his breath and pacing back and forth?"

Lucas went to the door and on inside into the warmth and the light. Benjamin met him in the hallway. "You smell like potpourri," Benjamin said.

"Is that those bowls of like wood chips and stuff people leave out to smell up a room?"

"Yeah, that's the stuff."

"I've been up seeing Christopher. He's living like King Tut up there. Jacuzzi. TV. Free food. Potpourri. Real hard-core suffering."

Benjamin led the way toward the family room. "Is he going to be able to go on this road trip, do you think?"

"A road trip?"

"You know. The big skiing weekend thing in Vermont. Everyone's going, although no one bothered to tell me until just this afternoon."

"I have no idea what you're talking about."

"Aha!" Benjamin held up a finger as if he had just made a major point.

"Aha, what?" Lucas flopped onto the couch and unzipped his jacket. Zoey's house always seemed hot. Maybe his own house was just cold.

"I don't know aha what. Yet. But I will," Benjamin said craftily. "So you're saying you don't know about the ski weekend in Vermont."

"No. Why would I be going to Vermont?"

"That's what I'd like to know," Benjamin said.

Mrs. Passmore came in, carrying a cup of coffee. Lucas liked Zoey's mother. She was about ten light-years cooler than his own mother. In fact, both of Zoey's parents were from different worlds than his own folks. And looking at Zoey's mom made him think maybe twenty years from now Zoey would still be beautiful.

"Hi, Lucas," Mrs. Passmore said. "Where's Zoey?"

"Mall day," Lucas said. "I thought she might be on the six thirty and I'd just wait here for her to get home."

"You don't need an excuse to come over," Mrs. Passmore said. "You're nicer than my own kids."

"Good shot, Mom." Benjamin slapped a hand over his heart. "Aren't you late getting down to the restaurant?" he asked. "We can't start the big drunken party till you leave."

"I know, I know. Never trust anyone over thirty, as we used to say many years ago."

"You're not over thirty, are you?" Lucas asked disingenuously.

"Not in dog years, maybe," Benjamin said under his breath.

"See what I have to put up with?" Mrs. Passmore asked Lucas. She checked her watch. "Actually, I am late. There's some veal stew left over from the lunch shift in the frig. You two can nuke it up if you're hungry. Bye."

"Bye, Mom."

"Bye, Mrs. Passmore." Lucas waited till she was gone. "So, are you going to explain this Vermont thing?"

"According to Claire, everyone is going to spend next weekend at this condo she's lined up. In Killington. And as part of the *everyone*, your name came up."

"You mean, like I know about this?" Lucas asked. "Like I've said I'm going?"

"Exactly. Supposedly it's me and Nina, you and Zoey, Aisha and Christopher."

"Christopher didn't say anything about it."

"See? Claire is up to something," Benjamin said thoughtfully.

"Still, it could be fun," Lucas said. *Him and Zoey*. Him and Zoey and a condo a long way from any parental types. It was hard to see where there was anything terrible in that.

Of course. That's why Zoey hadn't said anything about it.

Well, she was being kind of selfish. Just because she didn't want him to have a chance to . . . to spend some private time with her.

"Maybe it's Zoey who's up to something," he said under his breath. Oh, this was going to be excellent.

I've got you, my pretty, and your Gap bag, too.

The line from *The Wizard of Oz* popped up in Lucas's mind as soon as he saw Zoey, trundling in, looking flushed from the chilly night air and carrying a bag from The Gap.

"Hi, babe." Lucas got up and took the bag from Zoey's hand and gave her a chaste kiss on the cheek.

"Hi," Zoey said, glancing at Benjamin on the couch. "What have you guys been up to?"

"We've been discussing whether quantum theory has any implications for broader epistemological questions," Benjamin said without missing a beat.

Lucas nodded agreement. "Also, we were wondering what kind of person would actually buy a Taylor Swift album."

"I have a Taylor Swift album."

"Yeah, but we decided you're okay anyway."

"How generous," Zoey said, sweetly sarcastic. "Come on.

You can carry my bag."

Lucas followed her upstairs, barely containing his excitement. He had her. He had her good. Ms. Open and Honest. Ms. You-should-have-told-me-Christopher-was-a-hound. Ms.—

Inside the door to her room, Zoey turned and put her arms around Lucas's neck and pulled him down for a real kiss. Instantly Lucas forgot that he was supposed to be playing it cool and standoffish. Then he remembered and started to pull away, but Zoey put her tongue in his mouth and he forgot again.

"I missed you," Zoey breathed.

This was the moment for a stern, disapproving look, but instead Lucas lay back on her bed and pulled her on top. It was several moments later that the first "uh . . . uh," was sounded by Zoey, and Lucas reluctantly stopped doing what he was beginning to do.

Damn. He'd had the moral high ground and he'd given it up. Now whatever he said, he would end up sounding petulant.

Zoey gave him the consolation kiss she always bestowed after she'd flashed her stop sign. "So what did you do this afternoon without me?" she asked.

"Went up to see Christopher."

"How is he?"

"Fine." The memory of his conversation with Christopher brought back all the guilt he'd felt at hiding secrets from Zoey.

Which, in turn, brought back the justifiable outrage he felt on learning that she'd been hiding something from him.

Only he would have to be very cool. Very subtle, or he would just look like he was pouting, or else like all he was after was a chance to get her away to a private condo with a private bedroom and no parents and probably a king-sized bed or possibly a Jacuzzi out on the deck under starry skies which would get Zoey into a bathing suit . . . at most. Subtlety. That's what was required here.

"So what's this about a ski trip you didn't tell me about?" he blurted.

Zoey looked surprised and, to Lucas's infinite gratification, embarrassed. Her throat was beginning to turn red, the blush easing up into her cheeks. She looked away. "Who told you about that?"

Well. He hadn't needed subtlety after all. "Benjamin told me. Obviously you decided not to tell me." *Fine, now don't overdo it*, he warned himself. But it was too good to resist. "Ms. Honesty. Ms. No Secrets. Ha."

Zoey gave him an appraising look. "I suppose you think you've really got me, don't you?"

"Cold. Signed, sealed, and delivered. After all the crap you gave me over Christopher and that blond chick. After that whole honesty lecture, and how between us we'd never need secrets. There's really only one thing I can say—nah nah nah nah nah nah."

"Lucas, the reason I—"

"Nah nah nah nah nah nah. Hypocrite."

"Are we going to discuss this like intelligent people?" Zoey demanded.

Lucas held up a finger. "One more. Nah nah nah nah nah nah."

"Are you done?"

"For now," he said, holding his head at a cocky angle. "Although I reserve the right to fire another *nah* or two if necessary."

"Look. The reason I didn't mention the ski idea was that I really didn't think you'd want to go."

"Yeah, right."

"Also, I didn't really want to go."

"You told me you love to ski," Lucas said, shaking his head in contemptuous disbelief.

"Yeah, but you don't even know how to ski."

"I surf. If you can surf, you can easily learn to snowboard. You should never lie, Zoey. You are so lame at it."

Zoey took a deep breath. "Okay, you *know* the reason I didn't want to go. I didn't want you to get the wrong idea."

Here it was, Lucas realized, like a gift from God—the

moment when he would get to trot out one of Zoey's favorite lines and destroy her with it.

"What you mean is, you don't trust me," he said in a sad little voice. He saw her wince. Yes! She was down. The referee had started the count.

Zoey sucked in air as if she really had been punched. "You enjoyed that, didn't you?"

"Yes, I did."

Zoey nodded. "Well, I guess I deserved it. I was a hypocrite."

Lucas grinned beatifically. Ah, life was sweet.

"So, uh, Lucas. How would you like to drive over to Vermont this weekend?"

"Gee, I think that would be fun," he said enthusiastically. "Almost as much fun as actually winning an argument with you."

Zoey gave him a dirty look. "Enjoy it while you can. You won't be winning the argument you're hoping you'll win this weekend."

"Let's hear it one . . . more . . . time . . . Nah nah nah nah nah nah."

6. First, rate your boyfriend's looks and attractiveness on a scale of one to ten, with one being equal to, say, Senator Lindsey Graham, and ten being a melding of Leonardo DiCaprio and Christian Bale. Then rate yourself. Finally, have your boyfriend rate you and himself on the same scale.

Zoey

First of all, whoever wrote this quiz is showing her age. Leonardo DiCaprio and Christian Bale could practically be my dad. Dads. Well, if they were melded, one dad. A cute dad, don't get me wrong, but still a slight bit aged.

Second of all, I don't really approve of concentrating on looks as being all that important. Although I guess the point is to see whether you and your boyfriend have some wildly different numbers. Like say you think you rate a nine, but your boyfriend says you're only a four. That might be revealing, I guess.

So I'll answer, but I'm answering under protest because I don't think this is a very feminist question.

I'd give me a six and Lucas a nine.

No, I don't have a poor self-image; I'm just being realistic.

I have nice hair and my face is okay, except that my eyes aren't perfectly lined up. But I don't exactly have major breast development. Not that I'm saying a girl's self-image should be based on the size of her breasts. I'm just saying that's one of the things society, and especially the male half of society, seems to get obsessed with.

Although why should I let society bully me into having a poor self-image? Really?

So, let me change those numbers. I'll give myself a seven. Lucas is still a nine. The only reason he isn't a ten is because I don't want him to get too full of himself.

Lucas

Zoey's a ten. No question. I'm maybe a seven or something, especially since her previous boyfriend was Jake. That guy looks like someone from a Soloflex ad, whereas I look more like I should be a bass player for some alternative rock band.

But Zoey's perfect. I mean, her face, her hair, her legs, her . . . not to mention her . . . whew. Never mind. Don't want to start thinking that way.

Claire

Oh, who cares?

Aisha

Okay, Christopher would say I'm an eight or a nine. See, he wouldn't want to insult me, but at the same time he wouldn't want to make me think I was too good for him. Also he'll say he's like an eight, maybe, although what he believes is that he's off the scale—a twelve or something. Infinity.

In reality, I am probably an eight. I think my eyes are too far apart and also my legs are kind of bony. Christopher, too, is an eight. He'd be a nine to even a ten except there's that huge bulge in his head where he keeps his extra ego.

Christopher

Aisha's a nine. I'm a ten. That puts me up by one, which is fine. You need that edge working in your favor. If Aisha were a total ten, she'd probably tell me to take a walk. Girls get that way when they're too perfect. Like Claire, for example, who is a ten but who I wouldn't go near if you paid me.

Nina

Can we use fractions? Because I'm just not sure I could be represented by an integer. I feel the need for fractions, which is odd because I don't normally crave fractions. Or perhaps a radical. Perhaps a square root. Or maybe we should employ parentheses in some way. (Parentheses are very popular in every math class I've ever taken, she adds parenthetically.)

To be serious, I'd have to say that I'm probably x squared minus y. Or the other way around.

But the real mystery is, how would Benjamin answer this question? All he can go by is what people tell him. Zoey has probably told him I'm a ten. Claire has probably told him I'm a two. That averages out to a six.

As for Benjamin, Benjamin is perfect. If Benjamin could see, he probably wouldn't have anything to do with me.

EIGHT

JAKE SLAPPED THE ALARM CLOCK, sank back down on his pillow for a second, then forced himself up. He threw back the covers, stood up, and stumbled to his bathroom. When he came back, he began stretching out methodically: neck, shoulders, legs. He dropped to the floor and did fifty push-ups, rolled over and did fifty stomach crunches, then repeated the sequence twice more.

He had always enjoyed exercise, but it had taken on a new meaning lately. In his mind it had become the antidote to everything that had gone wrong in his life. The antidote to the depression and the inner conflict between what he saw as his duty and his fatal desire for Claire. It was the antidote to drinking and all that drinking had led to—cocaine to recover from his hangover, the loss of self-control that had gotten him kicked off the team and landed him in bed with Louise, a girl he cared nothing about.

It was a miracle he hadn't caught anything, he realized. A dose of clap or crabs would have just about topped off the week.

He looked down at himself suspiciously. So far, so good.

Jake dressed quickly in shorts, sleeveless T-shirt, and running shoes. He went out through the sliding glass door and across the patio and began running down the driveway to the road. It was still fairly dark. Not black, but a deep blue, with the moon long since gone. He ran south along the concave arc of the beach. As he turned eastward from Leeward Drive onto Pond Road he could see the horizon, already bright pink. And by the time he had joined the coast road that followed the eastern shore of the island, the brilliant crescent of the sun had peeked over the rim of the earth.

He pounded on, stride long and regular, over cracked pavement and drifting sand, arms high, his breathing not yet labored, past the shuttered, boarded-up summer homes. He could see the church spire and the familiar buildings of North Harbor, a picture of brilliant gold where the sun touched and deep night shadows that had not yet been driven off.

He ran the perimeter of the island past the Geiger house, trying but failing to stop himself from looking up and noticing that the light had not yet been turned on in Claire's room. She was still asleep, luxuriant black hair spread across her pillow, dark, serious eyes still closed.

He forced the image from his mind and accelerated the pace past the harbor, waving to the fishermen emerging from

Passmores' with steaming paper cups of coffee. Zoey's father, Mr. Passmore, was standing with his own cup, dressed in kitchen whites, outside the back door of the restaurant, seemingly contemplating a spilled trash can.

Jake gave a nod and Mr. Passmore raised his cup in acknowledgment.

Another complete circuit of the island and he would have had a good workout. Down the western shore as sunlight ignited the glass and marble facades of downtown Weymouth, along the north shore of Big Bite pond past the still-sleeping homes there, up along the rugged, rocky beaches of the eastern shore.

He should turn through the town, avoiding the Geiger house altogether. But, he reasoned, it was easy to get a foot caught on the cobblestones. Safer to stick to the main road. He didn't even have to think about her as he passed. Didn't have to look. Just run and feel the slow burn in his legs and chest.

Claire saw him come past the second time. She had collected a cup of coffee from the kitchen and climbed up onto the widow's walk, as she did most mornings to watch the sun climb the sky.

She sipped the French roast and tightened the cord of her bathrobe against the breeze, a breeze that blew down from the distant and now snow-covered mountains.

Would he look up? she wondered. Yes, almost certainly.

He'd be trying not to, but he would look.

He turned onto Lighthouse, moving with an easy grace that was surprising in someone so large. Claire smiled and felt a little twinge deep inside. He was such a powerful-looking creature, unstoppable, uncontrollable. He looked like he would never tire. Like he could keep running forever.

He kept his eyes firmly fixed on the road ahead, and Claire felt a momentary, perverse sense of gratification that he had proven her wrong. But then, just as he was passing by below, he turned his head and looked up, scanning up the side of the house, finding her with his eyes.

Claire sipped her coffee and gazed calmly out to sea, giving no sign that she had noticed him at all. He ran on, then looked back over his shoulder.

Well, Claire thought dryly, maybe not entirely uncontrollable.

Five blocks away, Lucas, too, was having a morning cup of coffee and enjoying the crisp air. He stood on the deck behind his house, leaning against the railing. He caught a glimpse of Jake through a gap in the buildings and trees, shook his head in amusement, and returned his closer attention to Zoey's house, just below his on the hill.

He could see straight into her kitchen and the breakfast

nook. Both were brightly lit. Mrs. Passmore was sitting with her back to him, reading a paper. From this angle he could just see Benjamin's left hand resting on the table. Zoey was in the kitchen, wearing the Boston Bruins jersey she wore to bed, white legs, and bare feet. She was fixing a bowl of cereal. She went into the breakfast nook and sat down between Benjamin and Mrs. Passmore.

Now he could see part of her face whenever she leaned forward to take a bite of cereal. One foot was curled up under her.

Lucas sighed. He felt it was somehow pathetic that he should get such profound pleasure out of watching her eat Grape-Nuts, but he couldn't help the way he felt. Seeing her this way, when he could just watch and not have to act cool, not have to exchange banter, just soak up every detail of the way she sat, the way she moved, the way God-help-him that she chewed her cereal and her tousled, uncombed blond hair lay against her neck . . .

He was disgustingly in love with her. He wanted her like he wanted life. More at times.

She laughed at something and slurped milk down her chin. She caught it with her finger and then licked the finger clean, still laughing.

"Here." Mrs. Passmore handed her daughter a paper napkin. "You still have some on your chin."

Zoey wiped her face. "I have to get going." She took her bowl to the sink, ruffling Benjamin's hair affectionately as she passed.

She went upstairs and opened her closet door. Her eyes rested on a dress that had always been one of Jake's favorites. She was hoping to find an opportunity to approach Jake about the drug story she'd been given, and it probably wouldn't hurt to wear something he thought was attractive.

"No, Zoey," she chided herself, ashamed of the thought. That would be manipulative. If she was going to get Jake's help with the story, she'd get it honestly or not at all.

Except for the fact that *not at all* was just not an option.

She decided against the dress Jake liked and instead picked out an outfit Lucas liked.

She was climbing under the hot shower when the memory came back. A dream. Or at least a piece of a dream.

She had been skiing down a long slope. Lucas had been standing at the bottom, waiting impatiently for her. She had tried to veer off, but she found she couldn't avoid running into him. And yet it hadn't been a frightening dream. In fact, it had reminded her of flying dreams she'd had. More thrilling than scary.

That was all she remembered. Whether she'd managed in the dream to glide safely past Lucas . . . or not . . . she didn't recall. Either way, it didn't take Sigmund Freud to figure out the meaning.

She toweled off, replaced the outfit Lucas liked on the hanger beside the outfit Jake liked, and grabbed a sweater that neither of them liked.

Aisha was up, showered, and dressed earlier than usual. Which was to say that she would not have to make a mad run for the ferry. As she finished her breakfast she noticed her mother preparing a tray for Christopher. Aisha knew for a fact that Christopher was almost fully recovered and perfectly capable of coming downstairs for breakfast. But it was like some weird conspiracy between her mother, who seemed to enjoy treating Christopher like visiting royalty, and Christopher, who, of course, had no objection to breakfast in bed.

"I'll take it up," Aisha volunteered.

"It's no trouble," Mrs. Gray said cheerily.

Aisha got up from the table and lifted the tray. "He needs to start getting readjusted to real life," she said. She removed one of the two sweet rolls her mother had added and two of the four strips of bacon. "Besides, you're going to make him fat."

She carried the tray up the stairwell lined with colonial-era prints. The door of the room had a painted wooden plaque reading *Governor's Suite.* Aisha kicked the door lightly with her toe, rattling the plaque. No answer. She struggled to free a hand to open the door.

Inside, the curtains were still drawn and the room was dark. Christopher was obviously still asleep. She tiptoed over to set the tray down on the sideboard.

Aisha started to leave, but curiosity won out over good sense. She tiptoed over to the bed, nearly tripping on one of the rugs.

He was breathing heavily, his bare chest rising and falling slowly and, quite frankly, Aisha had to admit, attractively. It was impossible not to wonder what he had on beneath the quilt.

Too bad you're such a dog, Christopher, she thought. *If you weren't a two-timing, faithless weasel of a human being, you would be very, very fine.*

She leaned over and kissed him with feather-light lips. He groaned softly, but didn't open his eyes.

Was that for me, or for someone else? she wondered.

His food was going to be stone cold if he didn't wake up. Her mother would hate the idea of her food being eaten cold. Aisha leaned over him again, this time giving him a real kiss. A very real kiss.

A faint smile formed on his lips. His eyes were still closed. He moaned in a dreamy, not-yet-conscious voice. "Aisha?"

Aisha stood up and moved swiftly toward the door. When

she reached it, she looked back. He was stirring, becoming conscious.

Aisha, he had said, still in his dream of being kissed. Aisha smiled in satisfaction. Aisha, not any other name.

That had to count for something.

NINE

THE FERRY PULLED AWAY, CARRYING Nina toward another day of the garbage disposal of the soul that was eleventh grade. She stuck a Lucky Strike in the corner of her mouth and inhaled the smell of tobacco. On the bottom of the box it said "L.S./M.F.T." She'd heard somewhere that it stood for "Lucky Strike Means Fine Tobacco." Actually, the fine tobacco stung her chapped lips. It might be wise to switch to not smoking a filtered cigarette. It might be wiser just to break the habit altogether, only as long as she didn't light up, it was harmless enough. And it annoyed so many people whom she enjoyed annoying.

Suddenly the gentle conversation beside her took a nasty turn.

"When exactly was this big decision being made?" Aisha demanded in a loud voice. "The last I heard it was a dead issue. None of us was going skiing."

Zoey was looking uncomfortable in the hideous sweater that no one, aside from her, liked. "I know, but Lucas found out about the whole thing, then it was like I was trying to hide it from him."

"You *were* trying to hide it from him," Aisha said, cocking an angry eyebrow at Zoey.

"Benjamin told Lucas," Zoey said.

Nina sat bolt upright, dropping the cigarette on her lap. "Benjamin?"

"Yeah, so actually, if anything, it's Nina's fault," Zoey said to Aisha. "She was the first to cave."

"I didn't cave anything," Nina protested. "I never said a word about any of this to Benjamin. Now he knows? He'll think I didn't want him to go."

"You *don't*," Aisha said. She was acting exasperated.

"That's not the point," Nina wailed. "It'll be like I'm dumping him or something. I don't want to dump him. I'm not even sure he's my boyfriend yet. I can't dump him in advance like that. It would be preemptive dumping. That's illegal."

"So who told Benjamin?" Zoey wondered.

"Oh, man," Aisha groaned, still giving Zoey a dirty look. "So now Claire's going, you're going with Lucas, Benjamin is probably going . . . How am I supposed to keep this from Christopher?"

"I have to ask him," Nina said, feeling panicky. "I have to ask Benjamin like it was my idea all along. I have to ask him to go and spend a *weekend* with me up on some *mountain* some-where. And I don't even ski. I don't even like people who do ski."

"You could take lessons," Zoey said helpfully. "Or you could just hang out in the condo or the lodge with Benjamin."

"He doesn't even like me, I don't think," Nina said. "Now we're spending a weekend together?"

"Of course he likes you," Zoey said reassuringly.

"Did he say that?" Nina pounced greedily.

"I'm *not* going," Aisha said stubbornly.

"What did Benjamin say about me?" Nina persisted.

"He didn't say anything," Zoey said. "But you know he likes you."

Nina was far from satisfied with that answer. But what was she supposed to do? It would seem like a total slam not to ask Benjamin to go after Zoey had asked Lucas. She was trapped. Either she asked him, risking total, abject humiliation if he blew her off, or she didn't ask, in which case he would be hurt and think she was no longer interested in him.

And she *was* interested. Unless he *wasn't*.

She practically jumped up from the bench and made her way over to the spot where Benjamin was sitting, head back, sunglasses raised toward the sky.

"Benjamin," she said a little shrilly. "It's me, Nina."

He nodded. "Nina, you know you don't have to identify yourself to me. I know when it's you."

"Uh-huh," she said. "So. All set for the big ski trip?"

He turned his head, aiming the shades at her in his very convincing mimicry of a sighted person. "Ski trip?" he asked blankly.

What? He *didn't* know? Well, it was too late to change direction now. "Yeah, yeah. Big road trip. I figured you knew. It snowed in the mountains and like we were all going to get a condo and then Zoey and Claire can ski and the rest of us can sit around roasting marshmallows in the fireplace and take them to the hospital after they break their legs."

"Are you inviting me?" Benjamin asked.

"Of course I am. You're my . . . I mean, we're . . . you know."

"Friends?" he suggested.

It was not exactly the word Nina would have liked to hear. "Yeah. I mean, you know, Zoey asked Lucas, and I think Aisha's going to ask Christopher."

Benjamin shrugged. "Well, if everyone is going, I guess I'll go, too."

"Good," Nina said, feeling deflated. There it was again, that total lack of any of the feeling that had been there the night they'd kissed. Now it wasn't even like it had been, back when they were just good buds. "I'll tell Claire you're in."

She got up, relieved to be away from him. A feeling that did not promise much for the weekend. She found Claire downstairs, reading her Latin textbook and talking under her breath.

"You know that trip?" Nina asked without preamble.

Claire looked up from the book. "What about it?"

"I'm going," Nina said, feeling trapped and annoyed.

Claire nodded. "Good."

Nina did a double take. "Good?"

"Sure. Benjamin's coming, so I'm glad you're coming, too."

"Wait a minute, how do you know that Benjamin's coming?"

"I mentioned it to him yesterday and I got the impression he wanted to come."

"*You* mentioned it." *Of course. Who else*? Nina thought darkly.

"Yes. See? You say I never do you any favors. I knew you were kind of nervous about asking him, so I took care of it."

Nina's eyes narrowed in suspicion. "So you were being nice to me."

"Mmm." Claire returned to her book, but Nina caught the hint of a satisfied smile.

Nina nearly reeled from the implication. It was incredible, but there was no other reasonable explanation. Certainly not the lame explanation that Claire was trying to be nice. No. No, it was obvious what Claire was really up to.

Claire was after Benjamin. And judging from the way Benjamin had lied about his knowledge of the trip, Claire might already have been at least half-successful.

Zoey tossed the ball up over her head, drew back the racket, and brought it swiftly down. It missed the ball by six inches. The ball fell on her head and bounced off.

"Excellent serve," Aisha said.

"The sun got in my eyes," Zoey explained.

"It's overcast," Aisha pointed out. "And what kind of overcast is it?" she asked rhetorically. She raised her voice to yell down to Claire, who was on the far side of the court. "Claire! What kind of clouds are these?"

"Scattered cumulus. Is one of you going to hit the ball over here at some point or can Louise and I go change?"

"I'm trying," Zoey said. She threw the ball up again and this time managed to hit it with the racket. The ball flew up and, assisted by a tailing wind, sailed over the chain link fence that surrounded the tennis courts.

"Much better," Louise Kronenberger said. "Now we don't have to play."

"One of us should go get the ball," Zoey suggested.

"Why?" Claire asked.

"Claire's right," Louise said. "Coach Androgyny isn't around. And if she comes back, we just play dumb. Tell her we thought the match ended if someone knocked the ball over the fence."

The four girls drifted toward the net, cradling their rackets and looking around warily for signs of Coach Anders. On adjoining courts, other groups of girls played on, ranging from competent to very good.

"This is so dumb," Aisha said. "Who exactly was it who had the brilliant idea to put off our gym requirement till our senior year? We could have done all this *last* year and be free right now."

"Tennis beats basketball, anyway," Louise said. "I mean, later in life we can play tennis at the country club while our husbands are off at work."

Zoey rolled her eyes. "Are you planning on doing some time travel back to the 1950s, Louise?"

"No, I'm just planning on marrying a millionaire. It's much easier than having to work and support yourself. He goes off to his office and does his job, I go off to the country club and do the tennis pro." She laughed. "Who'll be having more fun ten years from now? Me, or you—Zoey Passmore the intrepid reporter, worrying about where to put a comma in a story about the problems of the clam-shucking industry?"

"Zoey will," Claire said, unexpectedly coming to her defense. "Louise, you'll have had three brats, be living on welfare, and hanging with some guy who rides a motorcycle."

"Huh," Louise said, completely unfazed. "So what's this biker look like?"

"Like you care?" Aisha muttered under her breath.

"Actually, I am pretty open-minded." Louise smirked. "Although lately I've been trying to decide which type I like more—the big, muscular, jock type"—she gave Claire a long look—"or the wiry, sensitive, bad boy." She fluttered her lashes at Zoey.

Zoey felt herself getting steamed. Louise wasn't just kidding. At the homecoming dance she'd been all over Lucas every time she got a chance. But there was no point in letting Louise see that she'd struck a nerve. Louise enjoyed getting under the skin of girls like Zoey. "The wiry, sensitive, bad boy will be spending the weekend with me at a ski lodge," she retorted.

"No! Don't tell me you're giving up your *virtue*! Not Zoey Passmore!"

Zoey felt a blush and realized too late she'd gotten teased into a pointless situation that was just going to get more embarrassing. What she should do was let it go. But with Louise mocking her, it was impossible. "No, I'm not you, Louise," she said. "We're all going skiing, *just* skiing. All of us together," she added.

"Oh. You mean all you virgin islanders?" Louise held up a hand. "Sorry. You're not *all* virgin islanders."

Zoey wanted to ask what she meant, but of course that was exactly what Louise wanted her to do. Besides, if Louise knew something—or thought she knew something—about one of the island kids, it was really none of Zoey's business.

Unless it was about Lucas. She narrowed her eyes in dark suspicion. Lucas had been homecoming king to Louise's queen. Had they somehow shared more than a dance?

"So, all of you are going skiing, huh?" Louise said. She sighed. "Sounds like fun. Is your friend Christopher going, Aisha?"

Now Zoey saw Aisha's eyes growing suspicious. "I haven't decided . . . um, I mean, yes. Yes, Christopher is going. With me."

"And Jake?"

Silence. Zoey glanced at Claire, who just looked bored by the conversation. Certainly there was no sign that Claire cared one way or another about Jake. Evidently it really *was* over between the two of them. Poor Jake.

"Damn, here comes Coach," Aisha said.

The four of them wandered back toward their corners of the court.

"She was just yanking you," Aisha said to Zoey. "You know Louise—she's on a one-girl mission to spread insecurity around."

"I'll bet that's not all she spreads around," Zoey said in a voice that Louise might just be able to hear.

TEN

THE IDEA OCCURRED TO ZOEY while she was changing from gym clothes back into her normal clothes. She dismissed it as unworthy.

But during homeroom the next day the idea came back, slightly changed so that it seemed not quite so unworthy.

By lunch she had grown more used to the idea, but she had to talk to Claire about it first and Claire had not joined them for lunch.

It wasn't until her fifth-period American Literature class that Zoey saw Claire. By then Zoey had grown comfortable with the fact that her idea was partly self-serving. True, but was also a good thing to do regardless.

She was standing in the hall waiting for Claire to arrive when Jake passed by. He smiled in the distant way he'd adopted since their breakup. She smiled back, turning up the brightness level a little, and telling herself it certainly wasn't unethical to be nice to Jake.

"Hi, Jake," she said.

"Hi, Zoey," he said. "How's it going?"

"Great. How about you?"

He smiled ruefully at some private joke and said, "Couldn't be better," in a tone loaded with irony. He walked away and Zoey saw Claire approaching.

"Hey, Claire." She took Claire's arm and moved her out of the stream of traffic. "I wanted to ask you something."

Claire waited patiently.

"It's about Jake."

Claire drew a deep *why me?* breath and looked at Zoey skeptically.

"Look, I know you two just broke up and all. But you know, this whole road trip to Vermont . . . I mean, if Aisha decides to ask Christopher, and I think she probably will, you know, if she gets over being pissed off at him, well, it will be all of us. You, Nina, Eesh, me, Lucas, Benjamin, Christopher . . ."

Claire glanced toward the classroom door, clearly impatient to get into class. "So?"

"It's like everyone on the island *except* Jake," Zoey said.

Claire sighed a long, slow sigh.

"I just thought it would be nice to invite him to go, too," Zoey said. "Unlike everyone but you and me, Jake actually does ski."

Claire turned up her mouth in a faint grimace. "Are you asking my permission to invite Jake along?"

Zoey shrugged. "I just thought it would be polite to see if you minded very much."

Claire tilted her head, considering the question. "I guess it might be a little awkward, but more for him than for me. I'm just going to ski, and I don't see how his being around would keep me from skiing."

"So you don't mind?" Zoey said eagerly. The final bell rang.

"If he wants to go, I'm not going to stop him," Claire said with weary disinterest.

Zoey followed her into class and went to her desk. Jake had glanced over, but not at Zoey. His eyes had darted to Claire and then away.

Poor Jake, Zoey thought sadly. *I wonder if he knows how little Claire cares.*

It would be a good thing for him to come along to Vermont. Getting off the island and especially getting back to being part of the group would do him good. Maybe Zoey and he could patch up some of the lingering bad feelings between them. Maybe they could become friends again.

And then Zoey could ask him about the rumors of drug use on the football team. Not that that was her motivation for asking him along on the trip. No, in her heart she was sincere in wanting to reunite the group, to smooth over the rough edges that had formed in the last couple of months.

But when all that had been accomplished in a spirit of total sincerity and friendship . . . then it would be perfectly normal for her to ask for his help with her big story.

Jake spent the class paying almost no attention to what the teacher was saying. Instead he occupied his time by wondering what Zoey and Claire had been talking about out in the hallway.

That it involved him seemed certain. He was sure he had seen Zoey mouthing the word *Jake* several times. The *J* was very distinct.

Then Claire had come into the room wearing that nearly invisible smile, followed by Zoey, who had looked somewhat troubled.

Had one or both of them learned about the drug suspension? Was that secret out already? Or, worse yet perhaps, had they learned what had gone on between him and Louise?

A thrill of fear went up his spine. *They were in the same gym class with Louise!* That was it. That had to be it. That's why Claire was smirking. That had been a smirk of contempt. And Zoey had looked troubled because . . . well, just because she was nice and didn't like seeing people do dumb things.

When the bell rang at the end of class, Claire made a beeline out the door. Zoey hung back, waiting for him like a defensive lineman who was determined to keep him from running the ball.

Great. She probably wanted to talk about it. Ask him *why* and *how*, and whether he needed someone just to talk to. He steeled himself. He would handle it with dignity and honesty. Or else he'd just lie and say Louise was a dishonest slut and no way would he ever have slept with her. No matter how drunk and depressed he was.

"Jake, um, do you have a minute?"

"Sure," he said, summoning up an insouciant cheerfulness. "What's up?"

"Well, there's this idea that maybe we'd all drive to Vermont and go skiing this weekend," she said. "You know, all the old gang. Me and Nina and Lucas and Eesh and Claire and Christopher and Benjamin."

Jake nearly burst out laughing with relief. "Sounds like fun," he said.

"Anyway, it wouldn't be the group without you. So I was wondering if you'd come."

This was definitely better than getting cross-examined about Louise or his suspension. But a weekend road trip? With

Zoey and Claire? And why was Zoey asking him? That was a very interesting question. He looked closely at her familiar face. Once he had been hopelessly in love with that face. It was still a very pretty face.

"I don't know," he stalled. "Where were you thinking of going? I don't think Sunday River's even open."

"We were going to go to Killington. Someone has a condo that Mr. Geiger knows or something." She waved her hand vaguely.

So. Zoey was asking him to go to Vermont for the weekend. *After* she had talked to Claire. Which meant either that Zoey had asked Claire's okay, *or*—aha!—Claire had asked Zoey to ask him.

Either way it could be trouble. He was *not* interested in spending time with Claire. Nor was he interested in Zoey any longer. In fact, he was getting used to being alone. Totally alone. No team, no girlfriend . . .

Just the same, though, he did enjoy skiing. And this was a *group* thing. He'd always been proud of the way the island kids tended to stick together.

"I don't have anything better to do," he said. "And if everyone else is coming, I guess I will, too."

7. How does your boyfriend feel about the other people in your life? Try to guess whether your boyfriend will say he (A) really likes; (B) somewhat likes; (C) is indifferent to; (D) somewhat dislikes; (E) can't stand: your closest friends, your mom and dad, your siblings, and your previous boyfriend, if applicable. Then compare your guesses to your boyfriend's actual answers.

Zoey

See? This is why I think sometimes these quizzes are a good thing. I've never really thought about how Lucas feels about all this stuff. I think for the most part that my friends are also his friends. Only to a lesser degree. For example, he likes Nina, but probably not as much as I do. Same for Aisha. I would say Lucas somewhat likes them. As for Claire, I know he doesn't trust Claire because there's a lot of history between those two—most of it bad. I won't say he can't stand her, though. More like D, somewhat dislikes.

He's barely talked to my dad, but I know he likes my mom. I think he sort of likes the idea of my parents. The way they're close and work together and are basically pretty cool. Sometimes cooler than I, personally, would like. And I know Lucas really likes Benjamin, although it's not like the two of them are best friends.

As for Lucas and my previous boyfriend, Jake . . . there's a lot of history between those two as well. They stay clear of each other, mostly. Polite but not friendly. Closest to a C.

Claire

My closest friends? I guess that would be Zoey and Aisha. I don't really know how Jake feels about Aisha; more or less indifferent, I guess. As for Zoey, I'm not one of those people who think that love, once it is formed, ever really goes away entirely. I think Jake still cares for Zoey. I also think Benjamin still cares for me. I even think Lucas, deep down inside, still has affection for me. And of course I still, from time to time, have feelings of tenderness for both of them. That's only natural. Things aren't always black and white. Usually they're shades of gray.

As to Jake and my father? Indifference. On both their parts. Jake and Nina? There's a healthy mutual dislike there, and always has been.

Jake and my "previous" boyfriend? That would be Benjamin,

of course. And it's an interesting question. Jake and Benjamin are polar opposites. Jake is physical, Benjamin is intellectual. Jake is direct, Benjamin is subtle. Jake is all about passion and duty and living out some ideal vision of what a "man" should be, and when he fails he's a wreck. Benjamin is brilliant, analytical, cool, with his emotions kept under such control that you wonder how long he'll be able to keep it up.

I doubt they'll ever be close.

Aisha

How can I answer any of this question? I'm not even sure how Christopher feels about me. All I can say is he <u>seems</u> to really like my mom and dad and Kalif. He <u>seems</u> to like my friends. But who knows how he likes them? For all I know, Christopher is trying to calculate some way to go after Zoey or Claire or Nina. I don't <u>know</u>; that's the problem. I have the feeling Christopher is the kind of guy who would have been happy being a pirate, being dashing and ruthless and always in pursuit of something or someone.

As for previous boyfriends, I don't have anyone who would qualify. I went out with other guys before, guys who would have been happy to be faithful to me, to be open and honest with me, guys I could trust. But Christopher was the first one I ever really fell for. .

And I'm supposedly smart. Right.

Nina

Benjamin and my best friend get along great. Of course, they are brother and sister. Benjamin and my dad get along great, too. They got to be friendly back when Benjamin was my sister's boyfriend. Benjamin and my sister? They don't get along as well as they used to, but I still have my suspicions about them. I mean, think about it. Why would Claire dump Benjamin for Joke? And the flip side is, why would Benjamin be happy with me if he ever got the chance to get Claire back? Jeez, when I put it that way, it's enough to really make me insecure. There's only one possible solution— kill Claire in her sleep. A stake through the heart should do it, but it will have to be sometime when the sun's up and her evil power is weakest.

ELEVEN

AFTER SCHOOL ON FRIDAY, ZOEY, along with Claire, Aisha, and Nina, went to the multistory parking garage where islanders kept their "real" cars. Real cars were the cars that were parked on the mainland. They were the usual assortment of automobiles, ranging from the Geigers' Mercedes to the Grays' more humble Taurus to the Passmores' big van, and generally came with luxuries like brakes and windshields. Unlike "island" cars, which were used only for putting around the island's few roads and were pitiful piles of junk.

They decided to take the Passmore van, since they planned to hit the mall for everything they might conceivably need on a ski trip to Vermont. But to Zoey's surprise, the van was gone from its usual space.

"One of my folks must have come over," she said, explaining the obvious.

"I'm not supposed to take my dad's car unless I clear it with him first," Nina said.

"You're not supposed to take it anyway, unless *I'm* driving," Claire pointed out.

The three of them looked at Aisha.

"Sure. Why not? I have the keys. Only, if I do decide to buy a pair of skis, where are we going to put them?"

"We'll strap them on top," Zoey said. "But you shouldn't *buy*. Wait and rent equipment when you get there. You may not even like skiing."

Aisha made a face. "I'll either be skiing or stuck in the condo with Christopher. I have no choice but to like it."

"You'll enjoy it," Claire said with atypical cheeriness.

They searched out Aisha's car and headed toward the mall, stereo blasting, Claire and Zoey in the back, Nina in the passenger seat in full recline mode.

"How did Christopher react when you invited him?" Zoey yelled from the backseat.

"Not as excited as I'd expected. I think he feels a little insecure about it. I mean, he's from the projects of Baltimore. Very little skiing goes on there."

"Did he ever skateboard?" Zoey asked.

Aisha shrugged. "No idea."

"Similar skills. But if he's still bruised, he might want to take it easy."

"He'll have a great time," Claire said, still eerily upbeat.

Suddenly something caught Zoey's eye. She turned quickly. "Hey. There goes our van." She wrinkled her brow. She was sure she'd seen her mother behind the wheel, but there had also been a glimpse of someone beside her. It wasn't Benjamin, since he, Lucas, and Christopher had planned their own guy version of a shopping trip. And her father would be at the restaurant on a Friday evening.

She shrugged it off. She opened her purse and looked in her wallet. Enough to pay for gas and for food when they got to Vermont, but not a lot left over for shopping. Unless she were to use her handy ATM card to raid her savings account, sin of sins.

There were certain things she needed. For a start, she couldn't sleep in her usual Bruins jersey. She needed something a little more substantial than that. Something substantial, but not frumpy. Somewhere about halfway between Sears and Victoria's Secret.

She took a small spiral-bound pad from her purse and jotted a note.

"What's that?" Nina asked. Reclining the way she was, her head was practically in Zoey's lap.

"My list."

"You and your lists," Nina said, mocking her.

"Hey," Aisha said. "Don't make fun of lists. I have a list. If

I didn't keep lists, I'd never get anything done."

Nina slapped her forehead. "*So that's* why I never accomplish anything. I remember once I'd been planning to find a cure for cancer, only I never wrote it down on a list. Sure enough, I forgot."

"So what's on your list?" Aisha called back over her shoulder.

"Oh, the usual. Little sample bottles of shampoo and conditioner so I don't have to carry big bottles."

"I have that, too," Aisha said.

"Me too," Nina added. "In my head. My head list."

"Actually, this is just a small part of my bigger list, which is the list of stuff to bring with me tomorrow," Zoey admitted. "Clothes, makeup, and all that."

"Black lace teddy?" Nina asked.

"No. In fact, I was going to shop for something warm. Flannel, maybe."

"You could get pajamas with feet in them, like when you were little," Nina suggested. "That would stop Lucas dead in his tracks."

"This is not about Lucas," Zoey said. "It's about staying warm. We don't know how well heated this condo is, or if there are enough blankets."

"Or enough beds," Nina said with a leer.

Zoey grabbed Nina's jacket and placed it over Nina's head.

"It's a fully stocked condo," Claire said reassuringly.

"So you think we'll see the guys at the mall?" Aisha wondered.

"If we do, it will only be for a brief moment as they race past in perfectly straight lines, buy whatever they came for, and take off," Zoey said. "You know how guys shop. Speed shopping."

"That's because they never buy anything," Nina said, her voice muffled under her coat. "Whereas I"—she produced a gold American Express card—"have the power to buy anything I want."

"Where did you get that?" Claire demanded.

"I asked Dad for it," Nina said, pulling her jacket off her face. "I told him I was thinking about changing my look entirely. I showed him a picture from a J. Crew catalog. You know, all clean and preppy looking. Sort of a blazer-chinos-pennyloafers look." She laughed. "Out came the old Am Ex."

"That's very devious," Claire said. "I'm proud of you. And as long as I get to use it, too, I won't even tell Dad how you manipulated him."

Zoey

1 flower print flannel nightgown (JCPenney)

1 3-pack of cotton underwear (JCPenney)

2 pairs L.L. Bean heavy woolen socks

1 pair ski pants

1 blue satin nightshirt (Victoria's Secret)

1 Swiss army knife

1 sample-size shampoo

1 5-pack of razor blades

1 ChapStick

Claire

1 pair ski boots

2 pairs ski pants

1 leather miniskirt (Target)

1 wool-blend sweater (The Limited)

2 pairs L.L. Bean heavy woolen socks

1 sample-size shampoo

1 pound French roast coffee

1 ChapStick

Aisha

2 books: <u>Skiing for Beginners</u> and <u>The New Guide to</u> <u>Skiing</u>

3 pairs L.L. Bean heavy woolen socks

1 pair gloves

1 Ace bandage

1 bottle Advil

1 pair ski pants

1 pair green satin pajamas (Target)

1 sample-size shampoo

1 sample-size conditioner

1 sample-size Crest

1 small loofah sponge

2 magazines: <u>Ski</u> with article on Killington and <u>Cosmopolitan</u> with article "Why Men Lie"

Nina

1 large bag peanut M&M's

2 pairs men's boxer shorts

4 pairs L.L. Bean heavy woolen socks

1 sample-size Afta Shave

3 temporary tattoos

1 Thighmaster

1 ChapStick

Trip Purchases: The Guys

Jake

I new binding

I pair new poles

I pair sunglasses

I hand-grip exerciser

I bottle Afta Shave

I ChapStick

Christopher

2 books: <u>Skiing for Beginners</u> and <u>The New Guide to Skiing</u>

1 pair gloves

1 bottle Listerine

1 bottle Safari cologne

1 box Trojan sensi-ribbed condoms

Benjamin

1 scarf (hopefully black)

1 bag Jolly Rancher watermelon candy

Lucas

1 bottle Scope

2 packs Tic Tacs

1 box Trojan condoms

TWELVE

ZOEY AND THE GIRLS RETURNED to Chatham Island on the last ferry and arrived back at nine twenty-five. Zoey said good-bye to her friends and went straight to the restaurant. It was Friday, and with Christopher not available to pick up shifts yet, both her parents would be working late.

Her father was in the kitchen, cleaning it up after the evening dinner business, leaving out only what he would need to send the occasional order of steamed shrimp or nachos out to the bar.

"Hi, Dad," she said, setting her several bags of purchases on the stainless steel counter. She gave him a kiss on the cheek.

Mr. Passmore wore his hair pulled back in a ponytail fastened with a twist tie from a bread bag. He wore a faded Albert Einstein T-shirt under a food-stained white apron. He was nursing a cup of coffee to one side, while he stretched plastic wrap over a steel tub full of what looked like soup.

"No one on this island appreciates a good gumbo," he

said. "Lobstah, steamahs, sometimes a good chowdah," he said, mimicking the Maine accent.

"So, you guys will be eating gumbo all weekend, I guess," Zoey said.

"What, you won't eat it, either? Oh, yeah. I forgot. The big road trip." He smiled. "Brings back memories of when I was your age and the road trips we used to take. Three of us drove from Dayton to Santa Fe in two days because we heard you could get peyote legally." He made a face. "Which is probably *not* the story I should have been telling you."

"We're just going skiing, Dad."

"Cool. But your mother wants to have a little talk with you."

Zoey let her shoulders sag expressively. "No drinking and driving, no drugs, no picking up hitchhikers—like there would be any room."

"Yeah, all that," her father agreed. "And my fatherly addition—if the red oil-pressure light goes on in the van—"

"Pull over immediately."

"Mmm. How much money do you have?"

"Well, I just went shopping."

Her father dug in his pants pocket and pulled out a handful of cash. "Looks like fifty-three dollars. Here. And don't tell your mom I gave you any. That way she'll give you some out of the register."

Zoey went out through the swinging doors into the dining room. She said hello to the waitress and found her mother behind the bar, waiting on half a dozen people.

"Dad said you wanted to give me a lecture before I took off," Zoey said.

"Well, you're not going now, are you?"

"First thing tomorrow morning. We're going to catch the seven forty. I figure you guys will still be asleep."

"Good guess." Her mother surveyed her customers. "Anyone ready? Tom?" When she got only negatives, she pulled Zoey aside into a corner of the dining room. They sat down at one of the tables.

"I just want to get a few things out on the table before you take off," her mother said.

"No drunk driving, no shooting heroin, no hitchhikers, and if the little red oil light comes on, I just keep driving till the van burns up."

"I know you know all that, Zoey, but I'm serious. No one drives drunk. Not you, not anyone. Even just one beer, you don't touch the key. Are we totally clear on that?"

"Mom, do you even realize that I don't drink?" Zoey asked.

"You don't? Ever?"

"I've had one or two beers in my whole life."

"Wow," her mother said. "I mean, that's good."

"I'm not the kind of person who would do something dumb like drive halfway across the country looking for peyote," Zoey said, batting her eyes.

Her mother nodded. "I know you're not. Anyway, just because *we* were stupid when we were young doesn't mean we're going to put up with *you* being stupid." She looked down at the tablecloth, picking at a spot of dried-on food with her fingernail. "Are you sleeping with Lucas?"

Zoey rolled her eyes and fervently wished she could just slip quietly from the room. She shifted position in her chair. "No, *Mother.* Of course not."

"Well, that's good," her mother said without much conviction. "I mean it really is. It's a big decision. And not just because you could get your heart broken. You also need to think about STDs and pregnancy."

"Is that all you wanted to tell me?" Zoey said hopefully.

"Look, I'm just saying that if for any reason you *do* decide to sleep with anyone, use condoms."

Zoey felt the heat in her face, but with luck, in the dimly lit room the blush wouldn't be noticeable. "Mother, I know all that."

Her mother reached across the table and laid her hand on Zoey's arm. "Of course you do. But I'm telling you again because I want you to remember. I know it sounds like I'm being a hypocrite, but the truth is I'd be happier if you didn't start having sex at all yet. I can't control what you do or don't do, I know that. So, all I'm saying is, *if* you decide to do it, use a damned condom because that way at least you greatly *reduce* the odds of catching anything *and* the odds that I'm going to become a grandmother."

"Yes, Mother," Zoey said, gritting her teeth. "By the way, did you give this same lecture to Benjamin?"

"No, your father took care of that. After I twisted his arm a few times."

"Oh." Zoey was disappointed. She'd been hoping to at least catch her mother being sexist. "Anything else?"

"Yes. When you use a public toilet, flush it with your foot and don't sit all the way down."

Zoey smiled. "Got it."

Her mother looked at her and shook her head a little wistfully. "You're a good kid, Zoey. I don't know how your father and I ever managed to have two such great kids."

"Benjamin and I can't figure it out, either," Zoey said. "Hey, I saw you driving around when I was on my way to the mall. Who was with you?"

Her mother's eyes flickered. Then she shrugged indifferently. "There wasn't anyone with me."

"I thought maybe it was a hitchhiker," Zoey said accusingly.

Her mother made a face. "Go on, get out of here. Take some money from the register. And have fun. Just not too much."

Zoey lay in her bed, looking up at the low, sloping ceiling. She should get some sleep because she would have to do at least some of the driving tomorrow and she hated driving with a lot of people in the car. She had a vivid imagination and always conjured up images of driving into a train, killing or injuring everyone but herself. That way she would have to be alive and healthy and go around visiting all the people she had hurt in the hospital.

She wondered how Claire dealt with knowing that she had been driving and was responsible, at least in large part, for the death of Wade McRoyan. She herself would never have been able to handle the guilt. But Claire was a different person than she was. Everyone was different.

Like in the way they dealt with guys—Claire, always so in charge and in control, dumping one, grabbing another. Like the way she had just blown off Jake with hardly a second thought.

Claire was like Louise Kronenberger that way—always cool, no matter what.

Although there were some big differences. Like, for example, Zoey was pretty sure Claire had never done it.

She smiled up at the dark ceiling. That's because guys were too scared of Claire to ask.

Unfortunately, Zoey did not seem to have the knack of being in control. She couldn't be imperious like Claire. And she certainly wasn't going to be easy like Louise.

What had Louise meant with that crack about not all of them being virgin islanders? Had she meant Lucas?

Zoey shifted onto her side and pushed down the covers. Suddenly she was hot. The dreamy, philosophical mood had evaporated. Sex, sex, sex. It was like there was some huge conspiracy—Lucas, pushing and pleading and practically begging; her own mother, ready to hand her a box of condoms; every magazine on the stands, with one article or another about better sex, or more sex, or different sex.

The whole world wanted her to have sex. Even *she* wanted herself to have sex a lot of the time. It would make Lucas so happy and so grateful. And it wasn't like there weren't times when she thought about it, and even played out various scenarios in her mind. Just doing it would put an end to the whole battle of wills between her and Lucas.

But she had experienced many of these same thoughts when she had been going with Jake. Jake had been no more subtle than Lucas. And back then she had thought about how it might be fun with Jake, and how happy he would be, and grateful, and how it would put an end to the test of wills.

She loved Lucas. She felt she loved Lucas even more than she had once loved Jake. And yet, what if she had slept with Jake and then they'd broken up? And what if, somehow, some way, she and Lucas ended up breaking up?

She shifted onto her other side and looked out the dormered window to see silver moonlight on the bare branches of the trees. Tomorrow morning—or maybe it was technically morning already—she was going off, for the first time, on a weekend trip, more or less alone with a guy. A guy she loved, who loved her. Only he wanted the love to be physical.

And the only question was, in the end, should she say yes or no?

A few blocks away, Claire was also awake. But when she'd realized she wasn't falling asleep, she had pulled on a warm parka and climbed up to the widow's walk. With chilly fingers she'd reached around the brick chimney to the one loose brick, pried it out, and found her diary. She huddled with her back against the railing and tilted the pages toward the light of the moon. Reading was impossible, but she could see well enough to write in a straight line.

Temperature: 41 degrees. Almost no wind. Clear.

Tomorrow's the big ski trip. My plan has worked so far. Jake will be there alone. I'll be there alone. I'm hoping that a week of solitude and believing he's lost me will help him get past all the stuff that's happened between us.

And then what? True love and happiness? I have no idea. I'd like to think so, but I have to take things one step at a time. First, get Jake back. Then decide what that means for the longer term. Tomorrow's the big day. I've never gone away with a guy before. Although having six other people along keeps it from being a honeymoon exactly. I'm a little nervous about it all. Surprising, since there's really nothing to be nervous about.

Claire closed the diary and slid the pencil back in the spine. Nothing at all to be nervous about. Except, if Jake still rejected her, it would mean . . . being alone, but that didn't bother her.

It would mean that he hadn't forgiven her. That she still wasn't free of a night not unlike this one, two years earlier.

8. Will your boyfriend say it is okay for him to (A) look at other girls as long as it is totally innocent; (B) look at other girls, deliberately make eye contact, and smile; (C) look at other girls as much as he wants as long as he doesn't actually ask them out; or (D) never look at other girls when he's with you.

Nina

Okay, <u>next</u> question.

Zoey

I guess I don't mind it when Lucas looks at other girls. Just looks. If he was like Christopher, looking with serious intent, getting phone numbers and all, then I'd be very upset. And I think Lucas and I are in agreement on this. I think he'll answer A. If he answers B or C, I'd be kind of not all that thrilled. But I'm not so insecure I'd want him to answer D. I guess that would be asking too much.

Although I never look at other guys when I'm with Lucas. Almost never.

Claire

I'm not bothered by guys looking at other girls. I look at other guys, so it's only fair that I should extend that same right to Jake. Besides, I'm not the kind of person to get all worked up into an insecure, jealous frenzy like a lot of girls. Either there's nothing to worry about, in which case it's a waste of mental energy, or there is. And if there is, then the relationship is over anyway.

Aisha

I wouldn't mind guys looking at other girls if they could at least do it with a little subtlety. You know, like the way we girls look at guys: quick, discreet, yet comprehensive. With guys it's like they're trying to memorize everything when they look at a girl. Like they want to be able to remember every tiny detail later on. Personally, I don't even want to think about why they're that way, but they are.

Now, Christopher would say he's free to look all he wants <u>and</u> go get the girl's number. Which is why I'm not so sure I should even be taking this quiz, because I'm not so sure I have a boyfriend. But as for just looking, that's no big thing.

Wait a minute. Yes, it is. I can't lie. It pisses me off.

It PISSES me off. Only I can't do anything about it.

Yet.

THIRTEEN

THE DRIVE

FROM WEYMOUTH TO PORTLAND, ZOEY drove and Nina took the front passenger seat. In the second row of seats, Aisha sat beside Christopher who sat beside Claire, who was wearing the leather mini she had purchased the day before. In the cramped space, her leg was pressed against Christopher's leg. Aisha was annoyed. Christopher glanced several times at Claire's legs, annoying Aisha still more.

Lucas, Jake, and Benjamin all sat in the far back, their shoulders cramped together. Lucas and Jake looked out their windows in opposite directions, having very little to say to each other.

Nina controlled the music and played the playlist she'd put together the day before. This got on Benjamin's nerves because he was sitting back by the speakers. It also annoyed Zoey, who hated driving with other people in the car. One wrong turn could lead to a lifetime of guilt and regret.

Outside Portland, Nina insisted they make a pee stop at a McDonald's.

From Portland to Portsmouth, New Hampshire, Claire drove. Zoey moved to the back, thinking it would put her with Lucas, but when Lucas came back from the McDonald's, he grabbed the relatively roomy front passenger seat. So Zoey ended up sitting between Benjamin and Jake.

Aisha and Christopher were still together, with Nina beside Christopher. Nina was wearing faded, baggy pants and boots, and Christopher showed no signs of looking at her legs. So Aisha relaxed. Until she realized that Christopher could, from his angle, look up at the rearview mirror and get a fairly scandalous view of Claire's legs.

Claire, however, was using the rearview mirror herself, to watch what looked like Zoey and Jake in friendly conversation. Lucas ate an Egg McMuffin and channel-surfed the radio endlessly, driving everyone crazy.

Nina wondered darkly if Claire's frequent glances in the rearview mirror were aimed at Benjamin.

In Portsmouth they lost their way trying to find Highway 4, resulting in a babble of helpful and conflicting suggestions that drove Claire, as soon as she had finally found the right road, to pull into a 7-Eleven and demand that someone else drive.

From Portsmouth to Concord, Jake drove, always a

competitive event for him. He played highway tag with a car from Massachusetts, at one point rolling down the driver-side window to tell the other guy he was, in the phrase Mainers reserved for drivers from Massachusetts, a *Mass*-hole.

Benjamin sat in the passenger seat and, out of sheer perversity, played an opera playlist until a group vote that he be forced to stop.

Nina, Zoey, and Aisha sat in the middle seat. Claire was in the back, sandwiched tightly between Christopher and Lucas, a situation that annoyed Jake, Aisha, and Zoey simultaneously. Snappish behavior began to break out all around, with arguments over music, how much the windows should be open or closed, heat, and driving style.

Nina suggested they should all join together and have a sing-along. She launched immediately into the Barney theme song, in which no one else joined.

Just past Concord, Aisha made a pee stop request, but Jake refused to stop. Zoey joined in the pee stop request. Benjamin, who was grumpy over the defeat of his opera, backed Jake. Nina joined Aisha and Zoey. Christopher lined up with the other guys and an argument on bladder differences between the sexes and its meaning in the world of sports, the military, and big business ensued.

At last Claire spoke up, told Jake in her quietly authoritative voice to pull over at the next rest stop, and he did.

Aisha drove from the rest stop to Lebanon, climbing into altitudes where snow clung to tree limbs and many of the cars were carrying full ski racks. Jake got the passenger seat. He turned to a rock station that faded in and out.

Christopher ended up in the far back with Zoey and Lucas. Lucas and Zoey held hands beneath the jacket draped over his lap. Christopher wished he could hold hands with Aisha, but Aisha was driving and, anyway, they didn't seem to be getting along all that well.

In the middle seat, Benjamin was stuck between Nina and Claire. Nina calculated the degree to which he was in contact with her versus the degree to which he was in contact with Claire. It *seemed* he was sitting closer to Nina, but there was no way of telling what was going on in his head. He might be paying much more attention to the contact with Claire.

They hit another McDonald's in Lebanon and Nina took over driving duties, because while no one had much faith in her driving, no one stepped forward to tell her so. Zoey took the seat beside her, watched the map, and clutched the dashboard fearfully each time Nina turned around to talk to someone in the back. The landscape had grown whiter all around as they climbed ever higher, but the roads remained clear.

Now Claire was in the middle seat next to Jake, both of

them carefully ignoring each other, though Claire let her skirt creep up her thigh and Jake kept leaning forward to rub his forehead in a way that let him glance at her and then hate himself for glancing.

Benjamin sat behind Nina, wondering why she seemed to smell of Afta Shave.

Aisha was in the backseat, not objecting to the fact that Christopher had made room for his shoulders by putting his arm around hers.

Lucas sat on the other side of Aisha, trying not to notice Claire's hair, draped back over her seat so that it fell across his knees.

By the time the van pulled up and parked in front of the cluster of wood-frame, two-story condominiums, everyone was exhausted.

FOURTEEN

CLAIRE BREATHED A SIGH OF relief as she surveyed the condo. They had made it. They were here. The Plan was working. And Jake had been mooning over her all the way up in the van. Except for that brief period when he'd seemed to be enjoying talking to Zoey.

The condo looked great. Upstairs were two bedrooms joined by a balcony that overlooked the tiny village of Killington. The downstairs featured a huge living room, a kitchen, and a second long deck with a redwood hot tub. From the deck the view was straight up the side of the mountain, a vast, rising expanse of frosted fir trees crisscrossed by dozens of white ski runs and the little red daisy chains of gondolas, looking like Christmas ornaments.

Zoey came up behind Claire and grabbed her arm as she was admiring the view. "There are only two bedrooms," she hissed in an urgent whisper.

"There's a fold-out couch there in the living room," Claire pointed out. "One bedroom has two double beds, and the other has one double. Altogether, with the couch, that's sleeping for eight people. What did you want? Bunk beds?"

"How are we going to divide up?"

Claire shrugged impatiently. "I assume it will be girls with girls and guys with guys. At least, *I* don't have any more exciting plans."

"Well, neither do I," Zoey said.

"Fine, so what's the problem? You share with Nina, I'll share with Aisha. Great. Now, let's get changed and hit the slope. I want to get back in shape quick. Before we leave, I want to be ready to try a black diamond trail."

"You're on your own, then," Zoey said. Trails were ranked in order of difficulty from green circle to blue square to black diamond. *Double* diamond trails were for professional-level skiers or the suicidal. "You're no better a skier than I am."

"Hey." Lucas, looking unsure of himself with hands in pockets, accompanied by Christopher. Benjamin had found a La-Z-Boy and had it in full recline. "Everyone's wondering where we should put our stuff," Lucas said.

"We figured guys sleep with guys, girls with girls," Claire said confidently.

Lucas and Christopher exchanged a shocked look and shuddered visibly. "Sleep with a guy?" Christopher said. "Not in this lifetime."

"You're just sharing a bed," Claire said.

"Who's sharing a bed?" Jake asked, arriving and slinging his bag onto the couch.

"Me and Nina," Zoey said, "Claire and Eesh. Then you guys work out whatever arrangements you want."

"Wait a minute," Jake said. "Like I'm going to be *in the same bed* as Christopher or Lucas? In what universe?"

"What's the problem?" Claire demanded. "*We're* sharing beds."

"You're girls," Lucas said. "Guys don't sleep with other guys."

Zoey gave him a dirty look. "Well, you can forget the other alternative."

"So can *you*," Aisha told Christopher in the same tone of voice.

"That's not what this is about," Lucas grumbled.

"Uh-huh."

"Right. There's some *other* reason," Aisha said. "You guys cooked this up together, didn't you?"

"Actually," Benjamin said, speaking for the first time, "it's just something that guys don't do. We don't wear pink. We don't use the word *cute*. And we don't sleep with each other. We're manly men."

Claire felt herself doing a slow burn. What was the matter with all these people? She was trying to set up a nice romantic weekend here and get in some skiing, and between Zoey's outraged chastity and the guys' terror of homosexuality, they couldn't get past stage one.

"Look. Here it is," she said. "Two of you guys have to volunteer to sleep on the floor."

"So *all* the girls get beds, but only half the guys," Jake summarized. "Nice try."

"Jake," Claire said, striving to keep her voice mellow, "the girls are willing to share, two to a bed. You guys *won't* share, so two of you get beds and the other two get six feet of carpet."

Jake shook his head. "Uh-uh. We all draw straws or cut cards or something. Four people get beds. Four get floor."

Aisha planted her hands on her hips. "I'm not sleeping on the floor just because you insecure males are terrified you might wake up in the night and discover that your hand is accidentally on another guy's butt."

Bad tactic, Claire realized. Very bad tactic. All four guys had looked panicked by that mental picture.

"Look," Zoey said. "It's you guys who are the problem here. If you'd share beds, we could *all* have beds."

"*We* are not the ones with the problem," Lucas pointed out. "See, maybe it's you girls with the problem. After all, you're the ones who won't share a bed with a *guy*."

Christopher gave Lucas a high five, but Claire noticed that neither Jake nor Benjamin joined in.

"Fine," Claire snapped. "Let's draw lots or whatever. Four people win. Then those four people can invite or not invite one of the remaining four to share. For my part, if I win, I'll sleep with Zoey or Aisha."

Nina chose that moment to come wandering in from the bathroom. "Excuse me? Claire? Is there something you've been hiding from me all these years?"

"Let me have your pack of cigarettes," Claire demanded.

"Smoking *and* sleeping with girls?" Nina asked archly. "Boy, you sure change when you get away from home."

Claire snatched the pack from the pocket of Nina's jacket. She extracted eight cigarettes, ignoring Nina's protest. She broke four of them in half, throwing away the excess, leaving her with four long and four short cigarettes.

"You know, you could have done that with just six ciga-rettes," Aisha pointed out. "Four long, break the other two in half and use both halves."

"Thanks for that math update. Here. Choose. Long gets a bed. Short gets floor. I'd like to get up the mountain sometime before next month." She stuck the cigarettes out toward Jake. He pulled a long one.

In quick succession Nina, Lucas, and Christopher pulled long ones.

"Unbelievable," Zoey complained, staring at her short cigarette. "Three out of the four guys. That means two of the girls are on the floor. What are the odds?"

"Arrangements could be made for some lucky girls," Christopher said with a leer.

"What do you mean, *two* girls are on the floor?" Nina demanded. "I count three."

"One of the girls can sleep with you," Zoey explained. "Namely, me."

"Ha. I don't think so. I won fair and square. Besides, I contributed the cigarettes. You losers are on your own."

The seemingly endless bed debate had been followed by a nearly as long bedroom debate, with tempers, particularly Claire's, flaring. To Benjamin, she seemed once again to have some hidden agenda that she was impatient to pursue. But then again, maybe she just wanted to hit the slopes.

Finally, Benjamin found himself on the lower deck listening to the receding crunch of boots on snow, the voices growing fainter with distance. He trailed a finger through the hot water of the tub and felt the icy breeze on his face. He felt he could sense the awesome weight of the mountain towering above them. Could imagine the detail, filling in remembered colors, almost as if he were painting a picture. It might not be identical to the reality, but it was a good picture anyway.

Then he heard someone coming through the sliding glass doors, stepping out onto the deck. Nina. He should have realized that Nina hadn't left with the others. Instantly his mood darkened. She was trying to be nice, of course, but he didn't want her to be nice.

All the others had gone. The three confirmed skiers, Zoey, Claire, and Jake, had headed off at last to the lifts. Lucas, Christopher, and Aisha had gone off to sign up for either snowboarding or skiing lessons, figuring to try whichever was easier. Nina had stayed behind to be *nice*. The word for that kind of nice was *pity*.

Damn it, if anyone should know better, it was Nina. She knew him well enough. But maybe now that their relationship had changed, she was no longer ready to give him the rough, egalitarian treatment that he appreciated from her.

He didn't mind the being left behind. The simple fact was that there were limits on what a person could do without being able to see. He would never be an airline pilot, he would never be a marine rifleman, and he would never be a serious skier.

Being the person he was, he wasn't thrilled about having to close off possibilities, but he had adjusted. He dealt with it without self-pity.

But other people inevitably felt sorry for him. Felt they had to find ways of including him in things. And it was that pity that burned.

"What are you still doing here?" he asked as gently as he could manage.

"I don't ski," she said simply. He could hear her climbing up to look down into the hot tub.

"Neither does Aisha. You could learn, though." Nina was trying to be nice, he reminded himself.

"I'm not all that into physical stuff. I mean, I can barely dance, as you know."

"You dance fine," he said tersely. Surely she should be getting the message by now.

"That doesn't mean I can ski. Besides, I'd rather just hang—"

"Look, Nina," he snapped suddenly, "I'm a big boy. I can amuse myself. I don't need a baby-sitter."

He heard her sharp intake of breath. What surprised him was the prolonged silence that followed it. As it stretched on it became more unsettling. Was she looking at him? Ignoring him?

At long last, "Screw you, Benjamin." A voice with tears in it,

"Nina, I'm not trying to be a jerk, but I don't need you to hold my hand for me."

"Yeah? You know what, Benjamin? Just because you're cranky from the drive up here, and just because you wish you'd never gone out with me, that doesn't give you the right to dump on me."

"Wait a minute, what are you ranting about? This is about you feeling sorry for me because I can't go and ski."

"No, that's *not* what it's about. I know better than to ever show anything like pity for The Great Benjamin Passmore, Sightless Wonder Boy."

"Fine, then you understand. So go off and enjoy yourself."

"You know, you're right. I was under the stupid impression that I might enjoy myself by being with you. But that was before I realized what a jerk you are."

He heard the door slide open.

"You said whatever happened, we'd always still be friends, Benjamin. But all it took to put an end to that was one lousy kiss. Yeah, one *lousy* kiss!" He heard the door slam, and then the ringing emptiness of the vast open spaces.

FIFTEEN

CLAIRE FELT THE FAMILIAR RUSH of anticipation as the chairlift scooped them up, lifting their skis free of the snow, holding them in a careless grip as it drew them up the side of the mountain, swaying and wobbling high above the skiers below. It was an environment in which she felt so at home—cold, clear, quiet. Private, except for Zoey alongside her on the two-person chair.

They rose over birch and fir trees whose branches drooped under the weight of snow. And as they rose the panorama expanded, widening out across a dozen rounded mountain peaks, blazing sun winking and dancing along the wide white avenues of ski runs. Back down the mountain, the cars in the parking lot, the base lodge, the pristine village had all been reduced to Matchbox toys, or some too-perfect-to-be-realistic model.

Ahead a few dozen feet was Jake, ignoring the other person sharing his chair.

Claire allowed herself a moment of smugness. By the end of

this day the group would have broken down into its component couples. Zoey would have found a place to be with Lucas, Aisha with Christopher, Nina with Benjamin. Only Claire and Jake would be wandering alone, unattached. But with a hot tub, a clear starry night, a fireplace, the warm, mellow afterglow of a day on the slopes . . .

It was a pity to have to manipulate him this way, but it was his own fault for being stubborn. She loved him, he loved her. Just because he seemed determined to screw that up didn't mean she had to let him.

They reached the top after a fourteen-minute ride. Claire readied herself, slipping her gloved hands through the straps of her poles. Ahead Jake was obviously not waiting around to be friendly. He was already making his way toward the head of a trail, weaving confidently around other skiers. Claire muttered under her breath.

"What?" Zoey said.

"I said, there he goes." She grinned. "Race you to the bottom, Passmore."

Before Zoey could answer, Claire launched herself in pursuit of Jake. Jake had always been a more powerful skier, but Claire had greater finesse. She thought she could probably catch him, even pass him. If neither of them took a spill first.

Jake was schussing straight down the fall line, gathering

speed down the particularly steep early part of the trail. Claire dropped into a tuck position and went after him.

The suddenness of acceleration took her breath away, literally, and it occurred to her that she hadn't skied in seven months, that she was badly out of shape, out of practice, and trying to chase a guy with unbreakable knees down a challenging trail. The smart thing would be to take her time, get readjusted, get warmed up, practice a few moves, and *then* get serious.

But Jake was getting serious *now*. It had become a challenge. Jake was trying to get away. And she wasn't going to let him.

They were halfway down the slope when she saw Jake lose it in a mogul field, making a wrong turn that sent him tumbling. She laughed out loud, a sound instantly snatched away by the wind. That would teach him to be a hotdog.

Should she stop and help him retrieve the loose ski that had escaped into the trees, or just coolly fly on by with a superior smile? Or maybe the best thing—

She felt something wrong. Felt the skis flying out from under her. Hit hard on her right shoulder, rolled, twisted, skidded, slid out of control on her behind, tried to dig in her heels, misjudged, flipped forward, and came to a final halt with her head buried in the snow, limbs splayed.

She pulled her head up and spit compacted snow out of her mouth. Snow was packed behind her sunglasses, and she cleared it with her clumsy gloved fingers. And a healthy handful of snow was down her back, out of reach. She would just have to wait for it to melt.

"Are you okay?" Jake, sitting just a few feet away, leaning back against a birch tree.

"Aside from feeling like an idiot? Yeah."

Jake went back to reseating his boot in the binding of his runaway ski. "You know, you're not actually supposed to stop by using your face that way."

Claire was crawling forward to retrieve her own skis, which had stopped in the trough of a mogul. "Go ahead and laugh," she said sourly.

Jake grinned. "I think I will. I mean, that was a bad fall. I thought you might have snapped your neck. But then I realized you were just demonstrating the new 'ostrich' stop, where you stop by suddenly sticking your entire head into the snow."

Claire laughed despite herself. "I was trying to beat you to the bottom."

"I might have been showing off," Jake admitted. "And it was going pretty well there up until I went airborne."

"Oh, great," Claire said. "Look at this." Zoey was gliding calmly past in a shallow traverse, giving a nonchalant wave. She yelled something and grinned.

"What did she say?" Jake asked.

"Tortoise and the Hare,'" Claire said. "You know, the kids' story about the race between the rabbit and the turtle, where the turtle wins because she doesn't try to show off when she's totally out of shape?"

Jake used his poles to push himself up. He came over and, after planting himself firmly, gave Claire a hand up.

"You know, if we cut across here we can catch a nice, gentle trail," Jake suggested, sounding almost shy.

"After you, tortoise," Claire said happily.

It was going better and faster than Claire had hoped. She had spent the afternoon skiing with Jake. Sometimes they ran into Zoey, but without any spoken agreement or acknowledgment between them, Claire and Jake had become partners for the day. Riding the lifts together, always staying within sight of each other, challenging each other with stunts that rarely ever worked.

But she was aware that it was a shaky truce. She had caught him watching her admiringly from time to time, but that didn't mean much. The question had never been whether Jake was attracted to her. The question was whether he was ready to let go of the past and get on with living his own life.

In other words, to do what she wanted him to do.

By the time the sun began to drop below the peaks, they

were both worn out and chilled. They spotted Zoey a distance away, heading toward the ski school, and caught up with her.

"Hi," Zoey said. "You two champions do any more of that trick skiing you were demonstrating earlier?"

Claire gave her a dubious look. "I suppose you didn't fall once."

"Not more than six or eight times," Zoey said. "Never face first though. I prefer the popular butt fall. Let me ask you this— are your shins killing you?"

"You need to lean against the front of your boot more," Jake suggested. "I always used to tell you . . ." He let the sentence drift away. Claire knew he'd been the one who'd taught Zoey to ski. They'd gone fairly often, back when they were boyfriend and girlfriend, sometimes with Jake's parents, once or twice with the Passmores.

"You were a great teacher," Zoey said sincerely. "I was lucky to have you."

Had there been an emotional subtext there of some kind? Claire wondered. Probably not. Zoey had a low threshold of subtlety. She was just being nice, telling Jake that she was still his friend. And that was good. Probably.

They came to the base of the novice slope and Zoey shielded her eyes, looking around for Lucas.

"There's Aisha and Christopher," Claire said, pointing.

Christopher was sidestepping stiffly up a gentle rise while Aisha was snowplowing down, looking nervous about moving at just over walking speed.

"Let's race over and make them feel like rank, pathetic amateurs," Jake suggested, grinning wickedly.

"That would be rude," Zoey said. "Let's do it."

The three of them got up what speed they could and stopped just short of Aisha, throwing up as much snow spray as possible.

"Show-offs," Aisha muttered.

Christopher schussed woodenly down toward them, unable to stop until he was several feet past them. He looked back over his shoulder. "So this is what white people do for a good time, huh?"

Jake shrugged. "There has to be at least one sport white people are better at."

"For now," Christopher said. "Let me get a few more lessons and then we'll see. So far, all I know how to do really well is fall down."

"You'd have a long way to go before you could fall any better than Claire did," Jake said with a laugh.

Claire slapped his arm with her glove. "You went first."

"Where's Lucas?" Zoey asked.

"He just left a little while ago," Aisha said.

"Oh. He didn't like it?"

"Huh. He went nuts. He decided to do snowboarding and he's just been crazy. It's like he found religion or something. Bouncing around on those humpy things—" She made a wavy motion with her hand.

"Moguls," Zoey supplied.

"I think he wore himself out. He took off for the condo to thaw out his feet."

"Which is just what I'd like to do," Christopher said. "I'm not totally back up to a hundred percent . . ."

"Excuses, excuses," Aisha teased him.

"Let's all head back. Thaw out, then go see about food and nocturnal entertainment," Jake suggested.

"Nocturnal entertainment?" Christopher repeated, adding an exaggerated lascivious leer.

"Absolutely," Aisha said with a wink at Claire. "Too bad you're not a hundred percent, though. I couldn't be very entertained by a guy who was just, what, seventy percent?"

"There's a club for kids who don't have fake IDs," Jake said. "It's usually full of freshman scrotes, but we could just ignore them. And the music is okay."

"We're there," Claire said. A little music, a little dancing. Yes, she was truly a genius. It was all going like clockwork.

SIXTEEN

THEY ARRIVED BACK AT THE condo, laughing and teasing, and ran into a stony wall of bad temper. Benjamin was in the living room doing the frostily polite routine Claire remembered well. She guessed it was possible Benjamin felt left out of the day's activities, but that wasn't like him at all. He knew what this was going to be like. It was more likely that he was pissed off by the Black Keys, pounding from the floor above.

Claire went upstairs and found Nina, listening to music on her computer and looking like a storm cloud. Nina glanced up at her resentfully and went back to reading a magazine.

Claire peeled off her ski clothes and began digging in her bag for something warm and soft. She found a heavy gray felt bathrobe and slipped into it gratefully. "Have a good time today?" she asked Nina.

Nina's response was a sneer. *Okay*, Claire thought, *trouble in paradise*. She went over and turned the music down to a more reasonable level.

"Turn it back up," Nina snapped.

"Nina, not that I want to sound like Dad, but there are other people around, and other people next door, too."

"What, did *Benjamin* ask you to come up here and turn down the music?"

"No, actually, Benjamin didn't have much to say."

"He had plenty to say to me," Nina grumbled.

"I'm guessing there was a . . . disagreement?"

"No. No disagreement. We agree. We agree totally."

Claire sighed. Her muscles ached and various parts of her body were tender and bruised. Plus, the familiar cold-induced lethargy had begun to steal over her, making her dopey and thick. "Why don't you two work it out? I'm going to go jump in the shower."

She headed for the bathroom.

"I have nothing to talk about with that weasel! Maybe *you* should talk to him, Claire!" Nina shouted after her.

Ten minutes later, feeling somewhat more alert, Claire went back to check on Nina. Not that she cared about Nina's spat with Benjamin, but she did want to keep things running along smoothly.

But back in the room she found Nina deep in passionate conversation with Zoey and Aisha. Zoey was interrupting every few minutes to say, "Look, I can't get between you and my brother."

Aisha was listening impatiently. "So why don't you just grab him, sit him down, and say hey, what the hell is the deal with you, Benjamin? Cut to the chase."

"Oh, like you do with Christopher?" Nina pointed out.

"That's different," Aisha claimed. "Benjamin's easy to talk to."

"You know something? I'm tired of hearing about what a saint Benjamin is," Nina said. "Everyone thinks he's perfect. But I'll tell you, he can be pretty snotty when he wants to be. And rude. And mean, too."

"Benjamin, mean?" Zoey asked disbelievingly. Then she held up her hands. "Sorry. I'm not involved."

"He should just come right out and say—" Nina suspended her sentence when she realized that Claire was in the room. "Never mind."

Claire sighed and slipped out of her robe.

Nina gave her a dirty look. "And I wonder why Benjamin isn't really interested in me," she said pointedly. "He's still pining for the lost ice princess and her twin icebergs."

Claire pulled a sweater on over her head. "Leave me out of it, Nina. This sounds like it's between you and Benjamin."

Nina looked away, obviously embarrassed by having come right out and been vocal about her jealousy. "Yeah, right," she muttered.

Claire pulled on pants and a pair of new socks. "Nina, why don't you just go and apologize to Benjamin for whatever idiotic or annoying thing you did to make him mad. Tell him it's just the way you are, that you're somehow genetically programmed to be a pain in the ass. He'll believe that. I know *I* do."

Lord, she thought as she headed down the stairs. *You try to arrange a simple little seduction and it has to turn into a three-ring circus.*

Aisha felt slightly ridiculous, standing in front of a sliding glass door just inches from darkness and below-freezing temperatures when she was wearing nothing but a bathing suit. But she couldn't wear a parka into the hot tub and, having never experienced a hot tub outside, and being sore from a day of skiing lessons, she was determined to make the run.

The only question was shoes. It was only about five steps to the tub, but the wooden deck was covered with tracked, dirty slush. The problem was, if she put on shoes to run to the tub, she would have to pause to take off the shoes, and that would leave her exposed, bare flesh to the wind for extra seconds.

"Go for it, Aisha," Lucas said, leaning over her shoulder to look out. "I'd join you, but I'm afraid Zoey and Christopher might both get the wrong idea."

"It's cold out there. Normally I don't wear a bathing suit when it's twenty degrees."

"Soon as you hit the water you'll be fine," Lucas assured her.

Aisha took a deep breath and slid open the door. "AHH-HHH!"

She ran on tiptoes, scampered up the side, and plunged neck deep into the steaming, churning water.

Lucas stuck his head out the door. "Of course, what I forgot to mention was that the real problem comes when you decide to get out." He gave a smile and went back inside.

Get out. Yes, Aisha realized, that could be painful. Still, for now it was heaven. She moved weightlessly around the tub until she located a strategically placed jet. Ah, yes. This *was* good for the tired muscles.

She leaned her head back against the side and looked off toward the mountain. Night had fallen, but the moon was still trapped behind the mountainside, backlighting the peak with a silvery luminescence. Overhead were more stars than Aisha had ever seen before, sharp and unblinking in the crystal mountain air.

A steady foot traffic moved from the nearby condos toward the base lodge and other restaurants and night spots. A group of middle-aged types in bright down parkas came walking past and gave her a friendly, mittened wave. She raised a hand from the warm water to wave back but instantly lowered it again. Yes, getting *out* would be the tough part. She might just have to stay in here forever.

She heard boots crunching on snow and pried open one eye to look. It was a guy following the same path as the middle-aged group, only this one was much younger. He smiled as he drew near.

"Is good night for this thing, yes?"

Aisha smiled, partly because she was just feeling good, and partly because his accent was sort of sweetly comical. "It's a beautiful night, yes."

He stopped and looked over the railing at her. "I am Pyotr. Peter."

"Aisha," she said. He seemed harmless enough, and she didn't want to be rude to a foreigner.

"Isha?"

"Aisha," she repeated her name more slowly.

"Peter," he said. "But in my country, Pyotr."

"Nice to meet you," Aisha said. It was a strange circumstance for meeting someone for the first time, but Pyotr-Peter seemed nice and was definitely cute, accent or no. He couldn't be more than eighteen or nineteen, she estimated. "What country are you from?"

"Estonia."

"Oh." She had no clear idea where Estonia was, but had the sense that it was in Europe somewhere. "Well, nice to meet you, Pyotr."

"Very pleasant meeting you also, Aisha. Shall you be going to a club or disco, I hope?"

"A little later, maybe," she said.

"Then if I have the luck, I will see you later." He smiled and headed off down the path toward the lodge.

Estonia. Now where on earth was Estonia? And what was a very cute Estonian doing in Vermont?

The glass door slid open and Christopher stuck out his head. "Why didn't you tell me you were coming out here? I would have joined you."

She cocked a finger at him. "You've just answered your own question."

"Funny. Come on, we're all going to get something to eat."

"I can't get out," she said.

Christopher's face lit up. "You mean you're . . . you don't have any clothes on?"

Aisha rolled her eyes. "Little one-track minds," she muttered under her breath. Were guys in Estonia like this? Probably not. They probably spent all their time wondering where on earth they were. "Actually, no, Christopher, I don't have anything on. And I'll get out, but I want you to close your eyes and not peek."

"Okay," he said quickly. "No problem."

"You *swear*?"

"Cross my heart. Jeez, Aisha, I'm not some slimeball."

"Okay. If you swear. Close your eyes."

He did, covering them with his hand. Aisha stood up and dashed toward the door, dripping water that would be ice in a matter of seconds.

"You have a bathing suit on, you liar!" Christopher yelled in outrage.

Aisha ran past him and jumped inside. "How would you know, since you swore not to look?" She left him to think of an answer, slid the door shut on him, and threw the lock.

9. Will your boyfriend say that his dreams about you are usually rated G, PG, PG-13, R, or X? How about your dreams of him?

Zoey

Okay, who wrote this stupid quiz? I mean, I know it's a quiz for girlfriends and their boyfriends, but honestly, with some of these questions I don't even want to know the answers. And I certainly don't want Lucas knowing all of _my_ answers.

I think dreams are private. What your subconscious comes up with isn't something you should be telling people about. Really. It's just not anyone else's business. Not even Lucas's business.

Besides, I don't think dreams mean anything. Just because in a dream maybe you're . . . well, never mind. It's no one's business.

Lucas

There is a very useful saying I learned while I was in jail—I respectfully refuse to answer on grounds that it may incriminate me.

Aisha

I think dreams are out of your control, so they tend to be about a lot of different things, all mixed together. Sometimes a person shows up in your dream and it's like he's just part of the crowd. Other times, maybe he's the star player. But if you averaged them out, I guess my dreams wouldn't rate anything more than a PG. No biggie. There aren't any demons hiding in some dark corner of my brain.

As for Christopher's dreams, I hate to think. I guess, being realistic, that I do show up there sometimes in his subconscious. Sometimes I may just be the UPS delivery driver or something. Other times, who knows? Who wants to know?

Okay, I'd like to know. But not if he knew that I knew. That would be sick.

Christopher

The truth is, I very rarely remember my dreams. The ones I do remember are usually more like nightmares, and with those I'd just as soon forget.

The good ones fade as soon as I open my eyes, which is a drag. I think it would be cool to be able to have really great, out-there dreams—maybe a <u>Sports Illustrated Swimsuit Edition</u> meets the <u>Forbes</u> list of the 400 richest people and I'm around number six on the list and moving up dream. Come to think of it, that's my most frequent daydream.

Anyway, I hope I'm having great R- and X-rated dreams because I'd like to think the old subconscious is having a really good time, even if I'm not.

Nina

My dreams are all about fuzzy bunny rabbits. I believe that Benjamin also dreams about fuzzy bunny rabbits. Now is this quiz over with yet?

Okay, honestly, I used to have recurring nightmares. They were about what happened with my uncle, and they were not fun. I have them less now, but occasionally they'll still come bubbling up out of my subconscious. They're rated D for disgusting.

But I'll bet Benjamin has really cool dreams. I doubt that I'm in any of them, except maybe as a minor supporting actor. You know, like I could be the person watching helplessly as he falls . . . falls . . . FAAAAALLS! Aiyee!

But if he did happen to dream about me, I think it would

be like a G-rated thing. You know, okay to see with your parents. Bring the kids. When he dreams of Claire, it's probably more like PG-13, you know, but for sheer horror, not for sex.

Benjamin

In my dreams I can often see. Sometimes I can "see" people I've never seen in real life, people I didn't ~~nkow~~ know back then. Or I see these people changed, grown older or something. Sometimes these visions are so extraordinarily compelling that I can't help but believe them. I've "seen" Zoey this way, older than I remember her from when we were little and I was still sighted. I've seen Claire and Nina, too. All of them—Zoey, Claire, Nina—are very beautiful in my dreams. Maybe they're beautiful in real life, too. Or maybe I just have an artistic and optimistic subconscious.

But I don't have R-rated dreams, ~~tle~~ let alone X, because I'm simply too decent and mature and gentlemanly a guy for that.

And if you believe that . . .

Claire

There are a lot of storms in my dreams. Tornadoes and hurricanes and thunder. I'd love to see a real tornado someday. Be as close as I could get, hear it and feel it . . . I find those dreams very exciting. But they're G rated. And those are about the only dreams I remember. Sometimes a dream about my mom, but those are just sad. Sorry. Nothing very exciting here.

As for Jake? He probably dreams about football.

Jake

I have two kinds of dreams—R-rated dreams, which make me kind of spacey all the next day, and football dreams, where I can't make my legs run and the defensive linemen are all huge brutes who are going to crush me into the dirt and stomp me with their cleats.

Mostly I prefer the R-rated dreams.

SEVENTEEN

FULL OF BURGERS AND POTATO skins and nachos, they arrived at the club. Nina had been expecting the worst. She figured that an underage club in a ski area would be playing a mix of weenie tunes. And in her present mood, a single Justin Bieber song could cause her to run amok. Instead, they walked into a good sound system with Bastille blowing through "Pompeii."

"Good sign," Nina said. The first good thing to happen all day long.

"What?" Zoey yelled, cupping her ear.

"I said, thank God they're not playing the kind of stuff *you* like."

Zoey gave her a nasty look but decided against a comeback. Nina was near the edge and creeping closer all the time.

Lucas took Zoey's arm and led her away toward the dance floor. Aisha and Christopher followed them. Claire spotted a booth just emptying out and made a dash toward it.

A group of younger kids arrived at the booth at the same

time, prepared to put up a fight. But then Jake went up, jerked a thumb over his shoulder, and the younger kids slunk away.

"You're such a big bully," Claire told Jake. "It's very useful."

They sat down, Nina separated from Benjamin, who ended up on the far side, sitting beside Claire. *Coincidence?* Nina wondered. *Yeah, right.* She didn't believe in coincidence where either Claire or Benjamin was concerned.

Suddenly she felt depressed. Maybe it was the music, which had shifted into a melancholy John Legend song. The lyrics were all about mistrust.

Oh, yes. She suspected the whole reason behind this stupid trip was to give Claire an excuse to be with Benjamin.

Claire nudged Benjamin's shoulder and whispered something in his ear. At first he looked a little confused, or even embarrassed, but he slid out of the booth and let Claire lead him to the dance floor.

Nina followed them with her eyes. Oh, yes, maybe you could say hey, no big deal. Why shouldn't they have a dance? People danced with other people without it meaning anything. Out on the dance floor, Zoey was now dancing with Christopher and Lucas with Aisha. No biggie. Except that again, with Claire and Benjamin, nothing was ever innocent, no matter how innocent it looked.

Nina glanced at Jake. He looked like he was arguing with

himself. His eyebrows twitched from time to time, and his mouth even moved in muttered, unheard conversation.

Suddenly he looked over at Nina. His expression showed a half-formed, unwilling intention to ask her to dance. Nina shook her head no and Jake looked relieved.

The song ended and segued into some Tiesto. Zoey went over and danced with her brother. Christopher headed off to the restroom and Aisha came over and grabbed Jake, who went along meekly.

Claire sat down at the booth and took a long drink of her soda without acknowledging Nina.

Nina realized she was boiling. She'd been pissed off at Benjamin all day long. After storming out of the condo she'd wandered around the village, bored, which had just made her more resentful. Then, at dinner, when Claire had actually fed Benjamin one of her French fries, she'd gotten really steamed. Now she was so angry that she was unable to keep still, leg bouncing, hands drumming the tabletop. It probably just looked like she was responding to the music, but that wasn't it. Tiesto's beats were just feeding her anger, giving it shape.

It was a strange feeling. An unknown feeling. Not that Nina had never been mad before. But she had never been this kind of mad. There was a new element added, something desperate. Something that twisted her insides.

Not just anger. She knew anger. For years she had denied her anger at her uncle. Had denied her anger at her father for putting her in the position of being used by her uncle. Denied, especially, her unjustified but still real anger at her mother for having died.

No, not just anger. It was jealousy, Nina had to admit. That was the feeling. Rotten, soul-chewing jealousy.

Claire had had her chance. Nina had waited and hidden and suppressed her feelings for Benjamin for all sorts of reasons: from fear, from self-loathing, from guilt. But at last, she had gotten past some of that stuff, *enough* of that stuff that she had taken the huge emotional chance of telling Benjamin how she felt about him.

She had gone to homecoming with him and basically announced to the world that she was no longer the person everyone had known. She'd crossed the damned bridge, taken the risk, *kissed* him! And now . . . now it was like it all had never happened. Benjamin couldn't even seem to stand having her around. And Claire was the cause. She was certain of that. At least *part* of the cause.

"What did you and Benjamin talk about?" Nina demanded. The sound of her own voice surprised her.

Claire cocked a disdainful eyebrow at her. "Am I supposed to report to you?"

"I just want to know what happened."

"No."

"Damn you, Claire."

Claire looked surprised. It was dawning on her that this time her little sister wasn't just playing around. "What is the matter with you? Having a PMS attack?"

Nina's hand was trembling as she lifted her Coke to take a drink. There was no point, she told herself. She couldn't win a fight with Claire. And she didn't want to fight. What was she fighting *for*? For a guy who'd kissed her exactly once and then blown her off? The reasonable thing to do was just—

Only she wasn't feeling reasonable. "I know you're after Benjamin. I know that's what this whole stupid trip is about. You think you're so damned smart, Claire, but I know you set this all up."

Now Claire looked alarmed. She shot a glance toward Jake, returning with the others to the booth. Claire bit her lip, cursed under her breath, and quickly slid out of the booth.

"Running away, Claire?" Nina snapped.

Claire whirled. "I don't want to have a family fight in front of everyone. Outside."

Nina hesitated only a moment. All right. They'd do it outside. She jumped up and brushed past Zoey, ignoring her greeting.

Outside, the air was still and shockingly cold. Claire was waiting in the parking lot, arms crossed over her chest, looking, in the unnatural bluish lights, like Morticia in a bad mood. The bass from the music filtered out from the club but seemed to leave undisturbed the more profound, underlying silence.

"You want to run that by me again?" Claire said.

"You know what I said. You set this whole weekend thing up so you could go after Benjamin. I know you're still in love with him and you won't let him go. You think you're so brilliant, but I caught you, Claire. I figured out your game."

Claire pointed a finger. "Nina, I think you should calm down."

"I don't want to calm down!" Nina cried, her voice suddenly ragged.

"Look, you need to get a grip." Claire's voice had dropped to a low, deliberate calm. "This is kind of new to you, I know. The whole boyfriend-girlfriend thing. And you are overreacting."

"I am not," Nina said. Tears filled her eyes. "I'm not stupid, you know. I know Benjamin likes you better. Everyone likes you better. Big surprise. But I really—" Her voice choked.

Claire moved closer. Nina turned away, defeated and humiliated by the tears that were flowing freely.

"You're wrong about people liking me better," Claire said.

"You're wrong about everything you just said, and what you suspect."

"Forget it," Nina muttered.

"Look, Nina, here's the truth. Of course there is still something between Benjamin and me. Yes, I still look at him and think he's attractive. And, yes, I guess . . . no, I *know* he hasn't completely forgotten his feelings for me."

"At least you're being honest," Nina said in a tired voice.

"Things don't just end cleanly and completely between people who've been in love."

Nina nodded. "Yeah, well, it's not like I can compete with you. You decided to get him back; what the hell can I do?"

"I did not decide to get him back," Claire said.

Nina risked a glance at Claire's face. She looked annoyed. Annoyed was Claire's version of sincere.

Claire sighed and glanced back toward the door of the club. "Okay, I'll tell you, Nina. But for once in your life, you keep your mouth shut. I mean *shut*." She sighed again. "I didn't set up this weekend to get back with Benjamin. I set it up to get back with Jake."

Nina frowned. "You just broke up with Jake."

"Well . . . Look, he was all bent because he thought by being with me he was forgetting about Wade. And since I seemed to be trying to force him to forgive me, he'd gotten himself backed into sort of an emotional corner. You understand?"

Nina nodded, although she was mystified.

"So I dumped him. That way I knew he'd start missing me. Human nature—you can reject what's easily available, but you always want what you can't have."

"So . . . you pretended to dump him. You acted like you couldn't care less, and he—"

"He realizes what he's missing, finds a way to make peace with himself, and then, all that's necessary is"—she held out her hands, encompassing the dark mountains, the starry sky, the warm light of the village—"the right time and place. And with a loud popping sound he'll pull his head out of his butt."

Nina digested the information and felt the pieces falling into place. "You *were* flirting with Benjamin . . . but only to make Jake feel insecure."

"Very good, Grasshopper," Claire said sarcastically.

"Oh, you *are* rotten." Nina laughed suddenly. It was breathtaking. "You're more manipulative than even I ever realized."

Claire smiled her infrequent smile. Naturally, she thought Nina had just complimented her. "See, it's about me and Jake. Not about me and Benjamin. Although I will say one thing." Her voice softened and the smile grew wistful. "You picked a good guy to fall in love with when you picked Benjamin."

Nina nodded mutely. "I just don't think it goes both ways."

"You're on your own with that, little sister. The only advice I can give you is—think about getting your own head out of your butt and telling him how you feel. Be direct."

"*Direct*? Why? You aren't."

"I'm me. You're you," Claire said with weary condescension. "You have to work with what you have."

EIGHTEEN

AISHA HAD DANCED A FEW dances with Christopher and one with Jake, just because she felt like dancing and he was available at the moment. Then she'd danced with Benjamin and Lucas, being democratic about it. Then, feeling guilty because she'd neglected Christopher, she went looking for him.

She found him holding court, telling a small group of kids, a guy and two girls, a story about Baltimore. Looking more closely, she saw that one of the girls was wearing a silk Baltimore Orioles baseball cap. It went well with her tissue-paper-sheer top and long, bare, presumably cold legs. Possibly it was all just innocent talk about Christopher's old hometown, she told herself. Only Ms. Orioles kept touching Christopher's arm whenever she asked a question.

Yet she didn't want to go stomping up like THE GIRL-FRIEND, acting all proprietary about Christopher. Especially since they weren't even officially boyfriend and girlfriend.

"Hi. Is me, Peter. You recall?"

Aisha turned and saw him smiling at her. The dorky hat he'd been wearing was gone and so was the parka. Definite improvements.

"Estonia, right?"

He smiled, showing a nice lineup of pearly whites. "Do you enjoy to dance?"

"Sometimes."

"Maybe you have a boyfriend?" he asked tentatively.

"Funny you should ask," Aisha said. She glanced at Christopher, who was leaning in to hear something Ms. Baseball had to say. "If you're asking me to dance, the answer is yes."

They danced two songs. Peter wasn't a great dancer. Not embarrassing, but not great. He seemed to know it and made clumsy, self-deprecating remarks in fractured English.

Aisha checked on Christopher, but no, he hadn't moved. He hadn't come looking for her. In fact, he was asking Ms. Baseball to dance.

Fair enough, Aisha told herself. She herself had danced with Peter. Although Peter wasn't quite the dancer Ms. Baseball was.

"So, Peter, what's the deal with you?" Aisha asked. "What are you doing in Vermont?"

"Oh, we are living here now, in Ohio America. I am Russian from Estonia. In Estonia is not good to be Russian. Estonia people don't like us very good."

"So you're like a minority there."

"Yes. Like Negro people in America."

"African American. Or black. Mostly we don't say Negro."

"I offend?"

"No, not at all. I'm the ignorant one. To be honest with you, I don't even know where Estonia is."

He shrugged expressively. "You know where Ohio is, yes? That is my home now."

"So you're just here skiing, like everyone else. Are you any good?"

"Not so good."

Aisha sensed he was just being modest. "How *not so good*?"

He grinned. "I am maybe to be on the Olympic team for America." He waved a hand dismissively. "Probably not."

"No way. That's so cool."

"Very cold, sometimes, yes. You must have proper clothing."

Aisha laughed. "No, I meant *cool* as in—"

But he gave her a wink. "I was making joke. Do you ski?"

"I've taken one lesson." She held up a finger. "I can turn around in a big circle by plopping my skis down one after the other, I can go down a really gentle slope, sometimes even without falling down, and that's it."

"Then I must give you lessons," he said promptly.

"You? I don't think I could exactly afford to pay for an Olympic-level teacher."

"You teach me to dance"—he made a brushing gesture with his two hands—"and we are even."

"So where do you think Nina and Claire were running off to?" Zoey wondered aloud, taking a long swallow of her drink. She was hot from dancing.

Jake shrugged. "Who knows, with those two? They're the siblings from hell. With Claire and Nina together on this trip, you had to know there'd be bloodshed sooner or later."

"Where's Aisha?" Christopher asked as he returned to the booth. He scanned the dance floor, looking perturbed.

Zoey made a *who knows?* face. "I already lost Lucas in here somewhere." The club was wall-to-wall now, with bodies in motion to the music.

"This place is all right," Jake said into Zoey's ear.

She smiled her agreement. They were getting along, almost like old times. Well, actually, *not* like old times. In the old days they would have been here as a couple, making out, dancing most dances together, holding hands under the table. Now it was like they had begun to be friends again.

And it was all right to talk to old friends, Zoey told herself. About the weather . . . about mutual friends . . . about whether anyone on the football team was using drugs . . .

She made a face. Why did the idea of asking Jake about the story make her feel grubby? It was what reporters did, and if she wanted to be a reporter someday, she'd pretty well have to get used to asking people questions, wouldn't she?

On the other hand, another part of her wanted to write romance novels. It was that part of her that felt uncomfortable using a former boyfriend as a source. Maybe the two careers weren't as compatible as she hoped. Maybe *relentless reporter* and *queen of the love story* didn't go all that well together.

"You know, I'm glad we don't hate each other anymore," Jake said.

Zoey was touched. "I never hated you, Jake."

He nodded. "I know. I was just kidding."

"We're friends, right?" she asked.

He winked. "Absolutely."

Claire came back, as always managing by some magic to make a path through the close-packed bodies, like Moses parting the Red Sea. Nina was behind her, looking abashed and somewhat confused. Zoey saw the two Geiger sisters so often, in such familiar circumstances, that she seldom noticed how much alike they were. But when you saw them together, they looked like . . . well, like sisters, obviously. Both with luxuriant dark hair, though Claire managed to use hers to greater effect;

both with startling, almond-shaped eyes, though Nina's were lighter; both with a natural grace that Claire exploited and Nina seemed determined to conceal. Despite Nina's insecurity, Claire wasn't so much more beautiful. And yet the crowd parted for Claire and guys' heads swiveled around to watch her pass, while Nina had to push and shove to keep up.

Claire slid in beside Zoey. Nina sat beside Benjamin and affected an intense interest in what was going on out on the dance floor. She was drumming her fingers and biting her lip.

Suddenly she turned on Benjamin. "So you want to dance, or what?"

"Sure," he said.

"How about you, Claire?" Jake asked, sounding almost timid.

"I'd like to," Claire said neutrally. "But I have to hit the girls' room."

"Be prepared for a major line," Zoey warned her.

The DJ was on to a Beyoncé song that Zoey liked and she looked around again for Lucas.

"How about you and me?" Jake said. "I saw Lucas in deep conversation with some guys with purple hair. Snowboarders. You know, you've created a monster getting Lucas into that."

Zoey rolled her eyes. "I'm starting to realize it. That's all he's been talking about." Well, almost all he'd been talking about. She got up and walked with Jake out onto the floor. They danced a fast dance and then, more tentatively, a slow dance.

Holding each other only as close as was proper between friends, Zoey realized she nevertheless felt terribly awkward and uncertain. Not enough time had gone by for her to reach the point where she could touch Jake and feel nothing at all. She wished Lucas were around, but at the same time, she wasn't sure how he would react to seeing her with Jake.

The music had softened enough for conversation. But Zoey's mind was not on chitchat. The time was right. It was now, or maybe not for a long time. And she wanted to at least be able to tell Mr. Schwarz that she had gotten a good start on the story.

"Guess what?" she said brightly.

"What?"

"I got another assignment for a story for the *Weymouth Times.*"

"Cool. I'm proud of you."

"Yeah."

"So what is it? Another story on cafeteria food? I loved that one."

"No, actually, it's kind of a more serious story," she said, feeling a renewed wave of grubbiness at beating around the bush this way.

"Sounds impressive."

"It's about . . . well, I guess there are some rumors about drug use. On the football team."

Jake froze. His hands dropped away from her. His expression grew hard. He shook his head in shock. "Unbelievable."

"It's just a story," Zoey said, talking fast but not fast enough. The damage was done.

"Am I the biggest moron on earth?" Jake demanded bitterly. "I think we're getting back to a point where we're friends, and thinking, okay, this is nice because you know, even if it is over between us, I still really like Zoey. She's a cool girl."

"Look, forget it, Jake. I know *you* probably wouldn't even know if anyone on the team *was* using. I mean, I know you. That's not you at all."

"Nice try, Zoey, but even I'm not *that* dumb." He pushed her away and headed back to the booth, leaving her feeling appalled and ashamed.

Claire had just arrived back from the girls' room. Lucas wandered back and was sipping a drink, giving Jake, and then Zoey a cold, suspicious look.

"I'm out of here," Jake announced.

"I'll go with you," Claire said instantly. She hurried to catch up with him.

"Have a nice time with Jake?" Lucas demanded.

"Not exactly," Zoey said.

NINETEEN

"OKAY, SO WE'RE BACK IN the condo," Benjamin said in a *playing along with a lunatic* tone. "Now can you tell me what this is all about?"

Nina paced the floor of the dark living room, biting her thumb and wondering, quite frankly, what the answer to Benjamin's question was. She had dragged him out onto the dance floor, and then, still feeling edgy and dissatisfied and weirdly excited by Claire's strange confession, she'd dragged him back to the condo. She'd had an image in her mind at the time, something having to do with Claire's injunction to be direct—the queen of manipulation telling her to be direct!—but right now, alone with Benjamin, absolutely alone, no friends, no parents, nothing whatsoever standing between them . . . she had sort of lost the image. Or at least it had become bogged down with frustrating tendrils of reality. The worst of which was Benjamin refusing to play the role she had imagined for him.

Be direct!

"You want to tell me what the hell is the matter with you, you creep?" she demanded suddenly. Well, it *was* direct.

"The matter with *me*?"

"Yeah. Like . . . like why did you give me all that crap this afternoon? What was that all about?"

Benjamin made a frustrated sound. "Look, you know I don't like people feeling sorry for me."

"I wasn't feeling sorry for you. You twisted scrotal sac."

"Bull. Why were you hanging around here with *me*, then?"

"How about because I'd rather hang out with you than do anything else?"

Benjamin started to answer, then hesitated. "You're just saying that," he said at last.

"Oh, good retort," Nina said sarcastically.

He pushed his shades back up on his nose and exhaled slowly. "It can't be true that you just really wanted to be with me," he said. "Because, see, if that's true, then I was a real butt-hole." He shifted his jacket uncomfortably on his shoulders. Then he made a wry smile. "Of course, I don't think I was exactly a *twisted scrotal sac*."

Nina moved closer. He *was* a jerk, maybe, but when he smiled, when he looked at her, near her, in her general direction, whatever was the right phrase for what he did . . . he still made it hard for her to stay mad.

"I thought you were blowing me off," she said. "I thought. . . you know. All that."

"I thought you were, you know, signaling me to back off," he said.

"No."

"Me neither."

"Oh. Really?"

"Really."

"Really?"

"Really," he said.

"Benjamin . . ."

"Yes?"

"I, uh, I know you're not like in love with me, so don't say you are because I know you aren't, at least not yet, and that's cool." She twisted her fingers together. Be direct. Fine. Direct. "But I really do love you," she blurted in a rush.

He reached toward her. She waited while his hand found her face, stroking her cheek. His fingers touched the tear that had run down it. "Could I kiss you?"

Nina nodded, forgetting, as she sometimes did, that he couldn't see. But he drew her to him, with nothing but the light touch of his gentle fingers trailing down from her cheek to her neck.

This time she had no fears that old memories would come

between them. The only memory she had was of their first kiss. And as his lips met hers it was an instant made up of sweetest pleasure and utter relief.

"Let's see if in the future we can't both just say what we're really thinking," Benjamin suggested.

Nina kissed him again.

"You know," she said with a confessional laugh, "I thought Claire set this whole weekend up because she was trying to get you back. That's why I was so insane tonight."

Benjamin shook his head. "Nah. She set all this up so she could get *Jake* back."

Nina held him out at arm's length. "You *knew* that?"

"Oh, sure. But I let her think I hadn't figured it out." He grinned hugely. "Claire gets such pleasure out of thinking she's outsmarted everyone."

"You're as bad as she is."

"Probably," he admitted. "Maybe that's why even though Claire and I will always have . . . *something* . . . Maybe that's why we both need to have someone nicer and sweeter than ourselves."

"Like me?" Nina asked.

"Exactly like you," Benjamin said. "Except. . . you know, with better taste in music."

Nina kissed him again and drew him slowly down to the couch.

For the second time in the evening, Claire found herself outside the club. Some strange uncontrollable fate seemed to want to keep her out of the warm, welcoming interior and out in the frosty night.

She chased Jake, who was marching forward on his long legs, apparently oblivious to the breeze, which had begun to pick up, cold air tumbling down the slope. She had to run to catch up over ice and snow and between parked cars.

"Hey, wait up!" she called out. "I'll break my neck running after you."

He marched on several paces, but then relented and waited, still staring fixedly ahead.

"Thanks," she said.

He set off again, looking, especially with the steam coming out of his nostrils, like an angry bull.

"You want to tell me what happened between you and Zoey?"

Apparently not. At least not until they were halfway back to the condo, where he stopped so suddenly she ran into him.

"You know, Claire, I have to apologize," he said at last. "I always thought you were manipulative."

"Me?" Claire said in a reasonable facsimile of innocent astonishment.

"But I've come to find out Zoey's the one who really plays that game."

"Zoey?" This time it was genuine astonishment.

Jake stopped and turned to face her. "She set me up. I think she set up this whole trip just to loosen me up and get me off my guard."

"Really? Zoey?"

He nodded. He looked grim. "I guess maybe she already told you. I guess you already know about everything."

Claire shook her head cautiously. "I don't think I do, no."

"About my being suspended."

"Suspended . . . from what?"

"From the team."

Claire was shocked. "You were suspended from the team?"

"You didn't know?"

"No. I haven't heard anything about it."

"I wasn't in the game last night. Supposedly I have a pulled hamstring. That's the story. At least until people find out I was skiing over the weekend."

Claire shrugged apologetically. "I don't pay all that much attention to football."

He seemed at least partly relieved. "So maybe it's just Zoey. And the team. And a few others. Zoey probably told Lucas, too. But Lucas doesn't have many friends, so he probably didn't say anything." He started walking again, now at a more reasonable pace, hands deep in his pockets, hunched down inside the collar of his jacket.

"Maybe you could let me in on what's happening," Claire suggested.

He shrugged. "Maybe I should. Maybe you're exactly the person I should tell."

Claire waited patiently, listening to the sound of their footsteps on crisp snow.

"I did up a couple of lines of coke during the homecoming game," he said.

Claire tried to cover her sharp intake of breath by pretending to cough.

"I was hungover and out of it. You saw. I totally blew the first half. Someone . . . no point dragging him into it, but someone said I could do a little coke and straighten up. It worked for a while. We scored some points. Only the coach from the other team wasn't stupid. He told our coach he'd better do something about it. Coach basically told me I could take a piss test right there, and if I was positive I was gone for good from the team. Or—" He made a grim, cynical smile. "I could refuse the test and be suspended until I could take it and pass it. Then Coach covered the whole thing up, told the team to keep quiet." He rolled his eyes. "I pee on Tuesday."

"God, Jake. I had no idea this was going on." There it was again—that unfamiliar feeling of guilt she so disliked. While she had been playing out her clever plan, Jake had been in real, deep trouble. And she hadn't known. In fact, she'd dumped him the day after the team suspended him. Wonderful timing.

"Mmm. Well, Zoey tells me tonight that oh, guess what? She has a story assignment. From the *Weymouth Times*, no less." He waved his hand airily in mimicry of Zoey's nonchalance. "A story about drug use on the team. And oh, by the way, would I happen, by any strange coincidence, to know anything about it? Not that I would be involved in any way, oh no."

Claire almost burst out laughing, but stifled the urge. The notion of Zoey as ruthless interrogator was just so bizarre. Zoey probably *didn't* know Jake was involved. Knowing Zoey, it would have been a major moral dilemma for her even to bring it up with Jake.

"So you think she arranged this whole trip just to get next to you?" Claire asked.

"Now that I look back. I mean, *she* was the one who invited me. Plus she's been extremely nice to me the whole time."

Claire nodded sagely. She would have liked to clear Zoey

of his suspicions, but there wasn't any way to do that without confessing the truth. Oh well, Zoey would survive.

They reached the condo and, by unspoken agreement, stopped outside at the bottom of the deck. "I guess it's not really Zoey I'm mad at, though," Jake said in a low voice. "I'm the one who screwed up. Drinking. Doing coke." He shook his head in disbelief. "I have become a first-class screwup."

Claire stepped closer, not too close, just within the aura of his warmth. "Maybe I had something to do with all of that," she said. "I knew you were feeling, you know, conflicted."

"Nah, it's me. It's me. I can't blame anyone else. No one else forced me to hit the beer as hard as I did. That was me raising the bottles. That was me who let the team down. Me who . . . did other things."

"Everyone makes mistakes," Claire said. "Even the best people. And you are the best, Jake."

Jake bowed his head. "Yeah, I guess everyone does make mistakes. But it's easier to deal with your own mistakes when you haven't been a self-righteous jerk. Telling other people . . . how to live their lives. Refusing ever to forgive . . . other people . . . for the things they did wrong."

Claire held her breath. She hadn't made the connection until that moment. But Jake had.

"I know you didn't mean to—" He struggled to control

his voice. "I know it was an accident. You know, with Wade. I just wanted someone to blame. First it was Lucas. Then you. But like you said, *everyone* makes mistakes. Even big dumb straight-arrow jocks like me."

Claire slid her arms around his waist. "You're not so dumb."

"Yeah, I am," he said with feeling. "Any guy who would let you go, no matter what the reason was, is too dumb to believe."

Claire looked up into his eyes. "Jake, I am more sorry than I could ever tell you for what happened with Wade." Her own words, intended only to clinch the moment, suddenly struck home. It occurred to her that she was telling the truth. "There are just two things I deeply regret. One is that I never knew what my uncle was doing to Nina so I could protect her. The other is what I did to you and your family."

She brushed at a tear, amazed to discover it trickling down her cheek.

"I'm freezing," Jake said. "Let's go inside to continue making up. I don't think anyone's back but us."

Claire nodded. "Yes, let's make up for a couple of hours, at least."

Arm in arm, they climbed onto the deck and eased open the sliding glass doors. Claire heard a loud gasp. She turned on the light and saw Nina and Benjamin, clothing rumpled, faces flushed, lying on the couch still wrapped together.

"I'm . . . uh . . . I'm being direct," Nina said, blushing pinker.

"For the first time ever, she does what I tell her to do," Claire said to Jake, shaking her head. "Next I'm going to try telling her to leave home and join a cult."

TWENTY

"PEOPLE ARE DISAPPEARING AROUND HERE at an alarming rate," Zoey shouted over the sound of Nicki Minaj. "I haven't seen Nina or Benjamin in a while. And now Claire and Jake are both gone, too." She *knew* why Jake was gone, but as to the others . . .

"And I haven't seen Aisha in half an hour now," Christopher said, obviously frustrated.

"Did you piss her off?" Lucas asked.

"No, I didn't piss her off," Christopher said sharply. Then less confidently, "At least, I don't think I pissed her off. We were dancing. Then I happened to hear these people talking about Baltimore, so I got to talking with them about the old hometown and all."

"And these were *guys* from Baltimore?" Lucas asked.

"Some of them were guys. I mean, there was one dude. But it's not what you're thinking. They weren't even all that cool-looking or anything. The one was a total head-bag situation."

"I'm sure I didn't really hear you say that," Zoey said, shooting Christopher a withering look.

"Personally, I don't approve of that kind of sexist talk," Lucas said. He put his arm around Zoey. "I'm much too enlightened."

"I'm going to go look for her some more," Christopher said. "Maybe she went back to the condo." He got up and melted into the crowd.

"Great, now everyone will be back at the condo," Lucas said darkly. "No privacy at all for us. What if we want to discuss the meaning of life?"

"I'll bet that's just what you want to discuss," Zoey said. But Lucas was right. The condo would be way too crowded for Zoey to have to worry about anything happening. Which was especially good, because after the disastrous encounter with Jake, romance was about the last thing on her mind.

Lucas looked disappointed, almost glum. Then a light came on in his eyes. "So you want to get out of here?"

"Shouldn't we wait for Christopher and Eesh?"

"They're semi-adults. They can find their own way back."

They got up and walked out into the night. As they neared the condo they heard a strange, compelling sound—a brilliant soprano voice soaring from one impossibly high note to the next.

"I'm guessing that's Benjamin," Lucas said.

Zoey grinned. "No, Benjamin's a tenor."

They found Benjamin with Nina in the hot tub, Nina's computer belting out opera.

"Quick, Zoey," Lucas said. "The pod people have taken control of Nina."

Nina splashed a handful of water toward him, missing. "Hey, shut up, this is my favorite *area*."

"*Aria*," Benjamin corrected.

"Are I *what*?" Nina came back, laughing in appreciation of her own wit.

"No, that's not a pod," Lucas admitted. "It's still Nina."

Zoey pulled him away. "I don't think they want *us* hanging around," she whispered.

"Oh, yeah. Look, um, where are your keys to the van? I sort of left something out there."

Zoey found her purse and Lucas hurried away, looking like a naughty child planning a prank. She went upstairs and found one bedroom door closed. She considered knocking, but decided against it. From inside there were indistinct, low murmuring sounds that didn't sound like an invitation.

She went into the other bedroom and flopped back on a bed. The bed was slated to be either Lucas's or Jake's. She didn't much care, since neither of them was around. She wondered what was going on in the next room. Obviously it had to be

Jake and Claire. Unless, by some weird twist of fate, it was Jake and Aisha. That seemed pretty unlikely, but then, unlikely things had become commonplace lately, ever since Lucas had returned to Chatham Island and she and Jake had broken up. It really wasn't all that strange that Jake and Claire would be back together, having just broken up exactly a week earlier.

Lucas was in the doorway. "That's *Jake's* bed, you know."

Zoey shrugged. "I was tired. I flopped on the first soft flat surface I saw."

"Well, uh, look, I have a kind of surprise for you."

"A surprise?" She tried to sound excited, but she really was weary. The run-in with Jake had punctured her good mood. Jake thought she was ruthless enough to try to use him for her own selfish reasons. And he wasn't far from being right.

"Come on." Lucas took her hand and pulled her to her feet. As often happened, his touch revived her, at least a little. She slipped her arms around him and gave him a kiss.

"Not here," Lucas said conspiratorially. "Any second now Nina or Aisha or Claire or someone will come barging in."

"You have a better place?"

"Ha. It happens I do."

He kept her hand in his and led her swiftly down the stairs and out the front door to the parking lot. The van was running, exhaust billowing.

Lucas opened the side door, climbed in, and drew her after him. He'd had the heat running and it was perfectly warm. The seats had been reconfigured to make a little open area, just big enough for the two of them to lie side by side on the unzipped sleeping bag he'd laid out.

Zoey laughed appreciatively. "You went to a lot of trouble."

"Nothing but the best for you," he said. "At least it's private."

"Except for the windows."

"We'll just have to steam those up," he said.

With some reluctance, Aisha had accepted Peter's offer to run over to his hotel for a minute. First, she barely knew the guy. Second, she couldn't find Christopher to tell him she was leaving. Third, it was the kind of thing that Christopher, with his one-track mind, might misinterpret.

On the other hand, she'd reminded herself, when last seen, Christopher had been dancing with Ms. Baseball and keeping a very close eye on her every move. And Peter seemed like a nice enough guy. What were the odds he was a crazed Estonian ax murderer? But in case he was, she decided maybe she'd just wait in the lobby.

They had spent their time sitting on the overstuffed lobby

chairs, looking through a small photo album he had. Pictures of Mom and Dad. Pictures of his three sisters. Pictures of the old home back in Estonia that brought tears to his eyes. Pictures of the new home in Ohio.

That was it. No ax murdering. Not even an attempt to kiss her. He was just a sweet, polite guy who'd wanted her to have a cup of hot tea with him and look at pictures of the old, lost homestead.

Then, when she'd begun to yawn, he'd insisted on walking her back to the condo.

As they walked, it was impossible for Aisha not to compare Peter with Christopher. One gentle, the other brash. One modest, the other with half the world's supply of ego. Peter even had a girlfriend back in Estonia that he had been faithful to until she had written him to say she was dating a bus driver.

He didn't have the effect on her that Christopher had, didn't make her want to kiss him the way Christopher did. Didn't make her feel crazy the way Christopher always had and probably always would. But he was nice. It was like a reminder that nice, cute, gentle, sweet guys (who, if they skied competitively, probably had bodies like steel) were still out there in the world.

In other words, there was a world beyond Christopher.

The condo was dark and Aisha realized, with a shocked

look at her watch, that it was very late. The moon had set and there was no sound except for a car engine idling in the parking lot.

"I had fun, Peter."

"I like you very much," Peter said.

"Maybe I'll see you tomorrow."

"Please, yes."

To her surprise he leaned close and gave her a chaste peck on the cheek. "Good night, Aisha."

"Night." She climbed the steps to the deck as quietly as she could. Maybe she could get through the living room and upstairs without waking anyone up. But before she could put her hand on the sliding glass door, it opened.

"Where *the hell* have you been?"

Christopher. "Sorry, I hope I didn't worry anyone," Aisha whispered. "I kind of lost track of time."

"Why should I worry just because you disappear for hours and turn up with some guy who kisses you right out there in front of me?"

"Like I said, I'm sorry. But you're not my father, all right?"

"Where did you go with him?" Christopher demanded.

Aisha pushed past him into the warmth of the living room. In the dark she sensed another person, but peering around, she could see no one. Christopher was still fully dressed. Obviously he had been waiting up for her, no doubt fuming the entire time.

Well, well. So *he* was jealous.

"I went to his hotel room to look at some things he wanted to show me," Aisha said. Yes, she could have chosen her words a little more carefully, but why not let Christopher imagine the worst?

"You . . . You . . . to his . . ." Christopher sputtered. "Just what did he show you?"

"Is there someone else in here?" Aisha asked.

"Benjamin's on the floor," Christopher said. "He's asleep."

"Yeah," a voice said, "and I can't hear a thing."

"Look, don't try and change the subject," Christopher said angrily.

"Fine. Same subject. What were you and the Baltimore Areolas talking about?"

"Can you clarify that?" Benjamin asked.

"Some girl wearing a Baltimore Orioles cap and see-through T-shirt," Aisha said.

Benjamin chuckled. "That's pretty good, Aisha."

"Thanks."

"Okay, fine," Christopher said. "You don't want to tell me, cool. You don't have to."

"Good," Aisha said brightly. "Good night."

"Wait! Where are you going?"

"Up to bed."

"You really *aren't* going to tell me what you did with that dude? Don't you think I have a right to know? Don't you think you owe me some honesty?"

Aisha smiled contentedly as she climbed the stairs. Sometimes life just worked out so well.

TWENTY-ONE

THE VAN WINDOWS HAD BEEN well steamed.

They had made out for what seemed to Zoey a long time. Not that she was complaining. Only it didn't seem like Lucas was getting tired, and she was.

"Maybe we should go inside," she suggested.

"Too many people in there," he said. He kissed the hollow of her neck, something that never failed to send shivers through her.

"Mmmm. Yes. Only, look, we have to get some sleep,"

"Do we? I'm not tired."

She shoved him playfully. "You're never tired. You're the Energizer Bunny when it comes to making out."

"Don't you like it?" he asked.

"Of course I like it. Have I been acting like I don't?"

He shook his head. "No. But see, I don't want to go to sleep. I . . . look, Zoey. I want to make love. I even bought condoms because last time you said it was rotten of me even to suggest it unless we were protected and all." He fumbled around in the corner behind the front seat and pulled out a string of condoms, holding them up as evidence.

Zoey recoiled, scooting back away from him. Then, realizing how ridiculous her reaction had been, she started giggling.

"I don't think this is funny," Lucas said.

But Zoey couldn't stop now. She was giggling herself into hiccups.

"Damn it, Zoey," Lucas said sharply. "Don't laugh at me."

Obviously his feelings had been hurt, but still Zoey couldn't stop laughing. She was beginning to get alarmed.

He touched her, but she shook off his hand. He sat back, his eyes furious. At last Zoey got the spasms of laughter under control.

"I'm sorry," she said in a choked voice. "I wasn't laughing at you, Lucas."

"Yeah, it's real funny that I love you, isn't it? Big laugh."

"Lucas, that's not it," Zoey said. "I was just . . . I don't know, I was tense or something. It's been kind of a bad night. Jake and I—"

"*Jake*? What about Jake?"

"Nothing, nothing." She waved a dismissive hand.

"Look, Zoey, we're here together, we're alone, your mom or dad isn't suddenly going to show up . . . I mean, if we're not going to do it now, when are we going to?"

Zoey felt a wave of weariness mixed with frustration sweep over her. This day had started with the nerve-wracking drive, followed by arguments over beds, followed by too much skiing on out-of-shape muscles, followed by having Jake make her feel like a jerk. The best part had been the last hour, here with Lucas. Only now he seemed determined to ruin even that.

"Lucas, I told you. I don't know. I love you. I think you're amazingly hot. But I'm not ready yet to start having sex."

"Why? Can you just tell me that? Why?"

"Lucas, look, I've thought about this lately. I've been thinking about it a lot. I know a lot of people our age are doing it and all, and I know *you* want to. But, see, the thing is, I used to think about doing it with Jake, too, back when we were together. He used to be the one asking, and I was saying no. If I had slept with him, and then we'd broken up the way we did . . . I mean, it's not like it's just going to be one time, with one person. You think it will be, but if I'd slept with Jake, and then with you, that would be two guys right there, and I'm only seventeen."

"So I'm nothing more to you than Jake was," he said coldly.

"That's not what I'm saying," she protested. "But okay, how about this? If we slept together tonight, what about tomorrow night? What about every night from now on? It's not like you'd get tired of doing it. It would take over our lives. That's all our relationship would be about."

"You know, it is at least *slightly* possible that you might enjoy it, too," Lucas said.

"It's very possible," Zoey said softly. "Of course I would. Of course I'd enjoy being closer to you than I've ever been with anyone else, Lucas. I enjoy *everything* we do together, even the things where I tell you to stop. But whether I enjoy something isn't the only thing to consider. You're not the one who has to worry about getting pregnant, for example."

"I would always stand by you if something like that happened," he said fiercely.

"Oh, Lucas, see? That's what I mean. It's not something you have to think about as seriously as I do. First of all, if I got pregnant and *if* I decided to have the baby, are you going to support us? And pay for a baby-sitter so I can still go to college? On what? Minimum wage?"

He nodded slowly, but not as a sign of agreement. "In other words, we will never have sex."

"I'm not saying that."

"Then when? Give me a date or a time or something. College graduation? Next time Halley's Comet passes by? When? I mean, I thought when we decided to do this little weekend trip, that meant you were ready to be more grown up."

"I never said that. I never promised you; in fact I told you just the opposite."

"Fine. Not tonight, then. Tomorrow night? When?"

Zoey buried her face in her hands. "Damn it, Lucas."

"When?"

Her self-control snapped. "When I'm ready, that's when," she spat. "When *I* say that *I'm* ready."

"You know something, Zoey? Screw you."

"Lucas . . ."

"You're a very smart girl. You can come up with a million reasons why you don't want to make love to me. But I'm not going to wait around to hear them all. See, the hard fact is, I don't have to wait for you to make up your mind. If it's not you, then it will be someone else, Zoey. When you decide you're ready, you let me know. I *may* still care."

He slid open the van door, jumped out, and slammed it shut violently behind him. The inside of the van rang with the silence. Zoey slumped against the side wall and drew the sleeping bag up around her. She felt stunned, too stunned to think or analyze. It had all happened so suddenly. One minute they were bantering, the next kissing, and in an instant, *an instant*, it was all over.

All over with the guy she loved with all her heart.

TWENTY-TWO

IT WAS ALMOST MORNING BEFORE Zoey got out of the van. She'd had to turn off the engine for fear of getting gassed by the exhaust, and after that the temperature inside had dropped dramatically.

She had spent hours, sometimes crying, sometimes imagining one scenario after another—Lucas would come out and say he was sorry, that he hadn't meant it, that it was all some male equivalent of PMS. Or, alternately, she would go to him, crawl into his warm bed, and make love to him so gently and quietly that no one else in the room would even know.

But she knew neither scenario was going to happen. And after a while she cried no more, just stared blankly, feeling drained of all energy, grim, and utterly depressed.

As she stretched her cramped limbs and climbed out of the van, the stars were still visible in the sky, but the mountains could now be seen as darker masses against a somewhat lighter sky. Soon the sun would begin peeking through the valleys, and

Zoey wanted to be gone before then.

She went into the condo, grateful for the warmth. Christopher was breathing heavily, sprawled in a dream across the couch. Benjamin was rolled tightly in a sleeping bag on the floor. As silently as she could, she went to Benjamin and knelt beside him. She could hear the pattern of his breathing change. He knew she was there.

"Hi," she whispered.

"What's up?"

"Look, um, I've decided to go home early. They have a bus that runs from the village. It's not that expensive or anything."

In the gloom she could see his blank eyes searching, as though they might somehow see something. "What's the matter?"

"It's too complicated to go into, Benjamin."

"Oh. You and Lucas break up or something?"

"Something. I guess we did break up." Even now she couldn't keep the quiver out of her voice.

"I'm sorry, kid," he whispered. He found her and gave her a hug. "You don't have to leave, though."

She sighed deeply. "Lucas hates me. Jake hates me over something else. It wouldn't be any fun for me or for them."

"I still like you," Benjamin said.

"You're my big brother. You have to." She pressed the keys

to the van into his hand. "Tell everyone to stay and have fun. Especially you and Nina. Okay? I'll be fine. And make sure you get my skis home."

She hugged him tightly again and got up to go, feeling more alone than she had ever felt before.

10. Will your boyfriend say you and he will still be together a week from now, a month from now, a year from now?

Claire

Jake would say yes, yes, and yes. But then, Jake is a romantic. I don't like trying to guess the future—it never, ever works. Which is why life is interesting.

Aisha

If he's honest, I'm afraid he'd answer yes, yes, and no. I guess I'd rather it was either three straight yeses or three straight nos. I'd like to just know, one way or the other, so I could concentrate on more important things.

Nina

Benjamin would answer who knows? who knows? and who knows? For my answer I would have to check the Psychic Friends Network.

Zoey

~~I know Lucas and I feel the same about this—yes, yes, and yes.~~

TWENTY-THREE

THE BUS RIDE TOOK FOREVER. Killington to Boston, then a change of buses to go to Portland and a second change to get back to Weymouth. On the ride she slept a little and cried some more, hoping with what energy she could muster that Lucas would bitterly regret being such a jerk.

It was late afternoon before she caught the familiar ferry and saw the comforting silhouette of Chatham Island approaching. She was exhausted beyond belief, caught in an endless, gray dream of remembered conversations, secret wishes, and resilient hopes that clung to life despite everything.

She got off the ferry and briefly considered stopping in at the restaurant. But at this time of day her father would be in the kitchen and her mother would be at home, sleeping in preparation for the Sunday night bar shift. Showing up back home a day early would just worry her father. This was more a mother-daughter type of thing.

She slogged through the streets and almost collapsed with

relief on reaching her home. A good, long night of sleep and the events of the trip would all seem much clearer. Maybe Lucas would call and say all the things she still desperately hoped he would say. Maybe he had already caught the next bus and was on his way to her. Maybe.

She went in quietly, not wanting to wake her mother earlier than necessary. She dropped her bag at the foot of the stairs and made her way up.

At the top landing she heard a sound. Her mother's voice, a low murmur.

She went to her parents' bedroom door. It was open several inches.

"Mom?"

She heard a muttered curse. A rapid shuffling, another curse, this time a man's voice. A figure flashed past the open door. Running, pulling on a shirt in a frantic rush. A man.

A man, not her father.

Not *her* father.

But a man she had recognized beyond a shadow of a doubt.

WHAT ZOEY SAW

PART TWO

Dear Zoey,

Hi, it's me, your mom. Your <u>mom</u>. It seems very strange to write that to you because right now you're not even one day old and even though I've held you a couple of times, you don't seem quite real yet. At this point in your life you weigh less than eight pounds. You're mostly bald, although the hair you do have is like gold. We don't know the color of your eyes because you haven't opened them yet. Besides, you never know with babies. Your big brother Benjamin had blue eyes when he was born, but now they're brown.

I'm writing this book to you, my first little baby girl. I plan to write in it every birthday as you grow up, and then when you're sixteen I'll give it to you. You'll probably think it's lame and sentimental and be embarrassed by it, but that's tough. Someday when you're a mom with a brand-new beautiful baby girl, you'll understand.

Not that you have to be a mother when you grow up.

You can be whatever you want. As long as you're not a Republican. (Just kidding.)

Your father is right across the room now, asleep in one of the chairs. He was here during the delivery and didn't even get sick like he did when Benjamin was being born. He cried when he held you for the first time but tried not to let me see it.

I hope you like your name, by the way. We were torn between Zoey and Hillary, but Zoey sounded more laid-back.

I guess I don't know what else to say right now, and I'm pretty tired, too. You didn't want to come out and as a result I haven't really slept in about forty-eight hours.

But I wanted to tell you right here how much your father and I wanted you, and how much we both love you. I hope we'll figure out how to be good parents to you and Benjamin. Or at least not screw up too badly.

Love,
Your mom

ONE

ZOEY PASSMORE RECOILED FROM THE door, tripping backward, feeling for the door to her own room. Wave after wave of emotion, shock followed by embarrassment followed by revulsion. The silence of her room. The ringing silence of her room. Her face hot to touch, her heart pounding, her throat tight with a feeling close to panic.

The door to her mother's room had been open just a crack. Perhaps the latch hadn't caught. Perhaps *he* had been in too much of a hurry and had just been careless, swinging the door hurriedly, anxious to get on with . . .

Zoey tried to calm her breathing, sitting there on the edge of her bed, clutching the mattress with her hands, squeezing it, fingers stiff. Her chest felt constricted, as if she had to force each breath in and then couldn't exhale completely. The slanting afternoon light gave the room a grim, gray look.

Outside her room she heard a heavy tread and jumped. The sound of a large man tiptoeing down the stairs, trying far too late to be discreet. The third step squeaked and in that instant Zoey realized she hated him. Hated him and hated her mother.

If only she hadn't come home early. She should be with her friends in Vermont now. She should never have seen any of this. She didn't want to see this. She didn't want to know.

What would her mother say to her? Would she try to lie? Would she break down in tears and swear it would never happen again? Or would she say nothing at all?

A mental image of her father working in the kitchen of the restaurant, listening to some old rock and roll while he whistled out of tune and chopped parsley or sliced onions, came vividly to Zoey's mind. While her father had been working, only a few blocks away, her mother, *his* wife . . .

The enormity of the betrayal was too much to grasp. It was inconceivable.

A light knock at her door made her start. She quickly lay back against the pillows and snatched at a nearby magazine, trembling fingers scrabbling at the slick pages. "Yes?"

"Can I come in?" Her mother, of course. Now that *he* was safely gone from the house.

"Sure," Zoey said, her voice shrill and unnatural to her own ears.

The door opened. Her mother, hair hastily pinned back, wearing jeans and a plaid shirt. Her *husband's* shirt. "What are you doing back so early?" her mother asked, looking flushed, her cheeks red, her brow damp with perspiration.

"I wasn't having much fun there," Zoey said.

Her mother nodded. Normally she would pursue the matter, but this wasn't a normal conversation. "Oh. Well . . . I was . . . I was just in my room, watching TV. I heard you come in."

"TV. Soaps, huh?" Zoey asked.

Her mother managed a half-smile. "You know how I love my soaps. You probably heard them, you know . . ."

Yes, Zoey knew. Too bad it was Sunday afternoon and there weren't any soaps on. Too bad her mother hadn't prepared some better lie, because now Zoey could throw the truth in her face.

And then what? Tell her father? Go to him and say . . . what? I saw Mom in bed with another man, and you'll never guess who?

Instant divorce. The end of her family. The end of *her* family.

She met her mother's eyes. Her mother looked away.

"I guess I'd better take a nap," Zoey said. "It was a long night."

"Maybe later you could come down to the restaurant. We could talk about what happened on your trip."

Zoey rolled onto her side, turning away from her mother,

feeling small and ashamed. "I don't think so."

After a long while, Zoey heard the door close behind her.

A little over two hundred miles away and several thousand feet higher, Claire Geiger leaned into her turn and felt the edges of her skis bite, then slip. She adjusted her weight and regained her balance, accelerating as she tightened the radius of the turn.

Jake McRoyan was still ahead of her, throwing up a shower of snow, much stronger than she was. But had he read the slope correctly?

She widened her next turn, finding a patch of newly manicured snow while Jake fought his way over a small mogul field. Her way was longer but faster. Claire glanced left, saw that she was level with, then, in a flash, ahead of him.

She crouched low to gather momentum, then crossed his path just a few feet ahead of the tips of his skis. Close enough to hear his mock-furious shout. The words were whipped away by the slipstream, but the emotion was clear enough.

Claire slowed and the two of them came to rest, panting, in the trees off the trail. She brushed snow from the front of her suit, then removed one glove to run her fingers through her glossy black hair, combing out a fallen pine needle. She laughed triumphantly.

"That's the first time you beat me today," Jake said.

"The first time I really tried."

"Ha."

"Besides, it's our last run today, so it's the one that counts," Claire said, pushing her yellow wraparound shades back on her head. The slope was falling into shadow.

"Who made up that rule?" Jake demanded.

"Me."

"Then I get to make up rules, too," Jake said. He dug in his poles and brought his skis parallel with hers so that they stood side by side. "My rule is winner has to kiss the loser."

Claire smiled. "I guess I can live with that rule."

She leaned toward him, accepting the touch of his cold lips on hers, then, as tiredness was forgotten, his much warmer tongue in her mouth. She closed her eyes, which proved to be a mistake. Her balance went, and, still clutching him, she fell over, sinking into the snow as if it were a feather bed, Jake on top of her, legs and feet hopelessly tangled in their skis.

Claire tried to get up, but now Jake held her down.

"There's no escape. We may be pinned here until help arrives," Jake said. He kissed her again.

"My entire backside's frozen," Claire observed a while later. "I can't feel my butt."

"Can I?" Jake asked, leering outrageously.

"I still have my poles," Claire pointed out, brandishing one.

"And I'm prepared to use them."

Jake rolled off and levered himself upright. Then he reached down to pull Claire up. "Come on. Let's get back to the condo and grab the hot tub before anyone else does."

The tub was almost painfully hot on Claire's still-cold flesh and she had to lower herself in bit by bit, burning below the water, freezing out of it. The air around them was so cold that the water that splashed onto the wooden deck froze within minutes.

Jake was already in up to his neck, floating on churning bubbles and wreathed in steam. He was openly admiring her sheer white one-piece. *Savoring,* she decided. That was the right word.

It was still a little strange having a guy she cared for react to her that way. Strange after Benjamin, who had loved her without seeing her.

It wasn't necessarily a bad thing to have a guy think of you as more than sound and texture. Although, she realized with a certain sadness, Jake would probably never know her truer self, the thoughts and ideas and hidden motives, the way Benjamin had. Maybe no guy ever would again, because no other guy would ever be indifferent to . . . well, to the way she looked in a bathing suit.

"You're looking thoughtful," Jake remarked.

"What? You actually looked at my face?"

"Now that the rest of you's underwater, a brief glance."

Proving my point perfectly, Claire noted. Oh, well. It was naive to think that any one guy could ever be perfect in every way. And it wasn't like she didn't get a lot of pleasure from the sight of Jake's massive shoulders rising from the steaming water or from his long, corded arms stretched out around the rim of the tub.

"I was just wondering whether part of the reason Zoey left was because of the little scene you two had last night." A lie. Actually, she'd been thinking about it earlier, but she couldn't tell Jake the truth—that she had been thinking about his limitations.

A guarded look clouded his eyes. "I wondered that, too. Maybe I was too hard on her."

"I don't think you were too hard. Maybe she was just overly sensitive. After all, she *was* prying into something that's not really any of her business."

"Maybe she doesn't understand," Jake said thoughtfully. "So someone at the *Weymouth Times* heard rumors that someone on our team was using drugs. The rumor might not even be about me. I mean, it could be about some completely separate thing, right?" He looked over his shoulder self-consciously, glancing down the path in front of the deck.

"Probably all a coincidence," Claire said, pretending to

agree. "I don't think she'd have agreed to write the story if she'd thought you were involved."

"Don't you?" he said eagerly. "You mean I should just tell her?"

Claire shook her head. "No. It's too late now. If Zoey agreed to do the story, she'll most likely do it. She thinks it's integrity or something."

Jake nodded glumly. "Maybe she won't find out anything."

"Are you good at keeping secrets?" Claire asked, teasing.

"I don't know. I never had any until recently." Then, in a bitter voice, "The absolute stupidest thing I have ever done in my life."

Claire waved a hand dismissively. She was tired of this topic and wanted to luxuriate in the warmth. "Keep quiet and it will probably all blow over," she advised. Then she cocked an eyebrow at him. "Just don't try to keep secrets from me."

It was supposed to be a throwaway line, a joke. But there had been a flicker in Jake's eyes. She formed an impish, innocent smile. "You wouldn't ever keep secrets from me, would you?"

Jake shook his head. He looked so blatantly guilty that Claire almost pitied him.

So. Jake had something he wasn't telling her. Well, well. She could go for the kill right now, or just sit back and see how long he held out.

Jake looked around for the cold drinks he'd brought to the tub. Spotting them on the deck, he stood up, turned, and leaned far out over the side to reach, a V-shaped column of tanned muscle, rising wet and steaming from the water.

Claire felt a distinct rush of warmth that was not from the hot water. *Well,* she decided, *why spoil the mood?* Let Jake keep his secret for now.

How long Zoey had lain in her bed just staring blankly at her hand curled up in front of her face, she had no idea. She'd tried to think, to reason it all through, but her thoughts had come in disjointed bits and pieces that ran through her brain over and over and over again. Pointless, circular thoughts that wouldn't go away. Memories of a friend at school in seventh grade, confessing that her parents were breaking up; the framed wedding picture from her dad's dresser with him in pathetic sideburns and her mother in a white veil; visions of her friends when they found out—Nina, Lucas . . . Jake; her own breakup from Jake; her possible breakup with Lucas; heartbreaking visions of her father when he learned the truth; and Benjamin. What about her brother?

At some point she must have just shut down. She remembered that she had felt a weariness deeper than any she'd ever felt before. But still she was surprised that she had fallen asleep. And surprised that it was now completely dark outside her windows.

Downstairs the telephone was ringing.

She stood up, feeling dopey and strange, twisted by a subversive suspicion that she had gone to sleep in one world and awakened in another.

The phone rang again and she stumbled out into the hallway, padding on bare feet over cool wood and carpeting. The house was deserted, silent but for the ringing. On the fourth ring the answering machine came on. From downstairs she could hear the answering message in her father's voice:

> *Hi, we're not home right now, but since this is an answering machine, you can leave a message after the beep.*

The beep came as she was halfway down the stairs. This voice, too, was instantly recognizable:

> *Um, this is Lucas. I'm just trying to reach Zoey. I would really like to talk to her. So, um, Zoey, if you get this message, I mean, I really wish you would call because . . . I just, like, wish you would call, okay? I . . . um, I love you. Okay? So call me. Bye.*

He had mumbled the word *love*, no doubt anticipating that her mother or father might be the first to hear the message. She'd nearly run to catch him before he hung up, but something had held her back. She didn't know what to say to him, not now. Not when the entire universe had been altered and she was still trying to figure out what things meant. How could she know what to say to Lucas? How could she know how she felt about him?

She went into the kitchen and saw the little red message light flashing on the answering machine. Lucas's voice, bottled up there, ready to be replayed. Waiting for her to decide whether she would release it.

So much was waiting for her decision. Lucas waited for her call. Her mother must be waiting, too, for her decision. A family—no, *two* families—waited for her to tell the truth of what she had seen and destroy them. The world she had known, twisted beyond recognition and without warning by her own mother, now waited on her, Zoey Passmore, to complete the destruction.

She was entirely alone: no Lucas, no Nina, no Benjamin. No answers. No reasons. No explanations. Probably there was no explanation. How *could* there be a rational explanation for her mother doing this?

But if there were some reason, she decided, she would do whatever it took to uncover it.

TWO

LUCAS WAS SITTING ON THE bed in the condo, staring at the phone, when Nina Geiger went in tentatively, feeling awkward and out of place in the guys' room.

The sun had long since sunk behind the mountains, plunging the pristine little village into twinkling night. Downstairs the others—Aisha and Christopher, Claire and Jake, and Benjamin—were getting ready to go out to eat. Nina and Benjamin had considered staying in, a sort of protest over Zoey's absence, but in the end that had seemed silly. Zoey was a big girl. By now she was back home on the island, probably pouting and crying a little and raging at Lucas for being an insensitive lout.

The insensitive lout was looking haunted and depressed. "Still no one there. I got the answering machine," Lucas said without being asked. "I tried her this morning, no answer. I tried her at lunch, no answer."

"Did you leave a message?" Nina asked.

"Yeah," Lucas said snidely. "I said 'Sorry I tried to pressure you into sleeping with me; can we still be friends?' I'm sure she wouldn't mind her mom or dad getting that message by accident."

"That was sarcasm, right?" Nina asked. She spotted a plaid shirt hanging in the closet. "Is this yours? Can I borrow it for tonight?"

Lucas hung his head. "Sorry. I shouldn't take it out on you. Actually, this last time I *did* leave a message. I told her . . . you know."

"The *L* word?"

"Yeah. I'll sound totally pathetic if her mom hears it. Or her dad, oh man."

Nina busied herself with trying on the shirt in front of the mirrored closet door. Not bad. Looked kind of tough with the rest of her outfit and the eternally unlit Lucky Strike hanging from the corner of her mouth. "She'll get the message before her folks," Nina said reassuringly. *Maybe,* she added silently.

She was at a loss as to why she had come up here after Lucas. Her thinking had been that she would have talked to Zoey if Lucas had gotten through, but now that seemed like a fairly idiotic idea. What would she have been able to say to Zoey? Nina wasn't the reigning world's expert on relationships. What she really wanted was to get the complete story, the detailed word-by-word version that Zoey, as her best friend, was obligated to give her. But that would probably have to wait until Nina got home to the island.

"I guess Benjamin's pissed at me, huh?" Lucas asked.

The question surprised Nina. Lucas had asked it because she was Benjamin's girlfriend and therefore, presumably, an expert on his feelings. It gave Nina a little rush of pleasure that she was accepted in that role. "He just thinks the whole thing is kind of ludicrous. He doesn't think you're scum or anything. He just thinks you're . . ." The phrase Benjamin had actually used was "all hormones and no brain." But that would sound a little harsh. "He just thinks you're kind of impatient."

"Yeah, well, he's not wrong. I *was* impatient. And it is totally ludicrous. You know, she didn't have to run off, though. It's not like I was trying to force her or anything. I mean, I'm not some dog. But now everyone's giving me these looks like I'm Conan the Barbarian trying to jump Snow White."

"Conan the Barbarian tried to jump Snow White?" Nina shook her head. "Not in the Disney version I saw. So I can wear this? I won't get food on it or anything."

"Now what am I supposed to do?" Lucas held up his hands. "She won't even pick up the phone."

"Don't these little problems about . . . you know . . . come up all the time?" Nina asked. "Isn't this all just kind of a normal thing? Like no biggie?"

Lucas shrugged. "I don't know."

"Oh." Somehow she felt Lucas should know. But maybe he wasn't really all that experienced, either.

"I mean, sure, to me sex and all that should just be part of life, right?" he said.

Nina tilted her head back and forth noncommittally. Coming up here had been a mistake.

"I'm a guy, guys like sex. It's normal."

"I've heard that," Nina said.

Lucas spread his hands. "And girls like sex, too, right?"

"Did I just hear Claire calling me?"

His mouth was set in a bitter expression. "Zoey supposedly loves me."

"She does," Nina said confidently. "She's told me so."

A big mistake. Now he was peering at her eagerly. "What else did she tell you?"

"What else?"

"You're her best friend, and you girls tell each other everything. So she must have talked to you about us. What's the deal? Is she planning on being a virgin forever?"

"Ah. Oh, well, I'll tell you, um, Lucas . . ."

"I could use some input here, because it's like we're broken up but I still really love her. Only she never really tells me what she's thinking. At least not about sex. So I don't know. Is this it? Is it totally over? I can't deal with that. I mean, I really can't deal with that."

Nina saw what looked like tears welling up in his eyes, but Lucas turned away and raised his sleeve in what could, arguably, have just been wiping his nose. *That's the way guys are,* Nina told herself, aware that she was learning a great truth—*they'd rather you thought they were wiping snot on their sleeves than admit they were crying.*

A thought occurred to her, and she looked at the sleeve of the shirt she was wearing. It looked clean.

"Maybe you could call," Lucas said, suddenly animated by a new hope. "If she's there, she'll talk to you."

"I don't think I should get involved in this, Lucas."

"Come on, it won't be any big deal. Just call her, and then if she answers, you put me on."

Nina shook her head decisively. "Wrong. Unless I can borrow this shirt. In which case I'll try her later for you."

"It's Christopher's shirt, not mine. Go ahead and take it."

The lodge restaurant informed them that for a party of seven the wait would be forty-five minutes. If they wanted two separate tables of three and four, they could be seated immediately. That decision was easy—they were hungry. But the decision of how to break down into three and four was more complicated.

Nina and Benjamin wanted to be together. So did Claire and Jake. But Nina and Claire preferred not to be in the same group. Christopher wanted to sit with Aisha, but Aisha made a point of saying she didn't care whom she sat with. And basically, although no one wanted to say it out loud and hurt his feelings, no one wanted to sit with Lucas, who was walking around like a storm cloud on two legs.

Finally they broke up into a group consisting of Nina, Benjamin, and Aisha, and a second group of Claire, Jake, Christopher, and Lucas.

"Well," Nina said, settling into a seat near the huge fireplace that dominated the rustically decorated room, "Claire looks like the slut of the month. Her and three guys at one table."

"What does that make Benjamin here?" Aisha pointed out. "He has two girls." She opened her menu. "Man, do you believe these prices?"

"They're outrageous," Benjamin agreed. He had his menu upside down. "And I don't see anything I want, either."

"Do that to the waitress when she gets here," Nina suggested.

"Uh-uh, not me," Benjamin said. "I was raised in a restaurant family. My folks would kick me out of the house if they found out I hassled a waitress. Or tipped less than fifteen percent."

Nina leaned close to Aisha. "Is Christopher giving you death looks, or is it just my imagination?"

Aisha refused to look toward the other table. She shrugged. "I don't really care."

"Okay," Nina said. "So did you two have a good time skiing today?"

"She says, subtly prying," Benjamin remarked in an undertone.

"Was I being subtle?" Nina asked. "Sorry. What I should have said is, Eesh, what's the deal with you and Christopher? One minute you're on, then you're off, then you're on? You're confusing everyone."

"I wasn't with Christopher today."

"She says, answering an earlier question." Benjamin again.

"I had a private lesson with my friend Peter. Peter from Estonia," Aisha said. "He's trying for a spot on the U.S. Olympic ski team. I met him at the club last night. I'm going to have the fish." She closed her menu decisively.

"She's making Christopher jealous," Benjamin explained to Nina. "Do they have lasagna, by any chance? I feel like lasagna."

"Yeah. It comes with salad."

"Maybe I'm making Christopher jealous," Aisha said, "and

maybe I just happen to think Peter from Estonia is cute."

"Where is Estonia, anyway?" Nina asked.

"Or maybe I've just realized that Christopher isn't the only available guy in the world."

"It's a little country right between Latvia and Russia," Benjamin said. "Or else Lithuania."

"Like there's a difference," Nina said to Benjamin. "No, you're right, Aisha—there are lots of available guys around. Like Lucas, if he doesn't perform some very convincing groveling for Zoey."

Aisha waved a hand dismissively. "Oh, they'll work that out. Lucas's hormones just got a little out of control. A little testosterone poisoning."

Benjamin grinned. "Isn't that the same thing Christopher has? Must be going around. Like the flu."

Nina reached across and felt Benjamin's forehead. "Nope. No symptoms here yet."

"Funny, Nina," Benjamin said. "Funny, and I believe slightly insulting."

"Only slightly?"

Nina felt Benjamin's leg touch hers under the table. She confirmed the pressure and casually wrapped her ankles around his.

"The thing is," Aisha said, "it's necessary in any relationship for there to be certain ground rules. Some basic understandings. Like a constitution that lays out the rights and responsibilities of both people."

"And by making Christopher jealous you're basically writing a constitution?" Benjamin asked, incredulous.

"Exactly," Aisha said. "Just call me Thomasina Jefferson."

"Jefferson was Declaration of Independence," Benjamin said. "Not Constitution."

"Or was it Latvia?" Nina said.

Aisha was undeterred. "We the two people in this relationship, in order to establish a more perfect union, insure domestic tranquility, provide for each of us to always have a date for Saturday night, promote a common defense against being asked out by geeks, and secure the blessings of blistering hot make-out sessions—"

Nina fanned herself with her menu. "I can't wait till we get to the Bill of Rights." She wondered if Benjamin would want to make out tonight. Was he tired of it after last night? She wasn't. She'd never thought she'd feel that way, but she definitely wasn't tired of kissing Benjamin. In fact, she wanted to reach across the table and touch his hand right now.

"Article One—what goes around, comes around. Whatever you can do, I can do back, and harder."

Nina rolled her eyes. "Benjamin, should we just go ahead

and break up now, before I end up like Aisha or Zoey?"

"I'm fine," Aisha said. "Don't blame me just because Christopher's a faithless snake and I have to teach him a lesson. And it's not Zoey's fault that Lucas is trying to . . . to . . ."

"Test his equipment?" Nina suggested.

"I hope she's okay," Benjamin said, suddenly sounding concerned.

"Zoey? Come on, Zoey's indestructible," Aisha said.

Nina glanced at her watch. "By now she's gotten past crying over Lucas. She's already constructing some big scenario in her mind about how romantic it will be when she and Lucas make up."

"Yeah, you're probably right," Benjamin agreed. "After all, it's just a little lovers' quarrel. It's only dramatic because we're all here and in order to get some distance from Lucas she had to go all the way home. I was just thinking she has no one to talk to. But I guess she could talk to Mom."

Aisha made a disbelieving face. "Talk to your mom about her boyfriend trying to—"

"Catch up on his sex-ed homework?" Nina suggested. "Practice for his new job as a Trojan tester?"

Benjamin shrugged. "My mom's basically pretty cool. And Zoey gets along okay with her. As long as she doesn't ask my dad, no one will get hurt."

"You know, if I'd been raised in your family, I'd probably be a much more normal, conventional, and, frankly, boring person," Nina said a little wistfully.

"Yeah, but then you and I couldn't go out," Benjamin pointed out.

"I wouldn't want that," Nina said. She'd intended to toss off the line almost sarcastically. But it came out wobbly with sincerity.

"Me neither," Benjamin said, just as seriously.

"Good."

"Yeah."

"Definitely," Nina said, feeling a warm flush of contentment.

Aisha rolled her eyes. "You're going to make me lose my appetite," she said disgustedly. "You two are no fun anymore."

THREE

ZOEY HAD SLEPT SOME MORE and then gone out for a walk in the cool evening, wandering the utterly familiar streets of North Harbor, Chatham Island's little village, which felt utterly *unfa-miliar*. Were these really the same streets? Really the same small shops, many boarded up, awaiting the next summer's tourists? The same circle, with its grass stunted by the cold, ornamented by the small marble monument to the island's few war dead? The same grocery store window spilling overbright fluorescence onto the street?

It was as if everything had changed, but only slightly, around the edges, so that the illusion of normalcy remained but was ultimately unconvincing. It felt to Zoey as though every building had been moved off-center, that every wall had a newly discovered slant. The faces of the people inside the grocery store, harshly shadowed, were all faces of people she knew and yet alien, hiding darkness and deception.

Car traffic on the island was so infrequent that an

approaching car could be heard blocks away. Zoey heard the McRoyans' truck before it entered the circle. It could only be heading to the grocery store. Where else was there to drive on a Sunday night?

She meant to retreat into the shadows but for some reason stood her ground. The truck came into view—Fred McRoyan, Jake's father, and Jake's ten-year-old sister, Holly. The truck slowed. Holly caught her eye and smiled. Mr. McRoyan seemed not to have noticed Zoey and drove past.

Jake. Something about him tugged at her memory. There had been some argument with Jake, hadn't there? Up in Vermont, what seemed a lifetime ago now. An argument over something. Something of no importance now. So many things that *had* seemed important had now shrunk to insignificance.

Her house was still empty and dark when she returned, but Zoey drew her hand back from the light switch. There was something comforting about the darkness. She moved around familiar objects and through familiar doorways to the kitchen. The answering machine now showed three messages. She almost decided not to play them, but she didn't want them waiting on the machine for her parents to hear. She pressed the *play* button and again heard the same earlier message from Lucas. It was followed by a second message from him. "It's me again. Look, I'll be home tomorrow, but I'd like to talk to you tonight. Are you there? If you are, pick up, okay? All right, I was a jerk. Is that what you're waiting for? I'm sorry. Just call me, okay?"

Behind that message came Nina's voice. "Hey, Zo. If you're there, pick up. Come on, I know you're there. Where else would you be? Look, why don't you call Lucas? Everyone's treating him like dirt and saying he ruined the trip by being a horny little toad; sorry, Mr. and Ms. P., if you're listening. At dinner we made him sit in a corner and eat nothing but crackers. Anyway, he's major-league bummed, and he said if I called you and got you to call him he'd arrange to have Claire killed for me. So come on, Zoey. Please? Call the boy."

Zoey listened impassively to the messages. It was odd, really, how much things had changed. Yesterday evening the big question of her life had been whether or not she would sleep with Lucas. Now . . . She laughed mirthlessly. It wasn't *her* sex life—or lack of one—that had turned out to be important. Whatever she might have done with Lucas, it wouldn't have changed the reality of what was going on behind her . . . and her *father's* . . . back.

She should tell him. Her father had a right to know. Didn't he? At least that way he could *do* something.

Yes, he could do something. He could divorce her mother. And possibly destroy a second family as well.

No matter how often she tried to attack the question and

come to some kind of a conclusion, it always slipped away into a dense tangle of conflicting loyalties and speculation. And each attempt left her feeling dirty and even sick. It was gross beyond belief to even have to think about any of this.

Zoey went upstairs to her bedroom. She turned on the light and went to the deeply dormered window where she had a built-in desk. Her *father* had built the desk for her, and she had always loved the private, cozy little alcove. The window looked down the length of Camden Street through the silent, moonlit heart of North Harbor.

Her eyes were drawn to the yellow Post-it notes she used to tack quotations onto one side wall of the dormer.

The world is a comedy to those who think;
a tragedy to those who feel.

Yes, she should try to stick to thinking. Stay away from feeling. Zoey pulled down the note and the others beside it, crumpled them in a ball, and dropped them in her trash basket.

She sat down at the desk and opened the drawer. Inside was the journal she used to write her romance novel, or at least the first chapter. She'd written the first chapter over and over again, maybe twenty times. Glancing back through it was like looking back at a slightly distorted record of her own love life. Through most of it, the heroes had a lot in common with Jake. Then there had been a period where she had tried out different models. And the last attempt had featured someone much like Lucas.

All of it naive and ridiculous. Romance novels were just escapism for people who didn't want to face life the way it really was, where "romance" was a boyfriend angrily demanding sex, and where even marriage ended in squalid betrayal.

The journal made a loud noise as it dropped into the trash. Then she got up and searched through her bookshelf, finding the small pink volume half-obscured between larger books. *A Mother's Diary*.

She opened to the first page. A photograph of her mother, very young, holding an extraordinarily tiny baby. Below the photograph, her name— Zoey Elena Passmore. And written on faint pink lines, the time and date of her birth, her weight, her length from head to doll-size feet.

The pages were decorated with baby blocks and teddy bears and covered with handwriting. It was a notebook her mother had started on the day Zoey was born. She'd written Zoey a letter then, and since that time had added other letters, one on each birthday. On her sixteenth birthday her mother had given it privately to Zoey. Her mother had been a little sheepish, a little embarrassed. But when Zoey had read it, she'd cried.

It had been a testament to her mother's love and to the

enduring strength of their family.

Zoey turned to the second page. She read the first paragraph.

Dear Zoey,

Hi, it's me, your mom. Your <u>mom</u>. It seems very strange to write that to you because right now you're not even one day old and even though I've held you a couple of times, you don't seem quite real yet. At this point

Suddenly, a memory. She leafed ahead swiftly in the book. Something . . .

Yes. There it was, on the page devoted to her eighth birthday. "I heard about this island from a person I used to know a long time ago. He seemed to think it's the perfect place to raise kids."

A person I used to know a long time ago. The *same* person? That *same* man?

Zoey placed the notebook gently alongside her journal in the trash. It was part of the past now. Irrelevant.

Unless . . . Unless the past *was* important, at least in this case. "A person I used to know a long time ago." Was that where the explanation was to be found? Had Zoey just discovered something that had been going on for years? If so, then the situation was even worse than she'd imagined.

Her parents were both at the restaurant. There was no chance that either would be home in the next hour. Benjamin was hundreds of miles away in Vermont. She was alone in the house.

What she was now planning to do was wrong, but then, her mother was no longer a person to be talking about right and wrong.

The entrance to the attic was through the ceiling of her parents' walk-in closet. A rope pull with a wooden handle hung down. She tugged at it and down came the plywood stairs with a creak and a cascade of dust and mildew smells. Up, carefully, heart pounding. Fumbling in the dark for the light switch. Sudden illumination from a bare bulb whose harsh light didn't reach the farthest corners. Cardboard boxes, discarded furniture, her old dollhouse coated with dust. She sneezed violently. And again.

She knew just the box. She had found her mother up here once, years ago, sitting cross-legged on the wood floor, reading letters. Supposedly her mother had been getting down the Christmas decorations. It was her mother's job because her father had allergies. He couldn't stand the dust.

Her mother had quickly put away the letters and accepted Zoey's help bringing down the tree stand and the box of lights and gold-foil ropes.

Now Zoey found the box, knelt down, and opened it. A pile of old high school yearbooks. Notebooks. A black mortarboard from her mother's college graduation. Letters, held together with rubber bands.

Zoey lifted the letters. Letters from her grandmother to her mother. Letters from Jeff Passmore to Darla Williams, her mother's maiden name.

And in the middle of the pile, three letters.

From Fred McRoyan to Darla Williams.

To my daughter:

It's your eighth birthday, Zoey. We had a party here at our new house. We had cake and frozen yogurt, which melted. Couldn't get you all the presents you wanted because money is kind of tight right now. Your dad and I bought you clothes, mostly.

We just moved to this island a little while ago. Your dad and I think it will be a good place to raise you and Benjamin, and we're going to open a little restaurant, which is where all your birthday money went. Sorry, honey. We'll try and make it up to you later.

You're a very beautiful little girl, of course. Very mature for eight. You say you're going to be a veterinarian when you grow up. Either that or a philosopher. Where you got that idea I can't imagine. Your father, no doubt.

It looks like you're starting to make friends here. There's a little girl named Claire who seems sweet. Although she has a little sister who just drew mustaches on your old Barbie dolls. You got very upset. I guess by the time you're reading this you'll have gotten over it. But if it turns out the sixteen-year-old you can't stand this Nina girl, at least you'll know how it all started.

It's always strange when I write in this book. I mean,

263

here you are right now, a little girl, and I'm writing to you when you'll be a young woman. I don't have any idea what your life will be like then, although I hope it's wonderful and that you're happy. If we manage to stay here on the island, I believe it will work out. This is like a safe place in the world. A long way from all the things that could hurt you or Benjamin.

If not, I guess I'm to blame. I heard about this island from a person I used to know a long time ago. He seemed to think it's the perfect place to raise kids.

Anyway, so far I have a perfect little girl.

FOUR

ZOEY'S MOTHER WAS AT THE breakfast table the next morning, reading the paper as always, drinking coffee. Zoey's father was already down at the restaurant. It was the Monday of a three-day weekend.

Her mother said hello in her usual way. Zoey said hello back and fixed herself a bowl of Grape-Nuts. She sat down at the table, tugging at the back of the Boston Bruins jersey she wore to bed. She had halfway decided she wouldn't sit with her mother, but that would be cowardly. She wasn't going to start acting like she was afraid to be around her. It was her mother who should feel guilty. It was her mother who owed her an explanation.

But her mother just turned the page with a rustling of newsprint and sipped again at her coffee.

Zoey ate her cereal. Her mother drank coffee. The silence was like a vise that kept tightening, squeezing, increasing the pressure in the room.

Zoey choked on a mouthful of cereal and had to clear her throat repeatedly.

"You shouldn't eat so fast," her mother said from behind the paper.

"Don't tell me what to do," Zoey snapped. Resentment boiled up inside her. She glared at the blank gray wall of newspaper. There was a computer sale at Best Buy.

"Suit yourself," her mother said with supreme indifference.

"I will." God, how she wanted a fight. How she wanted to get it out in the open and tell her mother just what she thought of her. To hurl accusation after accusation, each phrase carefully crafted and rehearsed and replayed during the night when she should have been sleeping. Just let her mother say *anything* even remotely critical. Anything that would serve as an excuse for Zoey to unload the razor-sharp verbal spears.

Her mother sipped her coffee. Zoey ate her cereal, barely chewing, not tasting at all.

The phone rang and Zoey jerked. Her mother's paper responded as well.

A second ring.

"It's probably for you," her mother said.

"Maybe it's Daddy," Zoey said.

A third ring.

Her mother sighed. "I don't think your father would be calling me."

"Maybe he wants to find out what you're up to," Zoey said with a cold sneer.

A fourth ring.

The answering machine came on. Her father's voice on the outgoing message. A beep. A click.

"Hi, it's me, Lucas. Um, Zoey, in case you were going to call me here, don't, okay? Because we're coming home. We're leaving right now because it's started to rain. So I'll be home soon and we can, you know, maybe we could talk and work everything out, okay? I mean, look, I understand your feelings and I respect them, so don't get all down. Everything will be cool. We can—"

A beep. The message had run over thirty seconds.

Zoey was finished with her cereal. Her mother's cup was empty.

Her mother put down her paper, slowly, deliberately. She met Zoey's eye and didn't flinch. "Is there something you want to talk about, Zoey?"

Zoey stared at her. "What could I possibly want to talk about?"

"I don't know. You seemed—"

"You know," Zoey said quietly. Then, in a voice near a shriek, "You *know* what there is to talk about!"

At last her mother looked away. A bitter smile tugged at the corners of her mouth but failed. "You don't understand everything, Zoey. You're still just a kid."

"You're right. I don't understand. I wish I did, but I don't."

Her mother was quiet for a while. She sat with shoulders slumped and head low, staring blindly toward a corner of the linoleum. "Look, I love your father."

Zoey let out a short bark of a laugh. Of course she did. That's why twenty years ago she'd been getting letters from Mr. McRoyan and yesterday she'd been . . .

She hadn't read the letters. Not yet, and she wasn't sure she would or even could. But she didn't have to read them to guess that they were love letters.

"Well, believe what you want to believe," her mother said. "You will anyway."

"What if I tell Daddy?" The threat was out of her mouth before she realized it.

It didn't have the devastating effect she had expected. Her mother raised her eyebrows, then just looked thoughtful. "I don't know. Is that what you're going to do?"

Zoey searched for some fierce response, but none came to mind. She felt deflated. She'd never talked this way to her mother before, and far from being a liberating experience, it left her feeling hollow. "I don't know what I'm going to do."

Her mother stood up, lifting herself heavily from the table. She carried her coffee cup to the dishwasher. With her back to Zoey she said, "Don't be too quick to judge. Later in life you may find that living up to your high ideals isn't easy. That life is more about shades of gray than it is about black and white. And then you'll regret that you weren't more generous on the day you discovered your mother was just human."

FIVE

LUCAS DID MOST OF THE driving on the way back from Vermont. It was the best way to avoid being next to Jake and Claire, and Nina and Benjamin, who were holding hands and occasionally kissing and in general reminding him of the fact that he alone had managed to actually scare his girlfriend clear into another state.

Thank God for Christopher and Aisha, proof that at least part of the human race could act with some restraint. Although, given their unpredictable relationship, it wouldn't be surprising to see them all over each other suddenly. Aisha loved to talk about being logical and sensible, but there had never been more than about ten logical minutes between those two since they'd met.

Lucas hadn't slept much. He'd spent the waking hours of night swinging back and forth between self-righteous anger and self-pitying remorse. Now he was just feeling washed out, tired, sick of his friends, sick of himself, sick of everything.

He pulled off the highway, decelerating into the off-ramp, glad to be almost home.

Weymouth was surrounded by a ring of suburban sprawl, a jumbled wasteland of golden arches and red-roofed Pizza Huts, gas station price marquees, shabby banners over used-car dealerships, power lines, orange U-Haul trucks, discount stores, and mud-spattered cars. Within this ring was a second layer of older two-story homes, painted off-white and off-yellow and a shade that might have been a type of green or gray or just a deliberate attempt at ugliness. Bare trees and sparse, dying grass defined yards littered with Big Wheels and unused garden hoses.

Maine at this time of year, after the trees had lost their brilliant leaves and before the first cleansing snows, was not a pretty sight, Lucas decided glumly. Although, if Zoey had been beside him . . .

He veered to avoid a lunatic in a Volvo. Massachusetts plates, he noted. Inevitably.

They came to the edge of the city center, a small cluster of ten- and fifteen-story buildings that overlooked the Portside area. Here everything had been given over to yuppies and tourists — red brick, smoked glass, cobblestones, slick, understated corporate logos and professionally quaint hand-lettered signs.

"Damn it!"

Lucas glanced up in his rearview mirror. The outburst had

come from Christopher. He was turned around in his seat, staring hard at traffic moving in the opposite direction.

"Give me some paper and a pen, anything!" he demanded of Aisha.

"What is it?"

"Quick. Before I forget." While Aisha dug in her purse, Christopher began reciting a string of letters and numbers over and over again.

A license number, Lucas realized.

Aisha produced a scrap of paper and a pencil. Christopher scribbled furiously. "Got 'em. Got 'em. GOT the sons of bitches! Brice Street. That's where they turned."

"What have you got?" Nina asked curiously.

Christopher's eyes were cold. "It was them," he said. "I'm sure. I saw the guy driving, the skinhead, racist piece of crap. And now I have his license number." He waved the scrap of paper like it was a winning lottery ticket.

Lucas felt a sinking sensation. "Christopher, I thought you never got a good look at the guys."

"It was him," Christopher said staunchly. "It was that guy back there in that raggedy old Ford. One of them, anyway."

Christopher had been very badly beaten up in an attack by a gang of skinheads who had seen him talking to Zoey. Zoey had been unable to identify the assailants. But Lucas knew who was behind the assault—a damaged little creep he had known while he was in the Youth Authority juvenile jail. A little psychopath who had earned the nickname Snake for very good reasons.

"Now you can go to the cops," Jake said, becoming alert after a nap in the back. He too had caught the dangerous tone in Christopher's voice. "Give them the number. Let them handle it."

"Yeah, they were so good at handling it the first time," Christopher said sarcastically.

"You have a lead now," Lucas said. "They'll check it out."

Christopher nodded. "Uh-huh. You're right. That's what I'll do. I'll go to the cops."

"Don't do anything stupid," Aisha said in a low voice.

"Not me," Christopher said. He carefully folded the scrap of paper and put it in his pocket.

Benjamin took five minutes to say good-bye to Nina after they stepped off the ferry. It was slightly idiotic, since Nina would probably be over at his house within an hour, but basically he didn't care. He liked kissing Nina good-bye, hello, or whatever.

For Benjamin it was a relief to be back on the island. The island was familiar turf, a gridwork of streets measured out in steps and stored in his memory. It was a place he could move around confidently, without reliance on guides or even much on his cane. The path from the ferry landing to his home was one he knew well—so many steps to cross the square, so many steps up the slow incline of Exchange Street, a sharp right, watch out for the uneven brick sidewalk, so many more steps along Camden to the gate, to the door, to his room on the ground floor.

He slung his bag onto his bed, pulled off his jacket, hanging it on the seventh hanger from the left, and found the remote control for his stereo precisely where he had left it on the corner of his rolltop desk. He ran his fingers along the rack of CDs, found the section devoted to classical music, found the Braille tag on the spine of one CD, and inserted it in the changer.

Bach whispered in a corner. He adjusted the volume with his remote and Bach filled the room with elegant, deeply satisfying precision.

Finally. After an entire weekend of Nina's music—the Black Keys, Vampire Weekend, Jack White, Ellie Goulding . . . Fine music, but not Bach. He liked Nina. He liked her a lot. Maybe he was getting beyond liking. But he was going to have to do something about her taste in music.

Of course, she thought the same about him.

For a moment he tried to picture Nina. He had the bare facts. He knew that her hair was dark brown, that her eyes were gray. He knew that she was only of average height.

People said she was very pretty and then almost always

seemed to add a "but." Pretty, but doesn't act like it. Pretty, but seems to want to hide the fact. And the inevitable pretty, but of course, not like Claire.

But to Benjamin, who had at one time dated Claire and was now with Nina, the question of whether or not Nina was quite as beautiful as Claire was less important than the fact that when he kissed Nina, her heart pounded wildly, extravagantly. That her breath was burning hot against his cheek. That she sometimes made this little, involuntary, unconscious whimpering sound when he kissed the curve where her neck and cheek met.

Nina was hot to Claire's cold. Warm. Sweet. Funny. With very, very soft lips.

The knock on his door startled him, though it was gentle enough.

"Yeah?"

"I guess you're back." Zoey's voice.

"No one can fool you for long," Benjamin said. "Come on in."

The sound of the door opening, a long complaining squeak. Benjamin deliberately never let the door hinges be oiled. The squeaks were useful clues.

"Hi," Zoey said.

"So you did make it back. The way you kept refusing to return Lucas's phone calls, we weren't sure."

"I just didn't feel like calling," Zoey said.

Her voice was low, uncharacteristically grim. "You're not still upset over that, are you?" An unwelcome thought occurred to Benjamin. "Wait a minute. Something else didn't happen between you and Lucas, did it?"

"No. It wasn't like that. We just had a little disagreement."

Oh? Benjamin thought. *It's just a* little disagreement? Then why did she sound like her batteries were about dead?

"So. You're fine?" he asked.

"Sure. Why wouldn't I be?"

A definite false note. Maybe she just felt embarrassed over the way she had run off. It *had* been a little extreme. "You'll be happy to know that Lucas has been crawling around like he's lost the meaning of his life."

"Yeah, well . . . whatever. Are you hungry?"

Benjamin's jaw dropped open, but he recovered quickly. Okay. She didn't want to talk about Lucas. Fine. But she sounded nearly indifferent. Which made no sense at all. This was Zoey, after all. Zoey, who disappeared with Lucas into her room every afternoon and emerged for dinner humming and singing and twirling around and suddenly blurting out profound questions like, "Do you think love just keeps growing, or does it reach some ultimate point and that's as far as it can grow?" Or "Is love just a really strong form of like, or is it completely separate?"

Now it was ". . . whatever"? Something was definitely going on with his little sister.

"Yeah, I am hungry," Benjamin said. "I thought maybe we'd head down to the restaurant. Reassure Mom and Dad that I made it home alive and didn't even get a tattoo or anything."

"There's food here," Zoey said, too quickly. "I'll make you something."

Ah. Trouble with their parents? Zoey? Almost as unlikely as her indifference toward Lucas.

He shrugged. Whatever it was, it would come out sooner or later. Or more likely, given Zoey's naturally sunny disposition, her mood would just evaporate. And in the meantime, he *was* hungry.

"Okay. Let's raid the refrigerator."

SIX

"SO, CLAIRE, DID YOU AND Benjamin have a good time in Vermont?" Mr. Geiger asked, forking up a piece of salmon. "I don't suppose Benjamin could ski at all. Could he?"

Claire paused with her own fork hovering over her plate. She noticed the way Nina, sitting across the table, winced and gagged on a mouthful of soda. Janelle, the Geiger family's housekeeper and cook, cocked an ear as she set up dessert and coffee on the sideboard.

"I'm not seeing Benjamin anymore," Claire said.

"Oh." Her father looked confused. "Did I know that already?"

"It may have been mentioned," Claire said. Then, with a beatific smile at Nina, who was urgently shaking her head *no,* Claire added, "Benjamin's seeing someone else now."

Mr. Geiger shrugged. "His loss," he said loyally.

"But you might still get him as a son-in-law someday," Claire added.

"Really? Oh, I see. You think you'll get back together with him? That would be fine, I like that boy. Sharp as a bayonet."

Nina's eyes were narrowed, glaring daggers, so naturally Claire had to go on. "Yes, we all like Benjamin. Don't we, Nina?"

Nina stabbed her knife into her fish and twisted the blade.

"*Especially* Nina."

Mr. Geiger looked even more confused. "Why especially Nina?"

Claire shrugged. "She's the one who's going out with him."

Nina's appalled embarrassment was as rewarding as Claire had hoped. Nina loved to go around provoking other people, but of course couldn't stand to have details of her private life brought up in front of their father.

Mr. Geiger's eyebrows shot up. He looked at Nina. Looked at Claire. Looked back at Nina.

"She stole him away from me," Claire said sadly, fighting to suppress a grin.

Nina was turning red, nearly choking on her food.

"Broke my heart," Claire added for good measure.

"What heart?" Nina growled.

Mr. Geiger looked embarrassed. "This is . . . Not that I want to tell you girls how to run your romantic lives, but, well, it's a bit tacky."

"It's your own fault, Claire," Nina said. "Benjamin told you repeatedly that he was not ready to have kids."

Mr. Geiger stabbed his tongue with his fork.

Okay, Claire admitted to herself, *that was good.* You had to hand it to Nina—the little psycho was quick.

Nina held up her right hand and, using her palm to hide what she was doing from their father, gave Claire the finger with her other hand.

Mr. Geiger, apparently sensing that he had once again stumbled into the middle of the ongoing cold war between his daughters, sighed, gave Janelle a look, and concentrated on eating his dessert.

After dinner Nina pursued Claire up the stairs. "Hey, you're not really upset that I'm going with Benjamin, are you?"

"Not in the least," Claire said. Only a very partial lie. Mostly true. It would have been nice if somehow her previous boyfriends could live out their lives pining miserably, but that wasn't realistic. Lucas was with Zoey, Benjamin with Nina. When it grew tired between Jake and her, he'd probably find another girlfriend, too.

"Damn. I knew it was too much to hope for," Nina said.

Claire paused. "I *was* a little upset at first, because I couldn't imagine how, after being with me, he could find you at all interesting or satisfying. Then I realized it was just part of a bigger trend."

She left Nina behind on the second-floor landing and climbed toward her own third-floor room.

"Okay, like a moron, I'll bite," Nina said, pursuing her. "What trend?"

Claire shrugged. "Oh, people give up real butter for margarine, real ice cream for frozen yogurt, real steak for tofu burgers. I mean, they tell themselves it's almost as good as the real thing, but of course, we all know they're just trying to make themselves feel good."

"So, you're Häagen-Dazs—"

"And you're store-brand nonfat vanilla frozen yogurt."

"You're fat, then, and I'm nonfat," Nina said thoughtfully. "Okay, if you say so, but I never really thought of you as fat, Claire. Oh, maybe a little in your butt and those oversized buffers of yours. And, of course, your head."

Another good comeback. This is what came of Nina spending more time with Benjamin. She was growing more confident, harder to throw off-guard. It was very annoying.

They were at the door to Claire's room. "Scat," she said. "Shoo."

"I wanted to ask you something," Nina said. "Seriously."

Claire made a face. She didn't want to invite Nina in, but Claire had recently promised that if Nina needed someone to talk to, she'd be there for her. It was a promise made in the emotional aftermath of Nina's revelations about their uncle. And now Claire was stuck with it.

"Come in. Just don't touch anything or sit on my bed."

Nina followed her in and instantly flopped back on Claire's bed. "How come Dad doesn't get married again?"

"She asks, changing the subject with her usual grace."

"Seriously. I mean, he's not a bad-looking old guy. He has lots of money. That's his own hair. He owns several suits, although they all look the same."

"Just guessing, but maybe he doesn't want to get remarried."

"We should tell him it's okay with us if he does," Nina said. "I mean, next year you're out of here, off to college, thank-God-and-I'm-counting-the-days. The year after that, boom, I'm out of here, too. Then what does he have?"

"Hmm. A minus followed by a plus," Claire said. But actually, this wasn't the first time the question had occurred to her. Burke Geiger didn't have a lot of friends, let alone female friends.

"What did he do while we were away in Vermont? All he does is work and play golf."

Claire looked blank. "I don't know," she admitted.

"And when you and I are gone, it will be like that all the time. Who's going to be around to help him with his walker and buy him his old fart diapers and listen to his boring stories about how great it was when he had his own teeth?"

"Nina, Dad is forty-one."

"Yeah, see? He could live another twenty years, even more. And by then we'll both be off on our own. You'll be a bitter, lonely old lady living with cats."

"And I'll be bringing you magazines and chewing gum on visitors' day at the State Hospital for the Hopelessly Pathetic," Claire said.

"I'm just thinking we give the old man the big okay, you know? Say, 'Hey Dad, we think you're ready to start seeing girls. As long as she doesn't move in till we're out of here and she doesn't mess with my room.'"

Claire nodded. "Would you really be okay with that?"

"It's what Mom would have wanted," Nina said, suddenly serious. "She wouldn't want him to be all alone when we leave."

Tears suddenly appeared in Claire's eyes and she turned away, making a point of looking out the window. Damn. Behind her she heard a discreet snuffle. Their mother had been dead for five years. Maybe in another five the mention of her would no longer bring tears to her daughters' eyes. To this day their father couldn't speak of her without his voice wavering and strangling and dying away.

"Okay," Claire said. "But I'll do it. At the right time and place. I don't want you telling him he'll be senile soon." She made a face. "You know, Nina, I don't like this new, dippy-romantic personality of yours. You're changing for the worse, and I honestly didn't think that was possible."

The day had passed in a daze. Zoey had done her homework, preparing to make the first day back at school as painless as possible. She had watched bad daytime TV. She had eaten too much without tasting any of it. She had listened to music, but even with that, the pervasive sense of strangeness persisted. Halfway through a Taylor Swift album she loved, she turned it off and nearly threw it away. It was all mush and sentimentality. No bearing on the real world.

She had avoided dealing with things. But now, as night fell again, as she finished the dishes from her evening meal with an unusually quiet Benjamin, she was feeling rushed. She couldn't just go on avoiding things.

Upstairs in her room, Zoey almost pulled her notebook from the trash where it lay like a reproach. She needed paper.

She needed to think things through and get a grip. But she left the notebook and found an old yellow pad instead.

With a pen she wrote two headings at the top of the page:

Tell   Don't Tell

That's what it came down to. She could tell her father what she had seen, or she could keep quiet. There wasn't really any middle ground. She felt she should reach some firm decision very soon. Letting things hang was too nerve-wracking. And it would become increasingly impossible to keep Benjamin, who seldom missed anything for long, from prying.

Under Tell she wrote

The truth should come out.

Then, under Don't Tell,

Why should it come out?

Why should the truth come out? Should Nina have to tell everyone she met that she had been molested by her uncle? Should Lucas have to tell everyone that he had spent almost two years in a juvenile prison?

But Lucas had been there because the truth had *not* come out. Not until Claire had recalled the truth and admitted it had things started to get cleared up.

Under *Don't Tell* she wrote

Truth would probably cause divorce.

But again there was a counterargument. Under *Tell* she added

Sooner or later Daddy will find out.

The very thought filled her with incalculable bitterness and anger. It would be like a knife in her father's heart.

And the man her mother had been with! How could she have chosen Jake's father, Mr. McRoyan, over Zoey's father? Not to mention the fact that the man in question also had a family.

It was incredible. It was monstrous. It was a sin. That's what her religious friends, Aisha, Lucas . . . Jake . . . yes, that's what Jake would call it. A sin. Adultery. What a tired, old-fashioned word. Adultery. Divorce. The two went together, didn't they? And then what? Separate houses? Living with one parent and visiting the other on weekends, like half the kids at school?

Not her. Not *her* family.

Under *Don't Tell*:

Maybe it was just once and will never happen again.

Yes, maybe. Her mother knew that Zoey knew. Surely she would never do it again. And then life could go on like normal. Her father wouldn't have to know. Maybe her parents could still be in love.

Or maybe the answer could be found in one of the old

letters now stuffed beneath Zoey's pillow. For the thousandth time, Zoey thought about the letters. All through the night she had toyed with the idea of reading them. But did she really want to know what was in them?

She had to know, Zoey rationalized. Had to know what she was dealing with. She pulled out the letters and opened the first one with trembling fingers.

Dearest Darla,

I wish I could have written sooner, but they keep us jumping here, ha ha. Yesterday we took our first low-altitude parachute jump. Scared the hell out of me but it was fun, too.

I'll be getting a pass for next weekend so we can see each other, if you still want to. I guess I can tell you all about it then.

I know you probably are feeling a little uncertain because of what happened between us last weekend. I guess neither one of us planned for it to happen although I'm glad it did.

I know it sounds like I'm just saying this for self-ish reasons, but I don't think you have to be faithful to a guy who goes running off to hitchhike through Europe without you. How do you know he's being faithful to you? Answer: You don't. If it was me, I'd never leave you alone.

How are exams coming? Soon you'll have a college degree. Will you even talk to a lowly soldier like me? Ha ha. I hope you will.

Anyway, I can't write much more because it's lights out soon and besides as you can tell I'm not a very great writer. I just want to say that I really miss you, and really care for you. I have a picture of you up beside my bunk and all the guys say you're the prettiest pinup in the barracks.

So please write me back and tell me we can be together again very soon.

Love,

Fred

The door to her room opened a crack. An unlit cigarette appeared, followed slowly by Nina's face, making a dramatic appearance.

Zoey quickly crumpled the letter and slid it under her pillow, feeling a flush of guilt and resentment at Nina for showing up out of nowhere like this.

"Hey, Zoey."

"Uh, hi, Nina."

"Missed you, girl," Nina said. She flopped on Zoey's bed, making Zoey bounce.

"Yeah, me too," Zoey said, trying to sound convincing. She just wasn't ready to start dealing with people yet. She felt trapped in a weird space where normal laws of existence had been suspended. Having Nina show up was like having someone totally unexpected wander through a dream.

"So. Talk to Lucas yet?"

Zoey shook her head. "No, not yet."

"Cool. So?"

"So what?"

"So let's have the blow-by-blow, minute-by-minute. Let's go over the transcript of the fateful scene. I'll set it up. There's you, the shy yet plucky virgin. Then there's Lucas, the low-down horny dog. Take it from there."

"Oh, that."

"Duh. Like I wouldn't want to hear the whole story. I mean, it ends with the shy yet plucky virgin running clear into another state."

For a moment Zoey's mood lightened. It was hard to resist Nina's direct and completely disrespectful attitude. And the quickest way to get rid of Nina was to do what she wanted. If she tried to blow her off, Nina would turn relentless. "Look, I probably overreacted. Okay, we've had this ongoing—"

"Fight? War? Battle to the death?"

"This disagreement over, you know, the Big Question."

"You mean this is about whether or not Britney Spears's career is totally finished?"

Zoey felt her mouth smile. The first in what seemed like forever. Thank God for Nina. "That's right. We were fighting over Britney."

"Okay, so Lucas was trying to go where no man has gone before. He wanted to carry out an in-depth poll." Nina grinned, waiting.

"I assume you have one more?" Zoey said, playing her part.

"Of course. The three-part comic tautology rule must be observed," Nina said.

"Okay, let's hear it."

"He was gripping his bat, hoping to bang a home run and win one for the zipper."

"Are you done?"

"Actually, I have about eight more."

"The rule is three," Zoey said. "*Your* rule. Comic examples should come in threes, going from least to most funny."

"So basically I have it about right?"

"Basically."

"And you said *no*," Nina prompted, showing impatience with Zoey's delaying tactics.

"That's about it."

"And he said ohplease ohplease ohplease."

Again Zoey smiled. "Actually, he said I wasn't ready to grow up."

"Good shot." Nina nodded.

"And then he demanded to know when I thought I might be ready."

"And you told him—?"

"I'd let him know."

Nina laughed and gave Zoey a slightly off-target high five. "Excellent."

"And then he got mad . . ."

"And you were upset, huh?" This, in a gentler tone of voice. "Tears? Sobs? Vows of revenge? Plans to make him regret it?"

"I guess I was upset," Zoey said, almost wonderingly. At the time it had seemed a terribly difficult problem. Insoluble.

Nothing compared to what had been waiting for her when she got home.

Nina nodded. Then she looked her friend in the eye. "And it's because of this that you threw your romance notebook and your quotes and that book your mom gave you into the trash?" Nina looked significantly at the trash, then back at Zoey.

Zoey froze. The question had taken her completely by

surprise. She'd forgotten about the trash. She knew her face was growing red. "That's right, Nina," she said. "I guess I thought maybe Lucas was partly right. Maybe it *is* time for me to grow up."

SEVEN

"YOU KNOW, YOU COULD STAY one more night," Aisha said.

Christopher was looking disconsolately around the room, at the huge carved mahogany four-poster bed, the expensive rugs, the lush draperies, and especially at the oversized incredible bathroom with its raised Jacuzzi. They had just come upstairs from her mother's farewell dinner for Christopher. Mrs. Gray was sorry to see him go. Mr. Gray was relieved.

"Nah. I have to exit to reality sometime," Christopher said. He was holding a black nylon zippered bag that contained his belongings. "Back to my one room with the kitchenette in the corner and the bathroom down the hall."

"You have an excellent view there," Aisha said. "The beach. The lights of Weymouth."

"Uh-huh. And I share a moldy stall shower with the other three guys on my floor."

Aisha patted him on the back. It was obviously hard for him to leave this room, which wasn't exactly a surprise. The room was the prize jewel in her mother's bed-and-breakfast. In summer it rented out to tourists for five hundred fifty or so a day. After Christopher's assault, Aisha's parents had allowed him to stay here and recuperate.

The truth was, Aisha herself would have liked to take the room. Her own was considerably less magnificent.

"Oh, well," Christopher said with a shrug. "I'm out of here."

"I'll walk you downstairs."

The night was chilly. A breeze whistled through the bare oak trees and sighed through the needles of the pines. High swift clouds scudded beneath a half-moon.

Christopher piled the bag on his battered bike. "If it keeps getting colder, I'm going to have to buy an island car."

"This is Maine, Christopher. Believe me, it keeps getting colder. Six weeks from now you will not still be delivering papers by bike. Trust me on this."

"Yeah, I guess you're right. Back home in Baltimore you just have a bad month or so."

"You know what they say about Maine. We have two seasons, winter and July. Check the bulletin board at Island Grocery. Someone's always selling an island car. And remember, if it costs more than three hundred bucks or if the seats aren't ripped to shreds, people will think you're showing off."

Christopher grinned. "This is about the only place where I could actually afford to buy a car that would fit in." Island cars were inevitably salt-eaten, rattling, beaten, dented wrecks that ran on half their cylinders, dragged their mufflers, and had license plates from 1990. On Chatham Island, there wasn't much need for driving. People kept their real cars in covered parking garages on the mainland.

"Well, in the meantime be careful. The streets get slippery sometimes."

"Worried about me?" he asked with a winning smile.

"Not really."

"Back to school for you tomorrow. And work for me," Christopher said.

"Uh-huh."

"Interesting weekend. I think if I hadn't still been sore and stiff, I could have really gotten into the whole skiing experience. Plus, if I was rich enough to be able to afford that condo and the meals and the lessons and the ski tickets."

Aisha knew she should just let it drop. He was obviously trying to keep the conversation going. Hoping for what? A kiss? "Yeah, I think it would be fun if I could ski as well as Claire and Zoey. But just taking lessons wasn't any big thrill."

"Really?" He cocked an eyebrow. "Even the lessons you got from Peter the Estonian wonder boy?"

"He did show me a few good tricks," Aisha said, keeping a straight face. Ha. Take that, Christopher I-can't-be-tied-down-to-one-girl Shupe. Mr. That-blond-girl-was-just-someone-I-met.

"Yeah, I'll bet he did." Christopher seemed about to say something else, but instead he just raised his bike and shouldered his bag. "Listen, tell your mom and dad thanks again, okay? Anything I can ever do to repay them—"

"My mom loved it. She has the hospitality gene. Can't stand it when there's no one around to take care of and show off her decorating to."

He nodded. "So." He nodded again, looking down at the ground. "So, I'm going." He pushed his bike across the yard, but at the gate he stopped. Carefully he leaned the bike against the post and came back, walking resolutely toward her.

"I forgot something," he said.

"What?"

"This." He took her in his arms and kissed her. By the time he released her, she was gasping for breath.

Christopher walked away, a new swagger in his step. He stopped at the gate and looked back. "Remember that the next time you're thinking about Peter from Estonia."

"Wait a minute," Aisha said, stopping him in his tracks. She walked across the yard. "I forgot something, too." She reached up with both hands, placing them on his face, and drew him down to her. She kissed him softly, gently, then with more fire and still more. She let a hand drift down slowly over his chest, around his lean waist, over his hard butt, drawing him closer still. Then she released him.

"Now," she said. "*You* remember *that* the next time you want to be a big macho jerk who treats women like they're just numbers to be added up."

Aisha turned sharply and headed back to the house. And if it weren't for the fact that her knees were wobbly and her heart was hammering, she would have felt very pleased with herself.

Lucas was on his deck, looking down toward Zoey's house, when he heard their front door open. From his vantage point he could see only the back of the Passmore house—the unused spare bedroom upstairs, the dining room, kitchen, breakfast nook, and family room downstairs—all of which were dark.

But he could recognize the voice that floated over the roof of Zoey's house. Nina. Saying good-bye at the front door.

Good. With Nina gone, he could decide whether he was going to get up the nerve to go down and see Zoey. Nina emerged from the lee of the house and was visible briefly, walking with head down along the street. He heard the sound of the door closing.

He should go down right now. Talk all this out before she

297

decided to go to bed early or something. But what was he going to say? That was the problem. Was he going to promise never to try to get her to sleep with him?

Yeah, right. She'd certainly believe that. About like she'd believe that he had decided to become a priest.

No. There wasn't any point in b.s.'ing her. Zoey wasn't stupid. The only thing that would do any good would be to tell her that he would leave it entirely up to her to decide *when* or even *whether*.

But man, that grated on his nerves.

The door opened again, and this time Zoey emerged around the side of the house. She was carrying a white trash bag, which she stuffed into the big plastic garbage bin.

Lucas stepped back silently from the deck rail, melting into shadows. Zoey was staring at the trash as if it had some powerful significance. Her features, in shadow, lit only by refracted moonlight, looked sad. It would have been impossible to interrupt her at this moment, Lucas decided.

Finally, with a dismissive shake of her head, Zoey went back inside. A moment later the kitchen light came on. Zoey went to the refrigerator and, to Lucas's utter amazement, pulled out a beer. She used a towel to help twist off the cap and took a deep swig. Then she made a face. But doggedly she took a second drink. She stared for a while at the bottle, again with a sad, faraway expression.

Lucas heard the whispery sound of a bike coming down Climbing Way, the road that led up the ridge of the hill behind Lucas's home. There was a low squeal of brakes.

In the kitchen below, Zoey took a third drink, barely a sip this time, and drained the rest of the beer into the sink. Lucas smiled. Zoey would never have much of a future as a drunk.

The kitchen light went off.

Behind him Lucas heard a sound. He spun around.

"Ha. Scared you."

Christopher appeared from around the corner of Lucas's house. He was carrying a black nylon bag. He leaned his bike against the deck railing.

"Spying on Zoey?" Christopher asked. "Does she dance around naked down there or something?"

Lucas rolled his eyes tolerantly. "No, but Benjamin does."

"Don't make me sick."

Lucas glanced at the big bag. "Moving out of the Royal Palace?"

Christopher made a face. "Had to happen sooner or later."

"Not necessarily," Lucas said. "If you could keep from pissing off Aisha—"

"Look who's talking. Have you seen Zoey yet?"

Lucas shrugged.

"That's what I figured."

"It's kind of hard . . ."

Christopher immediately broke out laughing.

"It's kind of *difficult*, you sleaze."

"Uh-huh." Christopher shifted uncomfortably. "So, look, Lucas—"

That tone of voice was too familiar to miss. "You'd better not be about to ask me how you can get a gun again," Lucas warned. "We've been over that."

Christopher shook his head. "No, I respect what you said on that. I was just wondering if you know how to trace a license number."

Lucas turned and looked at Christopher. "Give it to the cops; they'll know how it's done."

"Isn't there any other way?"

"Give it to the cops, dude."

"Screw the cops, man," Christopher said heatedly. "This isn't about cops. All right?"

"Chill. My old man's asleep up there." Lucas jerked his head over his shoulder. "I don't want to have to deal with him on top of you."

"Sorry. But see, this isn't something I can just shake off." He stuck a finger in Lucas's face. "Those pricks put me in the hospital."

"Go to the damned cops," Lucas said tersely.

"So they can do what? Bust the guys *maybe,* and *maybe* they stay locked up for twenty-four hours before they make bail and come out looking for me? I'm not that hard to find. It's not like there are a lot of black guys in the area."

Lucas started to argue, but there weren't any arguments he could make. What Christopher didn't realize was that Lucas knew exactly who had beaten him up. Knew their names and records and associates. And he had concealed that information precisely because he was afraid that if he rolled over on the guys, they'd get out on bail and come after the people he cared about. Zoey, to be specific.

Lucas sighed. "I can't tell you that's not how it works out. That is how it works."

"So I either just shut up and take my beating, or what? I move out of the state? I'm not getting pushed around by some skinhead punks."

Lucas was silent. What the hell was he supposed to do? Christopher was his friend. The skins were psychos who'd sooner or later end up shot, serving life, or overdosing on any number of deadly substances. But in the meantime they were dangerous. There was no way he could get into the middle of this. He didn't approve of violence. It sounded naive, but he didn't. He didn't even watch violent movies. Still, if it was down to choosing sides . . .

"You know, Christopher, how sometime some guy might run into your car, then drive off?"

"What?"

"I'm saying suppose your car gets hit by someone who just drives off but you happen to see his license plate number."

Christopher nodded slowly.

"There must be some way to trace a license plate in a case like that. Probably the Department of Motor Vehicles. I mean, if someone did that to my car, I guess I'd call the DMV."

Christopher smiled grimly. "You're a friend, man." He gave Lucas a friendly punch on the shoulder. Soon he was on his bike, heading off into the night.

Lucas looked back down at Zoey's house. The kitchen light was still off. His eyes were drawn to the white plastic bag that Zoey had thrown away, acting as if it was the most important trash in the world.

"I wonder," he murmured, "what that was all about?"

To my daughter,

On your tenth birthday.

I barely know what to write this time, Zoey. This has not been a good year for any of us. Next week we are taking Benjamin down to Boston to have the operation. The surgeon is supposed to be the very best in the country, but he says the tumor is almost impossible to reach. He says Benjamin may die. Or if he does survive, he may be permanently blind. I have never been so scared in my life.

I know I'm the mom and so I'm supposed to be strong and I'm really trying but oh, God, if something goes wrong.

We had a party for you, and all your friends came over. Nina and Claire and Kristen and Jake and even that poor little boy Lucas who lives up the hill. He seems so sad, although maybe I'm just projecting. The whole world seems sad to me right now. You father blames himself, because he didn't want to take Benjamin to see a specialist earlier. The doctors have told him it wouldn't have made any difference, but your father blames himself for everything.

We've tried not to tell you anything that will worry you, but you're such a smart girl. I've seen the way you've been so sweet to Benjamin, doing all his chores, bringing him cold cloths when he gets those headaches. I know you know

303

something is happening. I even know that you're trying to keep up a brave front and not let me know how upset you are. In school you wrote a poem about your family. It's hard not to think you wrote it to reassure me, and I guess yourself, too. Maybe I'm reading into it, but the part about everything being okay just broke my heart.

My Family
I am Zoey,
and I am the smallest,
My dad is the oldest,
and also the tallest.
My big brother
Benjamin's very cool,
And often walks with
me to school.
My mom is nice and
always says yes,
Except sometimes
When she has PMS.

We live on an island
out in the bay,
And I am happy,
I would say.

Even when things

are sometimes sad,

For me and Ben

and my mom

and my dad,

I know everything

will be okay,

Because that's what

My dad and my mom always say.

Your teacher says you're very gifted. You got an A-plus. Benjamin complained because you used "Ben." You know how he is about people shortening his name.

I guess the birthday party wasn't too much fun for you this year. I hope you'll understand later why we sometimes didn't give you all the attention you deserve right now.

At age ten you just amaze me by how graceful and grown up you are. Already the little boys, especially Jake, are giving you looks. Today at the party he shook up a bottle of Coke and sprayed you with it. I think it was a sign of affection.

Hopefully next year's birthday will be better. I'm optimistic.

EIGHT

THE FERRY PULLED AWAY FROM the dock at seven forty A.M., precise and on time as always. Fog hung still and low over the harbor, muffling the roar of the engines, yet paradoxically magnifying the churning gurgle of water as it rushed along the sides. During the night, clouds had moved in to hide the rising sun. It was as if they were all trapped inside a pearl, surrounded by shimmering translucence, unable to see farther than the deck.

The ferry sounded its foghorn as it rounded the breakwater and entered choppier water. Behind them the island had already disappeared. Ahead the mainland remained invisible.

Zoey wiped condensation from her forehead with the back of her sleeve.

"How does Skipper Too know where to drive the boat when it's like this?" Nina wondered aloud.

"Radar," Aisha said in a hushed voice.

"Or else just habit," Nina suggested. "He's done it a million times."

"Yeah, but how can he be sure there aren't other boats in the way?"

"We're bigger than they are. We just crush them."

Aisha shook her head emphatically. "Radar."

"Instinct," Nina said.

Aisha leaned forward to look past Zoey, making eye contact with Nina. "Did Zoey fall into a coma and no one told us?"

"She's probably just thinking deep, profound thoughts," Nina said.

Zoey forced herself up out of her reverie. She couldn't leave Nina to defend her. Nina knew the truth now, but Nina was weak at keeping secrets. "I just didn't sleep very well last night. I'm spacey."

"Oh, come on, you're spacey every day," Aisha teased. "Jeez, this fog is making my hair frizz."

Zoey managed a wan smile. "Radar," she said. "Plus every-one who has a boat around here knows where the ferry is at any given time."

"Told you she was thinking deep, profound thoughts," Nina said. "Uh-oh."

"Uh-oh, what?" Aisha asked.

"A sad yet horny figure emerges from the fog."

Zoey focused and saw Lucas coming toward them. She sighed inwardly, though there was at the same time a shadow of the familiar surge of warmth and excitement she always felt on seeing him. There was no point in avoiding him any longer. She got up heavily from the bench.

"Watch his hands," Nina whispered.

"Don't take any crap," Aisha advised. "Make him beg."

She met Lucas at the stern rail overlooking the wake. A pair of harbor seals floated contentedly, their sleek heads bobbing like buoys, watching the ferry pass with shrewd, intelligent eyes.

"Hi," Lucas said.

"Hi."

He made an indeterminate gesture with his hands. "I thought maybe we should talk."

"Okay."

"I, uh . . . I think maybe I came on a little too strong. You know. When we were in Vermont."

Zoey said nothing.

"Okay, I came on way too strong. Look, I don't want to break up. You don't want to break up, do you?"

Zoey shook her head.

Lucas sighed in obvious relief.

For a while they were both silent. Zoey stared into the blankness of the fog. "I shouldn't have run away like that," she said at last. "That was stupid. But then, sometimes I'm just stupid."

Lucas looked surprised. "You've never been stupid, Zoey."

"About lots of things," she said. About lots of people. Naive and young and stupid.

"It was my fault," Lucas said.

Zoey was surprised. Lucas's fault? Oh, yes. That. She waved a hand. "Lots of stuff, not just that. It's just that sometimes things aren't what you think they are. People aren't *who* you think they are."

"Look, I said I'm sorry—"

Zoey shook her head. "No, I'm sorry. I'm just weird because I'm tired and because the sun's not out. I always get a little depressed when it's like this. Plus first day back at school after a long weekend."

Lucas slid his hand along the rail. He placed it over Zoey's. Zoey intertwined her fingers with his. It felt so familiar, yet like something she hadn't done in years. Still, there was a reassurance there. She wasn't surprised when he moved closer. When he put his other arm around her waist.

She was grateful for the warmth. Even now, as faraway as

she was in her mind, his touch was comforting. If the last few days had been different, she would have been ecstatic that they were making up. She loved Lucas. She did. But that feeling had become overlain with darker feelings of more recent vintage.

His face was now close to hers. A face she loved, but one now strange to her. Yet his kiss was as soft and warm as ever. And she responded in the way she knew he wanted.

"You know when you said I wasn't acting very grown up?" she said when at last they had drawn apart.

He looked embarrassed. "I didn't really—"

"No. You were right about that," she said. "I've been a real child. A little girl."

Lucas seemed unable to come up with a response. He just looked uncomfortable.

Zoey smiled crookedly and squeezed his hand. "Never mind, Lucas. Not your problem."

Before first period Jake went to the gym. He had walked from the ferry landing up the street and then, as soon as he was out of sight of the others, he'd broken into an easy run, reaching school without breaking a sweat.

The coach was waiting in his office, a small, glass-walled area beside the equipment room. He looked up as Jake burst into the room, keeping his expression perfectly neutral.

"You ready to do this, McRoyan?"

"Yes, sir."

"You're sure? Because once I send off the sample, it's out of my hands."

"No problem," Jake said confidently.

The coach handed him a small plastic vial with a screw-on lid. "Don't need to fill more than half."

Jake took the bottle and went to the boys' locker room. When he was done he returned, feeling ridiculously self-conscious walking around with a little bottle of urine.

He set the bottle on the coach's desk. The coach nodded. "Kind of embarrassing, isn't it?"

"A little," Jake admitted.

"Good. You know I cut you slack on this, don't you?"

"Yes, sir."

"You're a good kid. Not a bad football player. I don't like to see a kid like you screw up the whole rest of his life by making one mistake."

Jake nodded. He felt strangely choked up. "Y'sir, Coach."

His coach stood up. He leaned across his desk, putting his face close to Jake's. "You've used up your freebie. You show up at any practice of mine, or any game of mine drunk, half-drunk, near-drunk, stoned, high, even thinking about being high, and you won't know what hit you. You'll be off the team.

I'll let Mr. Hardcastle know what's happening. And I will personally go to your father and tell him. Do you read me?"

Jake nodded. "I understand."

"Well, you'd better." The coach shook his head regretfully. "What happened to your brother is not going to happen to another one of my players, or to another one of Fred McRoyan's sons."

Jake realized with horror that there were tears in his own eyes. It had never occurred to him that the coach might feel responsible in any way for Wade's drinking and death. When he answered, his voice was shaky. "No, sir."

"Okay, then. Be at practice tonight. And I am going to personally run your ass off. Now get out of here and we don't talk about this again."

Jake turned away, feeling both relief and a nagging worry. He stopped with his hand on the door. "Coach?"

"What now?"

"Zoey Passmore . . . She and I used to go out."

"Do I care?"

"She takes journalism and sometimes she writes for the *Weymouth Times.* You know, their youth page or whatever it's called."

"I'm still waiting to hear why I give a rat's ass."

Jake took a deep breath. "She says she's doing a story on

rumors that there's drug use on the football team."

There was a long silence.

"What does she know?"

Jake shrugged. "I don't know. She asked me if I knew anything. I blew her off."

The coach gave him a long, cold stare. "Sounds like a personal problem, McRoyan."

NINE

LUCAS HAD BEEN RIGHT ABOUT the Department of Motor Vehicles, but it hadn't done Christopher any good. There were papers to fill out, and an ID he would have had to show, and some long story about filling out a police report on the alleged accident. None of which Christopher could do without leaving a huge, easy-to-read trail of evidence pointing straight to him.

Not that he was thinking that way, he reminded himself. That kind of thinking was for criminals. He was out for justice.

Instead, after getting off from his midday job as equipment manager for the school phys-ed department, he caught a city bus out to the part of town where he had spotted the skinheads in their car. He remembered the car. And he had the license number. And he had seen them turn down Brice Street, which, the map showed, dead-ended against the river after less than half a mile length.

He had slipped a box cutter into his pocket, a short metal

handle that held an exposed razor blade. It wasn't much of a weapon, but if the people he was after should happen to spot him, at least he would have some means of defense.

He got off the bus, finding himself in a neighborhood of shabby homes and corner lots marked by self-serve gas stations and mini-marts. As he walked down Brice, the habitations became more spread out, separated by empty fields, by stands of pine, then clustered two or three together. A frame house with a trailer parked alongside. A kennel from which floated the plaintive cries of bored, hungry dogs. A rusted green mobile home with equally rusted appliances in the side yard and a hand-scrawled plywood sign offering rabbits for sale.

From time to time as he walked, Christopher caught sight of the river, brown and slow moving. He walked on the balls of his feet, fists unconsciously clenched in his jacket pockets. This was a world away from the urbane, relatively sophisticated heart of Weymouth, and farther still from the gentleness of Chatham Island. Here, while the environment was utterly different, the *feeling,* the mood, was closer to what he had known in the projects of Baltimore. There was sullen, lurking danger here, waiting like carelessly strewn explosives for the spark to set them off.

Then he spotted the car around a curve in the road, just a

rear bumper protruding from the cover of trees. He stopped. In the low, slanting light it was hard to see clearly. In an hour it would be dark. In two hours he was due at the Passmores' restaurant to start the night shift.

An image of that familiar place, a gleaming, bright, stainless steel and tile kitchen, seemed like a vision from another planet. Here he was, creeping along the quiet road, his heart pounding, breath fast and rasping cold in his throat. Closer, closer.

Yes. The Ford. The correct numbers on the license plate.

He stepped over the ditch that ran beside the road and plunged into the scruffy pine woods. He circled, moving as silently as he could over pine needles, with thorn bushes snaring his ankles. Finally he crouched behind a tree, peering through a hole in the vegetation. He saw a frame house, not large, not painted in many years. A bare window. A woman standing there, head down, shoulders moving slightly. Washing dishes in her kitchen sink, Christopher realized.

He checked his watch. Not much time left if he was to make work on time. Now that he was standing still, he felt the cold. He had to pee urgently. A dog on a long chain walked by in the side yard of the house. It stopped and stared, ears cocked exactly at the spot where Christopher was standing.

Christopher froze. After an eternity the dog walked away toward the backyard.

In the window another figure, passing by behind the woman. Just a glimpse of a bare head reflecting harsh light, a short goatee.

A second window was illuminated. Christopher shifted his position slightly. And there it was, hanging loosely on a wall. Red, white, and blue in an *X* of stars—the Confederate battle flag.

Christopher nodded grimly. Maybe—*maybe*—if this had been the South, that flag might have stood for some twisted notion of local history. But this was Maine. As Yankee as a state could be. Here the stars and bars could only be the symbol of racism.

The shaved head and goatee stopped in front of the window.

Yes, Christopher told himself, that was him. That was one of the creatures who had beaten him, knocked him to the dirty ground, kicked and kicked and kicked . . .

Christopher pointed a finger at the unseeing boy inside. Pointed a finger and silently mouthed the word *bang*.

TEN

ZOEY REACHED INTO HER DESK drawer for an eraser and realized with a shock that there was an unfamiliar empty space there. The journal. It had been in that drawer forever.

She glanced at her trash can. But no, she remembered now. She had taken out the trash last night. The journal, with all her writing, and the book her mother had given her. Gone now. No point having second thoughts. They were both artifacts from a time in her life that was over.

She erased the error she'd made on her trig homework, wrote in the correct answer, and re-checked her calculation. Yes. That was right. Or at least it seemed right. Math of any kind was not her strongest subject. Tomorrow morning on the ferry she'd check with Aisha. Aisha was taking calculus and regularly complained that the class moved too slowly.

There was a knock on her bedroom door. "It's me." Lucas's voice.

Zoey hesitated. "Come in."

Lucas was wearing a rough oversized sweater that made him look smaller than he was. Not quite vulnerable, that would be overstating it, but adorable. His long blond hair was wind-blown, his cheeks pink from the cold outside. His lips were a little chapped.

He came and stood behind her and rested his hands on her shoulders, looking down at her work. "Homework?" he asked.

"I'm all done," she said. "I just finished." She could sense his hesitation. He wanted to kiss her, but there was still an uncertainty between them, no doubt made worse by Zoey's preoccupation with other matters. Matters like the two still-unread letters under the edge of her mattress.

She felt his lips on the top of her head. She tilted back, raising her face to him, closing her eyes. Yes, his lips were a little chapped, and his hand, stroking her cheek, was cold.

She broke free and stood up, intending to continue kissing him from a more comfortable position. But he was staring at the walls of her dormered window.

"What happened to all your quotes?"

She shrugged nonchalantly, but she was aware that a blush would soon be appearing on her face. She had forgotten that others might notice a difference in her room. "I don't know. Decided it was time for a change."

"Oh." He nodded. "I liked them. Always had something

new to think about whenever I came up here."

"You always think about exactly the same thing whenever you're up here," Zoey said, hoping to distract him.

He made a wry smile. "I think about that everywhere, not just here. But I liked that quote about school. About it being unhappy and dull . . . what was it again?"

Zoey picked up her *Portable Curmudgeon* and flipped to the page. She held it out for Lucas.

"School days, I believe, are the unhappiest in the whole span of human existence. They are full of dull, unintelligible tasks, new and unpleasant ordinances, brutal violations of common sense and common decency." Lucas laughed delightedly. "H. L. Mencken, I don't know who you were, but you're my man. 'Dull, unintelligible tasks.' Think he attended Weymouth High?"

There was a louder knock at the door. A deep male voice. "All right, break clean in there."

"Come in, Daddy," Zoey said quickly.

Lucas shot her a mildly disgruntled look.

"Lucas!" Mr. Passmore said in mock surprise. "Imagine finding you here."

"What's up, Mr. P.?"

"Have I mentioned that you can call me Jeff?"

"Yes, sir," Lucas said.

"But I'm way too old for you to call by my first name,

right?" Her father winced and sent Zoey a droll look. "I just wanted to see if you guys wanted to come down and watch TV. *Modern Family* is on in a few minutes. And I feel like I haven't seen you much lately, between work and you going off for the weekend."

Zoey hurried to her father's side. "I'll come watch TV with you. Come on, Lucas."

"We'll do popcorn," Mr. Passmore said, enticing Lucas, making up for the fact that he was depriving Lucas of his girl-friend.

"And beer?" Lucas asked, giving way gracefully.

"Don't mind if I do," Mr. Passmore said. "And of course there are soft drinks for you."

They trotted downstairs, joining Benjamin and Nina in the family room. Benjamin and Nina were close together on the couch, hands intertwined. Lucas pulled Zoey down beside him on the love seat, and Zoey's father flopped back in the La-Z-Boy.

"Well," Mr. Passmore said with a wistful smile, "I'm the only one without a date."

After Nina and Lucas had gone home, Benjamin and Zoey stayed with their father. They watched some more TV together, and during commercial breaks that Mr. Passmore muted with the remote control, they exchanged brief bits of conversation.

Zoey was sitting on the couch, leaning back against the armrest with her legs up and covered by a throw. Her father was in profile, focused on the TV. His usual ponytail was unfastened so that his dark hair hung loose, not quite reaching his shoulders. At the front his hairline had started to recede. He wore a nondescript gray T-shirt and an old pair of painter's pants and heavy wool socks on his feet. He was drinking a Bass from the bottle and scrounging for the remnants of popcorn in a glass bowl.

Did he know? Zoey wondered. Did he at least suspect?

Did he sense the seismic forces building up beneath him, waiting to bring down his world?

"Glad Christopher's on the job again," he said, muting a car commercial. "It's nice to be able to kick back a little."

"He's probably glad to be back at work, too," Zoey said.

"He works hard. Man, when I was his age I only worked till I could afford my next set of Pearl Jam tickets and gas money to get there."

Zoey smiled affectionately. "Do you ever think of doing that again? I mean, Pearl Jam is still around."

Her father laughed. "Yeah, I think about it. Although nowadays I think about maybe getting a room at a nearby Marriott instead of sleeping in the back of a van or in a field somewhere."

He shrugged. "I don't know if your mom would be up for it, either."

Zoey became alert. "Did you guys used to do stuff like that?"

"You mean back when we had lives?" he asked dryly. "Sure."

"What do you mean 'when we had lives'?" Zoey asked. She didn't want to sound like she was pumping him for information, but she was.

"Before they had us," Benjamin interjected.

"No, it was more the restaurant," Mr. Passmore said. "Since we got that, we haven't had time for much. I feel like I barely see your mom, except at work. And I don't see much of you two, either."

He put the sound back on the TV and they listened to a local news story about a bus wreck.

"When did you guys decide to get married?" Zoey asked.

She noticed Benjamin cocking an eyebrow quizzically. "Right after they found out Mom was pregnant with me," he said.

"Very funny, Benjamin," Mr. Passmore said.

"Yeah, and true. I can count, you know."

This wasn't a big surprise to Zoey. She and Benjamin had figured out this titillating bit of information years ago. Their parents' anniversary came three months after Benjamin would have been conceived. "Was Mom your only girlfriend?"

Zoey's father gave her a surprised look. "What is this, Twenty Questions?"

"I was just curious."

For a fleeting moment her father's eyes grew vacant, faraway. But then, just as quickly, he shook off the passing mood. He covered it by affecting a swaggering tone. "I wasn't totally unpopular with the young ladies."

"Anyone special?"

Benjamin was doing the subtle tilt of the head that was his version of staring. He was concentrating on Zoey, a quizzical smile tugging at the corners of his mouth. She was going to have to stop this questioning or Benjamin's suspicions would be fully alerted.

"Special?" her father repeated the word. He shrugged. "Nah. Not really. Just your mom. She was the one who had guys after her all the time."

"At the same time she was going out with you?"

Her father turned the La-Z-Boy and looked at her. "Oh, no you don't. You can't use your mom and me as guides for how you deal with Lucas. Do as we say, not as we did."

Zoey formed a sheepish smile.

"But—now don't tell your mom this—but I do think she

had some other guy going at the same time as me."

Zoey nearly gave it away, but fought to maintain control of her features. Her voice wobbled a little, but she plowed on, hoping her father wouldn't notice. It was Benjamin, she knew, who wouldn't miss her emotion. "Another guy, huh?"

"Some jock or marine or something. So I heard. Never knew the guy's name. It was while I was away for a time. Backpacking around Europe while your mom was still in school." He smiled wistfully. "Fortunately for me, it all worked out, huh? I don't know what I would have done if she hadn't been in my life."

To my daughter,

Well. Didn't you get an odd present for your twelfth birthday? Two days ago you came to me, very adult and ladylike, and said, "Mother, I believe I have started my period." I knew it was something major as soon as you said "Mother" because you never call me that.

You handled it so much better than I did when it happened to me. With me there was crying. But then, my mother never was good at telling me all the facts of life, whereas we've always tried to be honest with you. I remember when you were five you asked us how babies are made and your dad found an excuse to leave the room, so I had to tell you.

Anyway, I was very proud of how grown up you were the other day. Your dad became depressed, of course, because to him it means you're growing up, which means he's growing older. Also, he's so nuts about you, and he doesn't want you to turn into a teenager. He probably remembers what we were both like as teenagers. And for that matter after we were teenagers.

I guess this means you've made the first big step from being a girl to being a woman. I know you'll be a wonderful woman because you've always been such a great kid. This last year you've had to deal with Benjamin and his therapy still taking everyone's attention away from you. Not to mention that Nina and Claire's mom died and that has hurt you terribly.

I hope you'll do a better job with your life than I have in some ways with mine. Maybe I can help you make fewer mistakes because I've definitely made some. Not that I'm ever going to tell you about them. I wouldn't want to give you any ideas.

Soon you'll be a teenager and then you and I will probably have trouble. Most teen girls have hassles with their moms. God knows I did. I think it's when you're a teenager that you start to realize that your parents don't actually know everything. But I hope you and I can beat the odds and go on being close, because I love you. Even if you weren't my daughter I would think you were pretty cool.

ELEVEN

Zoey's room, 6:31 a.m.

THE RADIO ALARM WENT OFF a minute late. For a moment Zoey was confused. The song on the radio was from one of her favorite albums. She recognized the Beyoncé lyrics immediately.

It was like a message. An omen. The message was grim but strong. She would do whatever she had to do.

One thing had become clear as crystal last night—the first and most important thing to do was protect her father. He was the innocent person in all this and he was the one who would be hurt the worst.

It's so clear now, she thought as she quickly dressed. As if the last of the confusion had been left behind in her dreams. Now she knew exactly what to do. She hefted her books, slung her purse over her shoulder, and headed for the door. Then she went back to her bed, bent down, and removed the letters from under her mattress. The last thing she needed if she was going to succeed was for her mother to find the letters.

Benjamin walked at her side, moving along the familiar path to the ferry like a sighted person. Except that Zoey knew in his head he was counting, making each step as nearly identical as possible, and keeping track on some subliminal level of all the tiny clues that only he noticed—the interval of coolness and warmth that was the sun peeking between gaps in the houses; the welcoming good-morning bark of the Brashares' big Labrador, Danny; the smell of the fresh doughnuts frying that meant they were passing Island Grocery.

"Sunny today?" Benjamin asked.

"Mostly," Zoey said. Her mind was still on her mission. It would take courage.

Benjamin grumbled good-naturedly. "That's one of the things I miss about going out with Claire," he said. "You ask her about the weather, you get a full, complete answer."

Claire Geiger had a somewhat strange obsession with weather, up to the point of sitting out in the middle of thunderstorms from atop her widow's walk.

"So," he said

"So what?"

"So, you going to tell me why you were giving the old man the treatment last night?"

"What treatment?"

"Like you were interviewing him to see if he should be a contestant on *The Bachelor*."

"I was just curious. I mean, he's our dad, but how much do we really know about him?"

This struck Benjamin as very funny, fortunately for Zoey. "Yeah, who knows what dark secrets the old man is hiding?"

"There's Nina up ahead."

Benjamin accelerated, caught his toe in a sidewalk brick, and barely kept from tripping.

Zoey snickered.

"That was not because I was excited about seeing Nina or anything," he said gruffly.

"Uh-huh."

The ferry, 7:48 a.m.

From across the deck of the ferry, Jake was watching her. Obviously something was bothering him. She hoped it wasn't what she feared it was. She didn't see any way he could possibly know. But secrets were hard to keep on an island as small as Chatham Island.

She squeezed out from between Nina and Aisha, who were

arguing over whether Justin Timberlake was cool or full of himself. Lucas was against the far railing. When he saw her get up, he started toward her with a smile on his face. But then, realizing she was going to Jake, he backed off, his expression coldly mistrustful.

"Hi, Jake," she said.

"Hey, Zoey," he said guardedly.

"You're not sitting with Claire?" she asked, by way of making conversation. She wanted him to have a chance to bring up whatever was bugging him. She wanted to hear him first, decide what he knew before committing herself.

"She's busy reading," Jake said, sounding mildly annoyed. "Sometimes I get the feeling I may not be the center of her existence."

"Claire is the sun and moon in her very own solar system," Zoey said.

He made a half-smile. "So. How's the big story going?"

"The big story?" Good grief, she'd practically forgotten. Mr. Schwarz, her journalism teacher, would kill her if she blew it. "I haven't had any time to work on it."

He nodded. He was looking at her through narrowed slits. Skeptical. "What are you going to do next? You know, on the story."

She shrugged. "I guess I'll talk to some of the other guys on the team."

"I doubt if anyone will have anything to say."

"Maybe not. Um, Jake, are you pissed off at me?"

"Why would I be?"

"I don't know."

"No, Zoey. I don't have a problem with you." Belligerent.

"Okay. And . . . and you don't have a problem with Benjamin, or anyone else in my family?" She tried out a lighthearted tone.

He looked quizzical. "What?"

"Nothing."

Journalism class, first period

As she was on her way out, Mr. Schwarz beckoned to her. She sighed and went over by his desk. Mr. Schwarz was the best-looking male teacher in the school, but when he was impatient or annoyed with someone, he tended not to look quite as cute.

"Getting anywhere with that story I gave you to do?" he asked, crossing his arms over his chest.

"Not yet," Zoey admitted. "Although I asked my friend, my

source, you know, the guy I said I knew who's on the team?"

"Jake McRoyan," Mr. Schwarz said.

"Uh-huh," Zoey admitted. Somehow mentioning Jake by name had seemed indiscreet. It made it too personal and unprofessional. "He says no way. He says he would know."

Mr. Schwarz stared at her. Then he took a deep breath. "Keep digging, Zoey."

"I was going to talk to some of the other guys on the team."

"Good idea. You might also try checking to see who on the team may have missed games or turned in a poor performance lately."

"That's a good idea," Zoey said. She glanced at the clock. It would be a run to make trig.

"Okay. Go," Mr. Schwarz said, dismissing her and looking cuter again for a moment.

Good ideas, Zoey thought admiringly. *Check on who had missed a game recently.* Too bad she'd been out of town over the weekend. So she hadn't seen the game.

And, of course, neither had Jake.

Jake?

No. Impossible.

Except that the week before at homecoming, Jake had

seemed . . . *No. Not Jake,* Zoey thought, trying to dismiss the idea.

But if it *was* him—if Jake *was* the person who had been using drugs . . .

She groaned. Like life wasn't complicated enough right now?

TWELVE

"YOU KNOW, I'M SEVENTEEN," AISHA said. "I'll be graduating soon. Off to college. And my point is, I don't think I'll suddenly decide at this time in my life to become a gymnast." She adjusted the water to be a little warmer and rotated slowly so that the shower could rinse the soap from her body. "Tell me why I would want to risk breaking my neck vaulting."

"You could be the next what's-her-name," Zoey said, stepping out of the water gingerly and running on tiptoes to her towel.

"She could be the next three-foot-tall anorexic?" Claire asked archly. "I doubt it."

"What are you talking about?" Zoey asked.

"Gymnasts. They're all the size of munchkins and eat nothing but rice cakes."

"Exactly," Aisha said, turning off the water. She buried her face in her towel. "So why are we doing gymnastics?"

"Why are we doing any of this?" Claire demanded.

"Because the school district says we have to and we didn't get it out of the way last year like we should have."

"Do you guys realize you have this same conversation every day?" asked Louise Kronenberger as she slipped on a sweater.

"We find it comforting," Claire said.

"Maybe we should try to get into it more," Louise suggested. "Like the guys do."

"They're in their locker room snapping each other with towels right now," Claire said. "Is that what you think we should be doing?"

Louise got a dreamy, faraway look in her eyes. "No. But you've drawn a nice word picture, Claire. It conjures up some interesting mental images. Does Jake have gym this period?" she asked innocently.

"I don't think you want to be imagining Jake," Aisha warned. "They're back together."

Louise grinned. "But it's so easy for me to *imagine* Jake." She batted her eyes. "I can even imagine a crooked little scar right . . . but then, I'm letting my imagination run wild." She looked in the mirror, patted her hair, and gave a good-bye wave.

Aisha noted the sudden narrowing of Claire's eyes, but she instantly regained control. The girl was cool, there was no question about that. But of course Claire knew there had never been anything between Louise and Jake. At least, Aisha was pretty sure there had never been anything between Jake and Louise. That would be hard to imagine. Jake was the last of the major straight arrows, and Louise . . .

Aisha finished dressing and went outside, skirting the edge of the polished gym floor. Christopher worked in the equipment room and it wouldn't hurt to stop by and say hello, since she had a few minutes.

The equipment room was a dark, not exactly fragrant place with metal shelves lined with things like volleyball nets, tumbling mats, jumbled piles of white plastic football pads, racks of baseball bats, and every type of ball known to man or woman.

Christopher had a clipboard in one hand, a pencil in the other, and earphones over his ears. He was intent on counting and hadn't noticed her.

Aisha crept up behind him and slid her arms around his waist. He jerked at first, but then relaxed without turning around. She kissed the back of his neck. He pulled off the earphones.

"Is that you, Natalie?"

Aisha slapped him on the arm. He spun around.

"I was kidding. Just kidding." He rubbed the spot.

"I knew you were kidding."

"Then why did you nearly bruise me?"

"Because I'm sure you've done something to deserve it," Aisha replied. "What are you doing?"

"While I was off, it seems a certain amount of equipment managed to disappear. Three basketballs, a catcher's mask, and a croquet set."

"Croquet set? Why do we have a croquet set?"

He shrugged. "Why do we have six bowling balls and a jigsaw puzzle of a cat playing with a ball of yarn? It's not my job to ask why. I just keep track of the stuff and keep it in shape."

"Well, I guess I'd better get going," Aisha said.

"Where to?"

"Homeroom, then lunch." Aisha considered an idea that had popped into her mind, rejected it, considered it again, and rejected it again. Then she went ahead and said it anyway. "You know, if you ever wanted to have lunch together—"

"Don't you eat in the cafeteria with the other females of the Chatham Island club?"

"Usually. But there's no law saying I have to. We are allowed off-campus, you know, and there's Burger King and the Dashing Deli."

"The deli's all right," he said. "We use their rolls at the restaurant. Mr. Passmore says they're the best bakery around. I'd love to have lunch with you there, Aisha. I wish I'd thought of it. How about tomorrow?"

"Why not today? It's Wok Wednesday in the cafeteria. They pretend it's Chinese food except that I don't think there's anything very Chinese about cut-up pieces of Salisbury steak mixed with bean sprouts."

Christopher winced. "Can't do it today," he said.

"You have to eat," Aisha pointed out. "You do get a lunch hour, don't you?"

"Yes," he said. Then he glanced away. "Only today I have to do something else." He looked down at his clipboard.

"Fine," Aisha said. "I can take the hint."

"Wait." He grabbed her arm. "I'd really, really like to take you to lunch tomorrow."

"I'll check my schedule," Aisha said. *And maybe,* she added to herself, *I'll just check out what you are doing during lunch today.*

"So where's Aisha?" Nina asked, taking the seat across from Claire and next to Zoey. She set down her tray and took a long look at what the cafeteria ladies had given her.

Claire shrugged indifferently. "Not my day to keep track of Aisha." In about ten seconds Nina would come up with something gross to say about the food. Ten, nine, eight . . .

"I don't know, either," Zoey said.

. . . seven, six . . .

"Wait! Someone barfed on my tray," Nina said, wrinkling her nose.

Four seconds to spare. "Every day," Claire said wearily.

"Every day what?"

"Every day you have to say something disgusting about the disgusting food."

"I don't have to," Nina argued. "It's just that they make it so easy. I mean, you know what this stuff looks like?"

"Please don't tell me," Claire said, knowing full well that nothing short of an anvil dropped from a great height directly on Nina's head would stop her.

"Like what's left after someone's been dead for a month and the worms have gotten to them."

Zoey pushed away her food. Nina gleefully took a big bite. Claire forked up a bite of hers, giving Nina a defiant look.

"Why don't you go sit with Benjamin?" Claire asked. "I'm sure he'd appreciate your descriptive talents."

"I didn't want to mess with tradition," Nina said airily. "We always sit together. Although without Aisha it kind of changes the balance a little. Basically, it means too much of you."

"Maybe *I* should go sit with Benjamin," Claire said, sending a long look from under lowered lashes in his direction. "That shirt looks good on him. Did you pick that out for him, Zoey?"

Zoey did a snap back to reality. "What? Oh, yeah. You know, the guys' store that's next to Express at the mall?"

"Maybe I *should* go over and say hi," Nina said, standing up with her tray. "Since Aisha isn't here and Zoey's obviously off in the ozone, anyway."

Claire allowed herself a small smile of satisfaction. Unfortunately, Nina's description of the main course had had an effect. She ate her bread and apple and drank her juice.

"Can I ask you a question?" Zoey asked suddenly, breaking in on Claire's contented silence.

"Go ahead."

"Do you think Jake ever used any drugs?"

Claire came fully alert. Jake had told her about his one nearly disastrous encounter with drugs. And of course she knew all about Jake's drinking—more than the one or two occasions Zoey and the others knew about. "Jake?" she said, sounding incredulous. "Why would you think that?"

Zoey looked thoughtful. "You know how sometimes I write stories for the youth page of the *Weymouth Times*?"

Claire nodded.

"They asked me to check out rumors that there's a drug problem on the football team."

Claire let loose a stream of silent curses. But outwardly she showed nothing. Or at least she hoped she showed nothing. Zoey wasn't stupid.

"So I asked Jake about it when we were up in Vermont and he got all pissed off."

"He's loyal to his teammates," Claire said.

"That's what I thought, too. But then I started thinking about how he missed the game last weekend."

"He went with us to Vermont."

"The game was on Friday night. We left on Saturday morning."

Claire finished chewing a bit of apple. There was an "official" story for why Jake hadn't played that game. But Zoey wasn't going to buy it for a minute. Still, it was the only story Claire had available. "He said something about a pulled muscle."

Zoey shook her head. "He was skiing all weekend. Skiing hard, too."

Claire concentrated again on her apple. Well, it had been worth a try. Now she wished she hadn't manipulated Nina into leaving. Zoey might not have brought all this up with Nina around.

Zoey leaned forward and pitched her voice at an intimate level. "Look, Claire, I think maybe those rumors are actually about Jake."

She could deny, or pretend to be indifferent, or she could tell Zoey the truth and try to get her to drop it. And the longer she hesitated indecisively, the more suspicious Zoey would become. "I don't think this is any of my business," she said at last.

"You're going out with Jake, Claire. If he's been doing

drugs, that has to be your business."

"What exactly do you want from me?" Claire snapped. "You want me to help you write your little story?"

"God, it *is* him," Zoey said. She covered her mouth with her hand.

"I didn't say that."

"I wish someone had told me before I agreed to do this thing," Zoey said.

Claire gave up. There was no point in denying it now. Zoey knew. "It was just the one time, Zoey. They suspended him from the team for a week until he could pass a urinalysis, which he did yesterday. That's really not much of a story, is it?"

"Is he okay?"

"Do you care if he's okay?"

"Of course I do," Zoey said. "I still care about Jake. We were together a long time."

She was obviously sincere. Perhaps a little too sincere, Claire decided. Things must not be total perfection between Zoey and Lucas. "If you care about Jake, then drop it. He knows sooner or later some of the people here will find out about it, but you know how he is with his father. If his father ever found out, Jake would feel like the lowest form of garbage."

"His father." Zoey nodded grimly. "He cares too much what his father thinks about him."

"People usually do."

"Do you?" Zoey asked sharply. "I mean, do you really care that much what your father thinks?"

The question made Claire uncomfortable. What did this have to do with Jake? "I suppose I do."

Zoey nodded. "Parents are just people, you know."

"I had heard that somewhere," Claire answered dryly. "What are you going to do about this story?"

Zoey's eyes flickered. She had been off somewhere, thinking about something else. "I don't know. I don't want to hurt Jake. It's important to me that he doesn't get hurt. He's part of the reason why—"

"Why what?"

Zoey made a forced smile. "Never mind. I'll have to think about it."

Aisha waited just inside a glass-windowed side door to the school. From here she could see the gym doors. Dozens of students were passing across her field of vision, but she was sure she'd notice Christopher if he came by. She didn't wait long to spot his tall, lithe form, moving quickly to slide between slower-moving groups.

Aisha opened the door and went after him. There wasn't much likelihood that he would notice her. Christopher always walked and moved like he was on an urgent mission. The problem was keeping him in sight. Several times she had to break into a trot.

He left the campus and headed down the street, past the Burger King, where most of the rest of the crowd veered off. Christopher kept moving until he was well into the downtown business area, crossing the commons, teeming with lunching secretaries and young executives. He went down Fifth Street, plunging into a grubby neighborhood of row houses fronted by overflowing trash cans and decorated with spray-painted graffiti.

Aisha began feeling conspicuous, no longer shielded from his view if he should happen to turn around. Plus, she was beginning to realize that she would have a very hard time explaining this bit of spying to Christopher.

He slowed, seemed to be checking a street sign, and ducked into an alley.

Aisha hesitated. Maybe he had spotted her and was waiting just within the alley to jump out and yell "Aha!" And really, she was way, way past the point where she could try to pretend it was just a chance encounter. She'd never been on this street before, didn't know anyone here, had no conceivable excuse for being here.

Except for the excuse that she was spying on Christopher. Trying to find out why he hadn't wanted to have lunch with her. Frankly, she'd expected to find him sharing a chicken salad with some little bimbo he'd met. She certainly hadn't expected him to go this far from school. And if he was meeting another girl, this was an odd place to do it.

She went ahead, walking as inconspicuously as possible to the mouth of the alley. When she reached it, she sidled against the wall and looked around the corner with a motion that reminded her of a Bugs Bunny cartoon and made her feel like a complete idiot.

She jerked back her head. Christopher was only ten feet or so away, standing close to a twentysomething white guy with long sideburns.

She could hear snatches of a low, muttered conversation. Christopher's voice. ". . . serial number or anything?"

"That's all . . . totally clean."

"Two bills?"

". . . fifty."

"And you'll throw in . . ." Christopher.

"Two fifty . . . and a box of . . . points."

Aisha strained. The sound of her own heart pounding in her ears was making it hard to hear.

Then she heard a sound with perfect clarity. A harsh metallic sound. Then a click. "That's all there is to it."

"Here's . . . money."

"Cool . . ."

". . . never seen me." Christopher's voice.

A laugh. "Never seen anybody, my . . ."

Aisha realized she had stopped breathing. For a moment she was paralyzed. The deal had been concluded. Christopher would be stepping out of the alley any second.

The sound of footsteps. She bolted, racing around the back of a car and crouching down below the windows. Looking left, she saw sideburns, hands shoved deep in his pockets, shoulders hunched. Then, in the other direction, Christopher. One hand was in the pocket of his coat, and the coat sagged on that side.

Aisha stood up. She was trembling. It was impossible not to know what had happened. At first Aisha had told herself Christopher was buying drugs. The truth was so terrible that even that would have been a relief. But there was no question. Christopher had bought a gun.

My dearest Darla—

I am so sorry for the way I reacted when you told me your news. I was angry and hurt but I shouldn't have yelled like I did. I guess I was afraid it would mean I would lose you and I don't want that to happen.

You said it couldn't be mine, that the timing doesn't work out. But it could be mine, if you agreed. No one would ever have to know. We could get married right away, before I get shipped out. That way you'd get what they call an allotment, part of my pay. Also, you could have the baby in a military hospital for free.

I swear to you, Darla, I would raise the child and love it like my own. It would be my own as far as anyone would ever be concerned. I don't want you to get an abortion just because you don't think the baby would have a father. And I also don't want you to leave me and go back to Jeff because of this.

I know we can work something out if you'll give it a chance. I'll be out of the army in three years. We could move to this great place I know called Chatham Island. It's a little island in Maine, a perfect place for raising kids and having a family. My own family lives near there, so I know people there and it's a great area.

Anyway, please think about it. I love you and will do anything to keep you.

Yours forever,

Fred

THIRTEEN

ZOEY HAD NEVER BEFORE SKIPPED school, but so far, it was proving much easier than she'd imagined.

First, she'd had to come up with a plausible story for Lucas. Lucas was in her sixth-period history class *and* her last-period French. They always walked from the one to the other together. There was no possibility whatsoever that he would somehow not notice her absence. None.

So she'd told him that she had gotten permission to leave early and work on her journalism project. He'd seemed puzzled, but the last thing she could worry about at this crucial moment was Lucas.

The time had come, and now that it had, it filled her with dread. What she was preparing to do was unthinkable. Except that she had to think about it and plan it out. How she would explain why she was there in his office. What she would say. How she would deal with his possible denial. What specific words she would use. Adultery? Betrayal? No. She was going to keep everything very cool and adult and simply tell him that he must never again . . .

What? God, it was impossible even to imagine discussing any of this. It was insane.

Feeling guilty, Zoey headed down the empty hall toward a side door. She had to ditch, she reminded herself. After school her plan would be impossible, with Nina and Benjamin and Aisha around. Besides, Mr. McRoyan might have left his work by then. And his work was the safest place to go to him.

Just at the door Ms. Lambert, her homeroom teacher, stepped out of a classroom.

Zoey froze. Her first attempt to skip school and she'd been busted!

But Ms. Lambert just smiled. "How are you, Zoey?"

"Fine," Zoey squeaked.

"See you tomorrow."

"Okay."

She was out the door. It was amazing what a spotless reputation could do for you. No one would ever suspect her of skipping school, so even on seeing Zoey brazenly walking out, the teacher had assumed she must have a good reason.

Zoey breathed a sigh of relief. Still, getting out of school was going to be the easy part.

She headed downtown, quiet now with all the worker bees

back in their hives till the big five o'clock rush to freedom.

Mid-Maine Bank owned the tallest building in downtown, fifteen floors. Mr. Geiger's office on the top floor had a terrific view of the entire city. Zoey had gone up there several times with Nina or Claire. The lower floors were rented to a wide variety of businesses.

Zoey went in through the green-marbled lobby to the brass elevator. Her heart was in her throat as she pushed the button, and she knew that when it came to the actual moment, she would never be able to stay as cool as she hoped.

The elevator bell dinged and she got off on the fourth floor.

The silent, carpeted hallway was lined with wood doors, each marked with the name of the company or person that rented the individual offices—WEYMOUTH SAIL; DR. OSCAR BRILL, OPTOMETRIST; VISITING NURSE ASSOCIATION OF WEY-MOUTH.

Zoey stopped at the door she was searching for.

She gritted her teeth. Her hands were sweaty, and she wiped them on her pants. Once through the door, she couldn't turn back. He would know why she had come. There would be no denying anything.

She put her hand on the knob, turned it, and stepped into the comfortable, modern offices of McRoyan Realty Holdings.

The receptionist looked up at her with a quizzical half-smile.

Zoey stared past her into the glass-walled office beyond.

It took several seconds for him to see Zoey, during which time the receptionist asked repeatedly why she was there, did she have an appointment, was she sure she was in the right place.

Fred McRoyan stood up slowly, levering himself up out of his chair, an older, heavier, but still-fit version of Jake. He stuck his head out of his office. "I'll see her, Ellen."

Zoey walked on stiff legs past the receptionist, blood rushing in her ears, breath rickety.

Mr. McRoyan closed his door behind her. "Would you like something to drink, Zoey? A soda? Coffee?"

"No, thank you."

He accepted that and went to sit behind his desk.

"Please . . ." He motioned to a chair.

She barely knew whether she had sat down or not. He rubbed his face with both hands, then folded them before him.

So much like Jake, Zoey realized. Had she ever noticed it so intensely before? It was like seeing the future—Jake in twenty years.

And nothing at all like Benjamin. No, there was no similarity there at all.

"What can I do for you, Zoey?" he asked.

Zoey took a deep breath. "I wanted to talk to you."

"Okay."

Here it was. "I want you to leave us alone."

He said nothing, just looked at her, or past her; it was hard to tell.

"I saw you the other day," she said. "With my mom."

He nodded. "I thought maybe you had."

"Well, I did."

"You weren't supposed to be there," he said regretfully.

"*I* wasn't . . . *You* weren't supposed to be there! Me? It's my house. I'm supposed to be there, not *you*." Her face was hot. Her fists were clenched.

"You're right." He held up two placating hands. "I expressed that the wrong way."

Zoey let out a curse that shocked her.

Mr. McRoyan pressed his lips into a tight line. "Zoey, would it help if I told you it was just that one time?"

"That's bad enough." She wasn't going to tell him about the letters. She had read them all now. She knew about his past, and her mother's.

"Yes, it is. I am terribly sorry that you walked in on that."

"Sorry you got caught, you mean."

"Sorry I have made you feel badly toward your mother. Your mother is a very fine woman."

Zoey sneered. "Yeah. Wonderful. Just stay away from all of us." She got up, intending to leave.

"I was in love with your mother."

She sat down again. So. He was going to tell the truth.

"A long time ago. She was still in college. I was in the army. Jump school. She had been seeing your dad, but he went off to Europe for a while to backpack and explore, I guess. Your mother and I—" He shrugged. "But I was on my way into the army and your dad came back. Anyway, that was that."

"Not quite."

"We never let anyone know. We've never so much as spoken of those days since you all came to live on the island. Then I guess something happened to make your mom feel . . ." He waved a hand. "Never mind. That's not the point. What I did was dead wrong and I am sorry."

That was it. He wasn't saying more. Zoey stood up again. "Just stay away from us. I don't want my dad to be hurt."

"I know."

"Good."

"Have you . . . Does Jake . . ."

"No," Zoey said shortly. "He's the other person I don't want to be hurt."

"Agreed." He stood up. "I know this won't mean much to you, Zoey, but I've always thought the world of you. I was sorry you and Jake didn't stay together."

"Good-bye," Zoey said. She wasn't sure what else to say.

She looked at Mr. McRoyan's downcast face. He looked sincere. Maybe this really could be the end of it all.

But then his expression changed. His eyes widened. It was as if his whole person collapsed. It was like those slow-motion films of buildings that were being demolished. A shudder, and all at once all the strength went out of him.

Zoey turned and, staring through the glass partition, saw Jake.

Jake stared at the scene before him. Zoey, looking startled. His father looking as if he'd learned the worst news of his life.

Zoey had done it. She had gone to his father to ask him whether he knew that his son was accused of using drugs. It was the only possible explanation.

Why? Why would she do something like this? For some stupid story? It was unimaginable that Zoey, of all people . . .

His father covered his face with his hands, leaning his elbows on his desk. Zoey came out, closing his office door carefully. She looked down as she came to him.

Jake grabbed her arm roughly and pulled her out, past the receptionist into the silent hallway outside. She didn't resist.

"What were you doing in there?" he demanded, almost frantic. If his father knew, he would be devastated. He would think Jake was on his way to becoming Wade. He would imagine the worst. He would lose all faith in Jake, and if that happened, Jake didn't know what he would do.

"I had to talk to your father," Zoey said stiffly.

"You didn't have to!" Jake cried.

"I had to protect my family," Zoey said. Her eyes were blazing now.

"Your family." Jake felt he must have missed something. Or else he was just stupidly failing to understand. What did his being suspended from the team have to do with Zoey's family?

"*And* yours," Zoey added.

"My family?"

"Yes. What happened was just about your father and my mother. It shouldn't break up our families. My dad still loves my mother, I know he does. I can tell, the way he talks about her. And I know he'd . . . It would destroy him."

Zoey was just rambling, staring blankly past Jake, almost as if she were thinking out loud. She was justifying something, explaining something to herself.

Jake shook his head in frustration. "What did my dad say?"

"He said he wouldn't let it happen again," Zoey answered. Then she peered at him, as though noticing him for the first time. "I didn't think you knew."

Didn't think I knew? Now he was utterly confused. How could he not know? This was about what *he* had done.

Wasn't it?

He took Zoey's arm again and drew her toward the elevator. They were both silent on the trip down. Zoey was like someone in a fever. Her face was flushed. She stared with bright, agitated eyes. Outside in the cooler air she gasped, as if she'd been suffocating.

Jake led her to a bench and sat her down. "I want you to tell me exactly what happened up there, Zoey," he said.

"Why are you here?" Zoey asked.

"I have study hall last period," Jake said. "You know that. And practice is starting late because Coach had something he had to go to."

"You weren't supposed to know," Zoey said again.

"That you were coming here?"

Zoey shrugged. "Any of it." Suddenly she put her hand on his. "I didn't want your family to be hurt, either."

Jake took a deep breath. "Look, Zoey, I only know some of it," he said, lying. He knew none of it. Whatever it was. "I want you to tell me what you said to my dad. Word for word. That way I'll be prepared, okay?"

Then Zoey told him.

FOURTEEN

AFTER LAST PERIOD CLAIRE WENT out to the football bleachers, expecting to do some homework while she watched Jake practice. He could use the show of support and besides, there was a magnificent, towering thunderhead, a cumulonimbus formation, to the south. The top was so high it had been sheared flat by the high-altitude winds. She could watch the sky, her greatest fascination, in between pretending to watch Jake.

Lucas went from last period to the football field, expecting to find Zoey. She'd said she was working on her story, and he knew that involved the football team. He also knew, and had known from the start, that Jake was the one who had been using. It was one of several secrets he had been keeping. People had an annoying habit of telling him their secrets—Christopher, Jake, Louise Kronenberger . . .

*   *   *

Claire saw Jake coming from the direction of town. Zoey was with him, walking close by his side. Why? Why were they coming from the direction of town, and why were they together coming from that direction?

Lucas saw them, too, and he was close enough to see that they were holding hands. Holding hands. Zoey and Jake. Jake, who never seemed to quite completely disappear from her life. It was the Freddy Kreuger of relationships—it never seemed permanently dead. He always had the feeling that beyond that next squeaky door, or just beneath the surface of that swampy pond, bingo! Up would pop Jake. And sure enough, here he was.

Claire noticed the hand holding, too. She had to stare hard to be sure, but yes, just then the two of them had swung their hands together, in unison. Unbelievable. Holding hands. With Zoey. No, no, this was not how things happened. Zoey might have Lucas when Claire was done with him; Nina might even have Benjamin when she was done with him. But she hadn't grown tired of Jake yet. When she did, then . . . whatever. But this was totally out of order.

Lucas saw Claire, far off across the field, over the heads of the bouncing cheerleaders practicing ragged cheers, a distant but easily identifiable figure on the bleachers. Claire was staring at the same sight he was watching—Jake with Zoey in deep, personal conversation. Jake touching Zoey's arm. Zoey nodding. Zoey grabbing his hand and almost shaking it, telling him something very earnestly. Jake nodding yes.

Then Claire saw it. Zoey and Jake in a long . . . long . . . very long hug. Breaking free and Zoey . . .

Yes, Lucas confirmed to himself. It had been a kiss. A kiss on Jake's cheek. Damn it. Damn him. Damn her.

. . . a definite kiss, Claire noted. Just a cheek, but a kiss just the same. Well. Added to Louise Kronenberger's little jab today, it was enough to make a suspicious person wonder. And she was a suspicious person. Was there a more cunning side to Jake? Was he not quite the simple person he seemed to be? Did he actually believe that she, Claire Geiger, was going to be used? By *him*?

No wonder, Lucas thought coldly. No wonder Zoey had been so distant ever since Vermont. Had something happened between her and Jake even there? He drifted back from the field, not wanting to be seen, melting back into the milling crowd on its way to the parking lot. There was no point in listening to some long string of explanations from Zoey. Or, worse yet, a confirmation of what he suspected.

Claire climbed down from the bleachers and moved swiftly out of sight behind them. She wasn't about to play the role of the poor, jealous girlfriend. So. So maybe Jake wasn't quite the straightforward, always-up-front guy she had imagined. No, maybe not.

She checked her watch. Still time to grab the four o'clock ferry home. Well, well. What exactly had happened? Had Zoey gone after Jake on the drug story and had Jake then turned her around? Perhaps Jake had put on a convincing show, telling Zoey that he still cared about her and how could she expose him to public scorn and so on.

Right. Jake put on a show. That was likely. Jake, who stammered like an idiot anytime he had to lie. Jake, being nefarious enough to pretend to care for Zoey just so she'd lay off the story? Uh-huh. Yeah, Jake was nefarious, all right. A real master manipulator.

No, the fact was that he *did* still care for Zoey. He always had, Claire told herself. Of course he did. Zoey was just his type. Snow White and the slightly tarnished Prince. They were perfect together.

She realized she was seething, walking down Mainsail

Street with a face for murder. She paused in front of a candy store and pretended to look at the display, while in fact she was checking her own reflection. Yes, far too much anger. Far too much emotion. Far, far too upset just because *her* boyfriend had been in a deep, intimate conversation with Zoey "I'm-ever-so-good" Passmore. Just because he had put his arms around her and squeezed her skinny, flat-chested body against his. And held her far too long.

She resumed her walk, laboring to keep her face blank, but still breathing like Darth Vader.

What a rush of emotion, a rational corner of her mind observed. *You're getting unusually upset, Claire. You're acting as if you're jealous, which is impossible.*

It took me by surprise, she argued with herself. *I wasn't prepared. I didn't expect to see it. Jake with Zoey!*

Lucas crossed her path, just in front of her. He was striding along with energetic concentration.

"Lucas," she called out.

He stopped and turned. "What?" he snapped. "Oh. It's you."

"You were back there, weren't you?"

His eyes were fierce. "Back there? You mean *your* boyfriend copping a cheap feel off *my* girlfriend? Yeah, I was back there."

"I'm sure you're misinterpreting things."

"Yeah, they were probably sharing some class notes. Or maybe discussing world peace."

Claire met his dark, mistrustful glare with one of her own. "Maybe we're overreacting."

"She's been cold to me ever since we came back from Vermont," Lucas snapped. "I thought it was over something else. She puts me through hell, makes me think it's me that's the problem, and all the time it's about Jake. She was even talking about him when we were there. Jake this and Jake that. And with all the stuff I know about Jake McRoyan, he ought to be more careful whose girlfriend he's playing grab-ass with."

Claire thought of pointing out that in no way had Jake been playing grab-ass, but that was of much less importance than Lucas's remark about knowing. "What do you mean, all the stuff you know about Jake?"

Lucas seemed about to answer, but then just looked sullen.

Claire took a shot in the dark. "You mean about Jake getting suspended from the team?"

"Yes, I know about that," Lucas admitted. "Unfortunately, people have this habit of telling me stuff, or else I just have bad luck and happen to be in the wrong places at the wrong times. Like about five minutes ago," he added bitterly.

"And I guess you know about Jake and Louise?" Claire said, holding her breath.

"Yeah!" Lucas said, excited. "I should just tell Zoey about that. Then see how much she likes Jake. He's not exactly the same old Jake she used to go out with." Then, calmer, he shot a glance at Claire. "I guess that must have pissed you off, too, huh?"

"Yes," Claire said, now cold as ice. "It must have."

Benjamin shifted the volume on his cell phone and adjusted his earphones. His favorite part of Bach's B Minor Mass was coming—the "Dona Nobis Pacem," a prayer for peace, as sublime a piece of music as he had ever heard.

He could feel the familiar vibration of the ferry's engines. There was a gentle and not too cold breeze, though once out on the water the temperature dropped a sharp ten degrees. He could tell the bay was choppy because from time to time the breeze would catch the top of a wave and hurl its cold spray against the side of his face. On the back of his neck he could just feel the slanting rays of a failing sun, sliding down behind the buildings of Weymouth. Everywhere was the smell of brine. And like distant echoes, he could hear through the music the calls of gulls following the ferry and hoping for a handout.

He felt a soft impact beside him, and the warmth of a body now touching his right arm. The scent of coconut shampoo and an unlit cigarette.

Nina. She was waiting till he was done with the music, perhaps watching his face, perhaps looking around at what sounded and smelled and felt like a beautiful world.

The music died away and he pulled off his earphones. "Hi."

"Hi. What were you listening to?"

"Swedish House Mafia."

"Liar. It was that Bach guy."

Benjamin smiled. "Swedish House Mafia are just Bach with more *f* words. Many more."

He felt warmth on his cheek, the undefinable sense of someone very near, then soft lips on his own.

"What was that for?" he asked, smiling at the flood of warmth that rushed through him. "Not that I'm complaining."

"I just felt like it. Is it okay when I just do that? I mean, does it embarrass you or anything?"

"You know what it does?" he asked. "It makes me think there really are things even better than music."

"Even Bach?" Mock surprise mixed with genuine pleasure.

"Hmm. Certainly better than Swedish House Mafia."

"I have a feeling that no matter which way I take that, it will work out to be an insult," Nina said.

Benjamin let his hand drift right, made contact with her leg, hovered discreetly above till he found her hand. He entwined his fingers through hers and then raised her hand to his lips. "I would never mean any insult."

Nina snuggled closer.

"How come you're not with the girls?" Benjamin asked. "Breaking with tradition?"

"Nah, Aisha and your sister are both in lousy moods. They don't even know I'm not there, probably."

"And *your* sister?"

"Claire missed the boat. Or else—oh, yeah. Wednesday's the day her coven meets."

Benjamin laughed. "Black mass?"

"She's going to conjure up the devil. She has him on speed-dial now. They're always chatting, exchanging helpful hints, recipes and so on."

Benjamin laughed again. He didn't really resent Claire for dumping him. Not really. But he did get a certain pleasure from Nina's occasional well-placed shots at her sister. After a pause he said, "Zoey has seemed preoccupied lately."

"Tell me about it. Her and Aisha both. Maybe they're having that thing when girls are around each other a lot and their periods start coming at the same time. Maybe it's synchronized PMS."

"An exhibition sport at the Olympics," Benjamin said.

"That was going to be my joke. You can't be stealing my punch lines."

"Or else what?"

"Oh, nothing," Nina said too innocently.

"Don't flip me off, Nina," he warned.

"Damn."

"So they're okay, though, right? Zoey and Aisha?"

A deep breath. "Zoey's your sister," Nina said, sounding a little cranky. "The deal is supposed to be that she doesn't spy on you for me, or me for you, and that we don't spy on her for each other. Otherwise, total chaos. The end of civilization as we know it. Besides, I don't know what her problem is. She made up with Lucas and all."

"Cool. Can you come over this evening to read to me?" he asked.

"Sure. Read what?"

He shrugged. "I don't know. Whatever I can come up with as a good excuse to have you with me."

"Okay." A lingering shyness in her voice.

Benjamin had to remind himself that for all her seeming boldness, underneath it Nina was still somewhat uncertain and even frightened in her romantic life. It made him want all the more to protect her.

He put his arm around her shoulders and held her close. There was something he wanted to tell her at that moment. A feeling that had been growing in him, becoming more certain, more powerful. He held back, though her nearness, the feel of her resting against him, the heartbreaking sweetness he couldn't fail to recognize just below the prickly surface, all conspired to make silence almost impossible. So he said the silent words in his mind. *I love you, Nina. I love you.*

"What?" she asked, sounding almost drowsy.

He kissed the top of her head. "I didn't say anything."

Zoey was aware that Nina had moved away to be with Benjamin. That was good. It was good that they were doing so well. Good for Nina that she had Benjamin, and good for Benjamin also. Her two favorite people in the world. Along with her father.

She was also aware that Aisha was in some kind of a funk, staring off toward the approaching island, not talking, not doing her homework or reading. And normally Zoey would have investigated, but at the moment her mind was filled with her own problems.

The scene between Mr. McRoyan and her had left Zoey feeling dirty somehow. And what had followed with Jake was even worse in some ways. She realized now that Jake had no idea what was going on between his father and her mother. Zoey had been the one to deliver that news to him, which wasn't what she had intended.

She had done nothing but make mistakes right from the start. She shouldn't have let her mother see how angry she was. She should have remembered that Jake sometimes stopped by his father's office. She probably should have just closed her eyes to the whole thing.

It was all part of what she now saw as her own naiveté. It was true—she wasn't ready to grow up. That was the reason for her fight with Lucas. And it was the reason she was behaving irrationally over this now. After all, half the kids at school came from broken homes. And it wasn't like she was a little kid who couldn't understand what was going on. She was seventeen, a high school senior. Soon she would be at college, making her own life away from her parents. What did it really matter if her mother and father broke up?

Except that it did matter. She didn't care if divorces and broken homes were commonplace. This was *her* family. Hers and Benjamin's. What would happen if there was a divorce? Would her mother or father have to move away? And who would Zoey end up living with? And where?

But the most terrible image, the one that kept appearing and reappearing in her mind's eye, was the image of her father when he found out the truth. That image seared her thoughts so painfully that she had to look away.

Zoey hugged herself, feeling lonely and overwhelmed.

Why wasn't Lucas here? It would have felt good to be in Lucas's arms now, as Nina was in Benjamin's. Only Lucas wasn't on the ferry. Neither, for that matter, was Claire.

Claire was probably at the practice, cheering Jake on. He would need all the support he could get. But where was Lucas?

If Lucas were here, he would make her feel better.

And he would drive from her mind the disturbing memory of the way she had felt when Jake had taken her in his arms.

FIFTEEN

CLAIRE STEPPED ON THE GAS and her father's big Mercedes accelerated into a turn. She downshifted and powered through, with trees flashing by on one side and a long drop to the surf-battered rocks below. She had to fight the centrifugal force that nearly tore her away from the wheel. A glance confirmed that Lucas was clutching the dashboard in a way that might well leave permanent marks.

"I'm not scaring you, am I?" she asked nonchalantly.

"Nah. What's scary about plunging two hundred feet straight down the side of a cliff so that we end up being a meal for crabs?"

They were driving around because neither of them could think of anything else to do. They were driving around because the alternative was getting on the ferry with Zoey and going back to the island. They were driving around together because the mere act of being together was a slap at Jake and Zoey

372

respectively and it made them both feel liberated.

Claire took the next curve slower. "I suppose you're think-ing about the last time you went driving with me."

Lucas gave her a cautious look. "Possible."

Their last drive had been two years earlier. Lucas, Jake's big brother Wade, and her. All three drunk. Claire driving. Into a tree, killing Wade, leaving her without memory of the event and causing Lucas's wrongful imprisonment.

Claire slowed down more. It wasn't as if Lucas had no rea-son to worry. By the next curve she was barely above the speed limit, and even had time to look at the scenery. This section of road wound along classically rugged mainland coast. Through the trees they glimpsed gray swells and explosions of white foam, the slow-motion destruction of the land by the sea as it chewed the cliffs into boulders and rock, and eventually, a mil-lion years in the future, into sand.

A brief glance toward the south showed the ferry, a tiny yellow, black, and white toy, crossing sparkling water.

"Let's keep driving till we're back in Vermont," Lucas said after a long silence.

"That's the other direction."

"That's where everything started to go to hell," Lucas said.

"I had thought the trip was pretty much a success," Claire

said. "Jake and I were together and everything was fine."

"Zoey and I weren't fine."

"I guess Jake and I weren't, either, given what we just saw."

"You know, you two guys were sort of broken up when he . . . you know, when he and Louise . . ." Lucas said, declining into a mumble.

"At a loss for words?" Claire asked dryly.

"Plus, he was hammered," Lucas offered.

"Uh-huh."

Another long silence, broken again by Lucas. "And you know Louise. She even came on to me, at the homecoming dance. I'm sure it didn't mean anything to her, and we both know it didn't mean anything to Jake."

"So did you take up her offer?" Claire asked lightly.

"No," Lucas said, laughing a little. "But I wasn't drunk and I hadn't just gotten suspended from the football team and I wasn't all messed up over a girl who—" He prudently let the rest of the thought go unspoken.

"A girl who was responsible for the death of Jake's brother," Claire concluded for him.

"Ancient history," Lucas said.

"Jake and Zoey were supposed to be ancient history, too," Claire reminded him. "History doesn't always stay buried. Old relationships never seem to completely die."

"Like you and Benjamin?"

Claire smiled her wintry smile. "He wasn't my *first* boy-friend." She waited for Lucas's response. It was slow in coming.

"Speaking of ancient history," he said softly, looking out the window.

Claire braked behind a slow-moving pickup truck. She craned her neck to look around it and see some of the road ahead. There were at least a couple of hundred yards of road clear of oncoming traffic. "Hold on," she said. She stepped on the gas and swung into the oncoming lane, accelerating past the truck and ducking to safety just a few feet from an onrushing car whose driver leaned on his horn and shook his fist.

"You have air bags in this thing?" Lucas asked.

Again, a long silence. Claire knew she should let it alone. She had made her little foray, bringing up old times, and Lucas had let it drop. And there was no good purpose to be served by bringing it up again.

Except that she was still coldly furious with Jake. Sleeping with Louise. The long open display of affection with Zoey. Unacceptable. She had gone through a lot to make Jake hers. And she didn't at all like the idea that after everything she'd done, he still had his thoughts on other girls.

She would have thought that of all the guys she knew, Jake would have been the one who was, well, easiest to control. It sounded harsh, but there it was. She had manipulated Jake, wringing from him his acceptance and forgiveness and, she had imagined, his devotion. And all the time he'd been savoring memories of Louise, and no doubt keeping in a secret part of his heart some lingering hope that he might get back together with Zoey.

"You were my first serious kiss," Claire said.

Lucas started as if he'd been caught in a guilty thought. Then he put on a careless tone and a no-big-deal smile. "You were my first, serious or not."

"You weren't bad for a first time," Claire said. It was pretty tacky, flirting this openly with Lucas. But then, he had agreed to go for a drive with her. And he was as pissed at Zoey as Claire was with Jake. "Do you remember it?"

Lucas shifted on the leather seat. "We were swimming, right?"

He remembered. That was obvious from the guilty look on his face and the way he kept changing positions.

"Yes, we were swimming down at Town Beach. You were very cute. You asked me in this squeaky voice if you could kiss me. And I said yes."

Lucas nodded.

"I remember you were surprised when I put my tongue in your mouth." She rolled her eyes. "And that suit I was wearing.

The top was like two sizes too small because I'd bought it the year before, and I was practically—"

"Um, Claire?" Lucas crossed his legs.

"Yes?"

"Why are you doing this?"

"Doing what?"

"Trying to make me get—" He sucked in a deep breath. "Trying to make me . . . You know."

Claire laughed. "I guess I'm pissed off at Jake."

"So you thought you'd make yourself feel better by seeing if you could get me all worked up?"

"Sounds so sleazy when you put it that way," Claire said. "Did it work?"

"Almost as well as it did back then," Lucas admitted. "God. I'll tell you, Claire. After that day on the beach I would have fought a swamp full of alligators armed with a Popsicle stick for you."

"I'll remember that if I ever have an alligator problem."

Lucas shook his head. "You know, you're a strange and not exactly nice girl, Claire."

"I know."

"It will never work with you and Jake, you realize. Not for long, anyway."

"You could be right," Claire allowed. But then, "long" was

a relative term. "Shall we head back?"

"Sure. I don't think driving around any more is going to make our problems go away."

Claire swung the car off onto the shoulder of the road, then pulled it into a U-turn.

"Just out of curiosity," Lucas asked, "how far were you prepared to go with me to get back at Jake?"

Claire smiled. "Maybe we'll find out someday. If you're right about Jake and me. And if I'm right about you and Zoey."

By the time the ferry had landed, Aisha had a plan. But she had to wait two long hours, during which time she paced back and forth in her room, sometimes listening to music, other times in silence so she could concentrate.

There was no doubt in her mind what Christopher had been doing at lunch today. He had bought a gun. As simple as that—he had bought a gun.

And there wasn't very much doubt as to what he intended to use it for. At the very least he would carry it around and wait for the skinheads to take a second shot at him. But what were the odds of that happening? The far more terrifying possibility was that Christopher actually planned to find the guys who had beaten him up and retaliate.

Just the thought of it made her want to throw up. Not

through any pity for the creeps, but because it would be the end of Christopher as the boy, and even man, that he had been.

At first she'd worried that he might be planning to do it tonight. But then she'd realized that Christopher was due to cook at Passmores' tonight. It almost made her laugh. Christopher might be thinking of taking human life, but he would never think of just dumping work.

It was insane. But then, it was an insane situation. One she was not going to allow to get any worse.

She went through the motions of dinner with her family, of doing the dishes, of pretending to start on her homework. Then, at eight o'clock, she gathered up the parcel she had prepared and went outside into the night. She rode her bike, coasting down the long slope of Climbing Way, cutting left to pedal past Town Beach, panting as much from excitement as exertion.

The lights of Weymouth sparkled and wavered across the black sea. Other lights—Jake's house, the few other still-occupied houses interspersed between the boarded-up summer rentals and small hotels—spilled faint illumination onto the sand-strewn road. As usual, there was no traffic on the road, unless you counted the ancient Irish setter who gave her a thoughtful look as she passed.

She pulled up in front of Christopher's rooming house and leaned the bike against the front porch railing. If she was lucky, no one would see her or say anything. But if the landlady was around, Aisha had a plan. She'd show her the parcel and tell her it was a gift for Christopher that she just wanted to drop off in his room.

She went inside and up the creaky, slightly creepy staircase to Christopher's door unchallenged. Tired sixties rock escaped from one of the rooms down the dark hall.

Christopher's door was locked, but she found the key she'd seen him hide beneath an edge of the stair carpeting. She opened the door.

"Christopher?" she asked the emptiness.

Silence. She closed the door behind her and snapped on the light. The room was octagonal, within a tower that formed the corner of the Victorian structure. He had a bed, neatly made. A small kitchenette in one corner, all the mismatched dishes cleaned and drying in the rack. A small black-and-white TV sitting on a chair with a wire hanger twisted into an antenna.

"So where would you hide it, Christopher?" she whispered. Talking to herself dispelled some of the strangeness of being here without him.

She crossed to his bed and lifted the thin mattress. A *Penthouse* magazine. No gun.

For a moment she considered the idea of taking the magazine and throwing it away. That would give him something to think about. But no, she was only after the gun. Dirty magazines didn't kill people or ruin lives.

She opened the dresser drawers, one by one. Top drawer was socks and underwear. Plain white cotton briefs. She was almost disappointed. Somehow she'd suspected Christopher might have gone for something more showy. In a way, it was reassuring. A guy who wore plain white cotton briefs couldn't be too crazy, could he? Certainly not crazy enough to use a gun.

"No, just crazy enough to buy one from some white trash dirtbag on the street. Perfectly sane. Nothing to worry about, Aisha."

Second drawer, T-shirts, two sweaters, gloves.

Third drawer, mostly empty but for a pair of shorts. And the last drawer held miscellaneous junk like paper, a few loose tapes, a pad of paper, scattered pencils and pens.

No gun.

Half an hour later she was as certain as she could be. The gun wasn't here. Could she have been wrong? Could it be that despite what she'd thought she'd seen, he didn't really buy a gun? Or . . .

A pathetic hope, probably, but he could have grown a brain at the last minute and decided to get rid of it.

Aisha lay back on his bed and stared up at his ceiling. The

paint was peeling back from a water stain.

Why did she care? It wasn't like she was in love with him, at least not anymore. Not since she'd realized what a snake he was. Only she did still care enough that she couldn't stand by and let him destroy himself. She did still care that much.

She felt defeated. She'd thought she was being so clever. She would find the gun, take it, and throw it off the point into the fast-moving current.

Only she hadn't found the gun. And now she would have to make the probably doomed attempt to talk him out of it.

Aisha got up, turned off the light, and lay back down again. When he came home, she would talk him out of it. She would do whatever it took to save him from himself.

Although she no longer loved him.

SIXTEEN

CHRISTOPHER READ THE TICKET THE waitress had slapped on the stainless steel counter. He moved to pull a broiler plate of fish from the reach-in, took off the plastic wrap, and slid it into the oven. He squatted, pulled the pan of steaks from the second reach-in, selected a nicely marbled strip, stood up, and tossed it on the grill.

Then he went to the walk-in, closed the door behind him, and pulled the gun from his pocket. It wasn't a big gun, or especially beautiful. Just dull blue steel, worn on the end of the barrel, a blunt little automatic. He pressed the button that ejected the clip and looked at the top bullet. A stubby brass casing topped by a dull lead slug, no bigger than the fingernail on his little finger. Thirty-eight caliber. Hollow point, so that the slug would flatten out on impact.

He had wanted a nine millimeter. Nines were the gun of choice in Sandtown, the Baltimore neighborhood where he had grown up. Everyone who was anyone had a nine. But no nine millimeters had been available, and a thirty-eight would do the job.

He put the gun back in his pocket. It was heavy and tugged at that side of his pants.

He checked his fish, turned the steak, made sure no other tickets were waiting, and went back to the walk-in. He took out the gun and struck a pose, pointing it at a box of lettuce.

"Bang," he said.

He whirled and aimed it square at a half-empty number ten jar of Thousand Island dressing. "Pow. Pow."

If only he'd had this when the skinheads had jumped him. He'd have liked to see the looks on their faces. "Going to kick my ass?" he said in a tough voice. "You'd better talk to my friend about that." He whipped the gun up from his side, leveling it at his remembered foes. At the guy he had seen through the window.

"Not so tough now, huh?"

He put the gun back in his pocket and went out to plate up the food. "Pick up!" he yelled.

He was impatient for the waitress to pick up the order. He wanted to check just one more thing on the gun. He wanted to be sure he knew exactly how to click off the safety.

The waitress came. Christopher ducked back inside the walk-in and took out the gun. Yes, he could do it with his thumb. It was awkward, but he could snap off the safety with his thumb. He did it several times. The feel of the gun became even more powerful when the safety was off. Now just the slightest pressure on the trigger . . .

He put the gun back in his pocket, suddenly feeling scared. What if it went off? What if he accidentally shot someone?

But had he put the safety back on? He took it out again and checked. God, the safety had been off! He clicked it on and put the gun away again.

Over the next few hours he took it out many more times. Too many to remember or count. He rushed through the final cleanup of the kitchen at the end of the night and did the minimal amount of prep work.

He went out front to check with Ms. Passmore and see if it was okay to leave. But the waitress was covering the bar. Ms. Passmore had stepped outside.

Christopher found her around the corner. She was deep in conversation with a man. Christopher was fairly sure it was Mr. McRoyan, Jake's father. Their low voices sounded tense and upset. He thought of backing away, but Ms. Passmore had spotted him.

"What is it, Christopher?"

"I just wanted to check with you before I took off."

"Go ahead. See you tomorrow."

On the way home from work, he pulled his bike to a stop to check the gun again.

He went up the stairs to his apartment. He had to take the gun out of his pocket again to reach his keys. He unlocked his door.

But what if someone had broken in? There wasn't any crime to speak of on Chatham Island, but what if? Maybe the skinheads had tracked him down, found out where he lived, and broken in. Maybe they were waiting for him right now.

Well, they'd get a surprise, wouldn't they?

He pulled out the gun, holding it in a sweaty hand. He opened the door.

There *was* someone inside!

Zoey recognized the knock on the front door. She put down the knife and the peanut butter, wiping her hands on a paper towel, and went to open the door. From the family room came the sound of the TV. From Benjamin's room came the sound of music, Vance Joy, which meant that Nina was still in there, though it was getting late.

Lucas stood under the porch light, looking truculent.

"Hi, come on in," Zoey said, trying to plaster on a big smile.

Lucas seemed hesitant, as if he wanted to kiss her but wasn't sure. Zoey solved the problem for him by leaning forward and giving him a quick kiss on the side of his mouth.

He smiled. "Peanut butter?"

"Oh, sorry." She wiped her mouth with the back of her hand.

"It's okay. I like peanut butter."

He followed her inside. She retrieved her sandwich and then led him toward the family room. He held her back.

"I thought we could go up to your room."

"Well, I was kind of keeping my dad company," she said.

"We hung with your dad last night," Lucas said plaintively.

Zoey flushed. Of course Lucas didn't understand why she wanted to be with her dad, she realized. He wanted to go upstairs and make out. But this wasn't the day for making out.

She slid a consoling hand into the pocket where he'd stuck his own hand. "Just a little while, okay?"

"I think we need to talk about something," he said doggedly.

Zoey almost laughed. Lucas wanted to *talk*? Not likely. "Sure you do," she said teasingly.

"I saw you and Jake at the football field today," he said.

"That was nothing," Zoey said quickly. Too quickly; it sounded suspicious.

"He was feeling you up in front of the whole school."

"He was not," Zoey said, outraged.

"You want to do this here, where your dad or Benjamin might walk out and hear everything we're saying?"

Zoey gritted her teeth. Just what she needed now. More grief from Lucas. She marched up the stairs, threw open the door, and sat stiffly on the edge of her bed, arms crossed, still, unfortunately, holding her sandwich.

Lucas closed the door behind him. He also crossed his arms and looked at her expectantly. "Okay, I'm listening."

"For what?"

"To hear why you were letting Jake grope you, that's what for."

"He was not *groping* me. Not everyone has your sex-obsessed mind, Lucas. Not everyone thinks a friendly hug is an excuse to start groping."

"Oh. So now he's better than me, right?"

"Maybe he's just not stuck on one topic all the time. Did it ever occur to you that what you saw may have had nothing to do with me and Jake?"

He laughed derisively. "Yeah, I figured when he was groping you it probably had to do with finding a cure for cancer."

"Sometimes you really make me mad, Lucas," Zoey said bitterly. Couldn't he get it through his head that this wasn't what he thought? She had hugged Jake because he was hurting after finding out about his father. And he had hugged her back because he cared about her and how she felt.

Lucas narrowed his eyes. "Did you get anywhere on that drug story?"

Zoey was taken aback. What was this about now? "What does that have to do with anything?"

"It was Jake, you know. Jake got drunk before the homecoming game and used some coke to get fired up for the game. I told you that night, only of course you didn't want to believe anything bad about Jake the Saint. And then you pretend you're going to do this story, only see, it would have to be about Jake."

"I know it's Jake," Zoey said flatly. "I found out this morning. Claire told me."

Lucas looked disappointed, but he redoubled his attack. "There's something else that even Claire didn't know about until this afternoon."

Zoey tried to look utterly indifferent, but Lucas plowed on.

"See, even Claire didn't know where Jake ended up that night after the game."

"You're going to tell me anyway, so go ahead."

"He ended up with Louise Kronenberger. *With* Louise. Very *with* Louise. Saint Jake, coked, hammered, and showing his muscles to Lay-Down Louise." He laughed cruelly. "Yeah, he's a much nicer person than me, Zoey."

Zoey covered her mouth with her hand. She felt like she'd been slapped. One more blow. Just one more rude surprise. Lucas, in a van in Vermont telling her he wouldn't wait forever . . . the monstrous sight of her mother . . . and now Jake. . . . It was like some busy demon was running around smashing everything she believed.

"Just leave, Lucas," she whispered.

"Wow, I'm sorry to tell you the truth about good old Jake. I'm sorry if I screwed up your plan to get back together with him."

Suddenly, surprising herself even more than Lucas, Zoey slammed her two fists violently down on the edge of the bed. "Everybody just leave me alone! Just leave me alone!"

"You're messed up, Zoey," Lucas said.

Zoey sagged, the violence burned out as quickly as it had kindled. "Yes. I am messed up," she said softly. "I am messed up beyond belief." Through sudden tears she saw Lucas's eyes soften. He took a step toward her. She put up her hand. "Don't. You can't help me."

"I—I could try," he said quietly.

"You've done a great job so far," Zoey said bitterly. "The person I should be able to turn to really only cares about whether he can get me to have sex with him. It's all anyone cares about, isn't it? You think people are your family and you can trust them, but that's all it is. Themselves. Just whatever they want for themselves. Forget everyone else and what they want, right? Someone else gets hurt, too bad. And they're doing all these things and don't even care. Oh, sorry, Zoey. Sorry if I destroyed your family and now you have to be thinking all the time 'what's next?'"

"Zoey, what are you talking about?"

"About . . . everything. Never mind. It's none of your business because all you want is to sleep with me, right, Lucas?"

"I love you, Zoey," he said in a quiet voice.

"Then it's settled. Come on, let's do it. Everyone else is, right? Why not?" She began tugging at the buttons of her blouse. "Come on, Lucas. You can do whatever you want and then you can go home and forget it, right?"

"Zoey, what is happening with you?" Quiet, worried.

"I'm growing up," she sneered, too full of fury to care that he was reaching out to her. "Isn't that what I'm supposed to do? Aren't I supposed to grow up and realize what people are really like?"

"Zoey, look—"

"No. Just get out, Lucas."

"I want to help."

Zoey sank back on her bed, utterly exhausted. "Just go away. Everyone just go away."

To my daughter,

On your fourteenth birthday. Well, you're definitely a teenager now. The day before yesterday we had a big fight because I told you I didn't think you should go to the movies alone with Jake. You told me I was hopelessly old, that I didn't understand that it was perfectly normal to be going on dates at almost fourteen. Wow. I want you to know that "hopelessly old" crack hit home. Probably because it's what I used to tell my mother.

I just didn't want you to start getting all involved with guys at your age. What you don't know yet (but will someday) is that they aren't just like girlfriends. Men can break your heart, and you can break theirs. Not that Jake is exactly a man. Remember last month when we found him stuffed in one of our trash cans and his big brother had tied down the lid?

Still, you haven't turned rotten or anything, despite being a teenager. You're still basically pretty sweet. Especially around Benjamin. He's been going through a bad time, realizing that he's fallen behind because of the surgeries and rehab and all, and now he's in the same grade as his little sister. But you've handled it with such style it really makes you dad and me proud. Sometimes we wonder how the two of us managed to produce such great kids.

You didn't want the usual party this year, so we dropped you and your friends off for pizza, movies, and video games. Then you realized, too late to do anything about it, that it would mean leaving Benjamin out. You were so devastated. You haven't learned yet that there are times when no matter how hard you try not to, you hurt people anyway. You're not very tough or cynical, Zoey. Maybe this will mean you'll always be easily hurt by others. But it will also mean you'll never be cruel, so it's a good thing.

Two more years and I'll give you this book. You've changed so much in just the last year I wonder what you will be then?

SEVENTEEN

AISHA WOKE DISORIENTED. NOT HER bed. Where was she?

A loud, questioning voice, tense, even threatening. A shape silhouetted in an open doorway.

Christopher.

"I said who's in there?"

"It's me," Aisha said. "It's me, Aisha."

The shape seemed to shrink to mere human proportions. He gave a relieved laugh. "Damn, you scared the hell out of me."

"Sorry. I fell asleep waiting for you." Aisha sat up.

Christopher didn't turn on the light. He came to her, sat down beside her, very close. "This is a very nice surprise."

Aisha accepted his kiss and returned it. His arms held her close. Her hand came to rest against something hard and cold. Recognition was immediate.

"What's that?" she asked.

"Nothing," he lied.

Aisha pushed him away. "It's not nothing."

"My keys."

"It's a gun, Christopher."

Silence.

She pushed him farther away and stood up. She searched for the lamp and found the switch. They both blinked in the sudden illumination.

"I saw you buy it," Aisha admitted.

Christopher looked alarmed. "Did anyone else see me, do you think?"

"I don't think so, no. You can still get rid of it and no one will ever know."

"Get rid of it?" He laughed incredulously. "Why would I want to get rid of it?"

"You have to get rid of it, Christopher. That's why I came here tonight. I was going to take it from you."

He stood up. His eyes were narrowed and suspicious. His right hand strayed unconsciously to the gun, a sharp-edged lump in his pocket. "I went to a lot of trouble to buy it, Eesh."

"Christopher, you can't do this."

"Can't do what?"

"Oh, don't treat me like I'm an idiot, Christopher!" Aisha shouted. "Don't you think I know what you're planning?"

"I'm not planning anything. I'm just planning that the next

time someone tries to jump me, I can protect myself." He smiled, softening his confrontational tone. "It's no big thing, Aisha. Back in Baltimore, back in Sandtown, everyone had a gun."

"Yeah, and it was a real paradise, wasn't it?"

His eyes clouded. His jaw was stubborn. "Look, I can't let it stand the way it is, Eesh." He shook his head as if he were helpless in the matter. As if he was really terribly sorry, but he had no choice. "I can't let it stand."

"Christopher, you can't do this," she pleaded.

"You don't understand," he said heavily. "I'm a man. A man doesn't let himself be hurt without hurting back. A man doesn't let himself be kicked and pounded on without making someone pay."

"Christopher, I thought . . . I mean, all the time you were at my house, all the time we were in Vermont, you seemed normal. You seemed like you were dealing with—"

"I *was* dealing with it," he blazed, rounding on her. He thrust a finger in her face, spitting the words. "I was dealing with it because I knew the day would come when I would make them pay. Perfectly calm, absolutely no problem, as long as I knew that the day would come. I waited. I can be patient when I have to be. I waited and said okay, Christopher, it's bad, but you hang in there and you'll get yours back. Now the time has come."

"Christopher—" she began, but he was past listening now.

"They kicked me, Aisha. I was on the ground and they kicked me and called me a nigger and—" He clasped his hands together, struggling to control the rage. Then, in a softer, yet more dangerous voice, "They spit on me, Eesh. People don't spit on me. No." He shook his head. "No, that doesn't happen. No one spits on me and calls me a nigger and just walks away thinking, hey, that was cool, let's go have a beer."

For a moment Aisha was caught up in his words, in a cold, hard anger. Yes, yes, make the bastards pay. She remembered her first sight of him in the hospital bed. At that moment, given the chance, wouldn't she have struck back as hard as she could? And, after all, would the world mourn the loss of another violent, hate-twisted monster? If the police couldn't do it, didn't Christopher have a right to exact his own revenge? Did they just have to take it and take it and never fight back?

But against all that was the single image that had formed in Aisha's mind and wouldn't go away. The image of Christopher with a gun in his hand, taking a life.

If he did that, if he killed, he would destroy himself as well. That action would take over his life, his personality. He would change to deal with what he had done. He would become hard and cold, just like the gun—lifeless, mechanical. Dead.

"It will be okay," Christopher said. "I'll be careful."

"No, it won't be okay, Christopher," Aisha said, feeling sick with the futility of arguing. Sick with dread. "It will be murder."

"It will be *justice*."

"You will be a person who has deliberately, cold-bloodedly taken a human life," Aisha said. "You won't be the same person ever again. You will never be able to undo or take back that action."

"Look, I'm not going to get caught," he said heatedly.

"Not by the police, maybe. But *you* will know what you've done. And I'll know. And God will know." All a waste of breath. He heard nothing. He understood nothing.

"God?" He laughed derisively. "So you're worried I'll go to hell?"

"Go to hell? No, Christopher, you don't understand. If you do this, if you kill, from the moment you pull the trigger you will *be* in hell."

Zoey pulled her Boston Bruins jersey on over her head and a pair of clean white socks on her feet. Her feet sometimes got cold at night. She slipped between crisp sheets and piled her two pillows behind her back. The only light in the room was from the small lamp by her bedside. The clock showed a little after eleven. She should be falling asleep now. She liked to get at least seven hours of sleep, and eight was better. Lately she'd been walking around in a blurry, half-alert state. She felt she hadn't truly slept since Vermont, a million years ago. And yet now, though her legs ached with weariness and her eyes were swollen and sandpapered, she was awake, staring blankly across the room.

It had been an unbelievably long day. It had started with resolve and determination to get control of her life. It had led to terrible scenes with Mr. McRoyan and Jake and ended with a jittery, nerve-wracked explosion between her and Lucas. It was emotional overload. Simply too much to fit into one day, one mind. And now she knew that if she turned off the light and closed her eyes it would all replay, over and over again in her brain, keeping her awake, overwhelming her with its complexity.

Too much. Lucas. Jake. Mr. McRoyan. Her mother and father. Too much.

She would wait until she was utterly exhausted, till she was woozy and passing out, unable to keep her eyelids up another second. Then, if she turned out the light, she might hope for a real sleep. A healing sleep of escape.

Normally she would write in her journal now. Only her journal was long since gone. Part of the landfill.

Or she might read. Except that as she scanned the shelves of her bookshelf, all she saw was one type of romance or another.

Escapism. Yes, she wanted to escape, but now all of that had become part of a grubby reality.

"No," she said wryly. "Romance is not what I need right now." She should have books about . . . well, anything but True Love. True Love wasn't doing too well around the Passmore household lately. Except for Benjamin and Nina, but the way things were going, who knew how long that would last?

She got out of bed and pulled her two favorite quote books from the shelf, then retreated to the heavy warmth of her quilt again.

You can close your eyes to reality but not to memories.

Not the best quote for her attention to focus on first, since it was precisely memory that she wanted to avoid.

Downstairs, she heard her mother come home. The door closing.

Neither man nor woman can be worth anything until they have discovered that they are fools.

The squeak of the third step. The sudden intrusion of memory. Of *him* hurrying away on that day. The image still made her skin crawl. How she had hated him. But earlier today, sitting disgusted and ashamed in his office, she hadn't felt the same surge of pure hatred.

The pure and simple truth is rarely pure and never simple.

She heard the door to her parents' room open, then close

softly. A hallway separated Zoey's room from theirs. She was trying to do just what the first quote had told her was impossible. She was trying not to remember what she had seen through that bedroom door. Trying not to remember Lucas's angry face in Vermont. Or his angry contempt tonight. Trying not to remember Mr. McRoyan and the way he collapsed on seeing his son. Trying—

A loud murmur of voices from the direction of her parents' room. Anger.

She switched off the light. She didn't know why; it just seemed like the thing to do. Like she could hide if—

A loud shout. Her father's voice. An eruption of more anger than she had ever heard.

Her mother's voice, scaling up, higher, higher, outraged, furious.

Zoey sat in the dark and covered her ears, but now the fight was raging unrestrained. Individual words could be heard, screamed at full volume. *Bastard. Whore. Son of a bitch.*

Others, still worse. Words that never should have come from the mouths of these two people whom she loved.

Zoey clamped a pillow over her head. She felt sick. She felt a deep, churning nausea. Her hands were trembling. Her skin felt crawly.

This had never happened before. She'd had friends who

talked nonchalantly about the fights their parents had, but *her* parents had never done this before. Not like this. Not with rage so strong it seemed to vibrate the walls. Not with fury, like some unpredicted hurricane.

Her legs were drawn up to her chest in a fetal position. The knuckles of her hand, clenched white, were in her mouth. She shook. She quivered like a person with a fever. She wanted to throw up, but she couldn't move, and still violent words tore through walls and pillows and all her pitiful defenses to rip at her heart.

It was happening.

It was happening right now, without warning. Like the shattering of an atom, releasing the forces of fire and wind and poison, her family was being shattered.

She could do nothing to stop it. She might have even helped bring it about.

Hatred, loose here in her own family.

A slammed door, rattling the windows. And then a shriek, right at her own door. Her mother's voice, like no voice Zoey had ever heard before.

"Are you happy now, Zoey?" Her mother pounded her fist on the door to Zoey's room, rattling it in the frame. "Are you happy in there, God damn you? Are you happy with what you've done?"

EIGHTEEN

IT WAS AFTER MIDNIGHT WHEN Zoey lifted her head from her tear-soaked pillow. The house was silent as she crawled from her bed. The sound of her mother's sobbing, coming through the connecting wall to the spare bedroom, had at last subsided.

She had to get out of the house. She had to breathe new, unfouled air. She had to escape from the horrible oppression, the palpable residue of explosive anger.

She pulled on jeans, tucking in her Bruins jersey, then a sweater, a coat. She would be cold, she knew that, because she felt as if her body was already half-dead, unable to generate warmth, all its resources long since exhausted.

She went gently down the stairs, preserving the quiet, temporary peace, afraid lest someone would wake and start the war again. For now there was silence, but for the wind scraping tree branches against the side of the house.

She reached the bottom of the stairs, and, as she had almost expected, Benjamin's door opened.

"Zoey?" he whispered.

Zoey went to him and put her arms around him. He hugged her close, and if every tear had not already been drained, she would have cried again. Instead her chest heaved with dry sobs.

After a long while she pulled away. "I have to get out of here for a while," she said.

"Yeah. Let me get my coat." Then he hesitated. "Is it okay if I go with you?"

She squeezed his hand. "Of course it's okay."

Outside there was air, fresh and cold. They stood in the front yard, midnight-blue figures trimmed with moonlight silver. Their breath rose as steam. They held hands like they had when they were little and Benjamin had been the one to guide his baby sister across the street.

Wordless, they walked out of the yard and down the street over cobblestones slippery with dew, past the gaping black windows of silent, sleeping homes.

They reached the sound of surf, just whispering on the sheltered sand of Town Beach. Doleful buoy bells tolled. Fishing boats at anchor creaked and amplified the slap of the swell against their sides.

They walked out onto the long concrete breakwater that separated the peaceful water of the harbor from the agitated surge of the open sea. Spray erupted to their left, falling over them as a salty rain, freezing and clean. Zoey breathed deeply, drawing each breath to its fullest.

"It was a good idea to come out here," Benjamin said. "The sound of the waves—"

"Yeah."

"Do you . . . Do you hear them like I do, I wonder?" Benjamin asked. "I mean, I hear the sea every day, but still sometimes it's like I've never heard it before. I know you can see it, too, but when you can hear it—*only* hear it—you can feel, or sense, or just know that it is so vast. So big beyond anything—" He fell silent.

Zoey sighed, a shuddering sound.

"Did you know about this?" Benjamin asked. "About them?"

"Yes."

Benjamin nodded. "I thought something was bothering you. I've been kind of thinking about other things, I guess. Nina, mostly."

"I found out when I came back early from Vermont," Zoey said. "I saw something I wasn't supposed to see."

Benjamin waited. He was good at waiting.

"I saw Mom and Mr. McRoyan."

"God, Zoey." He sighed. "That must have been bad."

"It made me *sick*." An almost violent response, surprising

her. She wouldn't have thought she had that much emotional energy left in her.

A strong surge exploded over the far end of the breakwater, Christmas-colored rain drifting down before the green and red warning lights.

"I did something kind of creepy," Zoey confessed. "I went up in the attic and found Mom's old letters. I found some from Mr. McRoyan from a long time ago. Supposedly he was in love with Mom while Dad was off in Europe."

Benjamin pursed his lips thoughtfully. "I heard something about Europe in all the screaming. It was all kind of confused. Europe and Fred and I think the name Sandra. But I'm probably wrong about that last part."

They started away from the breakwater, walking hand in hand along Leeward Drive. At this hour the only lights from Weymouth were the pale, almost orange streetlights. All of Chatham Island was dark.

As they walked, Zoey told Benjamin everything she knew. Everything she had done. Benjamin listened without comment until she was done and they turned to follow the road along Big Bite Pond.

"So Mom might have even ended up marrying Mr. McRoyan," Benjamin concluded. "Except that she was pregnant with me. I can't believe they've been together all this time without really loving each other."

"Maybe they have really loved each other," Zoey said. "Maybe it's just complicated."

"Yeah, it's complicated," Benjamin said with a faint whiff of his usual dry humor.

"What do you think will happen now?" Zoey asked.

Benjamin took a while to consider. "It's a pretty straightforward choice—they decide to stay together despite everything, or else they get a divorce."

"What if they get a divorce?"

He shrugged. "I don't know. There's the restaurant. The house. Us." He shrugged again. "I don't know."

"Who would you want to stay with?" Zoey asked.

"I'll stay with the island," he said as if he'd thought it through. "Maybe it's gutless, but last year of high school—I mean, I know the island. I know the school. I don't want to have to go somewhere new, somewhere where I don't know where I am. When I go off to college, that's one thing. I know I'll have to go through the whole process again, learning the streets, counting steps, learning what's safe, and so on. And on and on. But I don't want to have to scope a campus and a new home and throw in half a year of a new school. I have to be kind of selfish. I stick with the island."

"I can't believe we're even having this conversation," Zoey

said grimly. "But I'm glad I have you."

"One way or the other, Zo, we have to stay close. We can't let this ever get between us."

"You and me, Benjamin," Zoey said. Tears had edged her eyes again.

"No matter what." He made her stop. "Look, you do understand that none of this is your fault, right? You did the right things, at least as right as anyone could do with this stupid mess."

"Did you hear Mom? I mean, when she was pounding on my door—" Zoey tried to swallow the lump in her throat. "What she was saying?"

"Yes, I heard, sweetheart," Benjamin said gently.

"I . . ." A sob.

She felt Benjamin put his arms around her again, fumbling at first, finding her in his eternal night.

"I thought I was getting over this," she managed to say. "I thought I was all cried out."

"Not yet," Benjamin said. "Maybe not ever."

My darling—

I've just received your letter. I don't know what to say. I don't know what I can say.

You say you want to keep the baby, fine. I told you I would marry you and raise the baby as my own and give it all the love I can. You know that. You don't have to go back to Jeff just because you're pregnant with his baby. I mean, please, Darla, this is the nineties. We're not our parents, trapped in all kinds of stupid social demands. My parents got married and I don't think there ever was any real love or understanding between them. I've seen what that is like.

All that's really important is that I love you and you love me. And I know you love me, no matter what you say. You can tell me all you want that you have always loved Jeff but I don't believe it. I can't believe it because I'm not going to just go on thinking this was nothing but a temporary fling for you. I don't know what I'd do if I believed that.

What will I do if I don't have you? Do my tour and then move back to Maine alone? I always saw you there with me. Or anywhere, as long as there's you. I know you don't like the army, so maybe I could get an early out. Anything.

Please write me. You can't call for the next week because we'll be out on field maneuvers, but please write. If I see a letter waiting for me when I get back I'll know it's all going to be all right. Please, please don't let it end. Please write.

I know this sounds pathetic and desperate but I don't care anymore.

> I love you.
> Fred

NINETEEN

NINA HAD AWAKENED IN THE night, sweating and panting, after one of the nightmares. It was one of the usual, one she'd had many times before, full of dread and shame. They came a little less frequently now, since she had confronted her uncle over his molestation and since she had been seeing the shrink once a week. But they still came.

And yet they had lost a lot of their power. In the past she would never have been able to get back to sleep. And, sleeping, to have dreamed of far more pleasant things so that when the alarm went off, blasting some old Jimi Hendrix near her ear, she awoke a second time, content.

She started to turn off the alarm, then realized that the wailing guitar was certain to annoy Claire, whose room was upstairs. Claire was not a morning person. Neither was Nina, really, but Claire tended to walk around for the first hour of the day in a surly bad mood. And the rest of the day, too.

Nina got up, pulled on a robe, ran to the shower, and found

to her annoyance that Claire had beaten her to it. So she headed downstairs.

Her father was at the big antique pine table in the kitchen, wearing his inevitable charcoal gray suit and eating bacon and scrambled eggs. There was a small fire in the kitchen fireplace, and Nina took the chair closest to it. Through the French doors she could see a grubby, gray day that looked like rain.

"Bacon? Eggs? I guess you've stopped worrying about that cholesterol thing, huh?" She grabbed a huge blueberry muffin from the basket and poured herself some coffee.

Her father gave her a guilty look. "I have bran muffins practically every day. Plus, look, I'm having juice." He pointed to the glass of grapefruit juice. "And I hit the gym three times a week. And I lost four pounds. And why am I making excuses to you?"

"Excellent point, Dad," Nina said. "You shouldn't be making excuses to me."

"Then I'll just go ahead and eat this bacon."

"You should be making excuses to someone else. Only there isn't anyone else."

Her father chewed his bacon and looked at her suspiciously.

"You know, Claire and I were talking the other day, and she said that for an old guy you're not bad looking."

"How generous of her," Mr. Geiger grumbled.

"You have nice hair," Nina pointed out. "Although I do have two words for you—Grecian Formula."

"Gray hair is good for bank presidents," he argued. "It makes me look distinguished."

"Like people could feel safe giving you their money."

"Exactly."

"Aha! But who do you give *your* money to?"

Mr. Geiger rolled his eyes. "You know, you could just try asking, without all the preliminaries. How much do you want?"

"Whatever you have on you, Dad, since you're offering, but that's not really what I was talking about." She fixed him with a critical look. "You need to start dating. Claire is worried you'll end up like one of those old guys who sit on the benches at the mall and stare at people all day. Wearing a little hat and pulling your pants up to your chest and walking in little tiny steps, shuffle, shuffle over to spit in the trash can. All alone in some old people's home where perky volunteers from religious cults come on weekends and force you to play patty-cake and make ceramic ashtrays."

"Claire said all this?"

"She's just trying to be nice, Daddy," Nina said, with every possible appearance of sincerity. "Besides, I think she's right about you dating. What about when Claire returns to her home planet? What about when I go off to be a professional groupie?

You'll be here eating bacon all alone."

Mr. Geiger nodded reflectively. "I guess when you're both gone, I'll miss the cheeriness and optimism you bring now. You know, not ten minutes ago I was thinking, well, the bacon is crisp and life is good. Now I'm thinking of drowning myself."

"I have this teacher—" Nina said, letting it hang.

"Yes? Does he have something else depressing to add to the conversation?"

"She."

"Okay, she."

"No, I mean she's a *she*. Divorced. Twice, I think, but she doesn't have any kids."

"Oh. Too bad. Kids are such a joy," he said dryly.

"Mrs. Bonnard. She teaches English, and she's not bad looking. She has blond hair and she keeps in shape, although I don't think it's real. The hair."

"Let me guess—having trouble with your grades in English?"

"Dad! You're so cynical. Besides, what if she didn't like you? Then my grade could actually go down." Not by much, Nina admitted privately, since it was pretty close to the bottom already.

"I don't think I need any help getting set up," Mr. Geiger said firmly.

"That's what I told Claire," Nina said. "But she said you were getting old and kind of out of it. I said you were just like forty or something, but she kept saying that was pretty old if you were going to meet someone to be with in your old age."

"Claire said that?" he asked sourly.

"I told her you have all kinds of opportunities to meet women at work and you're still young and good looking. But she said, face it, all he really has going for him is that he has money."

"All I have . . . Oh, really? It's nice to know your sister has such a high opinion of me."

"Yeah. Well, anyway, all I was trying to say was that if you ever wanted to go out with someone, it would be okay with me." She smiled kindly. "Claire was the one who thought you needed help."

She got up from the table just as Claire entered the room, looking as annoyingly perfect as always, though her hair was wrapped in a towel.

"I hope you left some hot water," Nina said, grinning hugely.

Claire ignored her. "Good morning, Daddy."

"Oh, good morning, huh?" Mr. Geiger pointed an accusing finger at Claire. "Sit down, Miss High-and-Mighty. You and I are going to have a little talk."

Zoey and Benjamin left the house together, walking in strained silence down to the ferry. They had already discussed everything that could be discussed. They had considered skipping school but decided it would be smarter just to get out of the house. Even school was better than risking being drawn into the next round of the war between their parents.

Neither their mother nor their father had been at the breakfast table, and Zoey and Benjamin had hurried out early rather than risk an encounter.

As they passed the restaurant, they saw that it was closed. A man was rattling the door, perplexed. He spotted Zoey and Benjamin.

"Hey. How come you're closed?"

Benjamin answered for them. "My folks are a little sick."

"More than a little," Zoey muttered under her breath in an attempt at black humor.

"Hope it's nothing serious," the man called after them.

"Yeah, well, guess again," Benjamin said to Zoey, catching her mood.

"It's going to rain," Zoey said.

"Of course it is," Benjamin said.

"Closed the restaurant," Zoey said wonderingly. Her

parents had almost never closed on a normal business day. The last time had been during Benjamin's surgery, when they had shut down for a week.

A thin drizzle began to fall. They stood stoically side by side, both beyond caring about anything as minor as rain.

Jake had gone for an early morning run after doing his usual stomach crunches and pushups. He'd seen his father at breakfast. Neither of them had mentioned the events of the previous day as they sat at the table being fussed over by Jake's mother. Both he and his father knew that the subject would never be mentioned between them. But they also both knew that there had been a fundamental change in their relationship.

Jake had lived his life with an eye always on pleasing his father. Living up to his father's ideals. Being the son that Wade was supposed to have been, had he lived.

But that was over now. The full impact had not yet sunk in, but that stage of Jake's life was over. Whatever he did from now on would not be about pleasing or impressing his father.

He walked down the steep driveway and along the beach with thoughts slowly turning through his mind. Claire, Wade, Zoey.

A great many things had changed in a very short time. He had made a lot of mistakes. And he had finally learned that he had to forgive the mistakes of others in order to be forgiven himself. So in time he would forgive his father. But nothing would ever turn back the clock for the two of them.

He found Zoey and Benjamin together at the ferry landing, silent and gray in the cold drizzle. He stood near them, saying nothing.

There wasn't a damned thing to say.

Lucas was just leaving his house when he saw Aisha walking down the hill from the bed-and-breakfast. She normally took the little shortcut down to Bristol Street. He walked rapidly toward her to meet her before she turned off. Maybe she could tell him what was going on with Zoey. First the way she had blown up at him, then the startling explosion of late-night shouting from the Passmore house. It had been loud enough to wake Lucas's parents. His father had been on the verge of calling down to them to shut up, that people had to sleep.

"Hi, Aisha." She looked grim and downcast. Probably the horizon-to-horizon pall of gray cloud.

"Hi, Lucas."

"What's up?"

She shook her head. Nothing.

He fell into step with her. "Hey, Aisha? You don't have to answer this if you don't want to."

"What?"

"What's going on with Zoey? I'm lost here."

"Zoey?" Aisha looked impatient. "What do you mean?"

"I guess nothing."

They walked along, reaching Town Beach, just a hundred paces behind Jake. A light rain had begun. Lucas checked his watch. Ten minutes till the ferry. Hopefully the rain wouldn't fall any harder.

"Lucas?" Aisha said, surprising him.

"Yeah?"

"Lucas, did you tell Christopher how to get a gun?"

Lucas took her arm. "Are you telling me he has one?"

She stared suspiciously at him. Her eyes were red. "Did you help him get it?"

He shook his head. "No. He asked me to, but I said no."

Aisha started walking again. He looked up at the sky. A little sunshine would have been nice. He'd always believed that nothing really bad could happen to him as long as the sun was shining. This was a day for disaster.

TWENTY

BENJAMIN HATED IT WHEN THE weather drove them onto the lower deck of the ferry. It was overheated and smelled of paint, diesel fumes, and damp wool. The noise of the engines was much louder, blanking out the sounds of the water.

He sat on one of the outer benches, leaning his head back against a cold Plexiglas window. He had been with Zoey, but she had gone to the restroom. Nina took her place, but this morning he didn't even want to be with Nina. Silence was the best refuge from all the emotions of the long night.

"I got Claire so good this morning," Nina said gleefully, without preliminary. "Hey. Your hair's wet, you know."

"I noticed," he said. Not rude, but in such a way that she could have known that he wanted to be left alone. *Would* have known if she'd been the kind of person to read clues, to pay attention to subtleties. Claire would have known.

Something was rubbing on his head.

"What are you doing?" Definitely angry now. Even Nina had to see that.

"I'm drying your hair with my scarf."

"My hair's fine."

"You have wet hair. Why didn't you wear a hat or a hood or something?"

"Look, Nina, my hair is fine, okay? Leave it alone; my hair is fine."

The rubbing stopped. She fell silent. For about thirty seconds.

"So, anyway, I was talking to my dad, telling him he should maybe think about dating—"

Benjamin laughed, a harsh sound.

"That's not the funny part," Nina pointed out.

"It's irony. Perfect irony," he said bitterly.

"It is? Why?"

He waved his hand impatiently. "Forget it. It's a long and pretty sickening story."

"My favorite kind of story. Tell me all about it. It has to be more interesting than the homework I should be doing."

He shook his head. "I don't think so." Claire would have let it drop. But would Nina? No, of course not. She couldn't even tell that he was ready to lash out, that he was barely restraining himself.

"Come on, you have to tell me."

"It's really none of your damn business, Nina," he snapped.

A momentary silence, then, "Tell me anyway."

"Why?" he asked wearily. "I told you to drop it, so why do you insist on pushing it?"

The touch of her hand on his was surprising. "Because it's something really bad," she said softly, her lips so near his ear that he could feel her warm breath. "I can tell it's bad, Benjamin, and you need to tell me."

"You don't want to know." For some reason he felt near to tears. It was amazing. Where had that come from?

"If you tell me, you'll feel better."

Lord, now he really was crying. Good grief, how pathetic. He hadn't broken down all night with Zoey. He'd been strong and dealt with it. Now, with Nina . . .

"I'm sorry," he said, wiping under his shades. "Look, Nina, I don't want to lay all this on you."

"I'm your girlfriend, right? I'm the person you're supposed to tell things to."

He nodded, fighting a fresh wave of tears. "Yeah, you are my girlfriend." Yes, he thought with sudden clarity, yes. Claire would have known to leave him alone when he was snapping and defensive and wanted his privacy. But Nina had known better. She hadn't done what he wanted. She had done what he needed.

"Well, at least we have that straight," Nina said drolly. "I'm the girlfriend, you're the boyfriend. It's the traditional arrangement—one of each."

He smiled. "Yeah. And um, look, Nina?"

"Yes?"

"I love you, Nina."

"I'm really glad, because I love you, too, Benjamin."

Satisfaction in her voice? Yes. And a profound relief in his own heart. He would tell Nina, and then, yes, he would feel better.

"Now spill," Nina ordered. "And don't leave out any of the good stuff."

In the ferry bathroom Zoey threw up. She rinsed her mouth out with ice-cold water from the tiny tap. She found a piece of gum in her purse and chewed it.

Outside, she saw Lucas waiting for her.

"I want to give this one more try," he said, blocking her way.

"What are you talking about?" She still felt sick. Sick and weary enough that if her knees had simply collapsed, she wouldn't have been surprised.

"Us, Zoey," he said. "I want to know what's going on with us."

She shrugged. "I don't know, Lucas."

"Look, Zoey, I still love you."

For some reason this struck her as funny. "You do? Well. That's good. Love is a great thing. But you know, it's about half b.s. Maybe it's more like two-thirds b.s."

"Zoey, what is the matter with you?"

"You know how they say wake up and smell the coffee? I'm smelling it. Is it French roast? That's what it smells like. You wake up, you open your eyes, and hey, guess what? People aren't what you think they are."

"Zoey, are you drunk?"

She shook her head. "Tired is all. Tired of . . . everything."

"Look, come sit down with me. You need to sit down, babe, you're swaying back and forth."

"Oh, man," Zoey said with profound regret. "You seem so nice sometimes."

He smiled the smile that had made her love him. "Sometimes I am nice."

"Yep. Sometimes. Only who knows, right? You might know someone for years and years. Your whole life, maybe.

They seem nice. But who really ever knows? How? How can you know for sure?"

Lucas looked worried and confused. "I don't know, Zoey."

Zoey nodded, woozy, disgusted with herself, still sick to her stomach. Why wouldn't he just go away? She wanted to sit and go to sleep.

"I just need to know one thing, Zoey."

"Uh-huh."

"Do you still love me? If you do, then we can deal with everything else. But I have to know. I have to know if you still love me."

Something like awareness, consciousness, reawoke in Zoey's mind. He was waiting. Inches away. He looked scared and sad and hopeful. If she just said yes, he would let her be. And she did love him, didn't she? Wouldn't she, when this nightmare was over? Wouldn't that same feeling return, despite everything?

"I don't know anymore," she said. "I don't know anything."

TWENTY-ONE

"MORNING ANNOUNCEMENTS." MR. HARDCASTLE'S VOICE, crackling over the ancient intercom system, the background music of homeroom, almost always ignored.

Claire clenched her jaw and, without turning her head, watched Jake move to a vacant seat behind Zoey. He whispered something in her ear and she turned to give him a strange, tortured smile. He squeezed her shoulder and she patted the hand where it lay.

Then he got up and, with what subtlety he could manage at more than six feet and nearly two hundred pounds, moved back to his seat beside Claire.

"Attention, all seniors," Mr. Hardcastle went on. "A reminder that the first round of SATs is coming up very soon. Prep books and number-two pencils are available for sale at the school store."

A general groan at the mention of SATs. *Good,* Claire thought. She wanted to get the test over with, the sooner the better.

"Hi," Jake whispered, looking guilty.

"Was Zoey interviewing you about the drug story just now?" She said it just a little too loudly to be completely discreet. Jake looked around, horrified, but of course no one was listening; they were all lost in grim contemplation of SATs.

"She's dropping that," he whispered back.

"How nice of her," Claire said. "How ever did you convince her?"

Jake shot her a sharp glance.

Good, so her annoyance wasn't going totally unnoticed.

He shrugged. "I guess she decided it wasn't worth doing."

"Did she decide this while you were groping her on the football field yesterday?"

The bell rang and the class jumped to its feet.

"You saw that? I mean, it was nothing, Claire," Jake said, switching to a more normal speaking voice in the din of scraping chairs and loud chatter.

"I see lots of things, Jake. And what I don't see, I hear about."

A flash of pure guilt on his guileless face. "Like what?"

Like what? he asks. *Like what?* Claire sneered. "You know something, Jake? You should stick to being a big, straight-arrow jock. You're really not cut out for being clever." The remark was meant to wound, and Claire could see that it had.

"Claire, with Zoey and me yesterday, that's just something separate. It's . . . not anything like what you think it is."

"Oh, I know you still keep a little torch burning for Snow White," Claire said. "It's pathetic, but it doesn't lower you in my opinion nearly as much as the other. Louise, Jake? Yes, I know about that, too. Your first time, Jake, and it was stinking drunk with Lay-Down Louise." She gave him a contemptuous smile. "You must be so proud."

He would never do it. He would never do it. Aisha had repeated the phrase over and over again, reassuring herself, trying to make herself believe it. Christopher would never do it. Since the night before, the terrifying night before, with Christopher already deeply under the spell of the gun. All through the school day in a trance state, swinging wildly between relief and dread, each swing of the pendulum taking her farther and farther.

He would never do it. Christopher wasn't that kind of person. He would never do it.

She had looked for him at lunch and found him in the storeroom, hunched over, looking at it, scowling like a cat with a dead mouse. A strange, intense light in his eyes.

But still, she told herself, he would never do it.

As soon as the last-period bell rang, she ran to the gym. She would catch him before he left. She would do whatever it took.

She would knock him out before she would let him leave with that gun. If that didn't work, she'd tell the principal, even the police. Anything to stop him, although she knew that he would never do it.

And if he did?

What then? Could she turn him in to the police? Why? For doing to the scum just what they'd love to do to him? Would she see him destroyed when all he had wanted was justice?

But if she just let it happen, and then afterward kept quiet . . . then she would be a part of it. There was no greater sin, and she would be part of it. Part of evil. Not justice, the evil of bloodthirsty vengeance.

She arrived, breathless, at the equipment room. Coach Anders, the girls' gym teacher, was there, stuffing basketballs into a big canvas sack.

"Hey, hey. Now, why can't I get you to run like that in gym?"

"Sorry, Coach Anders." Aisha felt foolish. Of course she was running for nothing. This was all silly. "I was looking for Christopher Shupe."

"Oh, really?" Coach Anders put on a wise, knowing look "You two, huh? Well, that's all right. Christopher's a good guy. You know he has four jobs? People don't work like that any-more."

That's right, Aisha told herself. *People don't, but Christopher does because Christopher knows where he's going, and what he wants, and he doesn't let anything keep him from his goal of college and a life and a future.* "Um, is he in the back?"

"No, he took off."

Aisha's heart sank. "Off to his next job, I guess," she said brightly.

"He took the van over to pick us up a new volleyball net."

"The—what van?"

"The one we have for the phys-ed department."

Aisha rocked back, almost losing her balance.

"He just left," Coach Anders said. "Said he had a couple errands of his own, so I told him to take his time."

Lucas waited throughout the day for the apology he knew must come from Zoey. But in homeroom she'd only had time for Jake. At lunch, nothing. In history, where they sat near each other, still nothing. Last-period French, nothing. Not so much as a smile. She had torn out his heart and couldn't even be bothered to spare him a simple smile of encouragement.

And yet he didn't believe it was over. Something else was going on. Maybe it was all part of some long, drawn-out punishment for what had happened in Vermont. Maybe she was just trying to tell him never to pressure her again. Or maybe she was just being overly dramatic about the whole thing. If so, it was an unattractive part of her personality.

It occurred to him that whatever was troubling her might have something to do with the shouting he'd heard from the Passmore house the night before, but that was no excuse. In his home, hostility and anger were on the daily menu and he didn't take it out on Zoey.

He still believed she would come around. But at the same time he was humiliated about being treated this way, like a bad little boy who had to be punished for the sin of being a normal, heterosexual guy.

It wasn't over with Zoey; *that* he couldn't stand to believe. But the relationship needed an adjustment. Definitely. Zoey needed to be taught that he wasn't kidding when he'd said there were other girls out there in the world. Girls who wouldn't treat him like crap.

All this had been going through his mind as he walked, almost without thinking, from French class down the stairs and through the hall to Claire's locker.

Claire was removing some books from the locker. She had a look that, had he seen it in any other eyes, he would have thought was sadness. Perhaps disappointment.

"Hi, Claire."

"Hi, Lucas."

"So." He stuck his hands in his pockets. "Thinking of going for a drive again?"

Aisha dropped the key ring on the floor of the car and had to scrabble around to find it. Her hands were shaking so badly that she could barely insert the key, and as she backed her parents' Taurus out of the parking space in the public garage, she nicked the front bumper on one of the concrete support pillars.

She knew the van. It was painted in the school colors. If she could find it, she would recognize it. And after all, Weymouth wasn't such a large town, was it?

Only it had to be before the falling sun disappeared altogether. Already in the cloud-smothered gloom all colors were turning gray, and in the dark she would never find him.

"Silly," she told herself. "He's just acting tough. He's not going to do it."

She drove erratically, jerking to sudden stops when she spotted something like the van. Accelerating away from stoplights only when the impatient horns reminded her to move. She was dizzy from swiveling her head, looking this way and that. With each new street she passed, she was haunted by the possibility that she might have made a wrong decision, driven right past him, missing her chance to save Christopher by a matter of a few feet because of a choice to go left instead of right.

The early commute was starting, filling the streets with cars, slowing her progress, frustrating her decisions. One-way streets. Stoplights. Blocked intersections. A bus that wouldn't move. Horns. Headlights snapping on as the early darkness descended.

There! She stepped on the gas. Was it him? Could she catch him?

A shriek of metal on metal. She'd hit something! A parked car. But there was no time to stop; the van—was it the right van?—was gaining, taking advantage of a hole in traffic.

No. The van turned, and she saw that it wasn't him.

Somewhere a siren, too loud. Flashing blue lights reflecting in her rearview mirror, distracting her.

"Pull your vehicle to the curb."

The electronically amplified voice surprised her. She realized the police car had been behind her for several blocks. It was her they were after.

She pulled the car to the curb and felt as if she might collapse. Night was falling fast. The police would take their time writing her ticket. It was over. She was too late. She couldn't stop him in time.

Christopher drove the van slowly the length of Brice Street, waiting for darkness.

The gun was on his lap, protected, nestled there. Sometimes

433

he touched it, reassured by the coldness of it and yet disturbed. He had been in a state of nervous excitement all day. It was almost like being high. An exalted, alive feeling. A tingling in the skin and fingers, a buzzing in his head.

Kick me, will they? he repeated in his head, an imaginary conversation. *Kick me? Spit on me? I don't think so. Won't happen again, that's for damned sure. Won't kick anyone, ever again.*

The street ended at the river and he turned around, tires crunching over fallen leaves and the rusted coils of a ruined wire fence.

Back up the street, just a few feet now, creeping as slowly as the van would go.

He leaned across to roll down the passenger-side window. Maybe the bastard would make it easy. Maybe he'd come out to the street or into his front yard. Then he could do it through the window.

Hey, dude? Guess what, man? Remember the guy you were kicking in the balls? Remember that? Remember all the trash you were talking while you did it? You do remember? Good. Now suck on this. Not so tough now, are you?

He passed the house and pulled over to the shoulder of the road, a hundred yards farther down. He couldn't wait for the creep to come out. He couldn't have this drag on forever. The time was now.

He got out of the van, sliding the cold automatic into the waist of his pants, hidden under his jacket. He plunged into the woods as he'd done before, skirting around, the river now close on his left. In the dark he stumbled into a patch of thorns, which tore at his legs, fueling his rage.

He was at a pitch now, pumped, vibrating with impatient energy. Every muscle and sinew tight, eyes wide, nose flared, alive! He'd never been so alive!

The barking of a dog. But not directed at him. No, the dog was barking at the back door of the grubby house. Hungry.

Perfect!

The punk would come out to feed his dog. Any second now . . . yes! The door was opening.

He came out. He was wearing military fatigues and unlaced boots. He was carrying a bag of dog food and an open can.

"Hey, boy," he said, his voice utterly clear to Christopher's hyper-alert senses. "You hungry, boy? Yeah. Come on."

Christopher crept closer. Like a soldier closing in on his enemy. That's what he was—a soldier. Doing an honorable deed in a righteous war that he hadn't started but would damned sure finish.

TWENTY-TWO

CLAIRE DROVE IN A DIFFERENT direction this time. South, toward Portland. For a while neither she nor Lucas said much at all. Claire concentrated on driving and tried not to think about Jake. What Lucas concentrated on, Claire couldn't say, but he was grim and far away for a long time, hunched over, staring out the side window.

At last Claire pulled off onto a side road that dead-ended on a bluff overlooking the sea. She left the engine running, keeping the heat on.

She turned sideways on the seat. "Are you going to tell me why we're taking this drive?" she asked. "You didn't seem to enjoy the one the other day."

"Things change," Lucas said.

"Do they?"

He looked at her. The dark eyes had changed over the years, grown more wary, perhaps. Yet they were the eyes he had once looked into with something like love.

"Sometimes they change so much you feel like you've come full circle and back to a place you've been before," he said.

So. That's what this was about. She was a little surprised. Even a little disappointed in Lucas. "Full circle back to a beach a long time ago?" Claire asked, knowing the answer.

He nodded. "Back to a first kiss."

She should put an end to this. She really should. But the memories were strong for her, too. There had been a time when she would have done anything for Lucas Cabral. And it would be a down payment on paying Jake back. "Are you going to ask me as politely as you did then, Lucas, with your voice all squeaky and trembling?" she said, half-mocking, half-trembling with anticipation.

Lucas slid toward her, closer, close enough that the slightest movement would bring them together. "Do I have to ask?"

"No," Claire said. "You don't."

Christopher stood, drew up the gun, pointed it straight at the boy as the boy tossed the empty dog food can into the trash barrel.

"Don't move," he said.

The boy jerked and stared wildly.

"Don't move," Christopher repeated in a silky, dangerous voice.

"What do you want, man? What's going on? What is this?" Eyes wide, throat swallowing convulsively. Fear. Raw, stomach-churning fear.

"Remember me?" Christopher asked, grinning. He had moved closer. The gun was pointed right at that shaved head. Right at that sickly little mustache and goatee.

"No man, look, what is this, man? I don't have any money or anything. Honest to God, whatever you want you can have it, but look, don't shoot me. Don't shoot me, man."

"I'm the guy you were calling nigger," Christopher said, his voice rising, feeding off the fear.

"I don't know . . . just don't shoot me." Placating hands held up.

"You and your punk-ass skinhead piece of crap friends *kicked* me."

Was that a faint, dawning comprehension in those terrified eyes? Was the fear growing still deeper? Good. Good, let it grow. Christopher felt an urge to laugh out loud. The rush of power! Absolute power! He clicked off the safety. The skinhead knew what he had done. A dark stain was growing down the front of his fatigue trousers. There was the smell of urine and sweat.

"Look man, look man, no, look, don't man. Don't shoot me, man."

He was begging. Praying to Christopher like he was some

kind of a god. And with his gun, with his finger on the trigger, with the slightest pressure now, the difference between life and death, *wasn't* he like a god?

From far away the sound of a siren floated through the trees. The dog had started barking, jerking frantically at its chain. The skinhead had sunk to his knees, crying.

And the gun felt so powerful in Christopher's hand.

Zoey's parents were waiting in the living room when she and Benjamin arrived home. Her mother sitting, staring blankly, eyes red, skin pale. Older than she had ever looked.

Her father was pacing back and forth, biting savagely at a thumbnail. When Zoey and Benjamin came in, their father looked up sharply.

It was a moment of frozen time. No one said anything. No one moved.

Then her mother broke the spell. "Both of you sit down, please." A colorless voice.

Zoey sat stiffly. Benjamin found the easy chair across from her after some fumbling. They rarely used the living room, spending most of their time in the family room.

"We, um . . . we have something to tell you," Mr. Passmore said. He sighed shakily. "It looks like your mother and I will be separating."

Benjamin hung his head.

"A lot of bad things have been said and done around here lately," Mr. Passmore went on.

"I'm so sorry, Zoey," her mother interrupted. "Yelling at you like that . . . blaming *you*. I don't know how to tell you how desperately sorry I am."

Zoey bit her lip. "That's not what you need to be sorry for," she managed, in a grating, unnatural voice.

"Look, let's—" Her father raised a quieting hand, struggling to maintain calm. "Let's not make this any worse than it has to be. We've decided maybe we need some time apart. We're going to keep the restaurant going, at least for now, but I'm going to move out. Find a place . . ."

Zoey jumped up, rushing to his side. She threw her arms around him, holding him tightly. "Why should you move out, Daddy? It was her, not you."

"Zoey," Benjamin said, cautioning her, but without much conviction.

"This is your fault," Zoey said, directing a look of pure hatred at her mother. "You did this." Her mother blanched and recoiled. Her father pushed her away gently, holding her at arm's length.

"No, Zoey," he said. "I know what you saw. But that's not all of it. As much as I love you I can't have you thinking your mother was the only one in the wrong."

"Don't defend her!" Zoey cried in outrage. "She's destroying this family."

"No, Zoey. It's not that simple." He turned away and seemed to be struggling to gain control of himself. Zoey stood helpless, her arms at her sides, not knowing where to turn or what to do.

"This all goes back a long time," Mr. Passmore said at last. "You were asking the other night about when we first got together. I told you there had been another man in your mother's life. Well, I didn't know until . . . you know . . . but it was—well, I guess you know who it was."

"There was nothing between Fred McRoyan and me, not since we were married," her mother said fiercely. "We had put it all behind us. It was over." She shot a furious look at her husband.

Mr. Passmore nodded. "I accept that, Darla. I do."

"Not until I found out—"

"Let's not do this again," Mr. Passmore said. "I don't ever want to fight in front of the kids again. This is wrong." He took a deep breath. "There's something you kids don't know. While I was in Europe, backpacking around, while your mom was seeing . . . Fred . . . anyway, I also met a girl. An American girl who was traveling like me. We had an affair."

Zoey sank back onto the couch.

"And—and since then, I've seen her again. She lives down in Portland, and your mother, well, found out that I had seen this woman several times since we've been married. That's why she . . . well, you were getting back at me, right?" He directed this last question to his wife, putting on a bitterly cheerful tone. "And did an excellent job of it."

Zoey saw her mother's eyes were full of tears. She realized her own were, too. This was it—the destruction of her family. The end. Even more, the destruction of her parents, all their tawdry, humiliating secrets now laid out to sicken their children. Zoey wished she could just disappear. If she'd still had even an ounce of energy or will, she might have grabbed Benjamin's hand and run. But all she could do was watch and listen, helpless to change anything.

"You might as well tell them the rest," Zoey's mother said flatly.

Mr. Passmore nodded. "Yes. The rest. It seems while I was with this woman in Europe, well, it seems she became pregnant."

Zoey felt the world spinning around her.

"See, you both, Zoey, Benjamin, you have . . . a sister."

FIND OUT WHAT HAPPENS NEXT!

SISTER. THE WORD HUNG IN the air between them. Zoey's mother looked away, her mouth twisted in a bitter line. Her father hung his head, ashamed.

"Where does this sister live?" Benjamin asked.

"I don't know," Mr. Passmore said. "Her mother and . . . and the man she thinks of as her father live in Kittery. I was never supposed to have anything to do with my—with the young lady."

"How *Jerry Springer*," Benjamin muttered. "Or would this be more of a *Maury*?"

"I guess Lara—that's her name, Lara McAvoy—does know she has a biological father out there somewhere, but who, or where . . . I don't think she knows."

"This is not really what's important right now," Zoey's mother snapped in a brittle voice. Then, with an effort, she softened her tone. "The important thing is that you kids realize that both of us still love you and care for you. We don't want any of this to have to affect you."

Zoey laughed derisively. "Too late."

"Yeah, I think we kind of got affected," Benjamin said dryly.

"I'm just tired," Zoey said, shaking her head. "In a way I'm glad it's all out in the open."

Her mother leaned forward, trying to meet Zoey's evasive gaze. "What I said to you the other day, Zoey. About this being your fault. That was totally wrong. We're to blame. Your father and I, we're the only ones to blame."

Zoey stood up, wobbly with spent emotion and exhaustion. Outside, the night had fallen. Inside the room, no one had turned on more than a single dim lamp. Her parents' faces were in shadow, unknowable, almost unrecognizable in their masks of grief and shame and poorly concealed anger.

"Yes," Zoey agreed. "You are the ones to blame. But if you're waiting for forgiveness from me, Mother, you can forget it."

"People make mistakes," Benjamin said, so quietly Zoey wasn't sure she'd heard him.

"People make mistakes," Zoey agreed. "But they don't end up sleeping with men they're not married to on a tiny little island where everyone knows everyone else's business."

She was gratified to see her mother swallow hard. The barb had hit home. Good. They could say all they wanted that it was both their faults, but it had been her mother she'd walked in on. Her mother with Jake's father.

Zoey walked away. She heard Benjamin rise too and follow her from the room. Zoey began climbing the stairs, almost too exhausted to move her legs.

"Zoey?" Benjamin called out softly from the hallway.

She halted, waiting silently.

"People do make mistakes," Benjamin said.

The car swerved sharply around a cyclist, nearly invisible in the darkness, and fishtailed into a turn. In the backseat Aisha Gray was thrown against the door, bruising her narrow shoulder. But she didn't ask the driver to slow down. The speed of the car, now flying down the dark road, siren wailing, was Aisha's only hope.

"How do you know where we're going?" Aisha yelled at the detective on the passenger side, the older of the two men.

3

Sergeant Winokur.

He half-turned, and Aisha could see that his eyes were wide from the adrenaline rush. They glittered with reflected green dashboard light. His voice, though professionally measured, showed the raggedness of excitement, maybe even fear. "We *don't* know," he said. "But there are three possibilities. I put units on the others, too, as soon as you told me what was happening."

Aisha was confused. "Wait a minute; you *know* who these guys are?"

Sergeant Winokur nodded. "We've known from the start. We have a pretty good idea who's in these skinhead gangs." He made an annoyed face. "Actually, we were hoping these particular lowlifes would lead us to bigger fish."

"Just ahead, Sarge," his partner said, killing the siren.

"Yeah. Look, miss, you stay in the car and keep down. Do you understand? Head below the back of this seat."

Aisha nodded. Her throat was tight. Her chest was a vise around a pounding, fearful heart. "Don't hurt him," she pleaded. "Just don't hurt him, please."

The sergeant gave no response. He tried unsuccessfully to hide the fact that he had drawn an automatic pistol from the holster beneath his sport coat. The gun was low by his side.

The car skidded to a stop, headlights illuminating a crazed,

4

fleeting montage of dark tree trunks, a tilted mailbox, a gravel driveway, an old car, before coming to rest. Just up the street Aisha could see the van that Christopher had taken from the school's athletics department. She squeezed her hands together and prayed with all her might. Prayed like she had not done since she was a little girl.

"There he is."

"Yep."

Doors opened. Aisha looked up. Christopher walked blindly, head bowed, a stark figure in the blue-white glare of headlights. The gun hung loose in his hand. He seemed to be stunned, immobilized. He looked down at the gun, then up, straight into the headlights.

"Drop it." The sergeant rapped out the words. He stood behind the shelter of the open door, one foot still in the car, gun leveled at Christopher.

"Drop the damn gun!" the driver ordered.

Christopher still seemed confused, surprised, lost.

"I said lose the gun! Lose it right now or I'll shoot!"

Lucas's first kiss was tentative. Claire half-thought he might back away at the last minute. She half-thought *she* might back away, too. But neither did. And Lucas's lips met hers.

The betrayal was sealed. With that first kiss Claire had begun to pay Jake back for sleeping with Louise, for still secretly loving Zoey, and for the worst crime of all—for not really loving Claire.

But it wouldn't stop with one kiss. On the next kiss Lucas was bolder, taking her in his arms and holding her close. The feel of him was different. Not like Jake, not the wall of hard muscle, the bristly chin, the sense of physical power barely restrained.

Nor was this Lucas like the Lucas that Claire remembered from a long time ago, when his kisses had been sweet, his touch so gentle. This Lucas was more urgent, almost harsh.

And yet Claire felt her body responding swiftly to his touch. Her lips, her throat as he trailed kisses down to her collarbone, her heart as it pounded frantically. It was as if her body was somehow a separate creature from her mind. She felt a warm, spreading, intoxicating pleasure, but at a distance, not real.

He drew back just a little, catching his breath. His face was too near for her to see his features distinctly in the dim light from the dashboard. He was a blur with warm breath and dark eyes. He came closer still, and this time she opened her lips to him, and felt an answering increase in his own excitement.

It was strange. Such a combustible feeling, as if the two of them brought together would inevitably cause an explosion. And yet it was a cold fire whose warmth reached just the surface of her skin, tingling just the nerve endings while somehow leaving her mind unaffected.

Was she the only one feeling this strange disconnection? Was it some consequence of guilt? Was it concern for Zoey, for Jake? Did Lucas feel it, too? Was that the reason for his urgency? Was he racing to stay ahead of feelings of guilt?

She fumbled for and found the control button that lowered the plush leather seat into full recline with a mechanical whir. Her luxuriant black hair fanned out across the tan leather. Guilt, maybe, but sheer pleasure, too. Lucas was over her now, his weight pressing down on her, kissing her deeply, the two of them panting, groping, unrestrained.

His hands touched her, eliciting shudders of sensual response. His movements were so barely controlled, his fingers trembling, his breathing ragged.

Why not? Claire wondered. It was very clear what he wanted to happen next. *Why not?* It was a wild, passionate, insane moment. How often did anything like passion infiltrate even the corners of her dispassionate mind?

And if Jake could do it with Louise . . .

Lucas was undressing her with hurried fingers, driven by desire . . . no, by two desires.

The second of which was to hurt Zoey.

7

"Sister?" Zoey repeated the word into the mirror over her dresser. "Half-sister," she corrected, but that formulation made her uneasy. She'd always felt there was something ungenerous about phrases like half-sister, half-brother. Like you were making an issue out of it. Like you didn't quite want to accept a person.

"I *don't* want to accept *any* of this." Her eyes showed the signs of sleeplessness and tears, the blue surrounded and invaded by redness, lids puffed, expression dull and lifeless. Her blond hair hung lank and straight to her shoulders. She glanced at her clock. Ridiculously early to get in bed. And yet when had she last had a real night's sleep?

She began to undress, letting clothing fall on the floor, feeling a deep physical craving for her bed. In a strange way she was almost relieved. Things became simpler when you were too exhausted to think. She could feel her mind finally shutting down, her awareness like a diminishing circle of spotlight, smaller, smaller, releasing more and more into dark indifference.

She found her Boston Bruins jersey and slipped it on, reassured by its familiarity. At least some things didn't change. Her sheets were cool, her pillows soft. She stretched her legs out, feeling the tension in her every muscle. Her toes invaded the cold corners of her bed.

Her parents were breaking up. It was impossible to imagine that anything could stop the disintegration now.

And she had a sister, somewhere, maybe not far away, with no face as yet. An abstraction, but full of possibilities and problems that Zoey was simply too tired to contemplate.

Tomorrow she would have to begin confronting all the stories, the details, the trauma of this terrible day. But first . . .

. . . sleep.

TWO

"DROP THE DAMNED GUN!"

Christopher stood paralyzed. The bright light had come up from nowhere, and now voices were shouting. He looked down at the gun in his hand. It looked alien and alive. He opened his hand slowly and the creature slipped from his grip.

It was a shocking sensation, the emptiness of his hand, just fingers again. He shook his head, feeling like he'd been sleep-walking.

Strong hands grabbed him, a leg swept his feet from under him, and he was facedown in the gravel. Sharp rocks cutting into his cheek. Dirt in his mouth. His arms were twisted roughly behind his back. He didn't resist. He stared at the gun lying a few feet away, still more than just another artifact. Still like something living that had become a part of him.

Or was it the other way around? Was it he who had become a part of the gun?

He was jerked to his feet and pushed, staggering back against the hood of the car, blinking again in the lights.

"Christopher!"

Aisha. Her arms around him, her wet cheek pressed against his. Was she crying? Was he?

"I'm making the weapon safe," a far-off voice said.

Sirens and wildly swinging blue lights were coming down the road at breakneck speed. One by one they skidded to a halt in a shower of gravel.

"This weapon has not been fired," the first voice said.

"Oh, thank God," Aisha said. "Oh, thank you, God."

"I couldn't do it," Christopher admitted, feeling embarrassed and defeated.

"Check around the back of the house," a second voice ordered. "I . . . . Look, if the kid back there is in one piece, I don't need any formal statements from him at this time. You understand me?"

"Your call, Dave," the first man said, sounding doubtful.

"I couldn't do it," Christopher told Aisha.

"I know. I prayed so hard . . . I knew you wouldn't."

"I had him. I mean, he was scared, he was crawling and begging and all I had to do was pull the trigger—"

"But you didn't."

"I couldn't, Eesh."

Uniformed policemen were everywhere now. At least a

half-dozen cars were spread out across and on both sides of the road.

The first cop was back. He jerked a thumb over his shoulder toward the dark backyard, back to the sound of a frantically barking dog and a high-pitched, almost hysterical voice crying for revenge, screaming obscene threats now that the danger was past. "He'll live. Just shaken up pretty badly."

"Any evidence of shots fired?" Sergeant Winokur asked.

"No shots. No witnesses aside from the victim and this clown." He indicated Christopher.

"All right, Curt, see if you can't break up this party while I have a little talk with the tough guy here. All right, tough guy, come with me," the sergeant said to Christopher. He hauled Christopher by his pinioned arm, pulling him, stumbling, down the dark road, away from the barking and the flash of blue lights and the wailing threats.

"Where are you taking him?" Aisha cried.

"See this?" the cop demanded angrily. "Do you see what you've done to this girl who cares about you? She has to call us and come racing over here scared half to death?"

Christopher shook his head in confusion. It was all happening in a blur. They were in darkness now, walking across dead leaves and fallen pine needles. A branch scratched his cheek. A sound was growing louder. Water. The river.

"Sergeant, what are you doing?" Aisha cried again, still keeping pace, clutching at Christopher's other arm.

They stopped beside the river, an almost unseen but definite presence, running fast and loud, swollen with new rain and too-early snowfalls melting off the mountains.

Christopher was turned around. There was a metallic click and suddenly his arms were free of the handcuffs. He was aware of the police sergeant standing no more than a foot away. He could feel Aisha wrapped around his right arm.

"That punk back there is named Jesse Simms. He was the third individual involved in the attack on you. Within about twelve hours of the incident, we'd rolled this kid over on his buddies. We've been trying to use the other two to identify additional members of this particular skinhead organization."

"You knew?" Christopher asked.

"Yeah. Oddly enough, that's our job." The cop's tone was coldly sarcastic. "Sometimes we actually succeed. What was *your* job? What the hell were *you* doing here tonight with a gun?"

Christopher shrugged. "I . . . Look, they put me in the hospital, man."

"And the penalty for assault and battery is death now? Someone beats you up, you kill them? I'm curious, you know, since you're making all the laws now."

Christopher shrugged again. The sergeant was clearly angry

and growing more so. Christopher felt too drained to say much in his own defense.

"So you were going to kill him," the policeman accused.

"He didn't, though," Aisha said fiercely.

"No. What he did was commit assault with a deadly weapon. We could probably also call it kidnapping since he held the poor bastard with a gun to his head. But I don't think Mr. Simms will be wanting to press charges, because I'm going to tell him not to."

Christopher exhaled and for the first time realized he had been holding his breath.

"So. Tough guy. Why didn't you shoot him?" the policeman asked more gently.

"I don't know."

"It would have been easy. You had the gun. He was helpless."

Christopher felt a wave of nausea at the memory. Yes, he'd been helpless, crying, begging. "It made me sick."

"What made you sick? That he was scared? That he was begging for his life?" the sergeant bored in relentlessly.

"No," Christopher said sharply. "It made me sick that I made him beg."

"You enjoyed it. The rush of all that power from that little gun."

"No. Yeah, at first," Christopher admitted. "And then . . . Look, he deserved it. He's a racist piece of crap."

Surprisingly, the policeman laughed. "You know what? Lots of people deserve lots of things, kid. Sometimes they even get what's coming to them. Not all the time, but sometimes."

"And now what? Him and his friends will maybe spend ninety days in jail? Then it's right back out on the streets."

"That's about right."

"Maybe I should have killed him," Christopher said, but without conviction.

"And now you're ashamed because you didn't? You think you'd be proud if you had? You think you'd be standing here feeling like a big man because you took a life?"

"No," Christopher admitted.

"No. And you didn't get off on scaring that little punk. You know why? Because it takes a weak individual to enjoy causing fear. It takes a very small man to get pleasure out of another individual's pain. Maybe you just aren't a small enough man."

Christopher realized he was trembling, barely understanding what the cop was saying. All he knew was that a wave of relief so powerful it rattled him to his bones was sweeping over him. He had been so close to pulling that trigger.

Something was in his hand again: The gun. Emptied of shells, harmless, and yet so seductive.

"We checked you out after you first filed the complaint," Sergeant Winokur said in a quieter voice. "You work hard, kid. You have plans and you have a girlfriend here who is probably too damned good for you. And there was some provocation. So you're going to walk away from this one."

"Thank you," Christopher said in a whisper.

"Don't thank me," Sergeant Winokur said sarcastically. "I want a nice, clean case when we bust the rest of these punks. I don't want the jury having to deal with you playing vigilante. Now if you'd been found with a firearm, I wouldn't have much choice but to bust you and pretty much flush your life down the toilet. Do you follow me?"

"No . . . I . . ."

"What I'm saying is, that river is surprisingly deep way out in the middle."

Christopher nodded, comprehension penetrating his confusion. The sergeant gave him a long, thoughtful look. Then he turned his back deliberately and began to walk back toward the flashing blue lights.

"Thanks," Christopher called out after him. "I won't . . . you know."

There was no response. Christopher realized Aisha was still there, almost holding him up while his legs felt watery, his knees threatened to buckle. He felt weak as a newborn.

Aisha stepped away, waiting.

Christopher drew back his arm and found that he still possessed a reservoir of strength. The gun flew invisibly through the night. Seconds later there was a splash far out in the river.

"Let's go home," Aisha said.

"We can't do this, Lucas," Claire said a little breathlessly. "Not that I don't want to, but I think maybe it's a little far to take payback."

Lucas stopped his hand where it was but didn't pull it away. For a fleeting moment Claire wondered if he *would* stop. She had let things go way too far.

His voice was challenging. "That's all this is to you? Payback?"

"Oh, come on, Lucas, what is it to you?"

"It's . . . " He began cursing. He snatched his hand away, breaking contact.

Claire laughed. She used the button to raise her seat and began refastening everything Lucas had done such a good job of unfastening.

"You're cold, you know that?" Lucas demanded, sliding back across the seat.

"Uh-huh. I'm cold, but you've suddenly fallen madly in love with me, right? It isn't just that you're horny and you're mad at Zoey for refusing you. Or that you're worried about that long, very long hug between her and Jake? It isn't that you're thinking, 'well, I get laid, plus I get to pay Zoey back'?"

A semblance of humor returned to Lucas's features. "As revenge goes, it *would* be pretty effective."

"You and me. Could either of us have come up with a better way to piss off Jake and Zoey?"

Lucas laughed unwillingly, unable to resist the truth. "Still," he said ruefully, "it's not like I was just faking it."

"No, me neither," Claire admitted.

"You haven't exactly turned into a gorgon."

"We could definitely be dangerous together," Claire admitted. "But you're still in love with Zoey."

He shrugged and looked away.

"I think Jake is, too, at least partly."

Great, now she was feeling sorry for herself. Well, why not? Benjamin had obviously gotten over her a lot more completely than she'd ever expected. The level of affection between him and Nina was nauseating. And Lucas, and maybe even Jake, carried torches for Little Zoey Pureheart.

What did Jake feel for Zoey? What, if anything, did he feel for Claire? What, if anything, did anyone ever really feel for Claire?

Claire stole a glance at Lucas. Already the look of charged

excitement was fading, replaced by a sober, worried expression. That worry was sure to grow. In a few minutes it would begin to occur to him that Claire now held his relationship with Zoey in the palm of her hand.

Claire turned the key in the ignition.